KELVOO'S
TERRA

AN IMMIGRANT'S TALE

PHIL BAILEY

ISBN
978-1-7781024-4-8   (Hardcover)
978-1-7781024-5-5   (Paperback)
978-1-7781024-3-1   (eBook)

1. FICTION, SCIENCE FICTION, ALIEN CONTACT

To my number-one supporter and the love of my life, Cora, for her continued support of my illogical wish to keep writing science-fiction.

I would like to acknowledge all the individuals who played a crucial role in the creation of Kelvoo's Terra.

Thank you to my beta readers for helping me to refine the plot of Kelvoo's Terra to a point where it was ready for public consumption:

Sarah Bailey
Peter Ehm
Dave Eisler
Derrick Scott
Blake Thurston

Thank you Kevin Miller for your expert editing and immense improvement to the flow and impact of Kelvoo's Terra, and for helping me shed about 5,000 extraneous words.

Merci beaucoup Alain Berset, for your exquisite skill in crafting the 3D computer models of the main characters for the book cover.

Thank you Jan Westendorp, for your great work incorporating Alain's graphics and designing the cover of Kelvoo's Terra.

Gross External Kloormari Anatomy
Plate 1 - Anterior/Posterior View [1]

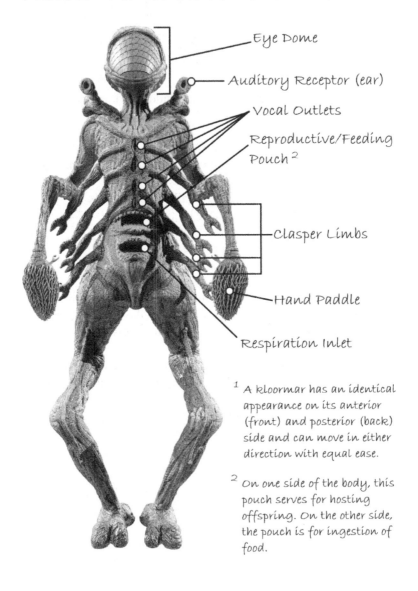

Eye Dome

Auditory Receptor (ear)

Vocal Outlets

Reproductive/Feeding Pouch [2]

Clasper Limbs

Hand Paddle

Respiration Inlet

[1] A kloormar has an identical appearance on its anterior (front) and posterior (back) side and can move in either direction with equal ease.

[2] On one side of the body, this pouch serves for hosting offspring. On the other side, the pouch is for ingestion of food.

Gross External Kloormari Anatomy
Plate 2 - Oblique View

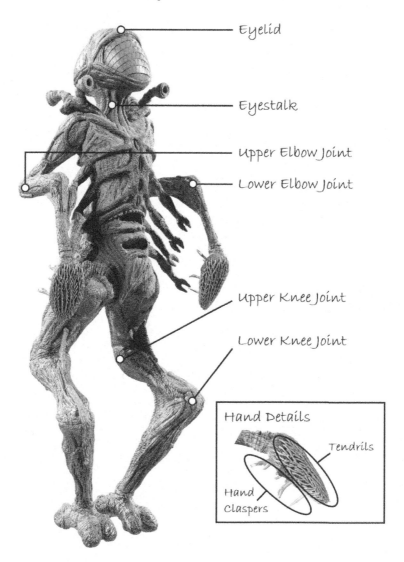

Eyelid

Eyestalk

Upper Elbow Joint

Lower Elbow Joint

Upper Knee Joint

Lower Knee Joint

Hand Details

Tendrils

Hand Claspers

PREFACE — MY TESTIMONIAL

When my written account of my experiences with humans was published under the title *Kelvoo's Testimonial*, my fear was that my story would end up unread in the Planetary Alliance's vast libraries. My hope was that my experiences might inform non-human species and serve as a cautionary tale for future dealings with humans. In reality, the impact of *Kelvoo's Testimonial* was swifter and more far-reaching than I anticipated.

Through much of *Kelvoo's Testimonial*, I chronicled acts of abuse that I, along with several other kloormari, endured when we were held captive by a criminal gang of humans on the vessel *Jezebel's Fury*. That part of my account did not impact Terra's relations with the Planetary Alliance nearly as much as the final chapters of my story, which led to the large-scale changes, known on Terra as the "Correction."

When my story was published, I didn't realize the extent to which the Alliance's trust and respect for Terran humans had been declining. The Alliance had difficulty with humans because they were so divergent in their values and personalities. Humans could not be relied upon to respond or take action in a consistent manner. Humans also exhibited self-centered tendencies, sometimes putting personal gain ahead of the collective well-being of others.

From the moment of their introduction, humans provided unique dimensions of culture and innovation to the Planetary Alliance. While not the most intelligent species, humans had unmatched imaginations and creativity. The innate capacity of most humans for kindness and empathy was viewed as something for other species to aspire to.

When Terran humans were accepted into the Alliance, Terran society seemed to model civility, order, openness, and diversity. At the same time, the Alliance was troubled that Terran peace had been achieved, in part, by the expulsion of tens of millions of humans from Terra a few hundred years before. These "outliers"—humans deemed to be violent, superstitious, or otherwise non-compliant with "normal" human values—were encouraged, and later forced, to relocate to two recently discovered inhabitable planets, named by the outliers as "Perdition" and "Exile".

The inhabitants of my village experienced humanity's best intentions when the Terran vessel, *Pacifica Spirit*, touched down to establish first contact with my species. I was fortunate enough to be one of ten kloormari selected to learn from the humans. Over the course of several months, I formed a close bond with our teacher, Samuel Buchanan, as he revealed the wonders of a universe that had been forever hidden behind the cloud-covered sky of my planet, Kuw'baal.

Shortly after the first-contact expedition departed, I, along with eight of Sam Buchanan's other students, became all too familiar with humanity's dark side when a human who called himself "Captain Roger Smith" landed on Kuw'baal. Through trickery and outright lies, the captain convinced me and my group to join a so-called "goodwill mission" to deliver aid to several planets over a six-month timespan. In honor of our human teacher, we referred to our group as "Sam's Team."

When Captain Smith took us aboard *Jezebel's Fury*, we learned that he was leading a crew of outlier humans, affiliated with a network of criminal gangs known as "The Brotherhood." Sam's Team was enslaved, and we were forced to support the crew on an interstellar crime spree. As peaceful beings, we were utterly unprepared for the intimidation and violence that we were subjected to and that the crew committed, even against their own species.

After learning that the human crew intended to murder us, we fought back and took control of *Jezebel's Fury*. We were subsequently rescued by a Sarayan warship and returned to Kuw'baal. At that time it seemed as though our abduction had lasted almost six months. Much to our shock, almost seven years had elapsed on Kuw'baal during our absence. An effect known as "time dilation" had caused us to experience the passage of time differently because the captain and crew had illegally used near-light speed velocities to commit their crimes and evade capture.

When we returned to our village, we barely recognized it. Our homes had been replaced by prefabricated metal structures, and a landing pad for visiting spacecraft had been erected on the mineral plain across the stream from our village. On the other side of the plain, a human settlement named Newton had been built.

Unlike our abductors, the settlers were not overt criminals. Most of the humans were friendly, though their attention was focused on the accumulation of wealth, something we kloormari couldn't fully grasp at that time.

Construction of a spaceport upstream from the village caused silt and other contaminants to foul the water. Algel, my species' only food, no longer grew in the stream. Human development and resource extraction had a similar environmental effect on other parts of Kuw'baal. While all of these developments were a shock to my fellow abductees and me, the greatest surprise was how accepting our fellow kloormari had been.

In part this was due to the fact that the changes had spanned the seven years of our absence, but for Sam's Team, the changes were sudden, profound, and shocking.

The human settlers had complex governance structures and a justice system that were utterly foreign to kloormari society. The humans designated our villages and some of the lands surrounding them as kloormari "homelands," where kloormari society could continue to exist as we saw fit. These homelands amounted to less than 1 percent of our planet's surface. All remaining areas of Kuw'baal were subject to human regulation. In exchange, a welfare system called "Indigenous Support" or "IS" was put in place, providing the kloormari with regular payments, apparently as compensation for access to our resources.

I viewed the changes as cultural genocide, but most of the kloormari had become preoccupied with the acquisition of the knowledge, entertainment, toys, and material goods that the humans provided. The inhabitants of my village didn't seem to mind the disappearance of wild algel from the stream, content to use their IS payments to purchase algel from human-owned farms or retail outlets.

Most kloormari understood the negative cultural and environmental impacts of human dominance, but three factors prevented them from taking action.

First, the kloormari had not been exposed to the worst of human behavior and were unaware of the damage that criminal humans could inflict on others. In contrast, Sam's Team had experienced human cruelty firsthand.

Second, confrontation had never been a component of kloormari culture. Those of us on Sam's Team, however, had been forced to learn how to confront our captors, which had been crucial to our survival.

Third, the kloormari saw their subservience to humans as a worthwhile trade-off for access to human knowledge and technology.

Rather than taking decisive action, the Terran authorities washed their hands of the situation, arguing that they could not remedy our problems since standard first-contact procedures had never been followed.

The story you are about to read begins seven years after the events described in *Kelvoo's Testimonial*. I wrote that story at the request of Trexelan, a sub-commander in the Sarayan military who wanted to present my story to the Planetary Alliance as they re-evaluated Terra's membership. As such, I wrote that story for Trexelan and the Planetary Alliance. However, I wrote the following story for all downtrodden, persecuted, and victimized beings on Terra and throughout the

Planetary Alliance. I hope it will make a meaningful difference for them.

PART 1: A JOYFUL BELONGING

ONE: THREE EAGER IMMIGRANTS

My human friend, Professor Jasmit Linford, came to my home shortly after daybreak while the girls were still fast asleep. He came to say goodbye.

"Could I at least accompany you to the shuttle?" I asked.

"I'd like that very much," he replied.

I felt awkward as the professor and I trudged in silence down the paved walkway from the village to the landing pad, and I could sense that Jas felt the same way. At that moment I wished that we had just said farewell on my doorstep.

The air was still, and the village was silent, as the residents had not yet stirred from their meditative states. The only sound was the crunching and scraping of my feet and the professor's shoes on the gritty downhill portion of the path as we approached the village landing pad. When we crossed the stream on the raised footpath toward the pad, we saw that Jas's personal belongings were being loaded onto the hovering shuttle. The three steps to the shuttle's doorway extended down onto the pad, waiting for the professor to board.

At the bottom of the steps, Jas turned toward me. He was taller and slimmer than most male humans. Some would describe him as gaunt. His hair was short, straight, and brown but interspersed with white around the temples and eyebrows. His chiseled face was clean shaven. I can't say whether other humans would have considered him handsome since I lack any understanding of the human capacity for physical attraction. When comparing Jas to other human males, I would guess that he had the look of an academic, combined with the ruggedness of someone who enjoyed the outdoors—not that I have any expertise on such subjective matters.

As we stood on the pad, face to face, Jas and I both tried to speak at the same time. "Please, Kelvoo, go ahead," Jas said after some verbal blundering from both of us.

I had planned to say goodbye, but such words didn't seem adequate, and I was not confident in my knowledge of protocol for the situation, so instead I exacerbated the awkwardness. "Would you like me to accompany you to the spaceport?"

3

Jas opened his mouth to speak, then blinked twice as if clearing his thoughts. "Of course!" he replied.

We boarded, Jas took a seat, and I folded my legs into a resting squat and put a wrist through the loop of a handhold strap. Then we resumed our clumsy silence.

As the shuttle hummed, ascended, and started to move forward, I distracted myself by taking in the scenery. To the left I saw the once bustling human settlement of Newton. Most of the town's homes and buildings were abandoned, but they were still maintained by a few kloormari in case they became useful in the future. The other structures were used by the remaining humans, most of them scientists, artists, or retirees. Some of the people had remained on Kuw'baal after the mass exodus of humans, and a few had arrived just before the Correction severely restricted all immigration.

Jas was one of a handful of humans with a visa to visit Kuw'baal for a limited time, and his visa was expiring that day. Visas were granted in the interest of scientific research or to help the kloormari heal and prepare for the possibility of gradual integration into the Planetary Alliance.

Thousands of sociologists had applied to visit Kuw'baal to study the kloormari, but Jasmit Linford was one of the few selected because he taught at the Interplanetary University on Terra. A main tenet of the university's mission was to accept, teach, and learn from a diverse body of students from the worlds of the Planetary Alliance. Jas was especially interested in attracting future kloormari students—especially me.

As the shuttle rose over the mountains and continued toward the spaceport, I saw Sam's Lake, its turquoise water nestled in the beautiful bowl-shaped valley. When control of Kuw'baal was returned to the kloormari, one of our council's first acts was to remove all traces of human mining exploration from the valley and create a park to preserve the land and the lake that had been named for Sam Buchanan—my teacher, mentor, and best friend from the human first-contact mission.

As the shuttle crossed the lake, my memories of Sam's suicide came flooding back. During my disappearance due to my captivity on *Jezebel's Fury*, Sam had blamed himself for the decline of kloormari society. He had spent years struggling to advocate for my species. As his fight became more desperate, he turned to alcohol to cope with his guilt and ended up living a squalid, solitary existence. When my teammates and I escaped and returned to Kuw'baal, Sam was overjoyed. He sobered up and assisted me in writing *Kelvoo's Testimonial* in a style that humans and other Alliance species could relate to.

With my story written, I looked forward to working with Sam to bring about positive changes for my species. I was blindsided and devastated when Sam decided to end his life to, as he wrote in his suicide note, "quit while I'm ahead." My inner conflict was unbearable as I struggled with sadness at my loss of Sam, combined with my anger for Sam's selfish, senseless act of self-destruction. Sam's suicide added years to the time that I and the other members of Sam's Team needed to heal and move on.

As the shuttle continued and Sam's Lake disappeared from view, my thoughts turned back to my first meeting with Professor Linford, when my friend, K'tatmal, had introduced us. At the time I was writing my doctoral thesis. Within an hour of Jas's arrival at the village, K'tatmal had brought him to me. K'tatmal thought we might have a few things in common since Jas's interest in sociology aligned well with my interest in human behavior. K'tatmal had been wise to introduce us since that introduction led to many months of mutual studies as well as deep academic and philosophical discussions, leading to a solid friendship.

As the shuttle continued its short flight, the mountains below us gave way to reddish plains, scattered boulders, and then undulating hills when we closed in on the spaceport, which was just twenty-six kilometers from the village. The spaceport was a marvel of human engineering, though most of it had been mothballed. I entered an almost meditative state as my thoughts turned to the massive engineering project during the Correction when the Terrans remediated the environmental damage caused during the spaceport's construction. Years later the wild algel finally returned to its former abundance in the village stream.

Jas finally broke the silence, snapping me out of my reverie.

"Kelvoo, are you absolutely *sure* that I can't convince you to take the university up on its offer?" he asked me for the thirty-fourth time.

"Jas, I'm not really sure about anything these days."

"After all, you've just earned your doctorate in psychology, specializing in human behavior," he reminded me. "It would be a shame to let all that education go to waste."

I had taken my doctoral studies through Jas's university via quantum entanglement communications.

"None of my education is going to waste," I countered. "Understanding, or at least *trying* to understand humans, has been a key component of my personal healing. Learning has also helped the other kloormari who were abducted by the Brotherhood gang, though each of them has studied in different fields. In fact, expanding our minds to better comprehend the universe is something that every kloormar craves and has benefited from.

"As I have said every time you have asked me, Jas, I am immensely honored that the Interplanetary University would offer me an in-person

5

teaching position, but I don't know whether I am ready to transition to a life on Terra. I don't know whether I could deal with the attention as the most famous—and some might say, infamous—kloormar in the universe. I don't know how well I might be accepted on a post-Correction Terra, I don't know whether I would even be any good at the job, and I don't know whether I have healed enough."

"Kelvoo, as I've said many times before, the best way to overcome fear of the unknown is to embrace such things, to *make* them known."

I was puzzled as to why humans kept repeating their previous statements when speaking with the kloormari. With our hyperthymestic memories, we retained every word that we had ever heard, but Jas was telling me once again to face the unknown. It occurred to me that perhaps the repetition was serving to sway me toward the possibility of considering the university's offer.

"Before I return to my homeworld, Kelvoo, I need to let you know that the board of directors sent a message to me last night, asking me to present a final offer to you. In light of your hesitation and your understandable and totally justified fears, the university would like to offer you a chance to make an open-ended, gradual immersion into academic life. They're willing to offer a contract with no set term. Any time you want to leave, you can do so without notice. They are also suggesting that you start by teaching a single course, giving you lots of extra time to adapt and settle in. To sweeten the deal, they'll provide a nice on-campus private residence for you and the girls. Speaking of the girls, I've told the board how bright Brenna and May are. That's why they would also offer Brenna a full academic scholarship, and May can attend our top-notch on-campus school for the children of faculty members and students. So, Kelvoo, what should I tell the board?"

"I'm sorry, Jas, but I still don't know. I would have to talk with Brenna and May to see whether they are interested."

Over the years I had learned the value of fibbing to humans. My statement to Jas was a fib to buy myself some time. I knew full well that May, and especially Brenna, desperately wanted to go to Terra. Both girls had lived through far more than an average human's share of difficulties, from the restrictive conditions on *Jezebel's Fury* to being orphaned when their father was executed. They had trouble integrating with other human children at school. Their classmates had looked down on them due to their origin from an "outlier" planet. As Jas had said, both girls were very intelligent. Brenna in particular had found the few other local humans her age to be uninteresting. I understood that a move to Terra might provide the kind of environment that would let the girls thrive both intellectually and socially.

6

As we approached, the spaceport's sprawling structure seemed stark and out of place against the sandy plain. The facilities looked deserted with no trace of movement except for a lone servitor bot, pushing a rotating broom to clear the streaks of orange dust that had blown onto a landing pad overnight. The only spacecraft in sight was the one that was scheduled to carry Jas and a few others to the interstellar transport orbiting high above the clouds. I knew that Jas was eager to return to Terra to reunite with his family, friends, and acquaintances.

I was pleased that I had accompanied Jas to the spaceport. Even though he had pressured me once again to relocate to his planet, the conversation had reduced the awkwardness of our goodbye. While I was reluctant to admit it, Jas's arguments were persuasive.

Our footsteps echoed from every surface as we entered the soaring, nearly empty terminal and walked to the only departure lounge that remained in service. Even though an hour remained before boarding, I was relieved when Jas extended his hand to me.

"Well, Kelvoo, shall we get this over with?"

I grasped his hand and shook it.

"Goodbye my friend," he said, looking directly at my eye dome, "You are by far the most interesting being I have ever worked with. Meeting you and getting to know you has been a privilege that I will always cherish, and I hope to see you again someday."

"Professor Jasmit Linford, thank you for your friendship, your support, and your invaluable contribution to my healing. I also hope that we will meet again."

Jas released my hand paddle and walked into the lounge. I turned and walked back to the shuttle, grateful that Jas's final words hadn't included yet another reminder of the university's interest in me.

On the return flight to the village, I pondered the university's offer for a full five minutes, which is an extraordinarily long time for a kloormar to concentrate on a single topic.

After I disembarked, I stopped on the raised walkway between the landing pad and the village path as I took in the sights, sounds, and smells of the village and the algel-fringed stream.

The villagers had awakened and were going about their day. Many were lining the banks of the stream, scooping their algel breakfasts into their feeding pouches. I was hungry and looking forward to joining them. The bright white sky illuminated the mineral plain's crystalline surface and the colorful buildings on the hillside and across the plain in Newton. I paused to listen to the rushing of the falls at the upstream end of the village, the babbling of the stream below me, and the slurping of the gelatinous algel as it was being scooped up and ingested. My olfactory receptors tingled with the smell of the fresh air and the moisture from the water and algel below me. I would always remember that moment, just as every kloormar remembers every moment from birth, but I felt compelled to pause and take it all in before I walked down to the stream bank and served myself a portion of fresh algel.

I continued along the path to the village. That's where K'tatmal spotted me.

"Greetings, Kelvoo. I see that you have disembarked from the spaceport shuttle. Have you been away?"

"Greetings, K'tatmal. I was accompanying Professor Jasmit Linford to the spaceport. I would like to thank you again for introducing him to me. The professor's visa was set to expire today, so he was compelled to return to Terra.

"Since we are speaking on the subject of Terra," I continued, "I am strongly considering accepting an offer from the Interplanetary University to teach on Terra."

"Has Kroz's relocation to Terra encouraged you to follow suit?"

I was unaware of Kroz's relocation to Terra, so I asked K'tatmal for more information.

"All I know," K'tatmal said, "is that Kroz is working on artificial intelligence in spacecraft control systems. Kroz accepted a position from a company on the Terran continent of Australia."

While the human first-contact team was visiting Kuw'baal, Kroz had taken a keen interest in software development. In fact, Kroz's expertise had saved our lives on *Jezebel's Fury*, so Kroz's choice of career made sense. K'tatmal, on the other hand, had specialized in Terran and interplanetary law and had played a key role in developing legal structures for kloormari dealings with Terra and other Alliance worlds.

"If I am offered a contract from the Interplanetary University, would you have the time to review it for me?" I asked. K'tatmal agreed immediately.

Later that afternoon I looked out through the front window of my home, waiting for Brenna and May to return. I saw them coming up the path as Brenna walked with her little sister after the school shuttle had dropped May off.

At seventeen, Brenna looked like an adult. She had reached her full height at fifteen. She was slim and physically fit. Her wavy black hair hung down level with her shoulder blades, blowing to one side in the light breeze.

While Brenna walked with long strides, May skipped along beside her. May had just turned eleven. Her dark hair was an explosion of tight curls that bounced with each skip. She was growing fast, with the top of her head now almost as high as her sister's shoulders.

8

Brenna was calm, restrained, and sometimes moody. In contrast, May was energetic, inquisitive, and prone to frequent laughter. Both were highly intelligent for their ages. Brenna cared a great deal more about other humans' impression of her while May was more independent and less concerned with social matters.

It had been fascinating to observe the girls' intellectual, emotional, and physical growth on a daily basis since I had been granted legal custody of them. Over the years I had grown to care deeply about these unique humans and, in my own limited kloormari way, I loved them very much.

When the girls entered the house, I requested that they take a seat. It would be an understatement to say they were excited when I asked them whether they were still interested in moving to Terra. It was rewarding to see Brenna's unabashed smile while May jumped up, clapped her hands, and bounced around the room, cheering.

Two days later, when I was certain that Jas would be back at work on Terra, I sent him a message via the interplanetary quantum entanglement network, requesting a copy of the university's offer and contract. His response showed that he was every bit as excited as the girls were. I took the contract to K'tatmal, who assured me that the only unusual aspect of the agreement was the degree to which they were willing to accommodate and welcome the girls and me.

***

Twenty-one days after Jas returned to Terra, Brenna, May, and I boarded the same spaceport shuttle that he had taken.

Once in orbit, we transferred to an interplanetary transport, which broke away from Kuw'baal and headed for the Ryla jump point. Twelve hours later, the ship leaped to the Terran jump point in line with the rotational axis of Sol. As the transport moved away from Sol and angled toward the orbital plane of its planets, the ship approached Terra from its northern hemisphere and assumed a circumpolar orbit. While we waited a few minutes for a shuttle to arrive, we stood before a large window in the main passenger lounge.

Compared with the pure white cloud cover of Kuw'baal, Terra's beauty was stunning. Its appearance was comparable to Saraya, which was the first inhabited world that I had ever seen as a visitor. Terra looked exactly as I had expected from the countless holos, vids, and images that I had viewed since first contact, but nothing could replicate the feelings that we had while orbiting the "real" world of Terra.

I stood and watched while Brenna and May leaned against the glass, cupping their hands on either side of their faces to block the reflections from the interior lighting, giving them the clearest possible view of our new home. All of the unknowns and all of my fears and doubts remained within me, but they were tempered by Jas's advice about making the unknowns known. The girls' excitement and awe was palpable as they gazed upon their species' homeworld for the first time. That alone made me realize that my decision was the logical and correct choice.

So, there we stood, three eager immigrants ready for the warm embrace and the boundless opportunities of an amazing new world.

TWO: HUMAN CUSTOMS

The orbital shuttle from Terra docked to the side of the transport, and its doors slid open with a gentle hiss. The shuttle disgorged its outbound passengers while we Terra-bound passengers waited to transfer. When the last being exited the shuttle, we saw Jas waiting for us just inside, a joyful smile on his face.

"How wonderful of you to meet us here in person, Professor Linford," I said, extending my hand paddle.

"That's *Chancellor* Linford to you, Professor Kelvoo!" he admonished, still grinning.

"How so?" I inquired.

"Well, there'd been a vacancy for the top job for quite a while. It seems that recruiting the most famous kloormar in history might have had something to do with my promotion!"

I offered my hearty congratulations to Chancellor Linford as I firmly gripped and shook his hand.

The gentle touchdown of the shuttle on Terra felt like coming home to a familiar place. I had studied Terra and humans to such an extent that, as we entered the arrivals complex, the sights, sounds, and smells were almost exactly as I had expected.

On one side of me, Brenna held my hand paddle as we walked. On the other side, May clasped my other paddle, her small fingers interlaced between the claspers on my palm. As we continued down the ramp, the corridor became more crowded as arriving passengers emerged from adjoining ramps. The increasing noise and chaos drove home the weight of my responsibility to care for and protect the girls. Brenna and May were buzzing with nervous energy, their heads swiveling to take in every sight and sound of the human homeworld that they had only heard about in stories and on the news. In their developing minds, Terra had mythical qualities, commanding awe and reverence.

At the bottom of the ramp, Jas held his Infotab close to a sensor, prompting a spaceport employee to meet and guide us to a holding area marked "Customs – VIP Arrivals." After the crush of the crowd, I was relieved to see that the four of us were the only occupants of the holding area. A burly human customs officer entered and then opened two doors on the opposite side of the room.

"The three humans will proceed to screening area alpha," he said in an officious tone. "The kloormar," he added, jabbing a finger in my direction, "will accompany me to area kilo for extraterrestrial examination."

Brenna and May's grip on my hand paddles tightened. "That's not a good idea," Jas replied. "I'm chancellor of the Interplanetary University, Mediterranean Campus. This kloormar is my special guest and is not familiar with Terra."

"Kelvoo had some very bad experiences with humans," Brenna interjected. "I want to go with Kelvoo!"

"Me too!" May shouted.

"Why the change?" Jas asked. "The last time I traveled back to Terra, kloormari visitors were being cleared alongside humans."

"Well, that changed last week," the officer replied. "Now we have new equipment for scanning kloormari. You have two alternatives. Your kloormari friend can come with me right now, or he can turn around, go back up the ramp, and return to the shuttle. Your choice!"

"It's alright. I'll go with the officer," I said. "I've read about Terran security procedures, and I'm sure everything will be fine." Having read the officer's badge, I turned toward him. "Please lead the way, Officer Montgomery."

Jas, Brenna, and May made their way toward screening area alpha as I followed Montgomery down a short corridor.

"I noticed that you referred to me as 'he' back in the holding area," I said to demonstrate that I wanted to be helpful.

"What?"

"You said, 'Your kloormari friend can come with me right now, or *he* can turn around.'"

"So?"

"I thought you might want to know that, as a kloormar, I am neither male nor female. I can contribute genetic material to create a baby, or I can host a baby inside my reproductive pouch."

"Look, buddy," Montgomery said without turning toward me, "they just pay me to process people—I mean creatures—I mean *beings*, OK? I'm not here to make nice with anyone or to bother being 'socially correct.'"

The corridor ended in a large room. It was three stories high and full of equipment, with a handful of customs officers milling about. Windows lined the sides of the room, showing humans being screened in the adjoining room on one side and a couple of Sarayans being processed on the other. The far wall consisted of floor-to-ceiling glass, which separated the screening room from a cavernous arrivals lounge, where travelers gathered after clearing customs.

"Got a kloormar for you!" Montgomery called out as we entered.

"Cool," an officer standing behind a counter said. "Put our guest in cubicle one while I fire up the scanner."

Clearly, kloormari visitors were still a rarity on Terra. The last time I had inquired, 1,507 kloormari were located on Terra, mostly to study or work as scientists or engineers.

Officer Montgomery ushered me into a cubicle with barely enough room for me to stand, then closed the door behind me. The walls hummed and emitted a soft bluish glow.

A sense of unease took hold of me. I analyzed my feelings, something I had practiced often over the previous seven years. I concluded that my anxiety was due to the impersonal way that I had been ordered about by an authority figure. The situation brought certain memories into focus, most of them relating to my captivity on *Jezebel's Fury*. I was relieved when the cubicle opened.

"Cleared," an automated voice stated.

"I'm Officer Sommers," the officer at the counter said. "I'll see you over here, please."

Montgomery and two others positioned themselves behind Sommers. "Please excuse them," she said, "we don't get a whole lot of kloormari through here. They're just curious. OK, let's see your ID."

I opened my Infotab pouch and produced a passport that had been issued to me by the Terran embassy outpost on Kuw'baal. As I handed it over, I noticed a bulge on the hip of each officer, partly concealed by their thigh-length blazers. As Sommers tapped my card on an ID scanner, Montgomery placed his hands on his hips, pulling back the sides of his blazer.

Sommers looked up at me in surprise. "You're Kelvoo?"

At that moment I recognized the holster, barrel, indicator lights, and textured grip of a blaster pistol on Montgomery's hip. The realization that each officer was armed suddenly dawned on me. In that instant, I— to use a Terran colloquialism—"freaked out."

My vision became blurred, ambient voices and sounds started echoing, my extremities burned, and despite my respiration rate reaching its maximum, I felt as if I couldn't take in enough oxygen. I was frozen with terror. Flashbacks from *Jezebel's Fury* filled all four of my brains. I relived the captain pointing his blaster at me. I saw the blaster fire that was directed toward me in the battle on Benzolar 3, and I revisited the horrific moment when, in an unthinkable fit of rage, I used a blaster rifle to kill Bazz, a crew member.

Officer Sommers' voice seemed to echo discordantly when she asked whether I was alright. At the same time, Montgomery's right hand moved back, a millimeter closer to his blaster.

Dropping to the floor, I used all of my limbs, including the eight clasper limbs along my midriff, to race down the length of the screening room, coming to an abrupt stop when I collided with the glass wall. When the customs officers pursued me, I was convinced that I had been duped into traveling to Terra and that I was about to be captured, tortured, and in all likelihood, murdered. I sprang to my feet and ran to the opposite corner of the room, upending furniture and knocking over any equipment in my path.

People in the adjoining rooms rushed to the glass to take in the spectacle. Some used their Infotabs to record the scene.

The wall I had entered through had an abstract sculpture attached to it, which extended to the ceiling, three stories up. Using all of my limbs, I scurried up the rods, panels, and textured metal outcroppings of the sculpture to the top. By that time Brenna and May had cleared customs and were in the arrivals lounge. Amid the jumble of images and sounds, I saw Brenna pressed up against the glass wall, staring at me in horror and shaking her head. Though I couldn't hear her, I saw that she was shouting, "No, no, no!" May stood beside her, crying. Jas was running back and forth, waving his arms and trying to get the attention of anyone who could put an end to the chaos.

Montgomery drew his blaster pistol and pointed it toward me. "What's the stun setting for a kloormar?" he shouted.

"For Chrissake!" Sommers screamed. "Monty, put your goddamn blaster away! That's Kelvoo!"

"Who?"

"Kelvoo! C'mon, Monty, don't you read or watch the news?"

"Hell no! I'll be damned if I'm going to get suckered in by that garbage!" Monty snapped as he lowered his blaster.

Perched just below the ceiling, I tried to calm myself. Jas had caught the attention of a high-ranking official who used an access key to open a door in the glass wall. She led Brenna into the room.

"It's OK, Kelvoo!" Brenna shouted. "You're safe!" She and the official picked their way to the base of the sculpture, stepping around and over the objects that I had strewn about in my panic.

"My name is Sheila," the official called up to me. "Sheila Yang. I'm the administrator of this spaceport. What happened, Kelvoo?"

"I don't know," I said between breaths.

"Please come down, Kelvoo," Brenna implored.

Still shaken, I descended the sculpture. On the other side of the glass, a huge crowd had gathered with people talking and gesticulating to one another.

Twelve security guards were let through the doors. They escorted Administrator Yang, Brenna, and me, forming a cordon around us as we

14

walked out into the arrivals area. I watched as Yang entered a ten-character security code to open a set of secured doors into a private lounge, where Jas and May were waiting for us. Yang called Sommers into the lounge.

Once I had calmed myself, I felt terribly embarrassed as I explained to the group that the sight of blasters and the memories they invoked had triggered my panic.

Yang asked Sommers if she knew who I was.

"Yes, Administrator," Sommers replied. "I've read Kelvoo's story twice, and I was deeply moved both times. Unfortunately, Monty—Officer Montgomery—hadn't heard of him—I mean, Kelvoo." She turned toward me with downcast eyes. "I'm so sorry, Kelvoo. I know how much you and your species have suffered at the hands of humans. I didn't realize who you were until you provided your passport. I completely understand your reaction."

Administrator Yang invited us to use the lounge for as long as we needed. She told Jas that his semi-orbital craft would be given priority clearance for departure whenever we were ready. Jas also told me to take as much time as I needed.

During the awkward small talk that followed, I wondered whether my efforts over the past seven years had been wasted. All of my meditation, all of my studies, all of the support from my peers, all of the help from human professionals, and all of the reforms and reparations from the Terran government clearly hadn't been enough for me to overcome my trauma.

"I'm ready," I said finally. "Let's go."

We walked down an empty corridor and outside to a secure landing pad where the semi-orbital was waiting for us. As I stepped into the blinding white light of Sol, Jas patted my shoulder. "Welcome to Terra, Professor Kelvoo." I didn't know whether he was trying to be ironic, sarcastic, funny, or sincere, as the subtleties of human communication still eluded me at times.

As we walked toward the craft, I looked back to find Brenna and May still standing on the pad where we had first set foot on it. Their arms were spread wide and their eyes were closed as they basked in the light as if wanting to absorb every photon. I realized that the girls hadn't been exposed to the direct light of a star for many years and, with their human memories, they must have forgotten what it felt like. Jas and I gave them a few minutes to soak up the moment.

THREE: A NEW HOMECOMING

The semi-orbital flight to the university was smooth and short. The craft accelerated in the energy beam as we cleared the atmosphere. At the cutoff point, the beam faded away. As our acceleration diminished, the graviton field was activated and began to intensify. As a result, the direction that felt like "down" shifted from aft of the vessel to the floor beneath my feet, giving the illusion that the craft was rotating.

In a matter of minutes, the vessel began its descent as it passed over the islands of Malta and Gozo, which glowed against the deep blue backdrop of the Mediterranean Sea. At an altitude of 20,000 meters, I saw puffy clouds below, reminding me of my first spacecraft journey when I joined the human first-contact team on the *Pacifica Spirit,* and I saw the clouded sky of Kuw'baal from above.

As we entered the Terran clouds at 3,000 meters, I recalled the wonderful experience of coming home to Kuw'baal after my abduction. I concentrated on those memories, so I could diminish my thoughts of the terrifying experiences that had led to my outburst at the spaceport. *I'm going home*, I thought. *I'm heading for my new home.*

The clouds vanished as we entered a clear expanse of sky and crossed the eastern shore of the sea over a wide, sweeping beach and sand dunes. The vessel banked to the south once the dunes gave way to rocky foothills and jagged, arid mountains. The scenery reminded me of the terrain near my home village, only far brighter. To the west, Sol's afternoon rays reflected off the deep blue sea, shimmering with flashes of gold. Continuing its curved trajectory, the craft turned back toward the sea, descended between mountains, and touched down on the university's landing strip. Like me, Brenna and May had their eyes glued to the floor, ceiling, and wall viewports along with the monitors showing the feed from the forward and aft vid cams for the trip's entire two-hour duration.

The landing strip ended in a circular pad at the edge of a rocky drop-off. A glass structure in the shape of a crescent lined the far side of the pad, overlooking the campus below. The doors of the vessel opened, and Jas led us to the reception building. Along the way, Brenna and May held my hand paddles. When the doors slid open and we entered the building, a group of six humans and one Mangor applauded.

Jas turned toward me. "These people are the facility's staff. It appears that they want to give you an impromptu welcome. They were only informed of your arrival moments ago on a need-to-know basis.

"According to your wishes, there will be no formal gatherings until you're settled in and an official announcement has been made." He turned to address the staff. "Alright, thank you for your enthusiasm. Our guests have traveled a long way, so please keep a respectful distance and please honor the confidentiality of this event."

The staff returned to their stations.

"Let's take a look at your new community," Jas said.

We walked through the rear doors onto a spacious deck at the edge of the drop-off, overlooking the university campus and the sea beyond it. As I stood at the railing, I saw that Jas had been true to his word about the local climate and how well suited it was to kloormari physiology. The temperature and the desert landscape felt like home. Although I wasn't going to experience rain almost every day, the breeze was laden with moisture from the Mediterranean, providing a comfortable level of humidity. The biggest difference for me was the expansiveness of the water and the brightness of the scene under the direct light, making the colors glow with a vibrancy that I hadn't seen since visiting a beach on Saraya.

As I stood at the railing, Jas gave me a quick overview, describing the major points of interest on the campus below. Most striking to me was the intense green that delineated the manicured, irrigated grounds and the way it stood out from the white and yellow sand and rocks surrounding it. The silver tanks and pipes of the desalination plant stood guard at the north end of the beach close to a large pier. At the opposite end of the beach, pilings extended two kilometers out into the sea and several kilometers along the shore, remnants of a massive atmospheric carbon-capture facility that had operated until two centuries ago.

After Jas finished describing the scene, I realized that I was so absorbed in my own reactions that I had been ignoring Brenna and May. *Are they excited by what they're seeing, or are they afraid to be in a strange place, so far from their homeworld of Perdition and, for the last seven years, Kuw'baal?* I wondered.

"How are you girls feeling?" I asked.

"This is the most beautiful place I've ever seen!" Brenna exclaimed without breaking her gaze from the sea.

"When can we go to the beach?" May asked.

"Let's get you settled in first," Jas said, motioning toward a car with its roof retracted. When we were fastened in, the car floated up over the railing and then descended over the drop-off and down the slope of the manicured, fragrant grounds of the campus toward the beach. We passed between student dormitory buildings, followed by apartments and semi-detached dwellings for faculty, and finally a gated enclave of houses. "Welcome to your home," he announced.

The car settled onto a pad outside a house that backed onto the beach. A patch of date palms gave way to a lawn in front of the house. Rows of olive trees lined the sides. The air smelled of vegetation with a hint of sea salt. We got out of the car and entered the home. The girls' luggage awaited them in the foyer. Having no need of possessions, with the exception of my Infotab and identification, everything I required was in the pouch on my belt.

Jas gave us a brief tour of our new home and familiarized us with the furnishings and equipment. I explained that, because of my anatomy, I had no need for chairs or a bed.

"I know," Jas replied, turning toward the girls, "but I thought Brenna and May might appreciate a few creature comforts."

Brenna smiled while May nodded vigorously. "For sure!"

Jas added that a room had been set aside as my study. All furnishings in that room had been removed, and only a combination algel incubation vat and dispenser had been added for my dietary requirements.

I complimented Jas on his excellent knowledge of the house. "I should know the place," he said. "I lived here before I visited Kuw'baal! I've just moved to the house three doors that way." He motioned to the north.

"Chancellor, please! You shouldn't have given up your home for us!"

Jas looked directly at my eye dome. "Kelvoo, I don't think you fully appreciate how special and important you really are, not just to this institution but to my entire species! As I've said before, your account of your experiences with humans has opened our eyes. Your perspective led to the Correction, during which humanity reexamined its culture, its relationship with the outliers, and our place in the Planetary Alliance. Moving to another house was the least I could do in recognition of your accomplishments. Besides, I was getting tired of the old place anyway!"

Jas explained that soon I would see the first payment of my salary on my Infotab. I reminded him that I had no use for SimCash or any other forms of compensation.

"Well, *you* might not, but I have a feeling the girls wouldn't mind a little pocket money," he said, smiling at Brenna and May. "I think you'll find out rather quickly that money is a necessity of life on this planet. I also know how much you care about your fellow beings. If you end up with plenty of excess SimCash, I'm sure you'll find many causes that you can support.

"You must be famished!" Jas said. "You haven't eaten since we left the interstellar transport this morning, and the girls only had a few snacks since then. I'm going to walk home, so you can have some dinner and get settled, but don't hesitate to call my Infotab anytime for any reason at all. The car we came in is university property, but you're free to use it as you see fit."

The moment the front door closed behind Jas, May bounded up to me. "Can we go to the beach now? Please, please, please?"

"As soon as we've eaten," I replied. "What would you both like for dinner?"

"Hot dogs!" May exclaimed.

"Yuck! I'll have fettuccine Alfredo and some green salad please," Brenna said.

"Servitor: activate," I called out, as per Jas's instructions. A panel in the kitchen ceiling slid open, and a Luxor P-1 domestic service bot floated down toward me, hovering about a meter above the floor.

"Servitor, this eleven-year-old human has the designation 'May,'" I said, placing a hand paddle on May's shoulder, "and this seventeen-year-old human's designation is 'Brenna.' My designation is 'Kelvoo.' Please provide hot dogs for May and fettuccine Alfredo and a green salad for Brenna."

What I thought was a simple request turned into a litany of questions and clarifications with the servitor requiring the number of hot dogs and the specific style of wieners and buns to be selected, along with condiment specifications. Similar questions were asked about the fettuccine. Finally, the servitor asked us to choose between "cooking performed by servitor," "cooking performed by household occupant," or "pre-cooked."

"How long is this going to take?" May asked. "I want to go to the beach!"

"Better make it pre-cooked," I told the servitor.

"Order placed," it replied. Two minutes and thirty-five seconds later, I stepped outside through the back door when a drone arrived from the campus commissary with the girls' dinner.

"Have dinner with us, Kelvoo," Brenna said. I asked the servitor for a bowl, filled it with algel from the study, then I joined the girls at the kitchen dining counter. While we ate, May suggested that we give the servitor a name.

"How about 'Bot' since it's just a bot?" Brenna suggested.

"I want 'Polly,'" May said.

"How about 'Pollybot'?" I asked, rather pleased with my creativity. I was even more pleased when the girls agreed to my suggestion. Brenna assigned the name to the servitor. When we left the counter, Pollybot washed my bowl and placed the food packaging into the reclamation receptacle.

"Time to sleep?" Pollybot asked.

"No, it's still too early for us," I replied.

"Clarification: I, servitor unit Pollybot, am inquiring as to whether I, Pollybot, should return to storage and enter sleep mode."

"Yes," I said. "Thank you." Some beings find it odd to use politeness when addressing bots, but I wanted to demonstrate courtesy for the girls' benefit. Pollybot glided to a spot below its storage compartment and rose through the ceiling panel, which slid shut behind it.

"Race you to the beach!" May shouted as she exited through the patio doors at the back of the house and charged for the shore. Brenna and I pursued her across the sandy dunes between clumps of beach grass, then over the warm, soft upper beach to the cool, wet, hard-packed sand fringing the sea. A stiff breeze blew spray from the white crests of the waves and pushed drifts of sand up the beach. May kept running until the frothing, foamy remnants of a wave rolled up to her feet, soaking her shoes and the bottom of her pant legs. Squealing with joy, May turned around, barely outrunning the advancing water. When the water started to recede toward the trough of the next wave, she chased it back until the next wave broke and washed ashore.

As May and Brenna laughed, frolicked, and played "catch the wave," I let the surges break over my feet, up to my lower knee joints. The feeling of the sand shifting under my feet, the freshness of the briny air, and the push and pull of each wave took my mind back to the beach on Saraya where I had traveled with Sam Buchanan and the first-contact expedition, when my experience with humanity had been joyful and enlightening.

I entered a semi-meditative state while Sol took on its timeless red glow as it sank toward the horizon, signifying the end of the most eventful day since my captivity ended and I had returned to Kuw'baal seven years before. A sizable wave came in, reaching my upper knees and almost throwing me off balance, but I was able to adjust my stance without interrupting my pleasant state of mind.

I heard a distant, muffled human voice calling my name, followed by a tugging on my arm. I realized it was Brenna. "May's in trouble! A big wave got her!"

Snapping into full consciousness, my eye dome took in all 360 degrees of the view. All I could see of May was her face, submerging and surfacing and gasping for air fifty meters from me. I tried to run toward her, but the resistance of the water and the shifting sand impeded every step.

"I'm sorry!" Brenna shouted. "I'm so sorry. I only looked away for a second!"

When I reached May and scooped her up, I was surprised by the degree to which her sodden clothes weighed her down. May coughed and took a deep breath as a wave knocked me over and pushed me closer to the beach. This was followed by strong suction pulling me back out to sea. While I was prone, I clutched May and dug all of my other limbs into the sand to resist being dragged. When the next wave hit, I rode it in while holding May's head above the surface. I managed to get my feet under me and stagger to shore while May's limp body hung over my arm.

"Is she OK, Kelvoo? Oh God, she can't be dead!"

Ignoring Brenna's wails, I took the applicable human first-aid steps that I had learned years before. I laid May on her side in the sand with her head positioned lower than her chest. As I used an auditory receptor to check for breathing and a tendril to feel her carotid artery for a pulse, May started coughing and sputtering between urgent breaths.

Picking her up again, I ran into the house with Brenna close behind. I pulled the Infotab from my belt and was relieved to see that it was functional despite its submersion in seawater. I tapped the contact icon for Jas, followed by "Send Location," so he would see that I was in the house. Then I told Jas what had just happened.

"Stay right there," he replied. "I'll summon a mobile clinic and then I'll be right over."

Jas sprinted over and then, just over a minute later, a red-and-white box about ten by ten by three meters descended from the sky and landed just behind the house. An emergency physician emerged as two bump-outs extended from the box, increasing the clinic's footprint. We carried May into the clinic, removed most of her wet clothes, then placed her on a scanning bed. The scanning arm swept over May and then returned to its starting position while an array of internal images and telemetry flashed across monitors that hovered over her.

As the physician examined the data, he introduced himself as Dr. Charlie Bergen. "Who's our patient?" he inquired.

"May Murphy. I'm her legal guardian, Kelvoo."

"Kelvoo? Not *the* Kelvoo every human in the universe knows about?" he asked in astonishment.

"Well, not exactly *every* human," I said, wondering when he would return his attention to May. "For example, there's one customs officer called Monty who doesn't know me from any other kloormar. Now, if it isn't too much trouble, what is May's condition?"

"Well, Kelvoo, I'm relieved to say that the girl's lungs are free from seawater, and her electrolytes are within the normal range. The only deviation from the norm is that the encephalascan indicates high levels of stress and exhaustion, as one might expect from a near drowning. I'm going to attach a bio scanner module to her chest, which she is to wear for the next twenty-four hours. This will alert the med center if there's any trouble, but that seems unlikely. All in all, May is one lucky kid!"

By that time May's fits of coughing had subsided, and she was able to sit up. Doctor Bergen and I walked back into the house with May where Brenna and Jas anxiously waited. Brenna took May upstairs to her room to help her change into night clothes. Meanwhile, Dr. Bergen told me how pleased he was to meet me.

"Are you just visiting for a short time?"

"No, we intend to be here for a while," I said.

"There should be a formal announcement about Kelvoo's presence in the next few days," Jas said. "In the meantime, please keep that information to yourself."

"Well, I hope to see you around the campus then," Dr. Bergen said before he let himself out.

Through the glass doors, I saw Dr. Bergen tap a command into his Infotab. The mobile clinic retracted its extensions, then he entered, and the assembly rose straight into the air despite the gusting wind. It headed over the palms, presumably returning to the campus medical center.

"Is there anything else that you need or anything more I can do for you?" Jas asked.

"No thank you, Jas. I think we just need some quiet time to relax and get some sleep."

"Of course. The three of you have been through a lot today."

When Jas left, Brenna took a seat on the end of a sofa. "Kelvoo?" she said.

"Yes, Brenna," I replied as I locked my joints in a relaxed squatting position beside the sofa.

"I just wanted to say that, well, even though it's been a crazy, scary day, I'm really glad you brought May and me to Terra and . . . I guess I just wanted to say thanks."

I was moved by Brenna's words, mainly because she was displaying a side that was softer than usual. Shortly after her thirteenth birthday, Brenna had become argumentative and easily upset. Sometimes she was needy, but other times she pushed hard to assert her independence. For example, she had been clamoring for me to let her go to Terra, but she demanded to go on her own because she "didn't need to be babysat by a clueless kloormar." Her teachers and social worker back on Kuw'baal had assured me that this was a typical rebellious phase that humans often went through at her age.

I wondered whether Brenna's words of gratitude were a reaction to her sister coming close to losing her life. Perhaps she felt guilty about letting her attention lapse while May played in the waves. Most of all, I hoped that Brenna was becoming more emotionally mature and was well on her way to fulfilling her untapped potential.

FOUR: THE GIRLS

Despite our exhaustion, Brenna and I talked well into the night while May slept.

I let Brenna lead the conversation. She started by recounting some of the events on *Jezebel's Fury* that unfolded after my kloormari crewmates and I had agreed to teach the girls how to read. Like most of the crew, the girls were illiterate at that time, back when the custom in some outlier communities dictated that there was no need for females to be educated. Girls in such communities were usually born with the expectation that they would perform household chores and bear children.

With no other friends on *Jezebel's Fury*, Brenna, who was ten, and May, age four, were extremely bored. Most of their time was spent on their Infotabs looking at pictures or playing games. Their inability to read frustrated their innate curiosity because, unable to read instructions, they couldn't fully utilize their devices. At the same time, my fellow kloormari and I were only engaged in mundane tasks whenever the ship was between missions. Wanting a better life for his daughters, the girls' father, "Murph," approached the ship's holy man to ask him whether the kloormari could teach the girls how to read.

"Just so they can read recipes or the Holy Scriptures," Murph assured the reverend.

When the priest asked us to teach the girls, we accepted immediately. Our motivation was not altruistic—we hadn't even met Brenna or May yet. We accepted the reverend's offer in an attempt to ingratiate ourselves to the crew.

Brenna and May's hunger for knowledge led them to ask many questions during their studies, which we answered to the best of our ability.

The lessons ended abruptly when the holy man learned of our answers to some of the girls' questions about God, answers that didn't match the reverend's teachings. He branded us as heretics while trying to convince the captain to put us to death. We were far too useful to the captain for that to happen, but we were barred from providing further instruction to Brenna and May. The girls were distraught. Fortunately, their literacy had grown to the point that they could read at a level equal to Terran humans of similar ages.

24

"May and I were so lucky that you taught us to read," Brenna said. "It made us realize that there was an incredible universe to discover. Every day we downloaded books from the InfoServer, and we'd spend hours reading and learning and loving every minute of it. We'd look up what we would be learning if we were in Terran school and then we'd study those subjects and test each other with questions. If you hadn't taught us, I don't know how we would have fit in at school on Kuw'baal. May would have been OK, I guess, but I would have been the only ten-year-old in kindergarten!"

In my conversation with Brenna, there were many aspects of our time on *Jezebel's Fury* that we *didn't* talk about. We didn't discuss the arrival of the Sarayan warship, which captured *Jezebel's Fury* and freed my kloormari crewmates and me. We also didn't talk about the fate of the human crew who, to my utter horror, were executed by the Sarayans as punishment for their interstellar crime spree.

Murph was among those killed. The girls' mother had died a short time before *Jezebel's Fury* set out on its final mission. Murph thought it would be a good idea to take his daughters "on an adventure," so they came along for the ride. He had expected to serve on the crew, make an immense amount of SimCash, and return to his homeworld of Perdition where he could provide his daughters with a life of luxury for the rest of his days.

With Murph's death, Brenna and May had no one to care for them. When they arrived at the human settlement of Newton on Kuw'baal, they were placed into foster care while the Terran social services system attempted to locate any living family members on the outlier worlds of Perdition and Exile. They concluded that the girls had no living relatives, so they remained in the care of a childless couple, Troy and Edna Gramm.

One topic that Brenna *did* want to discuss was the time that she and May had spent in foster care. "I hated the Gramms!" she exclaimed. "I also hated myself. I thought I was garbage, just some backward outlier human. May and I wanted to be like the Terran humans or even the kloormari, so every day we kept reading and learning, so we could become something better.

"When we were put in school, we were the smartest kids in our classes, but that didn't matter. The other human kids found out that we were outliers. I think our foster mom must've blabbed to some other parent. May was teased a bit but not as much as me because she was with younger kids. May just put up with it and tried to please everyone. Not me! I changed my mind and decided I was *superior* to those bullying little snots! I wanted nothing to do with them.

"One day, little Clarice Bychok came strutting up to me in the schoolyard, 'Hey, Bren,' she said, 'my mom heard that you came here from a bunch of outliers on a *spaceship*. Is it true? Was your daddy a criminal? Was your mommy one of those dirty outlier concubines?'"

Brenna's recounting of the schoolyard events brought back my memories of the persecution of the kloormari on *Jezebel's Fury*. As I imagined how Brenna must have felt in school, my body tightened with anger.

"I punched that little skank right in the nose!" Brenna continued. "She fell on her back in the dirt, and I jumped on her and started pounding her face. Half of Newton must have heard her screaming. I kept going until a teacher pulled me off."

"That must have been traumatic for you," I replied.

"Are you kidding, Kelvoo? It felt great! I'm glad I did it, and I would've done it again! Little Clarice was the only one who was traumatized."

I could relate to Brenna's reaction. I had felt the same way in the moment when I could take no more, and I used a blaster to vaporize the head of a sadistic murderer on *Jezebel's Fury*.

"I proudly told the principal, the social worker, and the Gramms exactly what happened. They agreed that Clarice shouldn't have said those things, but they also said I should've reported her instead of beating her to a pulp. Yeah, right! Anyway, they said I had anger issues and that I was anti-social."

I was familiar with the events that Brenna was describing—the social workers had briefed me. Nonetheless, hearing the story from Brenna's perspective was enlightening.

When Brenna continued, she revealed information that was new to me. "While I was suspended from school, I spent every hour in my room, studying. The Gramms said I needed to learn to socialize and that I should get my nose out of my Infotab. They also said that May and I should join some kids clubs or play sports or something. The social workers told them to let us choose our own activities, but the Gramms kept hounding us. One day, Ms. Gramm got home from the office in a grumpy mood. She saw us reading, and for no reason at all she yelled, 'What the hell is wrong with you two? You think you're better than us? Some people are just too damned smart for their own good!' That was a low point for me, but do you know what the hardest thing was, Kelvoo?"

I had several guesses, but from what I had read, I knew that when a teenager opened up, it was best to say as little as possible. "I don't know," I replied.

26

"The worst thing was knowing that we were on the same planet as you and K'tatmal and Kroz and Keeto and the other kloormari from the ship. Every day that went by without hearing from you convinced us that you had abandoned us and didn't care. One day I asked the social worker why you never visited. She said you were probably just getting on with your own lives and perhaps we should consider doing the same."

"Brenna, you already know what happened," I replied. "We were returned to Kuw'baal before you, and we had no idea of your location until K'tatmal learned that you were right there in Newton. When K'tatmal told our group, we *desperately* wanted to see you. I had promised that our group of kloormari would do whatever we could to take care of you and May. When I made that promise, I had no idea how we could help two Terran kids, but I meant every word of it. We *needed* to see you!

"K'tatmal contacted the local Child and Family Services office. They couldn't understand why a group of kloormari would care about a couple of human children. They told us that you weren't ready to see us. They said that the sight of us could reopen your psychological wounds and traumatize you all over again. Worst of all, they claimed they told you about our request for a meeting. They told us you said you weren't ready right now, but maybe it would be alright someday in the future."

"Lying scumbags!" Brenna cried.

"That's certainly what we realized when you came to the village," I said. "How did you manage to get to the village to contact us?"

"I told May I was planning to find you and I might be gone for a long time," Brenna replied. "May said it was too dangerous, and she was worried we would be split apart and put in different homes, so I didn't tell her anything more.

"I waited until after dark and then sneaked out the Gramm's back door. I took an extra jacket with me and grabbed my hoverbike. I used black tape to cover the bike's lights. Instead of crossing the mineral plain to go straight to the kloormari village, I went in the opposite direction, toward the hills behind the village. It was slow going because there was no light, so I had to creep along using the bike's sensors. When the bike's nav map showed I was on the side of a hill facing the village, I dropped the extra jacket. It was bright red and yellow, so I figured that people would see it and try to search for me out in the hills.

"I went around the village and then crossed the plain at the bottom of the steepest hills and the rockfall. The stream that goes under the rockfall was still flowing, and the plain was partly flooded from the rain earlier that afternoon. The bike's safety system wouldn't let me cross over water, so I waded through and carried the bike over the flooded parts. Luckily, there was a tiny bit of light from the village and the landing pad. When I got to the algel falls, I hid the bike between some boulders and then sneaked downstream along the edge of the water, ducking behind the bank. When I got to the first set of stepping stones, I ran across. I didn't know my way around, so I ran through the village until I saw the biggest building, which turned out to be the community structure. I was exhausted, so I curled up in the entrance and fell asleep."

"That must have been when Kwazka found you," I remarked.

"Yeah, I didn't know that kloormar's name at the time, but I asked where I could find any of the kloormari that had been on *Jezebel's Fury*. Kwazka said it looked as though I might be in trouble and offered to contact the Terran authorities for me. I begged Kwazka not to do it until I could see you. I explained that I had been with your group on *Jezebel's Fury*, and I had an important message for you.

"Kwazka asked me, 'Are you May or perhaps Brenna?' I said I was Brenna. Kwazka told me that most of the members of Sam's Team who were on *Jezebel's Fury* lived in a cluster of huts at the upstream end of the village. Kwazka led the way to your group's huts and told me that your group had chosen to live in traditional huts as part of your healing."

I recalled the moment when Kwazka brought Brenna to our group. We had just risen from our meditation. We were about to go to the stream to have some algel and then do some peer group counseling as part of our daily healing routine.

Brenna was distraught and furious when she saw us. "Why?" she screamed. "Why did you leave me and May? We thought you cared about us! We loved you and we thought you were going to look after us! Well, now we hate you! We hate your dull, cloudy planet, and we hate ourselves! I hope you're satisfied, and we never want to see you again!"

My studies of human nature taught me that, at eleven years of age, Brenna was unable to express her feelings calmly. Given the information that was available to her at the time, her reaction was understandable.

"When you explained that you'd been trying to see us and the authorities had lied to you, I knew you were telling the truth," Brenna said as we continued to reminisce. "I remember you calling K'tatmal right away. K'tatmal must have come over in two minutes flat! We were all talking about what to do next when a kloormari kid named K'pai came over and reported an Infotab alert about a missing human, which was me, of course!"

"That's right, Brenna. I had told K'pai about you and May in an earlier discussion about our kidnapping, so K'pai knew I would be interested."

"So that's when we all decided to go back to Newton as a group, right?"

"That's right. We waited until the Child and Family Services office opened and then we all marched over there. The staff was shocked by our actions but even more shocked to see *you* with us."

I remembered the administrator demanding to know why we had "taken" Brenna.

"We are here to return Brenna Murphy," K'tatmal said, "but we will not leave this office until our concerns are addressed. We have reason to believe that you have misled this human and her sister and that you have lied to us as well. We also believe we have grounds to file a complaint to the CFS oversight authorities."

I recalled the wide-eyed look from Brenna's social worker and the uncertainty of the administrator who was speechless at first and then decided to hear our complaint. The administrator agreed to a visit a few days later, during which Sam's Team could meet with Brenna and May, provided he was present along with Brenna's social worker and the Gramms.

"Oh, that was one *awkward* meeting!" Brenna said, laughing. "May wasn't sure what was going on, so she just answered questions. When May and I repeated the things we had been told and your group talked about the lies that the officials had spouted, the administrator and the social worker looked kind of terrified. I think they were afraid of losing their jobs! The Gramms looked like they were mad but trying to keep it bottled up, so their heads wouldn't explode!"

I reminded Brenna that the administrator suggested that Brenna's suspension from school might be revoked.

"Yeah," Brenna said, "and I told them that if they sent me back I'd punch Clarice in the nose twice as hard and then take off again!"

"That's when the administrator accessed your academic records on his Infotab," I replied. "I remember him saying, 'Er . . . yes, well I see that your grades are exceptional, so I suppose you could continue your education via remote self-study.'" I replicated the administrator's nervous voice when I quoted him, which made Brenna laugh.

She recalled that, for the first while, meetings were infrequent and were always supervised. Then the policy changed, allowing her and May to see us almost whenever they wanted, with no supervision.

"I've always wondered what changed their minds," Brenna said.

"It was my story," I replied. "That was about the time when my written account of my experiences with humans started becoming widely read across the Planetary Alliance. That was the beginning of the Correction, when the Alliance warned the Terran government that, if they wanted Terra to remain in the Alliance, they needed to change their attitude toward the outlier humans and stop the exploitation of Kuw'baal and the kloormari. Suddenly, the Newton CFS office thought it would be best to take a hands-off approach.

"That's also when the Terran resource companies started leaving. Most couldn't make a go of things if they had to share ownership and revenue with the kloormari, as the Alliance demanded. Ninety-three days after our initial meeting, Edna Gramm lost her job when the Victory Mining Consortium closed their operations."

"Yeah," Brenna said, "family services assumed the Gramms would just take us to Terra with them. I remember how furious my foster mom was when she packed our bags and pushed May and me into her car and sped over to your village. She dumped us right in front of your hut and yelled 'They're *your* problem now!' As she drove off, I yelled, 'Goodbye and good riddance, you old battle-ax!'"

"You and May must have felt terribly rejected," I said.

Brenna nodded. "Sure, but I've never been so happy to be rejected in my entire life! May might have felt abandoned, but from that moment on, our lives got *so* much better!"

"I remember how impressed family services was with your change in attitude and how much happier you and May were," I said. "They didn't know whether to place you with new human foster parents, but since humans were leaving the planet in droves and everything was so chaotic, they just avoided dealing with the situation. You and May had to stay in K'tatmal's home for a while since a simple kloormari hut wouldn't have provided the necessities of life, but a few days later, a villager named Kalala left for a research position on Saraya. That's when I moved into Kalala's 'modern' home, and the two of you moved in."

"May sailed along in school, and I kept studying with help from you and the other kloormari," Brenna said.

"You did exceptionally well. When you were fourteen years and seven months old, you passed your basic education with top marks. You graduated four years earlier than the average Terran human."

Brenna nodded. "That was when I started bugging you about letting me go to university on Terra. I wanted to go by myself, but I was below the minimum age. That was frustrating for me, and I'm afraid I became a bit of a brat toward you. Later, I heard that you had offers to move to Terra. When did those offers start coming?"

"Humans were trying to get me to Terra even before my story was published. They knew about me from the news story when I was interviewed on the *Orion Provider* during the first-contact mission. When word got out that I had been abducted and then I was back on Kuw'baal, everyone wanted a 'piece of me,' so to speak. It wasn't until I got to know Professor Linford, now Chancellor Linford, that I changed my mind."

"Why did it take so long?"

"I wasn't ready psychologically. No member of Sam's Team was. We still had a lot of meditation, study, and peer counseling to do before we could deal sufficiently with our trauma. Of course, that's not to say we were the only ones who were traumatized. I can't imagine the psychological impacts on you and May after *Jezebel's Fury*."

Brenna's face darkened. "You know, Kelvoo, we've been having such a good conversation. Let's not go there. I'm not ready to talk about that, and I don't know when I'll ever be."

I realized the conversation was straying into dangerous territory, and I wanted to salvage the discussion since it felt like a real breakthrough, so I changed the subject. "The last time I asked, you hadn't chosen what you were going to study. So, now that we're finally here at a Terran university, have you made a decision?"

Brenna's mood brightened. "I sure have! I'm going to learn something really, really important, and May can even take lessons with me!"

"But, Brenna, May is only eleven years old! What could she possibly do alongside you?"

"Swimming lessons!" Brenna announced with a grin. She broke into peals of laughter, which I interpreted to be a cathartic release of tension and suppressed pain. A sense of relief washed over me. It had been a long time since I had felt so relaxed talking with Brenna.

"Come on, Kelvoo," she said, "that's funny! Why aren't you laughing?"

"I can see why your statement was amusing given the situation at the beach this afternoon, but you know that a kloormar is incapable of laughter."

"I don't care!" Brenna giggled. "I just want to hear you laugh! C'mon, humor me. Let me hear you laugh."

As a kloormar, I could produce any sound that was audible by humans, but I wasn't sure which style of laughter to emulate. On the flight to Terra, I had overheard part of an entertainment vid that Brenna had been watching. The audio had included laughter from a large audience. I vocalized the same sound for her.

"That's awful!" Brenna exclaimed, laughing even harder. Pointing a finger at me, she let loose and fell backward onto the sofa in uncontrollable paroxysms of laughter, tears streaming down her face. It was several minutes before Brenna recovered and sat up again.

While Brenna's laughed, it occurred to me that for most our conversation we had simply recalled things we already knew. Still, I hoped that recounting our experiences might help Brenna to process and come to terms with all she had gone through on Kuw'baal.

By then we had been talking for hours, and the need for my nightly meditation was strong. Brenna's physical appearance indicated she was beyond ready for a lengthy sleep. Nonetheless, once her laughter subsided, I felt compelled to keep talking.

"You know, Brenna, I'm glad you want to learn how to swim. If the events at the beach today taught us anything it's that we're in a new place, and we need to take our time and put more emphasis on safety."

"Yeah, I guess," she replied.

"You need to understand, Brenna, that I am responsible for you and your sister, and the burden of that responsibility weighs on me. Even though I don't have a gender, most humans seem to see me as a male, so in their eyes, it's as if I'm your dad."

"What did you just say?" Brenna asked, her eyes widening in surprise.

I knew I had made a terrible mistake, but the reasons for Brenna's reaction escaped me, and the intensity of her pain shocked me to the core.

"Why in the hell would you say that? I thought we were having a nice conversation! Is this what I get for opening up and spilling my guts to you?"

"Brenna, please! If my mention of fatherhood disturbs you, I am truly sorry. I don't understand!"

"No, you don't! You don't have a clue! You are *not* my father, and you *never* will be!"

"I'm sorry! I didn't intend to imply that I was anything of the sort!"

"Don't you get it, you clueless kloormar? It's *your* fault my daddy is dead!"

"What?"

"You know exactly what I mean!" Brenna shouted. "If you and your friends hadn't shown up in the first place, the Sarayans wouldn't have captured us! May and I would have gone back to Perdition with my dad, and none of this nightmare would have happened!"

Brenna burst into tears, then stormed up the stairs to her room and slammed the door.

At that moment, the only thing that was clear to me was that Brenna was still in intense pain. The emotional inconsistencies and volatility of human nature had always puzzled me, but teenage humans were at a whole other level. Later that evening as I drifted into a meditative state, I was deeply hurt and utterly perplexed.

FIVE: ANNOUNCEMENT

Brenna and May slept through our first full morning on Terra. Likewise, I didn't regain consciousness until the early afternoon. During my meditation, I attempted to put myself in Brenna's position, but I couldn't understand how a few ill-chosen words could elicit such a visceral response and shut down what had been such a productive conversation. I was disappointed in myself since, having a doctorate in human psychology, I should have known better. It was as though all of my academic knowledge had no value whatsoever with actual humans, especially a human that I thought I knew quite well.

I thought about apologizing to Brenna, but I was indecisive since I had lacked the intent to offend her. I decided I *would* apologize for my insensitivity despite my honest mistake, in the hope that we could reopen our dialogue.

May woke up shortly after I did. She activated Pollybot and requested pancakes. I fetched a bowl of algel and consumed it in the kitchen while May ate and tried to make small talk with the servitor. Pollybot seemed to be even more inept than I was when it came to communicating with young humans.

Brenna entered the kitchen, looking tired and as far as I could tell, sad.

"Brenna, I—"

"I'm sorry, Kelvoo. I know you didn't mean to make me upset last night," she said.

"Would you like to talk about it?"

"No," she replied, then requested a muffin from Pollybot.

With my planned apology rendered moot, I picked up my Infotab and noticed a message from Jas, sent at 09:03.

Hi, Kelvoo. Please give me a call when you're up and about. Cheers, Jas.

He had sent another message at 12:14.

Hi again, Kelvoo. I'm sure all of you are taking some time to rest after a very eventful time yesterday, so I'm not worried about you yet.

34

Please give me a call when you can. If I don't hear from you by 13:00, I'll send a security staffer over to the house, just to be sure you're all OK. Thanks, Jas.

I tapped the "Call" icon beside Jas's name and, moments later, his face appeared on the Infotab. "Hi there," he said in a hushed tone. "I'm in a meeting, so please hang on a sec while I step into the hallway."

I wondered why Jas hadn't addressed me by name, but as he got out of his chair, I saw that he was exiting from a conference room full of other humans. I realized he didn't want to give away my presence on Terra, which was yet to be announced.

"Sorry about that, Kelvoo," he said a moment later. He asked how the three of us were doing, and I gave a perfunctory answer, understanding that he likely didn't want any details.

"So, Kelvoo, there's a whole lot of media buzz right now. Rumors are rife about you being on Terra, and some of those rumors have you right here on the campus. Fortunately, there are also rumors that you've been spotted in the Himalayan Mountains, on Vancouver Island, in Antarctica, and in a cornfield by the Dnieper River."

"Out of curiosity, do you know where the rumors originated?" I inquired.

"No idea. There are people back at the spaceport and several university staff and faculty who are in on our little secret. Word could have also been spread from the interstellar transport or the shuttle crew or maybe even directly from Kuw'baal. Who knows? The point is that we need to get ahead of the story by moving up the announcement. I had been leaning toward next week to let you get settled in first, but we can pull something together by tomorrow night. Do I have your go-ahead to announce your arrival tomorrow?"

"Yes, of course, Jas. I trust your judgment."

"You're the best, Kelvoo! You and the girls should stay in the house today. The answerbots in our call center are getting overrun with inquiries, and we've spotted some vehicles hovering above the upper boundary of our exclusion airspace. They'll be up there using telescopic sensors and imagers. They're recording vids of the entire campus in the hope that you're here and you'll go outside. We're trying to get a special order to expand the exclusion perimeter. Anyway, may I come over and see you after work, let's say at 17:30?"

I assured Jas that I would be pleased to see him that afternoon.

Having heard my conversation with Jas, Brenna switched on the holovision screen in the entertainment room and searched for news of

35

my arrival. May took her pancakes and planted herself in front of the holoscreen. I finished my algel before joining the girls.

One story after another cited anonymous sources indicating I was no longer on Kuw'baal and that I may have traveled to Terra. Some news sources showed a stock image of a kloormar with accompanying text, such as "Is Kelvoo among us?"

"That doesn't even look like you!" May exclaimed.

"Doesn't matter," Brenna said. "Most people are too dumb to notice the difference!"

After a few minutes, a breaking news story filled the holoscreen with the title, "Rampaging Kloormar causes havoc at spaceport!"

"We've just received a remarkable vid of a kloormar engaging in behavior that we would never have thought possible!" the announcer said. "Here's what a traveler recorded in the kloormari customs screening room of the Central Plains Spaceport."

It was clear that the vid clip had been shot through the glass wall from the arrivals lounge. I saw myself using all of my limbs to flee from the customs officers. Brenna and May must have been close to the person recording the vid since I could hear Brenna shouting "No, no, no!" and May crying. The rest of the audio consisted of shouts and exclamations from the crowd as well as a thump when I collided with the glass wall. The vid showed me getting up and running back to the far wall and climbing the sculpture to the ceiling. The clip ended with Officer Montgomery aiming his blaster pistol at me.

Brenna buried her face in her hands. "Oh, please, just kill me now!"

"I'm sorry, Brenna," I said, "but you know that's something neither May nor I would ever do."

Brenna walked away from the holoscreen, and May switched it to a program for young viewers. Brenna was able to distract herself with games on the home's entertainment console, but both girls expressed frustration at having to stay inside for the rest of the day.

Later that afternoon, Jas arrived pushing a small hovercart with a selection of human foods. "I hope the girls haven't eaten yet!" he exclaimed. The girls eyed the cart with interest. "We've got an assortment of cultured proteins and vegetables as well as a few treats," he said. "I don't know which of these items are suitable, Kelvoo, but since you're the girls' guardian, I'll let you decide what's best for their nutritional needs."

"It's alright, Jas. I'm confident that Brenna and May can be trusted to select the most appropriate nourishment."

Brenna helped herself to a slice of Boston cream pie and an assortment of chocolates. May took a bowl from the kitchen and piled it high with ice cream from the cart's refrigerated compartment. She added sprinkles, fudge sauce, whipped cream, and about twenty maraschino cherries. With their food in hand, the girls retreated to the kitchen.

"Oh, to be young again and have the metabolism to process sugar without consequence!" Jas remarked.

He took a seat in the living room, and I adopted a kneeling position across from him. He told me that everything was set for an announcement in the campus's Seaview Conference Hall at 19:00 the next evening. Staff who needed to know had been informed and sworn to secrecy "on pain of death," according to Jas. I assumed he was joking. Invitations to a special announcement had been sent to select guests as well as journalists from three "friendly" news organizations.

"The news outlets tell me they're sending their highest-profile announcers," Jas said, "which tells me you're the worst-kept secret in the history of this university!" He smiled. "I'll let the cat out of the bag at the event and then you can come onstage for a quick speech and to answer a few questions for the media."

"As we've discussed before," I said, "questions from the media are a source of great anxiety for me. Ever since I learned how to imagine, I've imagined Kaley Hart questioning me. Is there any chance she'll be there?"

"No chance whatsoever! Oh, she certainly had her months of fame and success after she covertly interviewed you and broadcast the location of your planet to the known universe, but when the consequences of her reporting started to impact Terra, she became a journalistic pariah. She ended up as an anchor at the only outlet that would take her—the Veritacity Network."

"I'm not familiar with that organization."

"Consider yourself lucky. It's just a small, gutter-journalism outlet that ekes out an existence by muckraking and pandering to the dregs of humanity. Do yourself a favor and don't ever watch it. It'll rot all four of your brains!"

I sensed that Jas was slightly upset, so I didn't pursue the subject. He went on to outline the sequence of events for the upcoming announcement.

"So, what do you and the girls have planned for tomorrow?" he asked once he was finished. I told him that we hadn't made plans and that the girls had found it frustrating to stay indoors.

"Tell you what," he said, "why don't I get a security detail set up for tomorrow? None of the rumors about you have mentioned the girls, so let's allow them to roam around the campus, since no one knows who they are. They'll have to be shadowed by security, but the guards will keep their distance and intervene only if they think there's any risk. I won't tell security that you're staying in this house. I'll just say there's a VIP who has two girls. The guards will watch the house starting at 06:00 and they'll keep the girls in sight when they go out. Just make sure that they're back here by 17:00 so they can prepare for the festivities."

"Are you saying that the girls will be allowed to attend the announcement?"

"Of course they will! After all, aren't they just like family to you?"

"Well, I think Brenna might differ with you on that!"

"Ah, yes! To be young again and rebel against the tyranny of authority!" Jas mused.

After he departed, I found the girls sprawled on the couches in the entertainment room. May was on her back, rubbing her distended belly and groaning. "I gotta tummy ache."

"Do you know the cause?" I asked.

"She went back to the hovercart and loaded her bowl two more times," Brenna explained. Her face had also taken on a pallid complexion.

"Oh yeah? Well, Brenna went back and cleaned out all the chocolate from the cart," May retorted.

Brenna asked me how my meeting with Jas went. I provided a brief synopsis and was sure to mention that they were invited to the announcement the following night.

"Yeah, I'm going to give that a hard pass!" Brenna said.

"Why?" I asked.

"I don't want the attention. I just want to be a normal student here without being defined by my history with you or Kuw'baal or the outliers or anything like that."

"Well, I'm gonna go for sure!" May said. "Will there be ice cream?"

"Probably not."

"Good! I don't need another gut ache!"

May's statement brought a smile to Brenna's face.

The girls smiled even more when I told them that they would be free to explore the campus the following day. Brenna bristled when I added that they would be under constant supervision for their safety, but she decided the intrusion was outweighed by the "illusion of freedom," as she put it.

The girls were still feeling the aftereffects of their overindulgence, so despite the early hour, they didn't hesitate to go to their rooms to rest and recuperate. I welcomed the opportunity to consume my evening algel and meditate in my study.

The next morning, the girls had finished breakfast by 07:15. On their way out the back door, Brenna asked for "a little pocket money," so I transferred 100,000 SimCash units to her Infotab.

A uniformed security team member was standing behind a shrub outside one of the neighboring houses. Her watchfulness was comforting to me.

With the girls being out, I spent most of the morning refining my plan for the course I would be teaching. At 13:28, May returned to the house. She explained that Brenna had met up with a group of students who invited her to join them for lunch. "They were just yapping away and laughing and being boring, so I told Brenna I was going back to the house. I asked one of the security guards to take me back home."

"Did the other students know who Brenna was?" I asked. "Did they see that the security people were watching over you?"

"Nah. Brenna told the group that her name was Glenda. The whole bunch of them were laughing and goofing off so much they didn't notice the guards at all!"

May went to her room to read. Brenna returned just before 17:00 holding a package. "It's a new dress," she explained. She took it out and held it up against her body.

"Very nice," I said, unsure how to react. Brenna smiled, so I was pleased that my response was acceptable.

"May tells me that you made some new friends," I said.

"I did! I met some really interesting people. *Way* more interesting than any humans on Kuw'baal! By the way, they're all pretty sure you're here, Kelvoo. They've heard that the university has a special announcement tonight, and I think they've figured it out!"

"So, what will you be doing while May and I are at the event?"

"Actually, I think I'd like to come along after all. That's why I bought a new outfit."

"Is there something that changed your mind?"

"The other students did. They love you! I couldn't believe it!"

"You couldn't believe that they love me?"

"Oh, come on! You know what I mean."

"Actually, Brenna, it does seem strange that so many humans would love me. After all, since I've become known across the Planetary Alliance, the humans have been through many difficult transitions. Most of the students here would have experienced changes in their lives while they were still children."

"Well, I told them I was from the outlier colonies, which wasn't a total lie. I asked them a few questions about how things changed for them during the Correction. Life was tough for some of their families for a while, but they all think Terran society changed for the better. Well I think *most* of them feel that way."

"Most?"

"There was one guy, Griffin. When we were talking about you, he turned away and didn't say much. I don't know; I think he's just shy. That's OK with me. He's actually kind of cute!"

"Oh, barf!" May replied, opening her mouth and sticking a finger toward the back of her throat.

"Well," I said, "with you being attracted to a male human, it's a good thing you had your fertility reversal prior to our departure from Kuw'baal."

"Oh my god!" Brenna exclaimed, giggling in shock. "I can't believe you just said that!"

"I don't know what you can't believe, Brenna. I'm just saying that it's important to avoid unwanted pregnancy if you have sexual congress with a male human. Of course, at some point if you wish to bear offspring, you can complete the means and competency tests and have your infertility reversed."

Brenna stood with her jaw hanging open. "OK, this conversation is *over!*" With that, Brenna and May went to their rooms to prepare for the announcement and subsequent festivities.

That evening, Jas, dressed in formal attire, ushered the three of us into his car, which took us across the campus to the conference center. Around the university's perimeter, we saw vehicles hovering or making their way to the northeast where a gap had been opened in the exclusion zone. The passengers were being screened, one vehicle at a time, to ensure that only invited guests were allowed through the gap. High above the campus, larger vehicles hovered with spotlights scanning the area around the conference center, casting bright white circles over the building and its grounds.

"That's the media trying to sneak a peek at you," Jas explained.

His car took us down a ramp to a secure loading bay below the conference center. From there we proceeded through large double doors, boarded a lift up to ground level, and walked along a service passageway into a cozy room, backstage from the Seaview Conference Hall.

A tall human, dressed similarly to Jas, let us into the "green room." Jas took the man's hands in his and leaned over to give him a quick kiss. Keeping his grip on one of the man's hands, Jas turned back to me. "Kelvoo, I would like to introduce you to my good friend, Simon."

"Simon, I'm very pleased to make your acquaintance, sir," I said, nodding my eye dome.

"Oh, no! The pleasure is all mine! I am so honored to be in your presence!" Simon gushed, bowing low.

I wasn't sure how to respond to Simon's effusive praise, so I changed the subject. "Based on the kiss, would I be correct in thinking that your relationship with Jas is more than friendship? Are you, perhaps, partners?"

"*What* did you just say?" Brenna asked. Her shocked reactions to my words seemed to be a trend that was gaining momentum.

Jas laughed. "It's alright." He turned to Brenna. "New non-human arrivals usually take some time to learn the topics that aren't discussed in certain situations." Jas turned back to me. "Don't worry, Kelvoo. None of our guests are going to judge you. For the record, though, Simon and I haven't been dating all that long, but things are moving along nicely. He's got a good, solid family conglomerate, and you never know; someday I might just apply for inclusion."

Judging by Simon's reaction, I guessed that Jas's statement was cheeky, and Simon was embarrassed, though he smiled broadly.

A monitor on the wall showed people filing into the conference hall and being guided to their assigned seats. The crowd was animated, chatting excitedly. A security staffer came into the room to show Brenna and May to their seats. I watched as the girls were placed in the first row.

At exactly 19:00, music started to play, and the lights dimmed.

"Shouldn't we be going out there now?" I asked.

"Not yet," Jas replied. "We want to wait a few minutes for the audience's anticipation to grow."

Three minutes later, he asked me whether I was nervous.

"Extremely!"

"Me too! Don't worry; it's natural. Besides, what's the worst that could happen?"

"Well, I might say something that is misinterpreted. I could inadvertently disgrace myself, my species, this university, and you! I could put my entire homeworld and the kloormari in danger, just like when I had my ill-fated interview with Kaley Hart! I could—"

"Sorry I asked!" Jas interjected. Then he smiled. "Don't worry, you'll do fine."

Jas didn't say anything further until a conference manager opened the stage door. "They're ready for you."

The music stopped playing, and the stage lights brightened. In the audience section, the lights were off, with the exception of a red glow over each exit. From onstage the front row seats were dimly lit, allowing me to see Brenna and May. The audience members behind the front row were only visible as silhouettes.

As planned, Jas and I stepped out of the green room and waited just behind the curtains on one side of the stage. Simon joined me there while Jas strode out on stage, to sustained applause. A microphone descended from the ceiling and hovered just below his chin.

"Honored guests, benefactors, members of the media, and friends," Jas said in a crisp, clear, well-practiced voice. "Welcome to the Mediterranean Campus of the Interplanetary University. You have been invited here to witness a great event in the history of this institution and, I daresay, a landmark event for Terra!"

As Jas continued with his platitudes, I took a closer look around the edges of the stage. Just past one side of the front row was a long table with three guests, seated apart from the crowd. Large cameras were positioned behind them, and other cameras were hovering over the audience or the stage itself. I concluded that the three guests were the media representatives. The cameras were large because, before agreeing to participate in the announcement, I had stipulated that the cameras must be clearly visible, unlike the hidden camera that had been used to surreptitiously interview me several years before.

Live broadcasts from the event were forbidden. Recordings of the event were to be cleared by the university and me before release. Any segments that misrepresented me or the university were to be deleted at my discretion, up to and including the entire recording. All of these conditions were intended to make me comfortable, but even so, I was terrified.

Sensing my unease, Simon struck up a conversation with me, asking about my home planet, my impressions of Terra, and how the girls and I were settling in. Simon struck me as friendly and empathetic, and I could see why Jas liked him.

After concluding his speech, Jas introduced me. "I am pleased to announce a very special addition to our teaching faculty. Joining us is an honors graduate with a doctorate in human psychology. Not only that, our new member has been at the forefront of the societal changes that have swept through this sector of the galaxy. Our new member's writings were, in fact, the key catalyst for those changes!

"Honored guests, benefactors, members of the media, and friends, it is my deepest honor to introduce to you the worst-kept secret in the history of this university, Professor Kelvoo!"

The audience roared its approval. I could tell from the changing angle of the din that the audience had risen to its feet in a wave from the front rows to the back of the house. I felt a hand on my shoulder. "That's your cue!" Simon said, nudging me with one hand and motioning toward the stage with the other. "Have fun out there!" He smiled as I stepped out into the lights.

Jas took a few steps back while applauding and smiling at me. I heard the roar of the audience, though I couldn't see them clearly. I also saw the journalists and their cameras. As I moved toward center stage, the microphone hovered close to the vocal outlets on my torso. As a kloormar with flawless recall, my speech was memorized and ready to go. I, however, was not.

The sights and sounds before me blended with the outpouring of appreciation from the crowd, along with their enormous expectations. All of it combined to overwhelm me to such an extent that my vocal outlets would not respond. My vision dimmed slightly, my extremities tingled, and my respiration rate soared in a manner reminiscent of the incident at the spaceport.

When the audience settled and took their seats again, silence permeated the room. I felt utterly exposed with all of my flaws laid bare. From the back of my eye dome, I saw Jas nodding toward me and mouthing, "It's OK." Brenna and May gave me wild-eyed stares. I decided to force myself to start speaking, but all I could manage was a squeak. Hearing concerned muttering from the audience, I tried a different tack. Instead of reciting my prepared speech, I decided to tell the audience what was happening inside my mind.

"I'm sorry," I said. "I find myself unable to deliver my prepared speech. I'm extremely nervous."

"Aw, c'mon hon!" someone shouted from the back of the crowd. "Ya know we love ya!" I recognized the voice immediately.

"Bertie!" I exclaimed.

"The one and only!" she shouted back, "I just wancha to know, I'm still steamin' mad about the spaghetti incident!"

At least half the audience burst out laughing, no doubt recalling my story about the zero-g spaghetti debacle from the galley of the *Pacifica Spirit*.

Bertha ("Bertie") Kolesnikov's remarks broke the spell. My senses returned to me in an instant. Hearing Bertie's distinct voice and unique manner of Terran speech comforted me and took me back to the best days of my early contact with humans. I wondered how many other members of the original human first-contact mission might have been invited. I looked forward to reuniting with as many of them as possible.

"I'm ready now," I said to the audience, then I started reciting my prepared statement. "I've been told that I should address you as 'honored guests,' but it is entirely *my* honor to be with you tonight."

I proceeded to thank the university and Jas for the invitation. I explained that it had taken me seven years on Kuw'baal before I felt ready to come to Terra. I also told the crowd that I had accepted Jas's invitation because of the university's acceptance of students from across the Alliance and outlier worlds as well as Jas's supportiveness and understanding of me on a personal level. I kept my talk brief, knowing that many human speakers tended to lose their audience's attention by rambling for too long.

When I reached my conclusion, the audience stood and cheered once more.

Jas stepped forward to stand beside me. He extended a hand, which I shook with my hand paddle. "Kelvoo will now accept a few *short* questions from the media," he announced.

Jas had assured me that the journalists would only lob "softball" questions at me. The first question certainly fit that description.

A woman wearing a tailored suit was the first one up. "I'm Liz Underwood from Atlantic News," she said. "Thank you so much, Kelvoo, for answering our questions. I would like to know how it feels to be loved and admired by so many humans."

"I feel like a fraud." My reply elicited a gasp from some of the audience. Brenna looked perplexed. Jas didn't seem to be fazed at all, though. "I can't understand what I have done to earn such love and admiration. All I did was write an autobiographical account of my interactions with humans, at the request of Sarayan Sub-Commander Trexelan. I doubted whether anyone would even read my work. I certainly didn't think it would lead the Planetary Alliance to reevaluate Terran membership in the Alliance and to demand such swift and sweeping changes!

"Terra had to endure the so-called Correction, in large part because of me. Because of my story, Terra was compelled to reach out to the outliers and welcome anyone who wanted to visit or even relocate to Terra. Because of my writings, thousands of Terran businesses and a million or more of their employees had to cease operations on my planet and return all lands and rights to the kloormari.

"While I support the Planetary Alliance's interest in righting the wrongs of the distant and recent past, and while I appreciate all of the positive changes for my species, I want all of Terra to know that I acknowledge the social upheavals and the economic impact that the Alliance's demands have had on you over the last several years.

"So, to answer your question, I find it remarkable to hear that I am loved and admired despite the sacrifices your species has had to make. I'm not deserving of your praise, but it comforts me, and it demonstrates that humanity, as a whole, is innately compassionate and moral."

My answer elicited another wave of applause and appreciation.

Additional questions followed. They were easy to answer, and my responses were well received. Finally, Jas indicated there was time for one more question, this one from James Sulawesi of the Vega Network.

"I don't like to ask this, Kelvoo, but a recent vid has been widely viewed showing a kloormar on what I can only describe as a 'rampage' in the Central Plains Spaceport. I've just received an update, indicating that you may have been that kloormar. Would you care to elaborate?"

The audience made it clear they did not like the question, and Brenna looked at James in anger. Jas stepped forward. "That question is inappropriate," he said, then turned to me. "You don't have to answer it, Kelvoo. If you like, we can end the Q and A right now."

"It's alright, Chancellor Linford," I replied. "In the interest of transparency and putting the question to rest, I will answer it. Yes, that kloormar was me. I had come to Terra believing I had sufficiently healed from my trauma. I also came with the understanding that Terra was free from firearms, with the exception of those carried by law enforcement. I did not realize that customs officers fit into that category.

"When I was proceeding through customs and I saw a blaster pistol on an officer's hip, some dark memories came to the forefront of my mind, and I panicked. I apologize to the officers, to the spaceport, to the witnesses, and to all of Terra for my outburst. It made me realize that my healing is still a work in progress."

I could tell I had the sympathy of the audience as well as all three members of the media. Jas announced the conclusion of the press conference and then invited the attendees to a reception in the Olive Grove Room across the hall.

As the crowd filed out, a security staffer escorted Brenna and May to the reception area while Jas and I walked back to the green room. Jas glanced at his Infotab and told me it was "blowing up" with requests to release the vid of the event. I told him it would need to be edited to exclude my stunned silence when I first came out. I also suggested discarding part of my answer to the first question when I called myself a fraud.

"I have to disagree, Kelvoo," he said. "I believe your vulnerability and self-doubt will have wide appeal. I think it reveals—and I hope you'll excuse the expression—your 'humanity.' I think your speech and your answers will put to rest any notions that you might be arrogant or interested in telling humans how they should live."

"Are there humans who think about me in that way?" I asked.

"Oh no!" Jas replied. "At least not that *I'm* aware of! I'm just saying that your presentation could dissuade some humans from thinking that way in the future."

I wasn't sure how to interpret Jas's comment, but I had a reception to attend, so I gave him the go-ahead to release the recording in its entirety, telling Jas I trusted his judgment.

45

SIX: REUNION

As we entered the Olive Grove Room, I noticed nine of the crew from the first-contact mission to my home planet. In addition to Bertie, I saw the *Pacifica's* navigator, Lynda Paige, systems specialist Audrey Fraser, exobiologist Li Huang, engineer Yuki Sakamoto, deckhands Rupert McKenzie and Rani Vysana, purser Max Magnusson, and researcher Michael Stone. They were gathered together, and they waved when they saw me. The sight of my original human friends filled me with pleasure.

Servitor bots hovered around the room, presenting trays of hors d'oeuvres and drinks to the guests. Brenna and May were sitting in chairs along a wall, holding plates piled high with food. Being of legal age to consume alcohol on Terra, Brenna held a glass containing a beverage that looked like sparkling wine. She seemed to be consuming it at a faster pace than the other guests.

Brenna, May, and my friends were situated toward the back of the room to allow space for the receiving line of beings who were just inside the entrance, waiting to be formally introduced. All were humans with the exception of two Sarayans and one Bandorian. Jas introduced each being to me. The guests were successful business people, popular celebrities, or top donors to the university.

When the formal introductions were over, I made my way over to my *Pacifica Spirit* friends. They led me to a bank of monitors that had live feeds from many of the original crew who couldn't attend on such short notice. They included Captain Kwame Staedtler and five others. We all reminisced about the wonderful times of friendship, learning, and discovery during the first-contact mission. All of my friends were familiar with my book, and they asked many questions about events after first contact. In turn, I learned about each of my friends and the inquiry they endured when they returned to Terra.

I made sure to spend time with Lynda Paige. I offered her my sympathies for how things turned out with her husband, Sam Buchanan. "The main problem was that he cared so deeply about the kloormari and your planet," Lynda said. "We both did, but over the years while you and the rest of your group were missing, Sam took all of the burdens of the kloormari upon himself. As he sank deeper into depression and turned to alcohol to cope, he changed into someone I didn't recognize. Kelly and I just *had* to get out of there.

"I feel so awful, Kelvoo. I can't say I'm surprised that Sam died young, but *suicide*? And right after you so kindly sought his help and gave him a new purpose? When I read the details in your story, I was devastated that you were convinced he had turned a corner in his life, right before he ended it."

"I feel awful too," I replied. "One of my first reactions to Sam's suicide was anger, combined with guilt about being angry. I still struggle with that, and I'm sorry."

"Please don't be sorry. Your anger was completely understandable. At his core, Sam was a kind, gentle soul who cared about others far more than himself. At the same time, he was unstable and infuriating."

"Are you sure you don't harbor any resentment toward me?" I asked.

"Of course not!" she exclaimed. "We're fine!"

"Lynda, could you please tell me about Kelly?" I asked. "When Sam told me that you and he had a son, and you named him Kelvoo Buchanan-Paige in memory of me, I was overwhelmed with emotion. Your son must be thirteen years old now. Please tell me, how is my namesake doing?"

"You could always ask him yourself," Lynda replied, looking over her left shoulder. As soon as I saw the young man's face, I recognized the shape of Sam's eyebrows and Lynda's mouth. "Let's go say hello," she said.

Kelly was seated to one side of my group of friends. He looked down as we approached, avoiding eye contact. He appeared to be uncomfortable.

"Kelly, don't you want to say hello to the kloormar who was your dad's best friend?" his mother asked. "Yesterday when we were invited, you said how interested you were."

"It doesn't matter," Kelly said. "I don't even remember my dad. He was just a drunk anyway."

I knelt so that my eye dome was level with Kelly's head. "You're right, Kelly, at least that's what he was when your mom had to take you back to Terra, but he was also my teacher and my friend. Whether you want to hear this or not, you carry part of your dad as well as your mom inside of you, but you have control over which aspects of your father you want to embody as you go forth with your life. There was a great deal of intelligence, kindness, and passion in your father. On your mother's side, there's her intellect and, I understand, a great sense of humor. Anyway, you have a lot to build on in your life, and I have confidence that you'll find a path to success and happiness."

Kelly glanced up at me. "Thanks," he said. Lynda also thanked me for taking the time to speak with her and her son. She said she had taken enough of my time and there were many others in the room who would like to chat with me. Sure enough, Jas had been hovering close by, and he let me know that some of his special guests would like to have a word or two.

While conversing with various dignitaries, I glanced over at Brenna and May. Brenna was on her third glass of wine, and May was eating a sausage roll, the crumbs from various pastries piled high on her lap.

Just as I was finishing a conversation, Jas stood on a raised platform at the end of the room to make another announcement.

"I want all of you to keep this confidential," he said, "but tomorrow, the university will announce that registration is available for Kelvoo's course, 'Human Nature – An Outsider's Perspective.' Space will be limited, so please don't breathe a word of this to anyone. Alright, let's get this party rolling!"

Music started blaring, and the guests cleared the center of the room, which had a wood floor. I walked over to Jas and stood close, so he could hear me over the music without others listening in. "Jas, aren't you concerned about word getting out and my course filling up before registration is formally opened?"

Jas smiled. "I'm counting on it!" he said in a tone that I interpreted as mischievous.

Some of my friends at the opposite end of the room motioned for me to join them. I strode over to them. "I'll be right back," I said. "I just need to check on Brenna and May."

My friends' eyes widened in surprise. "Wait!" Audrey Fraser shouted over the din. "Do you mean Brenna and May, the outlier girls from your story? The ones that you taught to read?"

"Yes. That's them over there," I said, motioning toward the girls.

"They're *here* on Terra? And you brought them to the party?"

"Yes."

"Well you can't just leave them sitting there all alone! Bring 'em over. We'd love to meet them!"

I did as Audrey instructed. As soon as the girls came over, my friends bombarded them with welcoming words and questions. I was worried they might upset the girls by bringing up their father's death, even if it was just to offer their condolences. Much to my relief, my friends were tactful and sensitive, including Bertie, who had been consuming alcohol at a greater rate than Brenna.

Some of the guests started engaging in a practice that I had always found pointless and perplexing. They danced in the center of the room, moving more or less along with the music, which had taken on a heavy, rapid beat. I stood and watched the dancers, failing to understand the point of their movements.

Bertie ambled to my side, grasped one of my hand paddles, and pulled me toward the dance floor. "C'mon, hon, let's you and me cut a rug!"

"'Cut a rug'?" I inquired.

"I'm askin' if you wanna dance with me, ya big doofus!"

"No thank you, Bertie."

"That wasn't a request, Kel! I'm not givin' you an option here. Come with me and start dancin'! It's OK. I'll show ya how!"

I had learned early on during first contact that Bertie was a formidable woman who was not to be trifled with. Reluctantly, I let her pull me onto the dance floor.

"OK, hon, watch me! See how I'm shiftin' my feet? Left, then right, then left . . . OK, you try it."

I did my best to replicate Bertie's movements.

"Yeah, you got it! You just gotta do it in time with the beat. That's better! OK, now move yer arms back and forth like this."

I moved my arms, but since I have an additional set of elbows on each arm, I had to modify the movement to suit my anatomy.

"Nice moves!" Bertie exclaimed. "OK, now bop yer head, er, I mean yer eye up an' down, up an' down. Wow! Yer a natural!"

By that time the other dancers had ceased their gyrations and joined the crowd that was gathering to watch the spectacle.

Bertie barked one set of instructions after another, each one involving increasingly intricate movements using different parts of my anatomy. Before long I was hopping about, clacking my clasper limbs together, whirling the lower sections of my arms in counter-rotating circles, and forming waves and ripples with the tendrils on the back of my hand paddles.

When the song ended, the crowd cheered and laughed, with the exception of Brenna and May, who looked appalled. I was starting to think that shock was becoming their default facial expression when they were with me in public.

Tired from the stress of my speech, the late hour, and my dance floor gymnastics, I assumed a kneeling position and conversed further with my friends, who were all seated. In the meantime, the dance floor became rather crowded.

Some of the guests were young, and some were older but had brought young family members with them. Several youths asked Brenna to dance with them. The first time she was asked, Brenna protested that she had never danced before, but she changed her mind at the urging of some of my friends. By the end of the evening, seven young males and two females had "cut a rug" with Brenna. Back at the house, before leaving for the event, Brenna had changed into her new sparkling white, close-fitting garment. It had a low front and a far lower back. Her hair was bound up at the top of her head with longer strands brushing the back of her neck. She had also applied smoothing compounds and pigments to her face.

I speculated that Brenna had purchased new clothing and modified her hair and face to increase her attractiveness. Based on the attention she had received, I concluded that Brenna had succeeded. It was gratifying to see her progressing through a normal phase of evaluating potential suitors, but at the same time, it made me feel concerned and protective toward her for reasons I could not define.

The festivities concluded at 02:15. As Jas and I said goodbye to the remaining guests, May procured a final pastry from an abandoned tray, and Brenna had one last glass of wine. As we walked down a passageway back to Jas's car, Brenna's path took on a weaving trajectory. "Better hold my hand, Brenna!" May offered. She guided her sister the rest of the way and then helped her into the car.

"I might have eaten too much tonight," May said once we were in the car. A moment later she threw up a portion of her stomach contents onto the floor.

"Oh my god, what a gross smell! I can't believe you just did that!" Brenna slurred. "Stop the car!" she shouted. By that time we were at the edge of the lawn beside the house. Jas stopped the car and lowered it onto the grass. Brenna stumbled out and dropped onto all fours, her hair falling out of its clips and supports. Then she also vomited.

"Looks as though the girls are having conversations with Ralph and Beulah," Jas remarked with a grin.

"I don't understand," I replied.

"You know—Rraaaaalfff and Beeeeeuuuuulah!" Jas said, imitating the sound of retching while reciting the elongated Terran names.

"Oh yes, Jas, I'm sure that is amusing," I said.

Jas helped guide the girls into the house, so they could clean up.

"Well, I'm going to leave the car here and walk back to my place," Jas said. "I'll send a cleaner bot over in the morning."

When Jas left, Brenna crawled to a washroom, leaving the door open. She was back on all fours with her head positioned over the waste disposal bowl and her hair matted with vomit.

I knelt beside Brenna. "It surprises me how humans are able to ignore past experiences, leading them to repeat behaviors with similar consequences," I remarked. "It was just the day before yesterday when you and May overindulged with food, making you both feel unwell. I know that humans have limited memories, but surely you remember the incident. To what do you attribute your choices this evening?"

Brenna turned her head toward me, glaring up at me through gooey clumps of hair. Rather than answer my question, she snapped her head back to its previous position and spewed her remaining stomach contents into the bowl.

SEVEN: SETTLING IN

In the days leading up to the start of my course, I honed and adapted my teaching material, based on my ongoing observations of humans. I had plenty of opportunities for human interaction since I was free to roam the campus. I especially enjoyed walking on the lawns in the dawn hours. The still morning air, the sensation of the blades of grass against the soles of my feet, and the refreshing coolness of the dew were very pleasant. My movements were restricted to the campus grounds, I was under the watchful eye of security personnel, and I had the attention of students and staff wherever I went, but despite these limitations, I had a wonderful feeling of freedom.

The girls also had greater freedom. Rather than being followed by a security team, each girl was assigned a "minder" for a few days. These were support staff who were in their twenties and were evaluated as being responsible and trustworthy. A few days later, the girls were free to roam the grounds as long as they stayed together. It was reasoned that they could be tracked via their implanted locators anyway, and when outdoors, they would be under the observation of the silent, ever vigilant drones that hovered above and transmitted their observations to the security AI.

I was permitted to attend classes and lectures in any discipline. I avoided doing so after the first three days because my presence proved to be a serious distraction. Everywhere I walked, students would wave and smile and give me words of greeting or encouragement.

I wasn't the only kloormar on campus. Two other kloormari had been students for more than a year. Before my arrival, Klandon and K'deet were merely regarded as a novelty and were left in peace. Once word of my presence spread, my fellow kloormari were constantly mistaken for me. The persistent attention was a distraction and an annoyance that the kloormari students had to endure. I have never understood why humans have such difficulty telling kloormari apart, since the patterns of our dermal speckles are unique to each individual.

Two days after my course was announced, I received a message from my old kloormari friend, Kroz. Thanks to Kroz's interest in technology and software during first contact, Kroz had saved the lives of the kloormari on *Jezebel's Fury* by overriding the vessel's control systems.

After escaping our captors and returning to Kuw'baal, Kroz studied technology extensively.

The message indicated that Kroz had relocated to the university and wanted to know whether we could meet. Not long after that, Kroz and I met at my home.

"What brings you to this university?" I asked.

"I decided to accept a long-term invitation from the university because of their renowned research into navigation and propulsion systems," Kroz replied.

"So, you're not here because of my 'star power'?" I asked. "You didn't come just so you could bask in my presence?"

"I don't understand, Kelvoo. For us as kloormari, another being's popularity doesn't factor into such a decision."

"I know, Kroz. I was intentionally making a ridiculous statement to try to construct a 'joke' that might amuse humans. I'm trying to mimic humor."

"I have no expertise or even the slightest concept of human jokes, pranks, or humor in general. Please do not attempt further humor with me."

An area of great expertise that Kroz *did* possess was in the field of artificial intelligence control systems. Kroz explained that inertial dampening fields could only be generated on vessels over a certain size. As such, smaller craft could only accelerate within the bounds of the occupants' ability to withstand g-forces. The same applied to maneuvering. Rapid changes in direction couldn't be made in small craft at high speed since doing so would crush those on board. Larger vessels could project a larger dampening field, so they had more of a buffer, allowing onboard software enough time to adjust the field as required.

The upshot was that while small vessels were capable of jumps through space, they couldn't accelerate and decelerate quickly enough to get to or from official jump points without traveling for weeks or months.

"I am working on AI systems that can adjust small dampening fields with far greater speed than current technologies allow," Kroz explained. "If the project is successful, my work could help revolutionize small vessel transportation!"

For the next two hours, Kroz went further into the details, which I found fascinating.

"I would very much like to see your project, Kroz."

"There isn't much to show you at the moment since we're just at the conceptual stage. I would be delighted to show you the project if and when we start building something."

Our meeting ended since Kroz was scheduled to be at the aviation center a few minutes later.

* * *

During our first evening on Terra, shortly after May's near drowning, Brenna had suggested that she and May should enroll in swimming lessons. Although she found the idea amusing at the time, her reasoning was solid, and I was concerned about the girls' safety. Shortly after that I mentioned Brenna's interest to Jas. The next day he told me that he had asked the university's head aquatics coach, Luna Chang, to provide private lessons. He said Coach Chang had protested the very idea of teaching two girls how to swim until she was offered a sizable bonus as compensation. I told Jas that I couldn't accept any favor that would deplete university funds or take an instructor away from her regular duties. Jas countered that having either girl drown would reflect poorly on the institution, especially when those girls had been in the care of the most sought-after professor in the university's history. I reluctantly accepted Jas's offer and arranged for morning lessons three days a week.

"How about you?" Coach Chang asked. "Or are you already a confident swimmer?"

"My apologies, but I have difficulty with humor," I replied. "Would I be correct in assuming that you are joking? I don't think that any kloormari have ever attempted to swim. I don't even know whether it's possible."

"Well, we'll just have to find out then!" she said.

On the first day of lessons, the car took us to the aquatics center. After letting us know how honored he was to meet us, the receptionist directed us to the pool where our lessons would take place.

When we stepped onto the pool deck, we realized we had the entire place to ourselves. When we talked, our voices echoed off the walls. The walls and the bottom of the pool were brightly colored, making the water appear unnaturally blue. A skylight allowed a shaft of light to illuminate half of the water, making dappled patterns on the bottom of the pool and creating similar reflections on the walls. The room had a high level of humidity, which I found very comfortable.

A human female with a short, slim build entered the room. She wore a black one-piece swimsuit. Her loud voice contrasted with her diminutive stature. "I'm Coach Chang, and you're Kelvoo," she said. I couldn't tell whether she was asking a question or making a statement. Before I could request clarification, she addressed the girls. "Which one of you is Brenna, and who is May?"

54

After the girls identified themselves, Coach Chang looked up at me. "Let's get one thing straight: I know you're the big, new hotshot celebrity on campus, but you're not getting *any* special treatment from me!"

"I'm grateful for that, Coach Chang. Since my arrival I have been fawned over and praised at every turn. It will be refreshing to be treated like a normal citizen."

"Well, I wouldn't exactly say you're *normal*," she retorted. "As for the two of you," she continued, turning to the girls, "why are you standing on the pool deck in your clothes? If you don't want me to push you in as you are, you'd better get into your swimsuits now!"

Brenna and May fumbled as they started unfastening their clothes.

"Christ almighty! Not here! Do it in the change rooms! What are you, savages?"

She motioned to a door, and the girls sprinted toward it. "No running on the pool deck!" Coach Chang bellowed.

"Please excuse the girls," I said. "They are outlier humans who, until recently, had only lived on Perdition, on space vessels, and on Kuw'baal. They have never visited a swimming facility before."

"Outliers, eh? Well, that explains a lot!" she huffed. "What about you? Where's your swimsuit?"

"I'm quite sure that no such suit has ever been produced," I replied. "Since my species has no external reproductive or child-feeding parts, we do not employ clothing. I live my life unclothed. I work unclothed and I sleep unclothed. I'm currently naked, and I will have to attempt to swim that way."

"Yikes!" she replied, grimacing.

The girls returned to the deck wearing their swimsuits, which they had just purchased, and carrying their towels and clothes in crumpled balls. They walked as rapidly as they could without running, dropping their clothes and towels in a corner.

"Don't you girls know how to use a locker?" Coach Chang asked. "Oh, never mind. Just get over here!"

We gathered beside the steps that led into the shallowest part of the pool. "In you go!" she ordered.

I waded in and stood in the water, which came up to my hip joints. Brenna was next.

"Oh, that's cold!" she exclaimed. Her remark seemed odd since she didn't seem to have any problem with the cooler temperature of the sea when we visited the beach.

"You know, sweetie, it's easier to get used to the cold if you just jump in all at once," Coach Chang said. Then she gave Brenna a shove, sending her flying into the water.

Brenna's screech was followed by a splash. A moment later she surfaced, sputtering. "I can't believe you just did that!" she shouted. I was relieved that I wasn't the only being that Brenna responded to with mortified indignation. I was also starting to warm up to Coach Chang, if not the pool water.

May held the railing at the top of the stairs, but she didn't want to step into the water. Coach Chang got down onto one knee on the deck next to May and put a hand on May's shoulder. "I understand, sweetie. I heard that you had some trouble at the beach, and now you're afraid to get back in the water."

May nodded.

"When was that?" Coach Chang asked, turning to face me.

"Seven days ago," I replied.

"Well that was . . ." She paused and thought for a moment, "Are you insane? There was a full-on westerly gale at the time! Christ on a cracker! What were you thinking?"

It was the second time that Coach Chang had mentioned the son of God from ancient Christian mythology. I wondered whether she might have been a devout follower of the old religion, then dismissed the thought. "I hope you will forgive me, Coach Chang. It was our first day on Terra, and we were unfamiliar with the myriad natural hazards on this wonderful planet."

"Hmph!" she exclaimed, then shook her head and turned back to May. "Tell you what, sweetie, we'll leave it up to you. You can overcome your fear and make yourself get in, so you don't ever have to be afraid again, or I can grab you, kicking and screaming, and damned well drag you in right here and now!"

May descended the stairs rapidly. While my sympathy for May was considerable, my admiration for Coach Chang increased. Knowing that human children benefited from structure and discipline, I considered changing my approach to the girls to emulate Coach Chang's techniques, but I realized that I lacked the fortitude to do so.

She advised us to take a few minutes to walk through the water and get used to it. Under Coach Chang's watchful eyes, we walked back and forth, venturing into deeper water.

The first exercise was to hold our breath and submerge our heads or, in my case, my eye dome, for a few seconds at a time. All three of us were nervous, but we complied. I realized I needed to keep all of my breathing inlets, vocal outlets, feeding pouch, and reproductive pouch sealed to avoid discomfort. I couldn't close my auditory tubes, but I learned that I could trap air inside them by pointing them down while I was submerged.

Coach Chang ordered us to open our eyes underwater. Brenna and May noted that everything looked blurry. In contrast, I found that my compound eye was able to see everything with perfect clarity.

As the lesson came to a close and we climbed up onto the deck, Coach Chang turned to me. "You know, I usually work with top athletes on the university's swim team—the best of the best! Teaching a couple of kids how to swim takes me back to my days as a student, when they asked me to teach water safety to toddlers."

"Those must be fond memories from your youth," I said, wanting to get on her good side.

"Christ no! It was effing hell!" she roared as she stormed off toward the changing room.

That evening, Jas called me to ask about the swimming lesson.

"The coach left quite an impression on all of us." I said.

"Yes, she certainly has that effect."

"Indeed! Her style reminded me of an angry military commander, as depicted in various ancient Terran vids. She was extremely forceful and demanding."

"I'm so sorry!" Jas said. "I'll have her replaced immediately!"

"No, please don't!" I replied, "I think she's marvelous!"

During our second swimming lesson, we learned how to "jellyfish float," or at least the girls did. No matter how large a breath I took, the density of my body made me sink to the bottom. No matter how I moved my limbs, I was unable to surface without getting my feet under me and standing up.

"I really don't see swimming in your future," Coach Chang said.

Regardless, I spent time in the pool during all of the remaining lessons. I found that if I held an exceptionally deep breath, I could stay submerged for between thirteen and fifteen minutes before feeling the urge to breathe again. I also learned that I could move along the bottom quite effectively. I tried walking on the bottom of the pool first, but the resistance of the water made for slow going. When I tried lying flat and using my four main limbs and all eight of my clasper limbs, I was far more streamlined and could move nearly as fast as walking upright on land. When I needed to breathe again, I would ascend the slope and stand up in the shallow end of the pool.

At one point, Coach Chang donned a dive mask to observe my technique. "Your little claspers move in waves, kind of like the sides of a cuttlefish!" she said.

"Is that good?"

"Hell if I know! To me you look like some kind of sea monster from a nightmare, for Chrissake!"

Before the end of our final lesson, all three of us had learned enough that we could be safe in the water. After that the girls would frequent the beach together, or Brenna would go with her new friends from time to time. I would also go for a "swim" along the sandy bottom, much to the chagrin of the security personnel. I found it relaxing to be immersed in a different environment and observe the marine life.

EIGHT: PROFESSOR KELVOO

My course began at the start of a new semester. That momentous day was also May's first day at the on-campus school, which was conveniently located close to our home.

At the last minute, Brenna decided to pursue an undergraduate degree in interplanetary linguistics. On Kuw'baal, three years before, she had asked me to teach her some kloormari words and phrases. When I explained that she wouldn't be able to reproduce the necessary sounds, especially in the ultrasonic range, she suggested that we could come up with a "simplified kloormari" language that could be used by either species.

I advised Brenna that it was much simpler and faster for a kloormar to learn Terran due to our perfect memories rather than having humans practice and learn a new language that was unfamiliar to both species. Brenna ignored my advice and told me that she wanted to try anyway, "just for the fun of it."

For several weeks we spent some of our time together coming up with a simplified version of kloormari that humans could pronounce. Brenna enjoyed the exercise, laughing as she tried to pronounce some of the words that she thought were "funny sounding." I found the exercise to be interesting from a purely academic viewpoint, but the hardest parts were butchering my language to suit human vocal limitations. Patience was also required to work with a human who needed constant repetition to record information in her memory.

In the end we came up with a few hundred words and simple sentences, such as the following examples:

Terran: I will meet you at the algel falls.
Simplified kloormari (SK): Ke soo ko te k'shluuk k'plat.

Terran: I met Ksoomu below the algel falls.
SK: Ke loo Ksoomu tun k'shluuk k'plat.

Terran: I am going to the Kloor-mart to buy a hovercart.
SK: Ke noo te Kloor-Mart ee buy hovercart.

The final example used three Terran words since the concept of a "Kloor-Mart" store, buying, and a hovercart had never existed for the kloormari before human contact.

Over time, Brenna appeared to lose interest in her project, but her decision to study language suggested that our previous activity had left a lasting impression.

On the morning of the first class, Brenna and May left a few minutes before me, so Brenna could drop May off at her school on the way to her class. As I left the house, I looked to the west and saw a multi-colored patch of sky through the trees.

To investigate, I walked toward the beach, where I saw a brilliant rainbow formed by a band of rain that was falling offshore. I had seen a similar effect on my visit to Saraya when I noticed the refraction of light in sprays of water that were blowing from the crests of ocean waves. That experience hadn't prepared me for the wonder of a fully formed Terran rainbow over the Mediterranean Sea.

The rainbow lasted for less than three minutes before the approaching clouds blocked Sol's rays. As I walked to my assigned lecture hall, a gentle wall of rain crossed the campus, drenching me. Rain was rare in that part of Terra, and there had been no significant precipitation since I had arrived. The rainbow had buoyed my spirits, and the rain, reminiscent of the daily downpours on Kuw'baal, comforted me. I was tempted to see significance in the coincidence of the rainbow and the dawn of a new chapter in my life. Then I reminded myself not to fall into the human trap of assigning meaning to the random overlapping of events.

Students stared as I approached the Humanities study hall, soaked from the rain. Some laughed when I shed the water from my body by shaking rapidly from my eye dome down to my feet. When I entered the lecture hall, students were filing in, occupying every one of the 112 seats. As Jas had predicted, all in-person spots had been filled even before the course was officially announced. Two hundred and fifty "live vid" spots had been sold, giving each buyer the ability to submit one written question per class, to be answered by me between classes. One million "view only" slots were also sold. My lectures were also available for free via public broadcast after a three-day delay.

I noticed Jas sitting to one side of the raised presentation area. As I approached, the students stood and applauded, and Jas strode over to greet me. "I know that teaching is new to you, Kelvoo," he whispered, "so if it's OK, I'm going to sit in on your first session just in case you need any assistance."

"You are, of course, welcome to attend all of my classes, Jas," I replied.

In the days leading up to that moment, I had been concerned that I would be nervous, but as I approached the hovering microphone, I thought about the rainbow, and it calmed me. Jas had told me not to obsess about the content of my course. "These students and the general public aren't really there for specific course material," he said. "They just want to be part of history and hear what you have to say. For your first class, just make your opening statement and then interact with the students by inviting plenty of questions."

"Good morning!" I began.

"Good morning," the assembly replied.

A student in the rear of the lecture hall shouted a very peculiar set of sounds. "Shhhsklthhh Puk'angh" is the closest I can come to spelling out what he said. The utterance transitioned from a high pitch (for a human) to a low growl. The other students, as well as Jas, reacted to the outspoken pupil with perplexed stares. It took me a moment to guess what the student was trying to do.

"Were you attempting to greet me in kloormari?" I asked.

"Yes!" the student replied, looking pleased with himself.

"I'm sorry, but it sounded as though you were injuring yourself."

When the students responded with laughter, I was pleased with my successful attempt at humor. The outspoken student grinned sheepishly.

I began my prepared opening statement. "Welcome to 'Human Nature – An Outsider's Perspective.' I think the name of this course says it all, since I'm here to share my observations of the human species. But why me? Is there something special about me that gives my viewpoint extra significance? Frankly, I don't know why I have the honor of standing here before you today."

The students exchanged puzzled looks.

"There is nothing special about me," I continued. "I have done nothing to deserve the praise and adoration and favors that have been lavished upon me. There is little genetic diversity among my species, so compared to my fellow kloormari, I do not have a superior intellect or any remarkable abilities. Each kloormar is, for all intents and purposes, much the same as the other.

"It is only my past circumstances that make me *seem* unique or special to other species. I happened to be the kloormar who rushed headlong toward the *Pacifica Spirit* as it touched down near my village on its first-contact mission. As a result, I was injured by a flying rock that was launched by the exhaust of the ship's engines. Because of that, I was taken onboard and was the first kloormar to interact with humans. As a student of Sam Buchanan, I happened to form a strong friendship with him. When Sam's students visited the *Orion Provider*, I was the one who was secretly interviewed by Kaley Hart, during what I thought was a normal conversation with a human, so I was the one that appeared on broadcasts across the Alliance. Due to my notoriety, I was sought out by the captain of *Jezebel's Fury* when he tricked me and eight other kloormari to board his vessel. Finally, Sarayan Sub-Commander Trexelan, requested that I write an account of my experiences with humans in what became known as 'Kelvoo's Testimonial.' It was these random events that put me where I am today. If those events had happened to any other kloormar, *that* kloormar could just as easily be the one standing before you.

"As you may know, I am an admirer of the works of the ancient human playwright and poet William Shakespeare. In his play, 'Twelfth Night,' Shakespeare wrote, 'Some are born great, some achieve greatness, and some have greatness thrust upon them.' I am not certain that Shakespeare's observation can be applied to the kloormari. Certainly, no kloormar is *born* to greatness. Who our parents were has no bearing on our status. In fact, since a kloormar is formed from the genetic material of several parents—even dozens at times—there is no single individual or couple that we would resemble.

"When it comes to *achieving* greatness, since first contact, many kloormari have entered fields of study and engaged in work that has led to breakthroughs. The kloormari, however, think of such accomplishments as the result of random chance, based upon the selected field of study, the skills that the individual chose to develop, and the circumstances of the work.

"Finally, there is the concept that some have greatness thrust upon them. That is precisely what has happened to me. I'm not saying I'm ungrateful. I'm just asking that you refrain from putting me on a pedestal and that you do not look to me for divine inspiration. I will do my best to share my knowledge in the hope that you will reciprocate and teach me as well.

"The chancellor," I said, motioning toward Jas, "has wisely suggested that our first lesson should consist of questions and answers so that we may become more familiar with one another and to help guide the remainder of this course. Let's begin with your questions so that, in subsequent classes, I can share my observations on human nature in a way that will be the most relevant to your interests and academic goals."

Almost every student indicated their wish to ask a question. The lecture hall's AI selected students at random, and the guest microphone made its way around the room. As the mic hovered in front of each student, the AI displayed the student's name on the main presentation panel. The questions were intelligent and, in many cases, interesting, since they made me look at my knowledge and experiences from fresh perspectives.

One of the questions concerned the murder of my child on *Jezebel's Fury*. Before I could respond, Jas intervened. "I had hoped that we would have had enough respect to avoid questions of such a sensitive nature, especially during the first class," he said, frowning at the questioner. "Kelvoo, you have no obligation to answer."

"I greatly appreciate your concern, Chancellor. I was aware—in fact I was *expecting*—such questions to come up, and I am fully prepared to answer them."

I answered the question and was relieved that I did so with my emotional response under control. I realized that in an academic setting I could recall traumatic events with a clinical detachment. I counted that as another milestone toward my psychological recovery.

A student named Priya Sanderson asked how I thought the outlier humans felt during the Correction when they were invited to have normalized relations with Terra.

"I'm sure there are a few students here who can answer that question better than me," I replied. "Who among you came here from the outlier colonies?"

"Excuse me! I'm sorry, Kelvoo," Jas said. "I should have explained before you started that this institution does not label its students. Each student's background is confidential. This campus is a safe space where we are all the same, regardless of species or origin."

I was going to change my approach, but as soon as Jas finished his statement, a student stood. "Excuse me!" he said. The guest mic zoomed toward him. His name, "Mickey Beene," showed on the panel. "I don't mind telling you that I'm an outlier. It's not as if I could hide it, given my accent and coloring!"

A chuckle spread around the room. Three additional students stood and identified themselves as outlier's too.

"To answer Priya's question," Mickey said, "we were ecstatic when Terra was opened up to us." Mickey's vowel sounds were elongated and consonants were clipped, sounding much like the crew of *Jezebel's Fury*. His pale skin and bright red frizzy hair was indicative of some earlier aspects of outlier culture that had different ethnic and racial groups living separately. "We were also nervous because we knew that the Planetary Alliance was effectively forcing the Terran government to deal with us and make things right, and we figured there'd be a lot of resistance from the people here. We were all surprised by how little resentment there was. That was because of you, Professor Kelvoo. Your story opened everyone's eyes to the truth, and that's why I'm so happy to be in your class today."

63

"Thank you Mr. Beene, you honor me," I replied. "I'm curious. In your opinion, what were the greatest benefits that came about during the Terran Correction?"

"Well, it depends. If you mean for me personally, it was being able to come to Terra to study. At the start of the Correction, the education system on Perdition and Exile were basic at best. Most of my learning was from all the reading that I did. I studied hard and finally passed the entrance exam for this place. I even managed to qualify for a bursary for my travel costs and tuition.

"If you're asking what the benefits were for the outlier humans in general, it was rooting out corruption. Our governments were full of graft and nepotism. Our educational system, health care, and infrastructure were appalling because politicians were lining their pockets instead of providing proper funding. Everyone knew who the guilty people were—you only had to look at their lavish homes and lifestyles to figure it out—but no one did anything about it. The Correction shone a spotlight on our people. With aid from Terra, we rose up and literally chased the crooks out of their offices!

"The Brotherhood gangs used to have their hooks into everything. Nothing was done without the Brotherhood getting their cut! I remember when the gang members on Perdition and Exile started getting arrested. There were too many to imprison them all, and we couldn't very well ship them to another planet, since we hated how our ancestors had been subjected to such treatment. In the end, those thought to be guilty of 'lesser' offenses were offered amnesty in exchange for publicly admitting to their crimes."

"And what about the gang members who were off planet at the time?" I asked.

"They were also offered amnesty on the condition that they came to Exile to hand over their vessels and the proceeds of their crimes. They assembled in their vessels in a large group, but instead of heading to Exile or Perdition, they jumped. Deep-space sensors couldn't pick up any space-time disruptions to detect where they had jumped to, so it must have been somewhere far outside the sectors monitored by the Planetary Alliance. No one's heard from them since. Maybe they had a secret base somewhere far away, or maybe they're out wandering through uncharted space. It could be that they're all dead. It's a mystery, but we sure as hell don't miss them!"

Mickey's perspective intrigued me, especially since a Brotherhood gang had caused so much suffering for my kloormari companions and me. Rumors abounded about how the Brotherhood vanished. Mickey's account was similar to most, and I found it quite plausible, especially because it lacked the hyperbole and embellishments of some of the more outlandish legends.

When the class had ended, I thought that it had gone very well. Jas agreed.

***

Before I started my academic career, I was concerned about being underutilized since I was only teaching one course. It turned out that my time filled up immediately. My students had more questions than the allotted time allowed, so I made myself available after each session to allow at least one question per student. After that I would return home to answer written questions submitted by the 250 students enrolled in the live vid program.

In the meantime, the girls settled in and continued their education. May enjoyed her school tremendously. She was pleased that most of her classmates were at a similar academic level, which made things more interesting for her. She made several friends, including two Sarayans and a xiltor. Since May's school included a mixture of species, no one bothered her about her outlier background, and her social skills seemed to be coming along well.

Brenna attended her classes and studied intently. She decided to resurrect her previous endeavor to create a simplified kloormari language, purely as an "academic exercise," and to practice and hone her knowledge of language components. She was dismayed that she had lost her previous notes, but she was relieved when I pointed out that I could reconstruct her work from memory. In one evening I dictated the simple dictionary and sentence structures that she had come up with years before. Then I transferred the transcribed data onto her Infotab. For a few weeks, we spent an hour or two each evening adding to Brenna's body of work. She would ask me to recite kloormari words and phrases. In many cases, I had to lower the frequency of the ultrasonic words or syllables, which changed the meaning somewhat, but together we worked out equivalents that humans could pronounce.

During the first semester, Brenna and May celebrated birthdays. On Kuw'baal, I hadn't understood the significance of marking each day when the orbital position of a planet coincided with a human's date of birth, so the first time one of the girls had a birthday, I did nothing to mark the occasion. The result was a surprising amount of sadness, disappointment and anger. For subsequent birthdays, I consulted with humans for advice and took the girls to stores in Newton for shopping. Adding to the confusion around birthdays was the fact that the orbital period (the timespan of one "year") differed between Perdition,

Kuw'baal, and Terra. In a sense, the girls had missed several birthdays during their time on *Jezebel's Fury*. Due to its near-light speed, years had passed during a trip in which the girls had aged only a few months.

May's twelfth birthday celebration was organized by her school teacher. I provided her with SimCash, so she could buy a gift for herself. Brenna refused my offer to arrange for a party and gift for her eighteenth birthday. Instead, she chose to go out with her friends.

As the months passed. Brenna set aside her simplified kloormari project and started coming home from her classes later and later. Sometimes she would spend the night at a friend's home. Most often that friend was Griffin Taylor. Sometimes when she was in a good mood, she would tell me things that Griffin had said or done. I would listen while May would roll her eyes in a way that only humans can. From Brenna's accounts, I learned that Griffin's parents were wealthy and highly influential.

From the moment I agreed to relocate to Terra, I wanted to visit as much of the planet as possible. Between first and second semester, I took some day excursions and a few overnight trips with the girls to fascinating places on various continents. In doing so, I caught the "travel bug." Wherever I went the residents of Terra were friendly, outgoing, and curious about me, whether they knew my identity or just saw me as another kloormar.

There was a long academic break after the second semester, so I traveled extensively. May accompanied me, but Brenna preferred to stay behind and "hang out with friends."

Given my studies of human psychology, I interpreted Brenna's wish to distance herself as a positive sign of normal development in her transition to emotional adulthood. In hindsight, I wish I had seen the warning signs in her increasing detachment.

NINE: ON THE YANGTZE

One of the memorable trips that I took with May was a multi-day voyage along the Yangtze River. At the river's headwaters, we boarded a vessel for the downstream cruise. The vessel was not one that hovered; it was an actual boat that floated on the water's surface, as Terran watercraft did in ancient times. I enjoyed the motion as the boat turned and rocked between rugged mountains through the swifter upstream sections of the Xiling and Wu Gorges. Farther downstream, May and I marveled at the magnificent cities and feats of engineering as the boat meandered through the wide, calmer waters.

A large contingent of visitors from the outlier planets was onboard. Now that Terra had opened up, outliers flocked to the "home planet" to visit areas where their long-dead ancestors had lived or visited. To the outliers, no part of Terra was more legendary than the Yangtze River.

During my captivity and May's residence on *Jezebel's Fury*, the crew had sung a song called "Home on the Yangtze." Even with my limited knowledge of Terra, I knew as soon as I heard the lyrics that they were a gross misrepresentation of the region. The song also promoted the violent overthrow of Terran authority. While I was trying to curry favor with the captain of *Jezebel's Fury*, I asked him about the song. He explained that it was written by someone with no firsthand knowledge of Terra. The song expressed the outliers' bitterness at the banishment of their ancestors from the homeworld, with the Yangtze serving as a utopian representation of Terra.

On the last full day of our cruise, the outliers congregated on the upper deck where May and I were watching the passing scenery. They were in a jovial mood, and many had been drinking. They decided to sing "Home on the Yangtze." I was concerned about the memories that the song would bring to the fore, not just for me but also for May. As the song started, May told me that she would like to go read in her cabin. I decided to remain on the deck as part of my efforts to face my memories head on.

Here is the song the crowd sang.

Home on the Yangtze, great river I treasure,
long may your course twist and turn.
Peace and contentment and wealth beyond measure.
To your broad shores I'll return.

Boating and fishing and swimming and staying
carefree in warm summer sun.
Pandas and lions and antelope playing.
Blue whales on their downstream run.

Yangtze oh Yangtze, they sent us away
far from your ice floes so grand.
Ripped from your warm embrace,
flung away into space,
off to a sad, distant land.

Home on the Yangtze, the girls are so pretty,
willing to please every day.
Doing as they're told, whether young or old,
I'll be back with them someday.

Basking in sunshine, drinking your waters,
I'll be the picture of health.
Panning your gold or picking your diamonds,
endlessly living in wealth.

Yangtze oh Yangtze, they sent us away,
far from your ice floes so grand.
Ripped from your warm embrace,
flung away into space,
off to a sad, distant land.

Home on the Yangtze, I'm coming back to thee
brimming with vengeance and wrath.
I'm going to smite those that took you away from me,
striking them down in my path.

Some fine day, we'll attack; I'll get my Yangtze back,
with God's grace vanquish the foe.
Rivers of blood, shall form a great flood,
blending with your glorious flow.

Yes, rivers of blood, shall form a great flood,
blending with your glorious flow.

The tone and tenor of the song were completely different from the rendition I had heard years before. The outliers eyed one another and smiled while singing about lions, antelope, blue whales, and ice floes, as if acknowledging the absurdity of the lyrics. For the final violent verses, the group sang in a loud, exaggerated manner with smiles and laughter. I assumed that the passengers found humor in the contrast between the grievances expressed in the song and the reality of what they had experienced on the trip.

When the song ended, curiosity got the better of me. "Excuse me," I said to an outlier, "but I'm wondering how the meaning of that song has changed for you since Terra opened up."

"Oh yeah!" the outlier said. "Don't get me wrong—I've always been a bit skeptical about the song, but now it's obviously ridiculous! Now, that doesn't mean that some outliers didn't take it seriously. The Brotherhood pretty much took it as their anthem!"

"By the way," the outlier said, "I'm sorry about how one of their gangs treated your fellow kloormar—you know . . . Kelvoo. Anyway, the name's Nate." He extended his hand toward me, then hesitated. "Er, do you folks shake hands?"

"Certainly. Just grasp the end of my hand paddle," I said.

"And you are?" he asked as he did just that.

"Kelvoo of Kuw'baal."

"What? C'mon. I'd heard that Kelvoo is some kind of professor at a university on the other side of Terra!"

"That is correct, Nate. I'm on leave until the start of the next semester."

"You're joshing me!"

"Have you ever heard of a kloormar 'joshing' someone?"

The astonished tourist turned to his group. "Hey, guys, it's Professor Kelvoo!"

I was immediately mobbed by outliers who were skeptical at first, then excited. The group assured me multiple times that my treatment by the "Jezebel Gang" was horrifying to every decent outlier. One woman said she hoped I hadn't been offended by the song, "We sang it as a joke because it's so silly nowadays," she explained.

Most of the group had a sufficient education to read at a basic level, and many had read *Kelvoo's Testimonial,* though some admitted they had to use an Infotab to look up some of the bigger words. Although the group treated me with kindness, empathy, and good humor, I was uncomfortable with the extreme adoration and reverence expressed by some of them.

The outliers invited me to join them on the upper deck that evening. "May I bring my human traveling companion with me?" I asked. "She's originally from Perdition, and her name is May Murphy."

The group was astonished. They knew about Brenna and May from my book. "Oh, those poor girls!" a woman said, tears glistening in her eyes. "Of course you *must* bring that sweet child with you tonight!"

I went to the level below and found May sitting on the bunk in her cabin, reading. "I have just had a wonderful conversation with the outlier group," I said. "We've been invited to visit with them this evening and they're very excited to meet you!"

To my surprise, May shook her head. "Oh no! I really don't want to do that!"

"Why not, May?"

"I'm scared of them!" she replied with a downcast look.

"Why is that?"

"Because bad people come from Perdition and Exile. That's why they got sent there in the first place! They're mean and stupid and a bunch of criminals. They're monsters!"

"But May, you and Brenna came from Perdition, and you're none of those things. Do you think you're a monster?"

May's eyes started to water, and her breathing pattern told me that she was on the verge of weeping. "I think I probably am."

"A monster?"

She looked up at me. "I don't want to be, but I won't be able to help it. My daddy wasn't very smart, and he worked with a bunch of very bad men. Sometimes I think bad things, and I wonder if it means I'm gonna *do* bad things," May's voice caught, and she started to cry. "I don't want to be an outlier, and I'm scared that if I'm with those people I'll want to become just like them."

At that moment it was clear to me that meeting the group of outliers could be a pivotal moment of healing for May. Up to that point, I had left most decisions involving May up to her. In a "cruel to be kind" moment, I got down to May's level and held her hands. "May, you are at a crucial age where you can choose whether to be a good person or a monster. To help you do that, you need to meet humans and other species of all different backgrounds and circumstances. Therefore, you *will* come with me tonight." I paused to let my words sink in. "Don't worry," I added in a softer tone. "I'll keep you safe."

May looked up at me with her watery eyes and to my amazement she nodded. "Thank you."

That evening when May and I went to the upper deck, the crowd swarmed around us. May gripped my hand paddle and stood close to me. Sensing her fear, the crowd backed away slightly. One of the women who had spoken to me earlier crouched beside May and smiled. "Don't worry, hon. We love you! You're one of us!"

May's eyes opened wide, and she shook her head.

"Please understand," I said to the crowd. "May left Perdition when she was only four years old. After that the only outlier humans she has ever been exposed to were the crew of *Jezebel's Fury*. Due to her experiences, May can't help associating outliers with suffering no matter what I say to the contrary. She's especially worried that she is destined to be a 'bad person' because of her origin."

"Oh, you *poor* dear!" the woman said. "We'll give you some space. You're welcome to talk with us and ask questions whenever you feel comfortable."

The crowd backed away. May and I walked to the railing and looked across the gently flowing water to a city full of towers, shining against the velvet-black night, their lights reflected in the dark water below. Over the conversations, I heard the water lapping against the hull while the ship rested at anchor. Periodically, outliers came and stood at the rail beside me to ask questions or tell me about themselves and their families.

Half an hour after our arrival, an outlier girl, perhaps seven years old, came up to May. "Hi, May. My name's Maisie, and I brung you a piece of cake, so you won't be afraid of us." May accepted the cake from the girl and quietly thanked her. Maisie's offering placated May enough that she greeted a few of the outliers, and soon after that, she engaged in conversation with some of them. By 23:30, May had let her guard down. She was smiling and laughing and looking greatly relieved.

At midnight, several thousand tiny drones flew out of the vessel's stern.

"It's showtime!" Nate shouted. "Let's gather together!"

The outliers spread out into a rough circle and joined hands. They invited May and me to participate. Nate held one of my hand paddles in his right hand, and May gripped me with her left hand. Little Maisie held May's right hand as we all watched the drones form images in the night sky. With fluid movement, the drones transitioned from one image to another, depicting flowers, animals, scenes of nature, and smiling faces. Images of humans, Sarayans, and other Alliance species flew and swirled. One image resembled a kloormar. The drones were equipped with speakers and made swooshing sounds as they flew around.

The drones proceeded to display three circles as points in a triangle. Shapes formed inside each circle, resembling the respective continents on Terra, Perdition and Exile. Letters formed above the planets, spelling out "Greetings to Terra from your outlier friends."

Music began to play from the drones. After a few notes, May's eyes lit up. "I know this song! We sang it in school!" After the opening bars, the circle of outliers, including May, gazed up into the night and sang.

Building bridges 'cross the sky. Building bridges, you and I.
Now we are no longer parted; here we stand.
Time and space kept us apart, now we're standing heart to heart,
face to face, as every race stands hand in hand.

Building bridges world to world, with the flag of love unfurled,
and the bliss of our reunion, strong and true.
Blaze of light across the night, let us all uphold our right
to live in peace together, me and you.

Though the distances are long, we'll build bridges tall and strong,
to span all our divisions from our past.
Take my hand and sing with me, of the joy of harmony.
May the bridges that connect us ever last.

As the outliers sang, the drones formed bridges spanning the three planets and displayed the words to the song, so others could sing along. Passengers on the top deck and the decks below joined in, as did I. As we sang, with lights shimmering off the river, I felt a warmth enveloping my entire body and a bliss that matched the joy I had felt years before when I first viewed my home planet from space. I only wished that Brenna had been there to share the experience.

As the party ended and the crowd dispersed, they wished us well. May and I received many invitations to visit Perdition and Exile, with our new acquaintances telling us how happy they would be to host us.

I walked May down to her cabin. Her smile hadn't faded since the start of the light show. As she stepped into her room, she thanked me for making her go.

I entered my accommodations in the adjoining cabin, helping myself to a generous portion of algel from my travel-size incubation vat. Instead of remaining there, I made my way back to a deserted section of the upper deck and locked my limbs in a squatting position for meditation. As I gazed upon the beautiful night sky and the city lights across the water, I closed my eyelid and allowed my recollection of "Building Bridges" to soothe me into my most contented, restful, healing meditation session since I had arrived on Terra.

***

A new semester and academic year began shortly after May and I returned to the university. I resumed my teaching and added swimming to my daily regimen because I found it helpful to use the muscles that were formerly exercised on Kuw'baal through manual labor.

When I arrived home after teaching, I would walk down to the beach—weather permitting, of course. If she felt up to it, May would join me. On rare occasions, so would Brenna. The girls would swim, and I would submerge and explore the undersea realm, crawling to shallower water to stand and breathe every few minutes. This activity caused dismay to campus security since I was completely out of sight and sensor range while submerged. I think a large part of the appeal of swimming was those moments of complete privacy.

I loved my work and my interactions with the students, feeling that I was learning as much from them as they were learning from me. We listened intently to each other, and we didn't hesitate to challenge one another, all while maintaining a high level of mutual respect.

Day after day I was surrounded by beings who supported me, liked me, and appreciated the information that I was sharing with them. More importantly, I felt that I was doing work that was valuable and beneficial to others. I was more than content. My state of mind could be described as a joyful feeling of belonging.

***

One day during class, a student named John stood and asked me a question. "How do you feel about the HI Movement?"

"I am not familiar with it, John," I replied. "Do you mean 'high' as in 'elevated' or 'high' as in under the influence of mood-altering chemicals or 'hi' as in the shortened form of 'hello' or something altogether different?"

While I asked for clarification, most of the students had neutral or slightly puzzled expressions, causing me to guess that they were also unfamiliar with the HI Movement. Some students looked concerned, offended or surprised by John's question. I heard a great deal of murmuring throughout the room.

"I'm referring to the Human Independence Movement. Sometimes it's just called 'HIM.'"

Most of the students stared at John. Some looked mortified; others shook their heads.

"Shut up," one student said through clenched teeth. Another made a slashing motion across his throat.

Noticing the strong reaction, John said "Oh! Um, never mind," before sitting down.

Before John was back in his seat, another student jumped in with an unrelated question. John looked puzzled by his classmates' reactions while many of the other students appeared relieved.

When I returned home, I used my Infotab to look up HIM. What I found was disturbing.

PART 2: CRACKS IN THE FOUNDATION

TEN: GETTING TO KNOW HIM

The Manifesto of the Human Independence Movement

WHEREAS:

1. The human species is indigenous to the planet Terra and is the only intelligent* species to have come into existence on Terra.

2. The human species, despite its history of internal conflict, has survived and thrived on Terra for over one million years prior to contact with, and without aid from, intelligent* species from other planets.

3. The human species has developed a distinct society, culture, and set of values that are core to human identity.

4. Each intelligent* species has an inalienable right to self-determination.

5. The introduction of alien species to Terra has led to changes in human society, culture, and values.

6. The continued presence of aliens on Terra will inevitably lead to further changes that cannot be accurately predicted, resulting in the potential for humanity's: a.) loss of identity, b.) loss of self-determination, c.) cultural genocide, and d.) eventual disappearance.

NOW, THEREFORE, the HUMAN INDEPENDENCE MOVEMENT hereby demands that the Government of Terra take the following actions, without delay, for the protection of the human species:

1. Withdrawal of Terran membership from the Planetary Alliance.

2. Identification and removal of intelligent* non-human species from Terra and all planets and other heavenly bodies as well as fixed and mobile spacecraft, whose human inhabitants or crew amount to over 50% of the total number of intelligent* beings therein.

3. Drafting and passing of laws to enable implementation of item 2 legally and peacefully wherever practical.

4. Permission for humans on Terra to own and carry arms without restriction for self-defense against domestic and/or alien enemies.

*References to "intelligent" are in accordance with Terran Government standards as defined just prior to commencement of Terran membership in the Planetary Alliance.

As I read the Human Independence Movement's manifesto, my mood darkened. I sent a message to Jas, requesting a meeting with him as soon as possible. Several minutes later, Jas replied that he would be home by 19:00, and I could drop by his house then.

In the meantime, I researched HIM. Their infosite was slim on details, with its main feature being a sign-up form and a merchandise catalog. The movement's logos were the words "HI" and "HIM" in red capital letters in a bold, blocky font. Among the items for sale in support of their cause was a jacket with scrolling letters in an electronic GarmentSign patch on the back, which spelled out "HI! I'm with HIM!" I had seen a young female student four days prior wearing such a jacket as she walked across campus. The thought of the movement infiltrating a place of learning was repugnant to me.

Outside of the HIM infosite, my search produced limited results. I found only two mentions of the movement in broadcast news segments. The first mention was highly negative. The other was neutral and was broadcast on the Veritacity Network, which Jas had referred to as "a small, gutter-journalism outlet that ekes out an existence by muckraking and pandering to the dregs of humanity."

At the door to Jas's home, I announced myself to the domestic AI at exactly 19:00. Simon, wearing only a white bathrobe, opened the door and let me in. "Will this take long?" he asked.

"I hope not, Simon."

He showed me through the foyer and down a hall to the right, which led to the main living area. Soft music was playing throughout the house. On the floor along the base of the walls were candles. I couldn't fathom why such ancient lighting devices were in use, and I was concerned about the potential fire hazard, but I had more important matters to deal with, so I didn't mention my concern.

Jas sat in a large, soft chair and swirled a beverage in a bowl-shaped glass. His shoes were off, and his feet were on the coffee table. "So," he said, smiling, "what trivial matter brings you my way?" I had known Jas long enough to recognize that he was joking, but the stress I was feeling left no room for me to appreciate his humor.

"Jas, I have just learned about an organization called the Human Independence Movement."

"What, HIM? What's that bunch of idiots up to now?"

"I read their manifesto, Jas. Did you know that they're calling for Terra to leave the Planetary Alliance? Are you also aware that they're seeking to remove non-humans from Terra?"

"Yup. Seen it, heard it, ignored it!"

"But Jas, why would you ignore a group with such destructive aims?"

"Because they're *nothing*, Kelvoo. They don't amount to a hill of beans. They're a joke! For the last two months, I've received threats from them every day."

"Why would they threaten you?" I asked. "You're not a politician, a government official, or a non-human! Why would they threaten the chancellor of a university?"

"Because we're an *interplanetary* university. We welcome students and faculty from several planets, as you know firsthand! They also hate us because their currency is fear and wild conspiracy theories while we deal with knowledge and facts, which expose their lies. Like I said, they're a bunch of idiots!"

"But, Jas, you've been threatened by them! Aren't you concerned for your safety?"

"Not in the slightest! They're fools, Kelvoo, but they're not stupid enough to make explicit threats of violence. If they did they'd be rounded up and facing a judge within minutes! No, they stay within the law by *implying* that my career *could* be in jeopardy or by saying, 'We're concerned for your safety. Who knows how some angry people *might* react to your actions?' and so on. I'd say there's no chance that they'd have the guts to actually *do* anything.

"Anyway, Kelvoo, the gist of it is that the HI Movement is *nothing*. It's probably just one middle-aged failure, living with his parents who has a mental defect that is just below the threshold for psychiatric treatment. HIM is nothing but a piece of fluff that will never amount to anything."

A hint of annoyance seemed to creep into Jas's tone. Simon approached him from behind and massaged his shoulders. Jas smiled up at Simon, then returned his attention back to me. "My point, Kelvoo, is that the HI Movement—or HIM or whatever you want to call it—is nothing more than an irritant. They operate within the law, so there's nothing we can do about them anyway. Don't let them get inside your head, er, your psyche. Really, Kelvoo, you'd be best off just letting it go."

I wasn't ready to let things go, so I kept asking questions, including how some Terran humans could have such feelings toward beings like me. I also asked what HIM was referring to regarding loss of identity or loss of culture or existential threats. I wanted to know how this bigotry had developed and how the justice system might deal with HIM if they became popular. Throughout the process, I became quite worked up.

"I hadn't realized that you had such an interest in Terran current events and politics," Jas remarked following my barrage of questions.

"Until now I didn't think that it was my place to get involved in such matters," I replied, "but now that I know there are humans who feel threatened— "

"Alright, I'll tell you what, Kelvoo," Jas said. "I'm part of an informal group of profs. We call ourselves the Sagacity Club. One evening a week we get together in the admin building. We bring in some food and we have a few drinks and shoot the breeze about current events, politics, and the general state of society. Our group includes a political scientist, a historian, a sociologist—that's me—a psychologist, a philosopher, you know, a well-rounded bunch of pundits and pontificators. Why don't you join us as my guest? You can share your concerns with the gang, and I'm sure they'll have plenty to offer on the subject."

"Thank you so much, Jas! That could be very helpful!"

"Good! Meet with us tomorrow at 18:00, and bring some of your algel with you."

"I'll be there. Thank you, Jas, I'll let myself out now," I said as I moved down the hall toward the foyer.

"In the meantime, don't worry," he called after me. "I'm sure there's nothing to be concerned about."

As I passed the window outside the house, I saw Simon taking Jas's hand and pulling him from the living area toward the back of the house. I surmised that Jas was in a hurry to get rid of me because I had interrupted some sort of activity that Simon had planned.

That night during meditation, I analyzed the information I had read about HIM and my reaction to it. My meditation was helpful. I determined that I might have exaggerated the risk, but I looked forward to my meeting with the Sagacity Club in the hope that I could gain additional reassurance.

ELEVEN: IN THE CLUB

In the late afternoon the following day, Jas sent me a message offering to pick me up and take me to the meeting. The ride to the meeting gave him an opportunity to apologize for brushing me off the night before. I let him know that he had reassured me, and I thanked him again for letting me discuss HIM and its mission with the group.

Jas and I arrived before any other guests. I was surprised by the level of security clearance required to enter the meeting room. Jas needed a special key card and had to place his palm on a scanner. He explained that the room held many rare and valuable artifacts. The room was remarkable, resembling a small library from Terra's ancient times. The floor was made from wood strips. Paneling and floor-to-ceiling bookshelves lined the walls. An ornate chandelier hung over a long wooden table at one end of the room. At the other end, a well-worn fabric rug was surrounded by overstuffed wingback chairs covered with forest-green simu-leather. The whole tableau seemed to have been taken from a scene in a historic vid.

"Are these authentic paper books?" I asked in astonishment as I reached to take a volume from a shelf.

"Don't touch!" Jas exclaimed. "They're worth a fortune! If you pull one out, it'll probably disintegrate!" He calmed somewhat. "Sorry, Kelvoo, this room contains the only collection of printed books within a thousand-kilometer radius of here. We don't have the luxury of actually *reading* any of them, but the scanned contents are readily available to the public." Jas went on to explain that the club was an attempt to simulate an academics' club of old. He said I would hear the attendees referring to one another by their last name. "It just adds a bit of fun," he added.

As each member entered the room, Jas didn't need to introduce me to them since I was well known to all. Jas did introduce each member to me, though: Dr. Martin Hoffman, psychologist; Dr. Rosa Schlenk, historian; Dr. Lembe Stark, political scientist; and Dr. Mary Sayed, philosopher.

The good doctors welcomed me heartily and peppered me with questions, which I was pleased to answer. Then the members took on a formal tone and used more precise language than I normally heard on Terra. I especially noticed the change in Jas's speaking style since I was familiar with his everyday parlance. I supposed that the affectation was to simulate an ancient conversational style, and I appreciated the precision in the formal yet collegial atmosphere.

During the back and forth, food and beverages were brought in by a servitor bot, and the group continued to question me between mouthfuls of food. My consumption of algel consisted of opening a vacu-pack that I had filled at home and squeezing its contents into my feeding pouch. The club members were intrigued to see me speaking through my vocal outlets while simultaneously absorbing my meal via a different orifice.

When dinner had been consumed and the plates and cutlery cleared, we made our way to the wingback chairs where drinks were served to the regular members. I took the opportunity to speak. "When the meeting is called to order," I said, "there's something I wish to talk about."

"Called to order, my dear Kelvoo?" Dr. Hoffman inquired. "Have we not been meeting for the last forty-five minutes?"

"We might be formal here," Jas explained, "but we're not *that* formal!" His comment was met with a few chuckles. "Please, Dr. Kelvoo, do raise your subject."

I proceeded to tell the group about the Human Independence Movement, followed by a presentation of their manifesto on a wall-mounted screen. I was surprised to learn that Jas was the only attendee who had heard of HIM, likely due to the thinly veiled threats directed against him. I asked the doctors whether we, and especially I, should be concerned.

"Balderdash!" Dr. Sayed exclaimed.

"Codswallop!" Dr. Stark added. "What say you about such people, Hoffman? What makes these HIM types tick? You are, after all, our resident psychologist."

"If you don't mind, Stark, I prefer the term 'head shrinker'!" Dr. Hoffman replied as the group guffawed. "Obviously, such types have deep-seated inadequacies," he continued, "leading them to lash out against those that they perceive as superior. These individuals feel impotent, so they project the illusion of power by inventing a threat and then calling upon the 'believers' to take action while they sit back and do nothing. As people, or perhaps I should say 'beings,' of fine academic standing, we all know the societal, economic, and cultural benefits of living and working with other sentient species. Only the poorly educated would think otherwise.

"You mustn't be concerned, Kelvoo. Movements, and in this case perhaps just one or two individual fools, tend to come and go. No one of any consequence is ever going to take them seriously, let alone take any of the action that this movement is suggesting."

"Well, there you have it, Kelvoo," Jas declared, "straight from the crack panel of expert gentlefolk! You have nothing to worry about!"

Dr. Rosa Schlenk, the historian, cleared her throat. "Sayed, Stark, Hoffman, Chancellor, we have not yet heard from *every* member!"

"The good lady is correct, and we beg her forgiveness," Jas said. "Please, Dr. Schlenk, grace us with your thoughts."

"Thank you, Chancellor Linford. History teaches us, my dear colleagues, that wars have erupted, genocides have been committed, and empires have risen and fallen due to movements such as this. As such, Dr. Kelvoo is quite right to take an interest in this matter."

"Be that as it may, Schlenk, you are referencing *ancient* history," Dr. Sayed replied. "Terra has been at peace for centuries now. We have a single planetary government, weapons have been all but eliminated, and the major causes of conflict—differences in race, language, religion, and country—no longer exist. In other words those things that had divided us—those things that unjust movements were based upon—are gone!"

"You are quite correct, Sayed, however, divisions can, and most often have, simply been invented to suit a movement's goals," Dr. Schlenk replied. "In this case, it is the non-human species on Terra that are being demonized as a threat to our existence. As educators, we see the absurdity of such claims, but we mustn't enclose ourselves in an academic bubble. I can assure all of you that millions of our fellow humans would want to believe this 'codswallop,' as you so aptly put it, Stark."

"Oh, come now, Doctor," Dr. Stark said. "Who would *want* to believe that our species is under threat?"

Dr. Schlenk shrugged. "All of the usual suspects. Those whose lives haven't gone as planned, those who feel isolated, and those who believe they are downtrodden or that there is something fundamentally wrong with society, but they can't quite pinpoint the reason or whom to blame for their situation.

"I'm sure you have all heard of the holo-game subculture with their addiction to violent games and vids. We know there are even throwbacks among us who would condemn our own chancellor here for something as innocuous as his intimate relationships with those of his own gender! Then along comes this absurd Human Independence Movement." Dr. Schlenk wrinkled her nose as she said the name. "They explain to the outcasts that the so-called 'aliens' have corrupted Terran society! Of course it makes no sense, but historically, people who believe in such movements aren't inclined to make an effort to investigate unless it's to find and repeat statements that bolster their point of view."

While Schlenk was providing her history lesson, Dr. Stark leaned forward, furrowing his ample eyebrows. My olfactory receptors picked up fumes from the brandy he was swirling in his glass.

"Let us consider this HIM organization for a moment," Dr. Stark said. "Do they have a point?"

"I beg your pardon, sir?" I replied.

"Are you and your ilk a threat to humanity?" he asked, turning toward me. "Does your presence dilute the values, culture, or identity of the human species here on our homeworld? Does this HIM group have a valid point?"

I was stunned by Stark's questions. "I don't know how to respond, Dr. Stark. Your questions take me by surprise, and I would need time to formulate a thorough response."

Apart from Dr. Stark, the other humans looked upon me with concern until Jas intervened. "Kelvoo, there's something you should know about old Starky here," he said with a chuckle. "He's a big believer in the Socratic method of teaching."

"And conversation," Stark added.

"Ah, yes indeed," I replied, "the method of challenging students or colleagues by putting forward contrary positions, thus prompting them to consider alternative viewpoints to better justify or to modify their own stances."

"Precisely, my dear Kelvoo!" Stark said, "Nonetheless, I recommend that you consider questions such as those I have raised. Seeking the answers will help you to understand, and if necessary, put a stop to actions against you that are born of ignorance and hate."

The assembled sages nodded in agreement.

"So, my good colleagues, what do we think?" Jas asked. "Do we still say that Kelvoo shouldn't worry about this 'HIM' thing?"

"It is nothing," Dr. Sayed, the philosopher, said. "Pay it no heed, Kelvoo."

"I can understand why you felt anxious when you came across HIM's manifesto," Dr. Hoffman, the psychologist, said, "but in my opinion, their so-called movement is probably just one or two disaffected individuals who are incapable of taking action apart from issuing statements and thumping their chests. Please try not to think about them, Kelvoo. Just know that you are appreciated and admired all over Terra."

I thanked him for his kind words.

"Despite challenging you with my devil's advocate approach a moment ago, I still say that this ridiculous movement is codswallop!" Dr. Stark added.

"I hope that my observations about past successes of movements like this didn't cause you too much alarm, Kelvoo," Dr. Schlenk said, "but I agree with Dr Sayed that Terran society has changed dramatically in recent centuries, and most of the things that have divided us in the past are no more. In fact, I would venture to say that it is precisely our contact with extraterrestrials that has helped humanity to cement its identity and become more united and confident than ever before. As such, I am confident that you do not need to be concerned."

"Well, Kelvoo," Jas added, "I don't have anything to add beyond what my learned colleagues have already said. This conversation has been a very interesting and thought-provoking exercise, though, and I thank all of you for your thoughtful input."

I thanked the members of the Sagacity Club as well, letting them know how valuable our conversation had been.

The group turned to discussing other matters, which were very interesting. I made a concerted effort to contribute my perspectives as a non-human. When the meeting concluded, each professor shook my hand and thanked me for attending. I felt truly appreciated in a way that transcended the fawning admiration of most humans. I thought I had been judged favorably based on my intellect, which I found rewarding.

Jas gave me a lift home. "I hope you didn't mind all the nonsense with the phony dialogue and stuffy intellectualism," he said. "'We just enjoy the role-playing aspects of the conversation. It may seem strange, but it's fun for us."

"While I don't understand the human concept of 'fun,' I did find the banter rather entertaining," I replied.

He smiled. "I must say, you were very good at it. You blended right in!"

"I'm glad to hear that. I recognized the mannerisms from human vids that depicted ancient academics during what I believe was the Victorian era. I simply mimicked that conversational style. I appreciated the respectful tone and the ability to put forward opinions in a frank but unobtrusive manner. We kloormari tend to converse with one another in a similar way, so it was comfortable and natural for me. I would be pleased to participate in a future meeting if the members see fit to invite me."

When Jas dropped me off at home, Brenna was waiting for me. She had a shoulder bag packed and was calling a friend to pick her up. When the call ended, she said she was heading out to spend the night at a friend's place.

May was in bed reading, and I wished her a good night before settling down for my nightly meditation. The reassurance from my fellow academics resulted in a meditative state that was both restful and productive.

After class the next day, Jas called me. "Today, the members of the Sagacity Club reached out to me. They were quite taken with you, and we would be delighted to welcome you as a member if you can spare the time. I should mention that they are also motivated to add some diversity to what has been a humans-only club. We've tried inviting other species before, but they found our verbal affectations too confusing and superfluous. I'm glad you enjoyed it."

I accepted Jas's invitation with gratitude.

TWELVE: KROZ, MIDGE AND MS. TAYLOR

Two hundred and thirty-nine days after arriving at the university, I was consuming algel in my kitchen when Kroz called my Infotab. "Kelvoo, do you remember me telling you about my project and saying I would let you know when I have something to show you?"

"Of course I do, Kroz. As a kloormar, you know I am incapable of forgetting."

"I know, Kelvoo," Kroz said, repeating the words I had used when I first met Kroz on the campus. "I was intentionally making a ridiculous statement to try to make a 'joke' that might amuse humans. I'm trying to mimic humor."

"I see," I replied. "Your words are humorous because your statement is clearly absurd. Furthermore, you repeated the words that I said to you regarding mimicry of humor. I think you did so in order to strengthen the 'joke' by turning my own words around and making me the recipient. Yes, Kroz. I'm sure you are highly amusing."

To up the ante, I repeated a statement that Kroz had made during our previous meeting. "I have no expertise or even the slightest concept of human jokes, pranks, or humor in general. Please do not attempt further humor with me."

"I suppose that if we were humans having this conversation, we would currently be incapacitated with uncontrollable laughter," Kroz replied.

"I should think so, Kroz, but after all these years, I still fail to grasp humor. Nonetheless, I am pleased that we are attempting to comprehend that inscrutable concept."

Changing topics, Kroz invited me to the aviation center after work the following day.

When the call ended, May gave me a funny look. "That sounded like a *weird* conversation!"

"Yes, May. We kloormari *are* weird, at least by human standards."

The next day, the car drove me to the reception building beside the university's landing strip. The strip was just outside the invisible security dome over the campus. The building intersected the dome's wall, so to leave the campus, I had to sign out inside the building. Cleon

O'Toole was at the security desk. He was familiar with me from the times I had left the campus to take various trips.

"Where to this time, Kelvoo?" Cleon asked. "Back to the Yangtze or perhaps some other far-flung corner of the planet?"

"Not this time, Cleon. I need to proceed ninety-three meters northeast of here," I said, motioning toward the aviation center.

"Alright then, safe journey!" he said with a chuckle.

When I entered the aviation center, Kroz was waiting just inside the main entrance. Kroz led me into a large hangar, past several aircraft, spacecraft, large assemblies of equipment, twenty manufacturing bots, and eleven human workers.

Kroz stopped beside a gleaming white saucer-shaped object about ten meters in diameter. Various hatches were open or absent, revealing mechanical, electronic, and quantum engineering components inside. The midsection was a disk about two meters thick, sandwiched between a three-meter-deep bowl-shaped lower section with an identical inverted bowl above it. The craft was cradled on scaffolding.

"Kelvoo, I would like to introduce you to *Midge*," Kroz said, motioning to the craft.

I was about to ask whether Kroz was suggesting that I greet an inanimate object when a voice resembling a human female emanated from the structure. "I am pleased to meet you, Kelvoo."

"Interesting," I said to Kroz. "It appears that *Midge* is the AI you were talking about, and the object before us is a small craft. It is fascinating that the craft is the shape of a flying saucer that humans thought extraterrestrials might travel in, many centuries ago."

"You are correct, Kelvoo. 'Midge' is the name of the AI *and* the craft itself. They are really one and the same. The similarity to a flying saucer is purely coincidental. The upper and lower sections are intended to project a spherical dampening field with a radius of thirty meters around *Midge*. I have been programming *Midge* to produce an equal opposing force against all inertial forces, fast enough that the vessel remains inside the dampening field's protective cocoon."

Kroz turned to the vessel. "*Midge*, narrate technical tour alpha—long form."

As *Midge* described its components and systems, Kroz led me up a ramp to the interior of the central disk. A circular column with a flared top and bottom took up space in the center of the disk, making the cabin resemble the shape of a human delicacy known as a donut. Four chairs with swiveling bases were bolted to the deck, and four others were stacked on a small hoverlift, ready for installation. Four other spaces had metal frames suited to supporting kloormari crew or passengers.

Midge's narration went into surprising detail, given its duration of only twenty-one minutes. Most humans would probably have found the presentation boring, but I was fascinated. This was followed by another two hours and twelve minutes in which I asked questions, and Kroz provided further details. One of my questions was about the estimated timeline for *Midge's* maiden flight.

"We are at least two to three Terran years from that point," Kroz explained. "After assembly, we must test with software simulations, followed by ground testing and then test flights. Keep in mind that *Midge* is only a prototype and will be replaced by a craft with more refinements. We will, however, transfer the AI to the new craft to retain *Midge's* knowledge and skills."

"I am relieved to hear that!" *Midge* exclaimed.

As I prepared to leave, I asked Kroz to keep me informed of new developments in the *Midge* project.

"Before you go," Kroz said, "how is your academic career progressing? I have heard that you are on friendly terms with the chancellor. I'm sure he is very pleased with the benefits that you bring to the university, especially the financial windfall."

"I haven't heard anything about the financial aspects of my work."

"Haven't you noticed that the university is expanding at a tremendous rate, with new buildings being constructed everywhere?"

"Yes, I have seen the construction. In fact, I have heard that some of the buildings have the latest technology, the finest luxury, and cutting-edge architecture. A faculty member mentioned that the builder bots have taken four weeks to construct some of the buildings rather than the standard two weeks, due to the added complexity. This is all very interesting, Kroz, but how does it relate to me?"

"Kelvoo, you are the most famous faculty member in the history of the university. You are arguably the most famous professor in any educational institution in the entire history of Terra! Student applicants are paying exorbitant fees to get on a years-long waiting list to attend school at the place where Kelvoo has chosen to teach! The university has changed its fee structure for the 250 live vid and the one million view-only slots to see your lectures. Now there is an AI-mediated auction for the spots with wealthy Terrans and others bidding amounts that none of the directors had ever thought possible."

"Well, Kroz, you seem to know far more about the subject than I do. Are my lectures still available for free after a three-day delay?"

"Yes, they are still free, but the delay has been changed to five days."

"Well, at least the public at large has access to my perspective and observations. But I am curious, Kroz, how do you know all of this?"

"I know, my friend, because I work here. We have a great many visitors from on and off-campus. Information, speculation, and gossip are plentiful here, and some of it involves you."

"Please, Kroz, tell me more."

"Well, a number of individuals are concerned that you are being exploited."

"I certainly don't feel exploited. What are their concerns based on?"

"They see the vast sums of SimCash coming into the university. Under transparency laws, they have accessed your contract with the university, which shows you receiving a salary only slightly higher than average for the teaching faculty."

"I think they must be confusing human and kloormari values. I didn't request any salary at all since I didn't see the need. I'm pleased now that I have some revenue so that Brenna and May can make purchases, and we can travel when we have the opportunity. If anyone expresses concerns to you about my possible exploitation, please assure them that I only require the ability to learn and to pass my knowledge on to others, and I am beyond satisfied with my situation."

"I am glad, Kelvoo. I didn't think you would feel exploited. I am also highly satisfied with my work and how my expertise has the potential to benefit many. By the way, since you mentioned Brenna and May, how are the girls doing?"

"They seem to be enjoying Terra immensely, especially May. Lately, I don't see much of Brenna. As an eighteen-year-old, she spends much of her time with a variety of friends."

"Has Brenna bonded with a potentially long-term intimate partner yet? I understand that this is something young adult humans strive for."

"Perhaps. Brenna speaks highly of a male friend named Griffin Taylor. He also attends the university."

"I am aware of Griffin Taylor," Kroz said. "The Taylor family has a long tradition of sending their offspring to this institution and providing generous financial support to the university. Their holding company, Taylor Group, is a customer of the aviation center."

"Customer?" I inquired.

"Yes. The aviation center is a public-private partnership. It makes a profit by selling customized air and spacecraft. The black vessel at the end of the hangar is the *Raven*. It is owned by the Taylor Group, and we are upgrading its propulsion systems."

Kroz paused before continuing. "Kelvoo, since Brenna is friendly and possibly intimate with a member of the Taylor family, there is something I should mention. It may be of no consequence, but I would be remiss if I didn't tell you about it. Two days ago, a high-ranking member of the Taylor Group—I believe she is one of Griffin's aunts—

stopped by for a progress report regarding the *Raven*. I don't know her given name—everyone here just addresses her as 'Ms. Taylor.' She was inspecting the craft with our sales director, Rashid Baylor, when she spotted me. A paint bot was working close to me using a compressor that produced a loud hissing sound. Rashid and she must have been unaware of our kloormari hearing and how we can isolate frequencies. Without intending to listen in, I happened to hear their conversation clearly.

"When Ms. Taylor saw me, she said to Rashid, 'Why would you have a non-human working here? Is the university enforcing some type of quota? After all, you're working on a vessel that must carry my family safely. How do you know you can trust these extraterrestrials?'"

"Did Rashid respond in your defense?" I asked.

"To some degree," Kroz replied, "but not with great vigor. I think he may have been worried about losing a very wealthy customer. Rashid told her that I was hired because my expertise is second to none and I was playing a key role in new technologies that would advance the aviation center's products and services. She replied that she would 'tolerate' my presence, provided that I did not work on, or even *touch*, the *Raven*. Rashid assured her that I was on a totally separate assignment and would stay away from Taylor Group projects."

"That is very disappointing, Kroz," I said. "It is our nature to be trustworthy, but there seems to be a small demographic of Terran humans that feels threatened by our increasing presence. Just recently, I came across the Human Independence Movement, also called the HI Movement or HIM. Their objective is to leave the Planetary Alliance and banish all other Alliance species from Terra!"

"Yes, Kelvoo, I have heard of HIM. In fact, I was about to mention it.

"As she was about to leave, Ms. Taylor said to Rashid, 'I hope you don't think I'm an awful person who would harbor prejudices against non-humans. I just have concerns about the increasing number of those types immigrating to Terra. I'm especially concerned about the kloormari, even though there are only a few of them *so far*. As I'm sure you know, they don't seem to care about money, so they'll work for subsistence wages. They learn quickly, and they're physically versatile. I *do* realize that these traits make the kloormari good workers. I mean, if Taylor Group started replacing human workers with kloormari, we could boost our productivity and profits through the roof! The thing is, Rashid, there's more to life than money. We need to work for the benefit of humanity and make morally sound choices. How is it moral to hire a kloormar when doing so could put three or four humans out of work?'

"Rashid told her that he didn't know how to answer that. Ms. Taylor reassured Rashid that he didn't need to provide an answer. 'Just think about it for a while,' she suggested.

"Finally, she told Rashid about the Human Independence Movement and suggested that he visit their infosite. 'You might find it interesting,' she added."

I was chilled when I heard that. "What did Rashid do?" I asked. "Did he tell you about the conversation?"

"No, Kelvoo, but I'm not concerned about Rashid. As Ms. Taylor was walking out of the building, Rashid shook his head and then turned to our chief designer, saying, 'She's a real piece of work, isn't she?' Our designer replied, 'To say the least!'"

I thanked Kroz for the fascinating tour. As I left, I reassured myself that just because one member of the Taylor family was a HIM sympathizer, it didn't mean that Brenna's friend harbored the same viewpoint.

THIRTEEN: THE BRENNA BLOWUP

As the car drove me home, I called Jas and requested a meeting at my house.

May was studying in her room when I returned. "Got a message from Brenna," she said. "She's gonna come home late again."

Ten minutes later, Jas arrived and made himself comfortable.

"What do you know about a student named Griffin Taylor?" I asked.

"Are you talking about a member of *the* Taylor family or just a regular run-of-the-mill Taylor?" he replied.

"I'm referring to the family that owns the Taylor Group. I understand they are major financial supporters of the university and customers of the aviation center."

"Yes, they were," Jas replied. "As I recall, Griffin is the second son of the majority shareholders. Why are you asking, Kelvoo? Is Griffin giving you trouble in class?"

"No, Griffin is not one of my students, but he *is* in Brenna's circle of friends."

"Are we talking about 'regular' friends or intimate friends?"

"I don't know."

"Well, either way, isn't Brenna lucky? The Taylors have more money that either of us would know what to do with! It's just too bad that they've pulled their funding."

"What do you mean?"

"For the last twenty plus years, four times a year, the university would get a huge chunk of its funding from the Taylor Foundation—they're the charitable wing of the Taylor Group. Anyway, a few months ago, the funds dried up with no explanation. Under previous circumstances, a cut in funding like that would have made me panic. Luckily, we now have all kinds of revenue coming in like never before."

"Is my presence contributing to the increased funds?"

"No, Kelvoo, I wouldn't say 'contributing.' I'd say you're the *sole* reason for the increased revenue!"

"Jas, am I being exploited by this institution?"

Jas's eyebrows shot up in surprise. "Wherever did you hear that?" he asked. "Did one of your students suggest that you're being exploited?" Rather than waiting for my answer, Jas continued. "Well, no matter. The only individual who can answer that is you, Kelvoo. Do you feel like we're exploiting you?"

"No, Jas, not in the least. The university has provided me with food and this shelter, along with sufficient funds to support Brenna and May and to travel and learn as I desire. I require nothing further."

Jas nodded in understanding. "Well, alright, Kelvoo, but let me be clear: if you *ever* feel like we're taking advantage of you or cheating you or failing to compensate you adequately, I want you to come straight to me *immediately*. If you would like an increase in your salary, a different house, or any other benefits, I have no doubt that the directors will agree to accommodate you."

I realized that the conversation was straying from the main topic that I wanted to raise, so I asked a question. "What I really want to know, Jas, is where the Taylor Foundation is making its donations. I assume that such a large charitable foundation contributes to a variety of causes. Is there a way to find out where their money is going?"

"Well, I don't know where you're going with this, Kelvoo," Jas said as he pulled out his Infotab, "but you've piqued my interest." Jas started tapping his Infotab screen.

"Are you able to directly access that information?" I asked.

"For sure! I'm taking a look on the Contribunet infosite. Terran transparency laws require non-profits to report the sources of their contributions. Normally, I would be more interested in looking up a non-profit's benefactors, but in this case I'm doing a reverse search, starting with the Taylor Foundation, and seeing where their money is going. OK, there they are. Hmm . . . let's look at their history . . . Oh! Now *that's* interesting! A year ago, the foundation was contributing to us and eleven other organizations. Then, a few months ago, they started reducing their list of beneficiaries except for one—the Earth Institute. As they dropped each non-profit, they increased their contribution to the Earth Institute. Now the institute is their *only* beneficiary. Not only that, the total amount of their contributions has tripled in comparison to the total amount they used to spend!"

"What a strange name," I remarked. "Earth Institute. Why would an organization be named using an ancient word for this planet that was used by just one of the old Terran languages?"

"That's not the only strange thing," Jas said, clearly intrigued. "I can't find any significant data about the Earth Institute. The only information showing is the minimum that is legally required. Even the list of directors and the institute's mission are just shown as 'pending.' You'd typically see that for a newly registered non-profit that's just in the planning stage, but in those cases their funding pool would be zero

95

or almost nothing. The Earth Institute has holdings worth over two trillion SimCash units!"

Jas put his Infotab down. "I'll have a word with security tomorrow, and I'll ask the investigations division to find out everything they can about the Earth Institute. I'll update you when I have more information. In the meantime, may I ask why you're so interested in this matter?"

"All I can say is that I'm concerned about Brenna. She's been quite disengaged lately, and I want to give her the space she needs to fulfill her potential. At the same time, I want to safeguard her against associating with people who might lead her down a troubling path."

"Say no more, Kelvoo."

"Oh, alright, I'll stop talking about it."

"That's not what I meant," Jas assured me, chuckling.

The next day, as my students were filing out of class after my lecture, Jas approached me. "Kelvoo, please let me give you a lift home," he said.

After the two-minute ride, as the car hovered outside of my door, Jas turned to me. "Our head investigator found a contact at the Earth Institute and posed as a wealthy potential donor. She was able to determine the institute's purpose." The words that followed hit me hard. "They're a façade, Kelvoo. The Earth Institute is a fundraising front for the Human Independence Movement! I'm sorry to say that the other club members and I might have underestimated the movement's scope. Nonetheless, I want you to understand that HIM only represents the tiniest portion of the Terran human population. Still, they obviously have power and money, and on this planet, money talks!"

As soon as Jas left, I send a message to Brenna's Infotab:

Brenna, when are you planning to come home? I have something I'd like to discuss with you.

Moments later, Brenna replied that she was out with Griffin and had decided to stay for the night at one of his family's homes. She said that she could drop by at 19:00 the next evening and have dinner at the house. I replied that I looked forward to seeing her.

That night, my meditation was fragmented as I considered the best way to discuss my concerns with Brenna. While my studies into human behavior were extensive, I felt ill equipped for the coming conversation, especially since I was dealing with a human teenager who was prone to outbursts of anger. To complicate matters, I hadn't spent much time with Brenna in recent months, and I didn't know how her personality and perspective might have shifted in that timespan.

I was not well rested the next day, and I was not as engaged as I should have been during class. I felt bad that I wasn't giving my best to the university due to my anxiety about the impending conversation with Brenna.

After work I asked Pollybot to prepare fettuccine Alfredo since that was what Brenna had eaten on her first night in our new home. I had decided that the best approach would be to keep the conversation as calm as possible while still expressing my concerns.

When Brenna arrived at 19:20 she said hello to me, then May gave her a hug. "Wow! Nice clothes!" May said.

"Oh yeah, thanks. Griffin's mom took me shopping. She's friends with Damon Nightingale."

"The fashion designer?"

"Yeah. She took me to his studio in Iceland. The pants and top are off the rack, but the jacket is custom fitted."

"Cool! And how about the big bracelet? Are the yellow parts gold?"

"The yellow is gold, and the silvery chunks are palladium. Griffin bought it for me!"

While May was becoming fully acquainted with Brenna's clothes and adornments, I filled a bowl with algel from my study and asked Pollybot to bring out the fettuccine. I positioned myself at the kitchen counter and announced that dinner was ready.

Brenna briefly regarded the serving dish full of fettuccine and Alfredo sauce. "Oh, yeah. I actually brought my dinner with me. I got it from one of the kitchen staff at Griffin's house just before I left. Sorry, but I'm kind of tired of pasta, and the carbs aren't so great for me anyway."

Brenna pulled a hot pack from her new bag, placed it on the counter, and broke the seal. Steam rose from the pack, revealing a greenish slurry with white chunks mixed in. May sniffed it, then wrinkled her nose. "What's that?" she asked in a tone that straddled the line between a question and an exclamation.

"It's spinach in truffle paste infused with saffron and k'k'mos extract with cultured protein slices."

"Yuck!" May replied.

"Hey, a girl's gotta watch her figure, you know! You'll understand in a year or two," Brenna assured her." Brenna turned to me. "I can't stay long, Kelvoo. What did you want to discuss?"

According to plan, I started with a question. "Brenna, are you familiar with the Human Independence Movement?"

"Oh sure! Griffin's told me all about it. What do you want to know?"

"I'd like to know what *you* think of it."

"It's fine. We humans need to look out for ourselves, you know!" She chuckled as if she regarded the subject as a source of humor.

"Brenna, have you read their manifesto? Are you aware that they want Terra to leave the Planetary Alliance? Do you understand that they are saying that beings like me are a threat to humanity? Do you know that they want all of the other Alliance species to leave Terra—by force if necessary? Do you realize they think humans should arm themselves, supposedly to defend against so-called 'aliens' like me?"

Brenna rolled her eyes. "Look, as a human, I get where they're coming from. They just want to protect what humans have built. They want to preserve the human culture and way of life. They feel as though humanity has become too dependent on outsiders."

"But, Brenna, what happens if they actually manage to get the laws changed? Would you be alright with them forcing me and all of the other non-humans off this planet, possibly at the point of a blaster? Are you fine with humans carrying arms in public?"

"Oh, Kelvoo!" she exclaimed. "It's *never* going to come to that! You're taking it way too seriously! If the HI Movement succeeds then sure, someday you might be asked to go back to Kuw'baal or wherever else you choose to go. HIM's members are people who want what's best for humans and everyone else. They just think it's better for each species to live in peace on their own planets."

"Then why are they spreading fear?" I asked. "Why are they depicting the Sarayans and the Mangors and the Bandorians and the Silupas and the Grovnexuns and the xiltors and the kloormari as threats?"

"Look, Kelvoo, these are just words. The movement is only trying to get attention to make their point. Once more humans get the message, HIM will be a lot more mainstream and a whole lot less radical sounding."

"I don't think you fully understand, Brenna," I said. "HIM is not the first such movement in human history. They are part of a pattern that has repeated itself over and over and over again. Movements like this arise by stoking fear among the population. It's always been about demonizing those who are different, using violence to achieve their means and then wielding their power for their own enrichment at the expense of the general population!

"Look, Brenna, chances are good that HIM will fizzle out and disappear, but it has come to my attention that HIM is extremely well-funded and that Griffin's family is one of the primary contributors."

"OK, now I get it," Brenna said, sounding perturbed. "You think I'm stupid enough that I would be in a relationship with a bad person! Well, you know nothing about Griffin, and he's nothing like you're imagining!" Brenna's voice grew louder as she continued. "I'm in love with him, OK? He's kind and caring, and he's totally in love with me, alright?"

"But Brenna, this is all so sudden and such a surprise. Why didn't you tell me this?"

"Why the hell didn't you ask me? I was telling you about Griffin all the time! Why didn't you take more interest in *me* and what *I* was doing?"

"Because, I was giving you the space that I thought you needed to thrive and grow. You chose to spend time with your friends, and you chose not to accompany May and me on most of our trips. You wanted space, and I didn't want to impose on you. I trusted your judgment."

"Oh, so now you don't trust me!" she shouted.

"Brenna, I'm sorry," I said in a tone that I hoped was soothing. "I'm sure you love Griffin very much and that he's a fine human. Why don't you bring him over soon? That way we can get to know each other and talk things through."

"Oh, hell no! You'll *never* understand him! You think you're some big expert in human behavior. Well, you're totally clueless, and it's all a crock!"

"Brenna, I'm so, so sorry that you feel this way. I just want to protect you from making a mistake."

"How dare you say you want to *protect* me? *You* didn't protect my dad from being murdered by the Sarayans, and *you* didn't protect me from going into foster care with those effing Gramms! Griffin was right! Humans and aliens like you need to stay the hell apart!"

Brenna reached for her bag.

"Brenna," I said in desperation, "I can see that my words have made you very upset."

"Don't you use that psycho-babble garbage on me!" she shouted. Then she grabbed her bag and made for the front door.

"Don't go!" May shouted. She had been sitting at the counter throughout the confrontation. "Please come back, Brenna! We need to talk more!"

Brenna bolted out of the house, and I ran after her. She jumped into a luxury vehicle that she had parked outside when she arrived. The hatch closed behind her, and even though there was no way she could have heard me, I was compelled to shout. "I'm sorry, Brenna! Please don't go. I love you!"

I saw the car's running lights as it raced uphill at a dangerously high speed. May came outside and held my hand paddle. I saw the car's lights again when it exited through the security field and was outside the campus. Then it rose and fled into the northern night sky. As the car's lights winked out over the crest of the mountains, I was left feeling empty and devastated.

For a moment I allowed myself to consider what Brenna had said. Perhaps humans and non-Terran species didn't belong together. After all, there I was, a kloormar holding hands with a little human that I was totally responsible for. I was just an insignificant speck on a strange planet. Kelvoo the great imposter, exalted by billions of humans as some kind of expert on humanity with humans lining up to see me and hear my supposed wisdom. I was the "great expert" on human nature, having thrust myself headlong into the role of being a parent to a couple of human girls, and it turned out I was an utter, abject failure.

FOURTEEN: ENLISTING THE MEDIA

I stood outside my home, staring at the night sky. May released my hand and went back inside. Over half an hour later, she came out and told me that I'd be getting too cold if I stayed outdoors. May was familiar enough with kloormari physiology to know that I could lose consciousness with enough exposure to cold.

My meditation that night was tortured. I ended it earlier than usual the next morning, using the extra time to write a lengthy message to Jas that provided a detailed account of my confrontation with Brenna. I was hesitant, thinking that Jas was likely tired of hearing my concerns about a human who wasn't his problem.

During class that day, I felt as if I didn't function well, though my students seemed as engaged as ever. After class, Jas surprised me by stopping by and asking if I wanted to talk at his house.

When we got there, he sat down to address me. "So, how are you holding up, Kelvoo? Any news about Brenna yet?"

"No, Jas. I feel as if I must do something, but what can I do without the risk of alienating Brenna even more?"

"Sometimes there's nothing you can do," Jas replied. "Brenna is eighteen, so legally, she can make her own decisions. Unfortunately, one of those decisions was to terminate her classes. She and Griffin Taylor are no longer students here. They both withdrew about an hour ago."

I was devastated. "Jas, what am I going to do? You say she can make her own decisions, but what if those decisions ruin her life and her future? I'm responsible for her and for May!"

I predicted Jas's reply before he spoke. "If Brenna's decisions ruin her life, then *she* chose poorly. Kelvoo, you are not responsible for Brenna any longer. She is an adult now."

"But why did she choose so poorly, Jas? What signs did I miss? Should I have spent more time with her? What should I have done differently?"

"I'm definitely the wrong person to ask, Kelvoo. I've never had siblings or any kids of my own. On the other hand, while I was just a junior prof, I counseled many parents who experienced the same issues as you. You are not alone, and you have always had the girls' best interests at heart. That's all I can tell you."

101

"But why would Brenna loathe me so much that she would defend a fringe movement that seeks to remove me and all other 'alien' species from Terra?"

"First off, I'm sure she doesn't loathe you, but I do think she's very conflicted. On the one hand, she associates the kloormari with her father's death, but at the same time, she sees how other humans admire you. I assume that Griffin and his family introduced Brenna to the movement, likely after she fell in love with him and started thinking that he was perfect and could do no wrong. Suddenly, along comes the HI Movement, which spells everything out in black and white: humans are good, but when they associate with non-humans, bad things happen! It's utter nonsense, of course, but something about it resonates with her, especially when she hears it from a guy she loves and a family that is the epitome of human 'success.'

"I've seen it so many times before. Just last week one of our law faculty told me about a couple of parents who came to see him. Their daughter had taken off to some retreat on Luna and cut off all contact. She went to follow some navel-gazing guru and 'discover herself.' It's just too easy for kids to get brainwashed these days!"

Jas insisted that I could only wait and see whether Brenna would "come around." He told me that I should just give it a few days.

I spent the following days staying closer to May. I was encouraged that she seemed to take comfort from my presence, but I worried that she was a time bomb, ready to explode with self-destructive fury as she grew closer to Brenna's age. I tried to discuss Brenna with her, but she told me that it made her too sad and she would withdraw whenever I raised the subject.

I told May's teacher about the situation, and to my relief, she alerted a counselor who spent some time with May. It may have been the counseling that prompted May to approach me one evening and tell me how worried she was.

May told me that, in the past, whenever Brenna was away for a day or two, they would correspond via their Infotabs. Sometimes Brenna would initiate communication, but it was usually May. Brenna always responded promptly and would take pleasure in sending May images of the places she and Griffin had gone, or things she had bought. Since the blowup, May had tried to contact Brenna at least six times per day. She had even pleaded with her to reply, but she was met by complete silence. May couldn't understand why Brenna had abandoned us. Neither could I.

The only comfort I could take was that I could always see Brenna's whereabouts on my Infotab due to her locator implant. She spent most of her time in the vicinity of the Taylor family's compound in Iberia.

Then, two weeks after she ran away, the signal from Brenna's locator stopped. So did my willingness to do nothing.

***

Prior to first contact between the humans and kloormari, I had no concept of imagination. It would have been strange for a kloormar to speculate about things that *might* be or that *might* happen. There was no need to think about anything except for past and present events and facts. It was my first human teacher, Sam Buchanan, who had introduced the concept of imagination and, as absurd as it seemed at the time, various circumstances led me to develop and use my imagination.

On the night when Brenna's locator signal vanished, my meditation was a shambles. That night my brains were overcome with imagination. I imagined Brenna wanting to come back, with the Taylor family holding her against her will. I thought about Jas's story regarding the student who had run off to Luna due to brainwashing, and I imagined Brenna being indoctrinated through psychological abuse. I imagined that Brenna had been taken because the Human Independence Movement wanted to hurt beings like me by luring and then harming a person who was dear to me. Worst of all, I imagined that Brenna was dead. I couldn't switch my imagination off as it tortured me with images of the horrible ways in which Brenna could have been murdered.

At 05:19 the next morning, in a panicked state of horror, I took action, using my Infotab to call the Atlantic News Network. Their corporate AI answered with a vid feed showing a bland but smiling avatar asking how my call could be directed. I asked for Liz Underwood, who was one of the three journalists at the announcement event when I started working at the university.

"Please identify yourself," the AI said, its face cheery.

"I am Kelvoo."

"One moment while I cross-reference your vid image with our database . . . Transferring your call to the editorial desk, North American continent, Atlantic Coast."

A young human male appeared on the screen. "Hello! The AI tells me you're Kelvoo! Are you *the* Kelvoo of Kelvoo's Testimonial fame?"

"Yes."

"OK, Kelvoo, the AI has successfully cross-referenced your image with the database. You are, of course, extremely important to us, but we get calls from a lot of sophisticated scammers, so I hope you can bear with me when I ask you to send your personal ID sequence from your Infotab."

I opened the security interface on the Infotab, entered my password, and let the device scan my biometrics and send my code.

"Thank you, Kelvoo. You've been verified!" the man said with great excitement. "By the way, my name's Matt. How can I help you?"

"I must speak with Liz Underwood."

"Oh. Well, Kelvoo, the thing is, we're located on the Atlantic coast of North America. It's almost 22:30 here. Liz was our anchor tonight, and she headed home about two hours ago after the evening broadcast. I see that you're calling from the Mediterranean campus of the Interplanetary University. If you have a story for us, we have crews close to you who can be there in half an hour."

"No, Matt. I must speak with Liz Underwood. I need her to interview me, in person, live on camera. I have an announcement to make that will be of great interest to all of Terra."

"OK, Kelvoo. Please stay right there while I do my best for you."

Matt muted the audio connection. On the vid feed, I saw him pick up an Infotab and make a call. In fact, he appeared to make three calls before he came back to his communications console. "Putting you through."

Liz Underwood appeared on the screen, sitting up in a bed, wearing nightclothes. Her hair was unruly, and her face looked rougher than it had when I saw her at my announcement and on newscasts. She blinked a few times. "Kelvoo! I'm honored that you called me. I assume you have a *very important* reason for calling."

"Yes. Thank you so much for taking my call. I have an announcement that I want to make as soon as possible. I don't want to get into the details now in case they leak out, and my message gets manipulated by others. I want to make the announcement live to all of Terra. I'm prepared to give you exclusive access to my announcement. I offer you my assurance that the story will be huge and very much worth your while."

"Well, I'm certainly flattered, Kelvoo, but at the risk of looking a gift horse in the mouth, why me?"

"We kloormari don't usually have a 'gut feeling' about people," I explained, "but from the moment you spoke to me when my position was announced at the university, I had a good feeling about you. I have also seen your newscasts and fieldwork, and I admire your professionalism. As you know, I had a very unpleasant experience with the media about fifteen years ago, so I need someone whom I can trust. I'm choosing to trust you, Ms. Underwood."

"Thank you so much, Kelvoo, and please call me Liz."

"When can we get together, Liz? This matter is of utmost urgency!"

"Alright, if we're going to have the most impact, we should meet where you are. Are you at the university now?"

I confirmed that I was at my home on campus. Liz told me that she would call the corporate hangar and have the company's semi-orbital vessel and the camera and sound bots prepped. She guessed she could arrive at the university's landing strip in about three hours. I asked Liz to call me when she was ten minutes from landing.

I wanted to make sure that my schedule was clear, so I could meet Liz as soon as she arrived. I sent a message to May's school to advise them that May might miss the first part of the day. When May woke, I told her about my plan.

I got the call from Liz at 08:10. "OK, Kelvoo, I'm ten minutes away. I'm sorry to tell you this," she added, "but I've been in touch with the network executives during the flight, and they're not going to allow our interview to be live on the air. They have no idea what you're going to say and for what purpose you're going to use the airtime. They *have* told me that we can shoot our segment, make sure we are both comfortable with it, and then release it immediately as a breaking news item if it fits the network's criteria."

"That will suffice," I said as I got into the car and directed it to take me to the landing strip.

When Liz emerged from the semi-orbital, her hair was styled, her face was smooth with pigments applied, and her attire looked professional. A young assistant, Jane, followed her but kept a respectful distance. Three cameras, two microphones, and several lights and reflectors hovered alongside Liz. After the perfunctory greetings and handshake, Liz asked me whether I had a preferred location.

I accompanied Liz through the security checkpoint to the other side of the reception building and out to the deck where Brenna, May, and I had stood when we took in our first view of the campus and the shining sea beyond. "I think this should meet the technical requirements," I said. "The morning sunlight will illuminate us as well as the background. Behind us is a view of the entire campus, so the setting will provide an appropriate context. Farther behind us, the sea will make an attractive but unobtrusive backdrop."

Liz smiled. "Have you worked in videography before, Kelvoo?"

"No, but I did some research while you were on your way here."

At that moment I realized that the conversation had provided a much-needed distraction from my anxiety, but as the cameras, lights, and microphones took up their positions, the reality of what I was about to say dawned on me. My intense worries about Brenna, my exhaustion, and my lack of meditation had me frazzled. Internally, I had to fight my distress, so I could focus on the task at hand.

Liz positioned me against the railing, facing the cameras while she stood beside me. When I told her I was ready, she told the cameras to begin recording, then looked into the lens. "I'm Liz Underwood from the Atlantic News Network. I was recently contacted by Kelvoo, Terra's most famous kloormar. Kelvoo has an important announcement to make and has granted us exclusive access."

Liz turned toward me as one of the cameras pulled back to widen its shot. "Kelvoo, please share your announcement with our viewing audience."

"Thank you Liz," I began. "As many of you know, when I relocated to Terra, two young human females accompanied me. The girls are named May Murphy and Brenna Murphy. The girls are orphans from Perdition with no known living relatives. I was granted legal guardianship of May and Brenna by the Terran authorities on Kuw'baal. Both girls moved to Terra with me willingly and enthusiastically.

"Two weeks ago, Brenna, eighteen years of age, left our home. I have neither seen, nor heard from her since then. Last night, her locator stopped transmitting. I'm desperate to find Brenna and bring her back home, where she—"

"Cameras, pause," Liz said. She dropped her broadcast persona and turned toward me in indignation. "Kelvoo, did you get me out of bed and have me fly an ocean and a continent away to announce that a teenage girl has run away? Do you know how many millions of teenagers do that every single day? Hell, even the smallest local news outlets don't cover runaways!"

"Liz, you don't understand."

"Look, Kelvoo," Liz said, softening her tone as she reached out and touched my upper arm, "I respect and admire you. I have a couple of kids of my own, and I understand how terrifying it would be for one of them to go missing. I just think that you might want to start with the local authorities first. I'm sure she'll turn up sooner or later."

"But Liz, her locator—"

"That doesn't mean anything. Runaways will sometimes cut out their locators, usually with the help of a friend. It's painful, but it's not too damaging. Sometimes they'll get hold of a local anesthetic or even find a medical professional for the extraction. You said she's eighteen. At that age there is no legal requirement to be locatable, so there's nothing you can do about that."

"Alright, Liz, but there is *much more* in my announcement. If I may continue?"

"Well, since we're already here, let's have you complete your statement. Then we'll see whether the network wants to air it. Let's start from where you said you wanted to bring Brenna back home."

"Cameras, resume recording," Liz said, and I returned to my statement.

"I am desperate to find Brenna and bring her back home where she belongs. I'm especially concerned because Brenna has become involved with people in a radical movement. I think it is likely that she was brainwashed and ran away in an irrational mental state."

"Excuse me, Kelvoo," Liz interjected, "what movement are you referring to?"

"They are called the Human Independence Movement or the HI Movement or HIM."

I didn't know whether Liz had ever heard of HIM. If she hadn't she covered it up well. "Please, Kelvoo, tell our viewers what *you* know about that movement."

"Their manifesto calls for the immediate withdrawal of Terra from the Planetary Alliance. They think the presence of non-humans on Terra is a threat to the values and culture of Terran humans. They are demanding the expulsion of non-humans, and they want humans to carry arms, so they can defend against the supposed 'threat' from beings like me! Your viewers don't have to take my word for it. They can see the manifesto for themselves at the Human Independence Movement's infosite."

"Well, Kelvoo, every so often we see small, fringe movements pop up. They usually fade away after a few weeks. My question is, why would Brenna associate with radicals like that, especially since she has lived among the kloormari and with you for so many years?"

"She is in an intimate relationship with someone. I learned that this person's family is a major financial supporter of the movement. I asked Brenna about it and suggested that she stop associating with such people. She downplayed the beliefs of HIM, and we ended up in a verbal confrontation. She ran out of the house, and I haven't seen her since."

"Who is this person that Brenna was in a relationship with?"

"His name is Griffin Taylor. I confronted Brenna after I learned that his family's charitable organization, the Taylor Foundation, has been a major contributor to HIM."

"Wait, Kelvoo, are you referring to *the* Taylor Foundation?" Liz asked. "Aren't they a huge contributor to this university and many other educational institutions?"

I explained that the foundation had been a major contributor, but now all the money that they used to donate, and more, was being directed to HIM. Liz asked why I chose to go public with my concerns.

"There is a Terran expression, Liz," I replied, "'Daylight is the best disinfectant.' I want to shine a light on the Human Independence Movement to make your viewers aware of their dangerous goals. I need

107

them to release Brenna and return her to me, if they haven't murdered her already."

"Kelvoo, do you really think that this movement would want to harm Brenna? Wouldn't she be more useful to them as one of their supporters?"

"Liz, I want to remind your audience that I have seen the good side and the dark side of humanity. I have studied for years, and I have a doctorate in human behavior. Movements like this have come and gone, and they do not behave rationally. If the Human Independence Movement strives to remove so-called 'aliens' from this planet, then they undoubtedly see a prominent 'alien' like me as the enemy! I think they would like to see me suffer, and I wouldn't put it past them to lure Brenna over to their side and harm her simply to hurt me!"

"So," Liz replied, "what would you like to say to these people if they're watching?"

"Let me see that Brenna is alive and well and then return her to me. If you have harmed or murdered her, I will do everything in my power to see that you are brought to justice and punished as severely as possible. Give up your ideology and goals. They are based on lies, ignorance, and hate. It will not end well for you."

"And if Brenna is alive and is watching," Liz said, "what do you want to say to her?"

"Brenna, if you can, please let me know that you're alright." A wave of emotion almost overcame me, and I had to push it down as I continued. "I love you. I know you don't believe that a kloormar can feel love in the same way as a human, and you may be right, but I *do* know that I would be devastated to lose you.

"Please think about your little sister. May is extremely worried about you. She loves you and misses you desperately. Whatever you may think of me, please let May know that you're alright, or better yet, come home to us.

"If you hate me so much that you can't bear to be in my presence, I will ensure that you can move into your own home, and May can visit you or live with you if she wants to.

"Finally, please understand that the people you are involved with are using you to further their hateful, hurtful cause. If you can find a way, please reach out. We love you, and we miss you desperately."

"Is there anything else you would like to say, Kelvoo?" Liz asked in a somber voice.

"I have no further statement, Liz, except to thank you and Atlantic News for letting me make this statement."

"Cameras, stop recording," Liz said. She dropped her on-air persona again. "That was a very powerful statement, Kelvoo. I apologize for cutting you off early in your announcement without waiting to see where you were heading. I guess I'm sleep deprived and prone to being cranky."

"I can relate to that!" I said. "Do you think my message will resonate with your viewers?"

"Without a doubt. On a societal level, they'll be saddened by the Human Independence Movement and its goals. Normally, I'd say that this movement is just another flash in the pan that will fizzle out, but if they're funded by the likes of the Taylor Foundation, we're going to have to keep an eye on them. On a more personal level, your statement packed an emotional punch when you brought up Brenna's sister and the effect of Brenna's disappearance on her."

"Yes, May is extremely upset and anxious about Brenna."

"Speaking of May, where is she at the moment?"

"At my home. In fact, I must return home soon, so she doesn't miss too much school."

Liz looked me in the eye. "Kelvoo, do you think I could ask May a few questions on camera?"

"I'm not sure whether May would be willing. She may be too upset."

"I only ask because your statement will be strengthened if we follow it up with a few words from Brenna's poor little sister. If we can get some good vid of May, our viewers' hearts will go out to her, and the impact of your statement will be reinforced tremendously."

"In that case, Liz, let's go talk to May and see what she thinks."

We walked to my car. Liz and her assistant, Jane, sat across from one another, allowing Jane to apply additional tints and treatments to Liz's face and examine her hair. There was no room for the production bots, so I asked the car to drive slowly while the bots followed.

Liz and I entered the house and Jane waited outside with the bots. May was in the living area reading on a sofa. She looked up over her Infotab screen to see Liz smiling at her. "Hi, May, I'm Liz."

"Oh yes," May replied. "I remember you from the night of Kelvoo's speech."

Liz got down onto one knee to interact with May at eye level. "How are you holding up?"

"I'm OK."

"I'm sure you're really worried about your sister, but these things usually turn out alright. If you don't mind, could I please ask you a few questions?"

May shrugged. "Yeah, I guess."

Liz tapped her Infotab, and Jane opened the front door, letting the cameras, microphones, and lights into the house. Liz sat next to May as the bots took up positions all around and above the sofa. May had a wide-eyed look of concern, "Um, what's going on?" she asked.

"Liz would like to talk to you and record it on vid, so it can be broadcast," I explained.

"OK, but why?"

"To help us find Brenna. We want people all over to know what's happening, so they can help us get in contact with her."

"Don't worry, May," said Liz. "Just ignore these bots. We'll just chat like we're good friends."

"But what if I screw up?"

"Then we won't show it. Your dad—I'm sorry, I mean Kelvoo—has told me so many good things about you, so I know you'll do great. Just relax and be yourself." I was surprised to hear her say that since I had told her very little about May. But I refrained from correcting Liz because I trusted her to do her job and aid in my mission.

Liz started her interview with simple questions about May's younger years on Kuw'baal. She wisely avoided the subject of May's past back on Perdition and on *Jezebel's Fury*. Liz progressed to asking May about moving to Terra, about school, about places she had visited, and about her life on the university campus. Liz's questioning was gentle, and sometimes she would elicit a smile from May as they talked about lighthearted moments from May's past.

Once May was more relaxed, Liz started asking about the circumstances of Brenna's disappearance. May's answers were heartfelt, thoughtful, and intelligent. I also admired Liz's obvious expertise in human behavior as she guided May and coaxed her toward an excellent expression of her feelings.

"Can you feel your sister's presence?" Liz asked in a surprising twist. "Are you confident that she's alive and well?" The first question disturbed me because it suggested the existence of a psychic connection, which was pure superstition. May was far more disturbed by the second question. We hadn't discussed the possibility of Brenna being harmed or dead, and May was not prepared to consider those possibilities. As May started to cry, Liz asked her whether she had a message for Brenna.

"Just come home, Brenna," May said, sobbing. "I miss you, and I love you."

Liz stopped the recording and looked up at me with a sad smile. "We're good, Kelvoo. I'd say we have everything we need." She gave May a hug, thanked her, then told her that she did "a super-good job."

"Can we get this broadcast *now*?" I asked.

Liz tapped a message on her Infotab before answering. "I'm sending the content to the network right now, but let me call Jerry Simmons, my executive producer."

Liz placed the call and then turned up the volume, so we could all hear.

"Hey, Liz!" he said. "So, was your junket to the Mediterranean worth the time and cost?"

"Yeah, listen, Jer. I'm with Kelvoo and his . . . er, I mean *Kelvoo's* daughter. Um, I mean *foster* daughter. Is that right?" She gave me a tentative look before continuing. "Anyway, Jer, I'm here with Kelvoo and May right now."

"Oh, OK then," Jerry replied in a more business-like tone.

"I'm calling because Kelvoo wants us to broadcast as soon as possible. To answer your question, yes, this story was worth the time and the cost. At its core it's a simple, heartfelt, missing-person story, but it's also about a new fringe group that is seeking to expel Kelvoo and all other so-called 'aliens' from Terra. They're probably just your typical bunch of nutjobs, but they has massive funding, including major backing from the Taylor Foundation!"

"What? *The* Taylor Foundation?"

"Uh huh! So, here's why I'm calling. I think we need to turn this into a special segment. I'm thinking sad background music, attention-grabbing graphics, and major urgency. Now, Kelvoo," Liz said, looking up at me, "the thing is that it'll take two or three hours for the studio to assemble a piece like that. Often, when we get an announcement like yours, we have to blast it out, so we can beat the other networks to the punch. In this case since you so kindly gave us an exclusive, I think we should take the time to give your story the impact it deserves. Believe me, it'll be worth it! What do you say?"

"Alright, Liz. I admire your skill as a journalist, and I trust you."

Liz turned back to her Infotab. "What do you say, Jer?"

"I'm with Kelvoo," Jerry replied. "I'm trusting you on this, so let's make a big statement! We've just received your content, and we'll get to work. In the meantime, we've got a decent number of other items coming in. When we add your story, it could be a big news day! Please get back here as soon as you can. We need to get you prepped for tonight's newscast."

Liz commanded the production bots to make their way back to the landing strip. Liz, Jane, May, and I piled into the car. We overtook the production bots as we flew to the landing strip. We said our goodbyes to Liz and her assistant. I instructed the car to proceed to May's school. May moved into the seat beside me for the three-minute trip.

"I hope you didn't mind Liz Underwood referring to you as my foster daughter," I said along the way.

May turned to look at me. Then she touched my arm and gave me a sad smile. "It's OK. I kind of liked it. I was just wondering, would it be alright if I started calling you 'Pa'?"

"You can call me whatever you want, May, but you should be aware that 'pa' is short for 'papa,' which typically refers to a male. As you know, a kloormar is neither neither male nor female."

"I know, but for me 'pa' would be short for 'parent,' so can I call you 'Pa'?"

"I would like that very much, May."

A warm, reassuring feeling flooded me. If I had a human's anatomy, I think I would say that my heart swelled with joy, tinged with sadness."

After dropping May off, I proceeded to the lecture hall with ten minutes to spare before the start of my class. Despite my exhaustion and continued anxiety, I performed better than I had in recent days. I took comfort in the knowledge that I wasn't helpless anymore. I had stopped waiting and had done something about Brenna's absence. I was confident that things were going to happen.

Things certainly did happen.

After my lecture, I stayed behind to answer questions and discuss topics with some of the students. Three hours and ten minutes after my class started, Jas entered the hall. "Good! You're still here," he said.

Jas told the remaining students that he had to meet with me in private. He led me down a hallway to an empty conference room. Jas closed the door behind us and then turned to me. "Kelvoo, I'm going to ask you this as calmly as possible," he said, enunciating each word. "What in the hell is going on?"

"Well, quite a lot, actually," I replied. "Last night, Brenna's locator stopped transmitting. I had no choice but to do something. Before class today, May and I were interviewed by Liz Underwood from Atlantic News."

"I know. I was in a board meeting when I got an urgent call from our media center. They sent me a recording of your interview, and I watched the first seven minutes of it before coming to see you. Kelvoo, why would you make a news announcement without clearing it through media relations first?"

"Because my statement was entirely personal in nature. It did not involve university business."

"Well, it's university business now! Inquiries and questions and urgent calls are flooding in fast and furious! Our call center answerbots are so overwhelmed that our comm systems are shutting down! But never mind that for a minute. Kelvoo, why did you tell the entire planet about HIM?"

"Because daylight is the best disinfectant," I said with much satisfaction.

"But you've just told billions of people about a movement that almost no one had ever heard of!" he said.

"Yes. When people know about their nefarious goals, the great majority of the public will oppose them."

"I don't think you understand, Kelvoo. Let's look at this rationally. Let's be optimistic and guess that only a billion people will see your announcement or any of the thousands of reports from other outlets. Now let's say that ninety-nine percent of those people think that the HI Movement is shocking and wrong. Conversely, let's say that just one percent find the movement's message appealing and worthy of their support. The result is that an obscure, largely unknown fringe movement suddenly becomes a force to contend with, now that it has ten million followers as well as trillions of SimCash units behind it!"

Jas's tone changed, and he looked at me with sympathy. Then he shook his head. "My God, Kelvoo, what have you done?"

FIFTEEN: BRENNA'S CALL

Jas's reaction jolted me. I started questioning myself. *Could Jas be right about my actions strengthening HIM? Did my panic and exhaustion cloud my judgment? Were my actions nothing more than a self-centered publicity stunt?*

Jas told me that, out of an abundance of caution, extra security would be set up around my home. May and I would have to be accompanied by security personnel wherever we went, at least for a while.

When it was time for May's school day to end, Jas and I and a bodyguard took a university car to pick her up. We drove with the windows set to tinted mode, so outsiders couldn't see in. I had to message May to let her know which vehicle we were waiting in.

After we picked May up, the car took us down a ramp under the main administration building and then we took a lift to the top floor and walked down a short hallway. Jas opened a tall pair of carved wood doors.

"Welcome to my offices," he said. I had never visited Jas's offices before. They were more like a suite with a main reception area, a conference room, an office, a kitchen, and a guest room with sofas, closets, low tables, and an entertainment center. With the exception of the kitchen, every room had a wall consisting of tinted floor-to-ceiling windows looking out across the grassy expanse of the campus's main quad.

"You and May will be spending the night here while we create a stronger security perimeter around your house," Jas informed us. "It's not as if HIM is equipped to harm you, but they could inspire an unhinged radical to take action. Tonight, security will be stationed on this floor and at the main entrance." Jas showed us the controller on the side of the sofas that would transform them into beds. He opened a closet containing two servitor bots at floor level and shelves holding bedsheets and pillows above. Jas asked us whether security could bring us anything from our home. I requested my algel vat, and May asked for her pajamas, toiletries, and a change of clothes for the morning.

I found it difficult to gauge Jas's mood, which seemed to alternate between annoyance and sympathy. He bid us goodnight and told me to contact him if I needed anything.

As soon as Jas left, May turned to me "Could we please watch the interviews that we did today?" I told May that, while I was curious, I was concerned that watching the vid could trigger a great deal of emotional distress in her. "I know you must have told the reporter how scary everything is, and I know that I might get really upset when I watch it, but I need to know what is happening," May replied. "I know that there are bad people out there, and we could be in danger. That's why we have to stay here tonight. I'm not a little kid anymore, but I know I'm going to be a lot more scared if I don't know what's going on."

May's logic was inescapable. I switched the entertainment unit on and performed a search for our interviews. As the vid clip started, May put a pillow on the floor and sat next to me while I locked my joints in a squatting stance.

As I watched, I thought that the network had done an exceptional job. After she returned to the studio, Liz had narrated and recorded an introduction, using some additional research that the network must have performed. That set the stage for the content involving May and me. My study of human behavior told me that the background music was subtle but well suited to the mood. The graphics were bold and attention-getting, and the editing was magnificent, with the close-ups of May's face being very effective during the most emotional parts of her responses.

"I can't believe I actually sound like that," May said.

"You sound wonderful," I assured her.

We stayed in front of the entertainment center and browsed the news networks until well past sunset. The headlines were dominated by coverage of Brenna's disappearance.

"Do you think people will do anything when they see the story?" May asked.

It didn't take long for us to find out. Out of the side of my eye dome I saw a telltale flickering of orange light. Fire! I leaped to the wall of windows, so I could see where the attack was coming from. What I saw was astonishing.

Out on the quad, hundreds of beings had assembled—humans and other species, students, staff, and faculty. Bonfires had been lit, and beings were gathered around them. Some in the crowd wore illuminated GarmentSign patches or held up panels. Some had even used old fashioned paper or cardboard. The signs bore slogans such as "There Are No Aliens—We Are All PEOPLE!", "Beings United for Peace," "Hate Has No Place On Terra," and "We love Kelvoo!" Several of the signs simply read, "Free Brenna!" A group gathered and started singing the song that May and I had sung with the outliers on the Yangtze cruise.

"Building bridges 'cross the sky. Building bridges, you and I. Now we are no longer parted; here we stand . . ." The group sang with gusto and excellent pitch control.

"That's the campus choir," May said. "They've performed at my school a couple of times."

We watched as the choir sang and the crowd swelled in size.

"We did the right thing, didn't we?" May asked.

"Jas might not agree," I replied, "but yes, I'd say we did the right thing."

About two hours later, it occurred to me that I should be monitoring the news for any developments regarding Brenna's situation. I tried searching for any vid or still images of Brenna, but all that came up was millions of instances of the image from Brenna's student registration, which Atlantic News had shown in their story, along with a smattering of images that a few of Brenna's friends had submitted to news outlets.

I picked up the entertainment center's controller and switched it to AI search mode. Then I spoke into the controller. "My name is Kelvoo. A human named Brenna Murphy was in my care and is missing. She is associated with the Taylor family and the Taylor Foundation. Scan all related content to date and then activate and sound an alert if new, relevant, verifiable content is available. Apply a higher relevance to new vid, image, or audio content."

I switched the display panels off and turned to May. "We should both try to get some rest now."

May asked me to get a pillow and bedsheets from the high shelves in the closet. "I don't want to bug the servitor bots," she explained.

May didn't press the button to convert the sofa to a bed. Instead, she took the bottom cushions from a sofa and laid them on the floor, so they were perpendicular to the window wall. She placed a sheet over the cushions and put the pillow at the base of the windows. May crawled under the sheet, not bothering to change into her pajamas. She laid on her back, staring at the ceiling.

"I'm going to have a hard time falling asleep," she said.

"I understand," I replied.

"I know I'm way too old for this, but maybe it would help if you could sing me a song."

"I'd be pleased to give it a try. Which song would you like?"

"You pick one."

"What kind of song would appeal to you?"

May took a moment to ponder her reply. "Tell you what, why don't you sing me the last song you've heard, except 'Building Bridges,' of course."

I began.

When disaster brings you trouble;
When your losses break your heart;
We will be there on the double,
to pitch in and do our part.

We'll restore your life and lift you.
We are here to help with pride.
Aiding folks like you is what we do,
Serving millions, far and wide.

Say goodbye to worry and your uncertainty.
The Terran Fiduciary Insurance Company.

"A commercial?" May exclaimed with a mixture of shock and laughter.

"You asked me to sing the most recent song, and I saw the commercial on a news network earlier."

"That's so silly!" May laughed. I was glad I could provide some levity for her, but my gladness was bittersweet. May's laughter reminded me of the time that Brenna asked me to simulate human laughter, which made Brenna laugh uncontrollably.

May settled herself. "Goodnight, Pa," she said. "I love you."

Since May had used a term of endearment, I reciprocated. "Goodnight, sweetie. I love you too."

I turned off the lights. A smaller group was still assembled outside, and the dying flames of the last bonfire lit the room with a warm glow. I assumed my meditative stance at the foot of May's makeshift bed. Then I closed the lid over my eye, except for a tiny slit at the bottom, so I could watch over May.

It occurred to me that I was truly fortunate—some might say blessed—to have this innocent yet wise person in my life as I watched her grow, adapt, and transform. I felt love both toward her and from her.

May rolled onto her stomach and propped her head up on her hands with her elbows on the floor, so she could watch our supporters outside. When the last of the crowd had left and the fire diminished to embers, May rolled onto her side and slept. I closed my eye completely and fell into a deep, restful meditative state.

It was fortunate that my meditation was restorative because it ended abruptly when the entertainment center sounded an alert at 05:04. I accessed the alert message: "A news item started at 05:00 and is currently underway. The news item appears to include content relevant to your AI search parameters."

117

I selected "Replay from start" from a list of options.

An announcer introduced the story as a breaking news update, with a statement from the Taylor Foundation.

May groaned and stirred. She sat up and rubbed her eyes when she understood what I was watching.

A Taylor Foundation spokesperson appeared at a podium and issued a statement. "While it is typically against the policy of the Taylor Foundation to respond to baseless attacks from questionable individuals, the statement made yesterday by the kloormar known as Kelvoo was so egregiously false, malicious, and scurrilous that we are compelled to issue a response.

"We call upon Kelvoo to issue an immediate retraction and public apology. Failure to do so will result in civil action for compensatory and punitive damages. We also call upon the protestors gathered outside all Taylor family residences and places of business to disperse immediately.

"We categorically deny any suggestion of brainwashing, kidnapping, or harm inflicted upon Brenna Murphy. Brenna is a great friend of the Taylor family, and she is with us of her own volition. To clear up this matter once and for all, Brenna Murphy will now make a statement."

To my intense relief, the camera pulled back to show Brenna standing at another podium about two meters from the spokesperson. She was well dressed, but she looked tired. As she made her statement, I could tell from her eye movements that she was reading prepared text from a holoprompter projection.

"My name is Brenna Murphy," she began. "I am under the care and protection of the Taylor family of my own choice and free will. With the full approval of the Taylor Foundation, I wish to confirm that the foundation has made contributions to the Human Independence Movement and is a supporter of their cause.

"I first learned of the movement from a Taylor family member several months ago. Before my arrival on Terra, I spent most of the past several years under the guardianship of an alien while living on an alien world. As such, I was, at first, resistant to the movement's goals and ideals. However, over time, and based on my personal experiences, I have come to appreciate everything that the Human Independence Movement stands for.

"Human and alien values are in conflict. This fact is undeniable and is perfectly illustrated by Kelvoo's reckless assumption that I was so weak-minded that I could be brainwashed and taken against my will. Alien thinking is inflexible and incompatible with our own. That's why, for the sake of all species and in the interest of peace, the human species *must* separate itself from alien influences.

"To Kelvoo, I say, leave me alone! I am happy to have been accepted by the Taylor family with great love and understanding. I do not wish to return to your home or your presence. I'm separating myself from you and your influence in keeping with the philosophy of the Human Independence Movement. In case you don't believe me, I will call you tomorrow at noon in the university's time zone, so I can tell you directly what I have to say.

"Finally, I wish to make the following statement directly to my little sister, May."

Brenna paused as if needing to compose herself and suppress her emotions. During her pause, May came over to me and clutched my arm. "I'm afraid of what Brenna is going to say."

"So am I, May."

"May, I love you," Brenna said. "I'm sorry I left so suddenly without saying a proper goodbye. Goodbye doesn't have to be forever. May, it isn't right that you're being raised by an alien, even if that alien is the 'almighty' Kelvoo! Kelvoo can't love you like a human can. Kelvoo can't teach you what it means to be human, and Kelvoo can't set a good example for you. The Taylors think you're wonderful and they would be so happy to welcome you into their family. I'm asking child services to turn you over to us. That way we can be together all the time! May, I love you so much, and I'm looking forward to being with you again.

"I want to conclude by thanking the Taylor family for all of their support and for allowing me to make this statement."

When the announcement ended, the news host introduced guests to confer and analyze what was said. I switched the entertainment center off, so May, who was visibly distraught, and I could discuss what we had just seen.

May and I talked until Sol had risen over the mountains to the east. Then we put the sofa cushions back in place and folded the bed linens. May got dressed and prepared for school, though I wasn't sure how I was supposed to take her there given the requirement for a constant security presence. Fortunately, I wasn't scheduled to teach that day.

May and I moved to the reception area and waited. I was about to call Jas when he and Simon arrived, looking tired and disheveled.

"Have you been monitoring the news?" Jas asked as he stood in the doorway.

I confirmed that we had seen the latest developments, including the statements by the Taylor Foundation and Brenna.

Jas turned to his right, and spoke into the hallway. "You can come in now."

A male and a female human entered. Jas introduced them as Helen Mataroa and Juan Springer. "Helen is a social worker who would like to get to know May a little bit. Juan is a crisis counselor who assists our faculty members now and then."

Helen smiled at May. "Hi, May. Can we talk for a bit?"

"No, I have to go to school now."

"It's alright, May; I've spoken with your teacher," she said. "You don't need to go to school today. Why don't you come with me so we can have a chat?"

"No way!" May exclaimed with wide-eyed terror. "You're not taking me anywhere! I belong with Kelvoo, and you're not taking me anywhere else! I don't want to be with my sister!" She backed away toward the guest room.

"No one wants to take you away, hon," Helen said. "Tell you what, why don't we go into the next room while Kelvoo and Juan chat out here?"

May looked around the corner into the guest room to ensure there were no exits that she might not have noticed the previous night. "It's alright, May," I said. "There's nothing wrong with talking. Just be open and honest with Helen, and I'll be right here if you need me."

Still hesitant, May sat on the sofa in the guest room while Helen made herself comfortable in a large matching chair. Juan sat in another chair, and I took a kneeling position across a coffee table from him. Jas and Simon left to give us privacy.

Juan and I discussed recent events, with many of his questions along the lines of "How did that make you feel?" Helen and Juan were obviously unaware of my hearing and multi-tasking abilities since I was able to hear and process the discussion in the guest room while simultaneously conversing with Juan. I hadn't expected to benefit much from Juan's counseling due to our species' psychological differences, but he did help me to analyze my thoughts and the resulting emotional effects. I was also pleased with the conversation between May and Helen.

After two hours, our sessions ended. Helen messaged Jas, and two minutes later he joined the four of us in the conference room. Helen spoke first.

"First, I just want to reassure all of you that under Terran law, we have to investigate when anyone suggests that a child is at risk in their home." She turned to May. "While your sister didn't exactly say you were in danger, I just wanted to make sure you're doing alright in case people come along later and say that we didn't do anything. Anyway, as far as I'm concerned, it's all good."

Helen turned to me. "Kelvoo, May loves you very much, and she knows how much you care about her. Brenna's statement about you being unable to provide proper support is false. I've spoken with May's teacher who assures me that May's ability to socialize with her peers and adults is better than average. While guardianship of a human child by a non-human is rare, it is my opinion that the relationship provides May with a unique perspective and is beneficial to her both intellectually and emotionally."

At that point Juan jumped in, addressing Jas. "I would like to say that Kelvoo cares deeply about May and her well-being." Then he turned to address me. "In our discussion, I saw that you are confused by Brenna's seemingly sudden change in attitude. You're also questioning your judgment and the fact that you didn't see any early signs of trouble, and you're starting to grow angry with Brenna. I want to be clear that this has nothing to do with any lack of understanding of humans on your part. The recent events would elicit exactly the same responses in most humans, even if they were Brenna's lifelong biological parents."

Helen smiled at May. "I want to be clear that no one is going to send you to the Taylor family or separate you from Kelvoo. For some reason the Taylor family has become associated with a bizarre movement." She turned to Jas and me. "Not exactly an environment conducive to raising a well-adjusted young person!"

May and I were relieved. She leaned over and hugged my upper arm while I held her shoulder.

"So," Jas said, "the only thing we have to deal with now is the call from Brenna in an hour and a half."

The five of us strategized about how to handle the call. We all agreed that we should record the call in case we had to combat any future misinformation about it. We also agreed that we would all be present, but everyone would be off-camera except for me. However, I would take the call in speaker mode, so all of us could hear. Helen and Juan could give me signals or written advice if they felt that they could help.

"What if she wants to talk to me?" May asked. "What should I say?"

"I think that would be OK if it's brief," Helen said. "Just be honest and say what you're feeling."

While we waited for the call, we talked about many things, including the potential rise of HIM and the ways in which Terra and our lives could be impacted.

Brenna's call came at 12:07. My Infotab was set on top of a desk with its camera pointing toward me. Jas, Helen, and Juan were sitting across from me. May was sitting at the end of the desk. Before I could say "hello," Brenna started in. "I don't have anything to tell you other than what I already said in my statement. I want to talk to May."

"Before that, can I verify that you are not being held against your will?" I replied.

"I already said I *chose* to be here. Now let me talk with May!"

"To show me that you are not under duress, I am going to ask you a question that your 'hosts' will not know the answer to. If you need help, just answer incorrectly. Your captors will not know that you're lying, and we will try to take you out of the situation with as little danger to you as possible. If you answer correctly, I will not bother you again. Just know that I love you regardless of what happens."

"Let me talk to May!" Brenna said, her agitation growing.

"When we were on *Jezebel's Fury* and you were learning to read, you were very proud to read the story of Henry the Barnyard "blank." What word should replace 'blank'?"

I was crestfallen when Brenna answered correctly. "Horse, OK? It was a horse! Now, I demand to speak with my sister!"

In an instant, my fear for Brenna transformed into anger. "Do you really think you're in any position to make demands? Who do you think you are?"

As I spoke, Jas looked concerned, but Helen and Juan were having silent conniptions. Both shook their heads vigorously. Helen waved her hands in front of her, and Juan made a slashing motion across his throat. I was undeterred.

"When you were living in *my* home, I gave you freedom to come and go as you pleased, then when I politely asked you to come over to discuss something, you delayed our meeting until the next day. Then you sauntered in, twenty minutes late, rejected the meal I had carefully selected, then when I tried to express my concerns in a calm, adult way, you kept dismissing me, and then you had a childish fit!"

By then Helen and Juan were on their feet, gesticulating wildly. Juan leaned toward me. "End the call!" he hissed. "Please end the call now!" Helen's head was clamped between her palms as she shook it. From the side of my eye dome, I saw May, her jaw clenched, as she glared at Brenna's image. As for Brenna, her anger had grown into full-blown rage, tears welling up in her eyes.

"How did you end up with such a vile, hateful bunch of humans?" I asked. "Did they buy you off with clothes and jewelry, or are you just following your hormones?"

Brenna's face was a portrait of fury as tears streamed down her cheeks. "Shut up! Shut up!" she screamed. "Shut up and let me talk to my sister!"

May decided to take matters into her own hands. She stepped into view of the Infotab's camera, clutched my upper arm, and pulled herself close to me. Seeing May, Brenna reached her hand out toward the camera. "I love you May!"

May looked directly at Brenna's image. "Go to hell, bitch!"

May released my arm and stomped toward the guest suite, breaking into sobs. Helen ran after her, hugged her, then gently guided her back to the desk across from me. Brenna lost her composure and ran out of view of the camera.

Jas, May, Helen, Juan, and I looked at one another in stunned silence. Before I had a chance to end the call, a human male in his mid-twenties walked into the frame and sat in front of the Infotab on Brenna's end. He smiled.

"Well, that went smoothly!" he said in a whiny voice dripping with smug sarcasm. "Well, well, well," he continued, "so you're the great Kelvoo! You know, Bren said you wanted to meet me. Well, here I am, alien scum! Take a good look at me now because you won't be seeing me or Bren ever again, unless it's when we cheer to see you and all the other alien vermin herded onto a barge and taken—"

At that moment I took Juan's advice and terminated the call.

"I assume that was Griffin Taylor," I said to Jas, who nodded his confirmation.

Suddenly, I realized that my respiration rate was at its maximum, my vision was darkened, and my extremities were tingling with furious anxiety.

"OK, let's all take a deep breath and release our tension as we exhale," Helen advised. We all took a few moments to compose ourselves. Then I turned toward May. "I'm really surprised by how angry you are toward your sister. Having grown up with her, I was concerned that you would feel some degree of sympathy for Brenna. Do you, perhaps, feel some empathy for her point of view?"

"No," May replied without hesitation. "You took us in, you took care of us, and you protected us. It was supposed to be our job to protect you! Brenna turned against you, so now it's *my* job to protect you."

The thought of this young human feeling the impossible responsibility of protecting me was overwhelming. My reaction was validated when I saw Juan and Helen blinking back tears.

I turned back toward the counselors. "I gather that my reaction to Brenna was less than optimal," I said. "In fact, I have seen vids that depict the stereotypical reaction of an angry human parent, and I'm surprised by the similarity of my reaction."

Juan shrugged. "What's done is done."

"Well, I apologize if my outburst made matters worse," I said.

May came over and gripped my arm again. "Pa, I'm sorry I used a bad word when I yelled at Brenna. I know you don't like it when I say rude things."

"It's alright, May. Just don't make it a habit, or you might end up giving people the wrong impression, but in situations where you're really angry, I'm not going to judge you for saying a bad word."

"I'm glad to hear that, Pa, because I just want to say that Griffin Taylor is a total dick!"

SIXTEEN: THE MULTIPLYING DIVISIONS

The evening after Brenna's call, May and I were able to move back into our home. The added security was unobtrusive, with the only noticeable changes being additional sensors along the roofline and at the edges of the lot. May resumed her attendance at school, and I continued teaching, though both of us had to be accompanied by a security detail wherever we went.

Jas was correct in one of his earlier predictions and wrong in another. He was right that my broadcast announcement would draw attention to HIM. Jas had also predicted that ten million humans might join HIM. His estimate was far from accurate. Within six months, over two hundred million people held a membership in the movement! Public polls showed that 2.8 billion Terran humans had a somewhat favorable or higher opinion of HIM. While this was a long way from a majority of the fifteen billion plus humans on Terra, HIM was by far the largest and fastest growing movement for societal change in Terran history. The movement was awash in donations and had over a quadrillion SimCash units in its coffers.

Branch offices of HIM started appearing. Rather than forming as virtual communities like other non-profits, HIM acquired or built physical offices and hired staff. Their members were encouraged to attend in-person meetings at their local chapter where HIM "coaches" would make fiery speeches to whip up support and intensify fear of the alien "invaders." New talking points would be introduced at meetings, which the devotees would use to try to drum up support in the general populace.

A year after they became widely known, HIM "devotion centers" or "DCs" appeared in strategic locations around Terra. To create a devotion center, HIM would purchase land that was at least two hectares in size and would build a compound with strong outer walls that surrounded enormous courtyards. The DCs functioned as a modern equivalent of ancient Terran monasteries or convents. In those times, humans who wished to devote their lives to the worship of their deities lived in isolated places where their lives revolved around constant self-reinforcing indoctrination in the dogma of their beliefs. So it was with devotion centers.

Members of HIM could pay exorbitant amounts to attend courses in devotion centers. If they had little wealth or they wanted to turn control of their lives over to HIM, members could live, work, and be instructed in a DC. To enter a devotion center in any capacity, HIM members had to prove their worth, usually by recruiting a significant number of new members. Next, they had to undergo a battery of psychological "truth" tests and brain scans to verify that their devotion was absolute. These conditions allowed the teachings inside the DCs to remain a closely guarded secret.

The media breathlessly covered HIM's growth. The more trusted, established media outlets, such as Atlantic News, Vega Network, and Terra Broadcasting, paid close attention to HIM and the threat that it posed to an orderly multi-species society.

The fringe networks, such as Veritacity, saw an opportunity in HIM. They had never garnered an audience beyond a small slice of the general population, so they decided to aim for a large segment of a smaller demographic. Early in the rise of HIM, they granted interviews to movement organizers and devotees in the interest of providing "balanced reporting" to counter the "one-sided view" of the major media outlets.

The Veritacity Network had its star journalist, Kaley Hart. Her secretly recorded "interview" with me over fifteen years before had revealed the existence of my species and the location of my planet long before the kloormari were prepared to adapt to a multi-species existence. The aftermath was disastrous for my species and led to the highly disruptive Correction on Terra. During the Correction, Kaley had been loathed for her role in betraying my trust and triggering the Correction, but with the rise of HIM, Veritacity leveraged her infamy by portraying her as an innocent journalist who was just doing her job while they painted the non-Terran species and the Planetary Alliance as ambitious, controlling, and vindictive. Veritacity convinced HIM to endorse their network, leading to a huge surge in their audience. With their new revenue, Veritacity started buying up other populist media outlets and hundreds of small news providers.

Eighteen months after the start of the HIM phenomenon, Veritacity claimed it had the largest audience among all Terran news networks. However, that fact, like most of the information emanating from Veritacity, was misleading since the *combined* audience for all of the major networks was far higher. Such details didn't matter to Veritacity, which constantly reminded their viewers of their position as the "number one news network" or "Terra's most trusted news source."

For an hour or two every evening, and for four hours or so on our days off, May and I watched the news from a variety of sources. The stories about HIM and related social upheaval were fascinating but also deeply troubling. Like an addict, I felt compelled to follow events closely.

I avoided watching Veritacity except for the times when my AI search found an announcement by, or about, Brenna. Brenna never agreed to be interviewed. Her announcements were pre-recorded and rare, which made them highly sought after. Veritacity had exclusive rights to broadcast Brenna's statements and would announce them in advance with great fanfare. Brenna's missives were, to my mind, lackluster and bland, as she simply regurgitated the latest talking points that Veritacity had been using to bombard its followers. She always ended with a statement assuring the audience that she knew what she was talking about due to her terrible past oppression as the victim of an alien upbringing.

Several times, Jas and I talked about whether I should go on the air to combat the misinformation, lies, and hatred. Immediately after the disastrous call from Brenna, the university assigned a media liaison to me. Every month, and whenever suggested, my handler, Victoria Janes, met with Jas and me. She was constantly bombarded with network requests to interview me or to obtain my statement regarding one matter or another. The three of us and the university's board all agreed that the benefits of any media presence from me would not outweigh the potential backlash. As a result, I stayed "above the fray," as Jas put it, and concentrated on my classes, though my students' questions always drifted toward HIM and the growing tensions in society. Much to my students' frustration, I constantly had to explain that I could not comment at the risk of inflaming the situation.

For many months, universities were relatively unaffected by the movement. It was as if the places of advanced education were islands of peace in an angry, tumultuous world. HIM and its followers dismissed institutes of higher learning as elitist and out of touch with humanity.

As HIM ascended, I attended my weekly meetings with the Sagacity Club. Dr. Rosa Schlenk continued to raise the similarities between the rise of HIM and other populist movements in Terran history, some of which became violent.

Dr. Lembe Stark, political scientist, continued playing devil's advocate, frequently raising some of the arguments and justifications being put forward by HIM. I understood that his intent was to encourage us to understand HIM, so we could better argue against the group, but as time passed, he became more vociferous in his arguments, and I started to wonder whether his anti-HIM sentiments were starting to waver.

Dr. Sayed, our philosopher, continued to argue that Terran society had changed, and humanity had evolved so much in recent centuries that HIM would never win over a majority of Terran humans. At many of our meetings, she would predict that the membership of HIM was at its peak and was on the brink of waning. Each week, however, she was proven wrong, but she remained undaunted in her assertions.

The club's psychologist, Dr. Hoffman, didn't have much to add to the topic of the Human Independence Movement. He typically stayed quiet and often looked bored while we discussed HIM, though he had much to say and contribute on most other topics of discussion.

As for Jas, he tended to take on the role of moderator. His position and thoughts on HIM remained steadfast and constant.

Overall, our group struggled to come up with reasonable explanations for the rise of HIM and the degree to which it had grown. The traditional news media was constantly seeking answers to the same questions. Their investigations targeted underground groups of gamers who enjoyed simulations of violence and conspiracy theorists who fantasized about overthrowing governments, but their numbers were insignificant. The general consensus was that a great number of humans had been keeping their discontent to themselves, or were simply attracted to the notion that society was rotten, and outsiders were to blame.

**

Twenty months after the Human Independence Movement exploded into the human consciousness, a semester had just ended. That was also when HIM opened a new on-campus location, a move that I felt violated the sanctity of the university.

When I heard the news from a student, I alerted Jas.

"I know," he said, "They've been trying to open a chapter here for several weeks."

"Shouldn't they be stopped?"

"I've tried, Kelvoo. We are, after all, the *Interplanetary* University, founded on the principle of multi-species inclusion. The board fought tooth and nail to prevent those idiots from establishing a beachhead here. In the end, however, we were hoisted on our own petard. Our own Bill of Student Rights permits students to organize into clubs or societies or movements provided that they are sponsored by a faculty member and that at least one hundred students petition the board. It took them a long time to convince a hundred students to do so, but they've done it, and it makes me sick to my stomach."

"But, Jas, what kind of faculty member would sponsor something so awful?"

"Someone you and the girls know well—Coach Luna Chang."

I was incredulous. Coach Chang's instructional methodology had been harsh but effective. I had viewed her blunt, abrasive style as a "tough love" approach. She reminded me of Bertie from the first-contact mission and how Bertie's rough exterior was a façade for inner kindness. However, I realized that Coach Chang's abrupt, rude exterior must have extended all the way to her very core. I wondered how she had managed to tolerate teaching me when her prejudices must have led her to despise my presence.

"Are you going to fire her?" I asked.

"I want to with every fiber of my being, but I'm not permitted to fire anyone based on their beliefs, no matter how repellent. Even worse, the university is obliged to provide HIM with a meeting space!"

The university granted HIM access to a long-neglected temporary structure that had once been used as an overflow classroom. HIM announced that they would launch their on-campus chapter with a march from their new "headquarters" to the main quad. A counter-demonstration was organized immediately. May and I attended, so we could witness the historic but sad event as it unfolded. Jas advised me not to go. I thanked him for his concern, and we went anyway, with two security guards accompanying us.

We joined a growing crowd outside of HIM's building and waited for the occupants to emerge. Only fifty-two of the one hundred petitioners filed out at the appointed hour, leading me to believe that some of the students had been coerced into signing. Coach Chang led the procession as they shouted slogans such as "Terra for Terrans" and "Aliens go home!"

As the small mob made its way along the path toward the center of the campus, we counter-protesters, at least two thousand strong, flanked them and drowned them out with slogans and signs of our own. I recognized some of the signs from the show of support back when Brenna ran off. There was even a "Free Brenna!" sign.

Taunts were hurled back and forth between the two sides. The overall din was intense enough that even I couldn't distinguish the words. A counter-protester stepped toward a movement member while shouting. The HIM member responded by stepping up to the counter-protester to scream in her face. In doing so, the member's sign accidentally clipped the head of the counter-protester. Shoving ensued, followed by a few flailing punches with both students falling over. Security personnel, including the two assigned to May and me, moved closer to us.

At one point, May and I ended up close to the front of the march. To avoid becoming separated, we held hands. I could feel May trembling as Coach Chang spotted us. I don't know whether she would have been able to distinguish me from any other kloormar, but May's presence was a giveaway. Coach Chang stormed toward us. "Why don't you go to the beach, have a swim, and drown yourself, kloomer scum?" she shouted. I ignored her, and we kept walking parallel to the group. So, Coach Chang decided to take a different approach. "Why the hell do they let you take care of a human kid, you alien piece of—"

"Because Kelvoo's my pa!" May said. "Because Kelvoo loves me, you ugly pig!"

As Coach Chang lunged toward us, the situation started to get out of control. I scooped May up and ran toward the edge of the crowd. Chang's advance was interpreted as an attack against May and me, which the counter-protesters could not tolerate. As I retreated up a grassy slope, the back of my eye saw a violent melee with punches thrown, kicks landed, placards tossed, and angry shouts, screams, and insults being hurled. Security tried to step in, but they were hopelessly outnumbered.

The battle lasted less than five minutes with about an equal number of HIM members and counter-protesters lying, crouching, or sitting as they nursed their injuries. Ambulances arrived, and medical attendants sorted through the injured, triaging those who were most hurt. May and I managed to slip away and walk back to our house unguarded.

Two hours later, May and I searched the news outlets for coverage. Vid clips of the battle had been submitted from student Infotabs and mini-drone cams. The major outlets described the skirmish as a disagreement between the main student body and a small group belonging to the university's new HIM chapter. The Veritacity Network and outlets of a similar ilk had a different approach, with headlines such as "Peaceful HIM Marchers Attacked by Intellectual Elites" or "Enraged Mob Assaults Innocent HIM Group" or "Violent Anti-Movement Attack: Backed and Funded by Interplanetary University?"

***

As the weeks passed, small skirmishes or shouting matches became more frequent on campus, along with acts of vandalism and occasional violence resulting in injury. Anti-HIM groups formed, and their memberships grew, but so did the number of HIM followers. Any time evidence was presented showing violence being initiated by a movement member, HIM would issue a statement such as the following: "The Human Independence Movement strongly condemns all acts of violence and property damage by groups and individuals on both the pro-human and anti-human side. We denounce, in the strongest possible terms, any such acts perpetrated by individuals claiming to be our members. At the same time, we acknowledge the frustration experienced by humans who are alarmed by the growing influence of the aliens and their deliberate, methodical dismantling of human culture and values. We call upon the government of Terra to restore peace by implementing our plan for the immediate removal of all alien species."

I wanted to counter the bizarre notion that supporters of a multi-species society were "anti-human." As strong as my wishes were, I didn't get involved. I couldn't think of any action that I could take—as an "alien"—that wouldn't exacerbate the conflict.

And so, the conflicts intensified, the misinformation grew into greater lies, the conspiracy theories became more outrageous, and the societal divisions changed from cracks to fissures to chasms. As Dr. Schlenk kept pointing out, similar scenarios had played out time after time in past centuries, and I felt there was nothing I could do to help.

Then, when all seemed hopeless, Terran election season started, and things *really* started going downhill.

SEVENTEEN: SHE'S NUTS

On the opening day of election season, Terra's two long-standing political parties, the Integrity Party and Unity Party, submitted a full slate of 500 candidates each. To the dread of most Terran humans, and all non-humans on Terra, the Human Independence Movement announced that it had formed its own political party. It was clear that HIM had been preparing to enter politics for a long time since it was ready to go with a slate of 500 candidates. Each candidate had far more than the million registered supporters required to qualify. HIM's new "Humanity Party" (HP), simultaneously announced its leader, Gloria Truscott.

Prior to the announcement, I had never heard of Ms. Truscott. Terran records indicated she was sixty-eight years old, though she claimed to be forty-five and as healthy as when she was twenty-five. She had been an actor with limited success. She had managed to launch a few startup business ventures with backing from investors, only to close shop in each case when the funds were depleted. Truscott had been involved with HIM from its early days, well before my announcement on Atlantic News turned them into a household name. It was rumored that she had been traveling from one HIM devotion center to another to spread the word and whip devotees into a frenzy of adoration and rage.

Every network covered Truscott's leadership announcement. May and I watched the live broadcast, which I can only describe as a surreal experience.

The opening scene was an empty stage with "Humanity Party" in large red holographically projected letters, five meters high, hovering above the back of the stage. In the foreground was an audience of thousands of humans, silhouetted against the stage lights. The crowd managed to maintain absolute silence.

A hoverlift, which was also silhouetted, descended from the rafters, bearing a human figure. A spotlight snapped on, illuminating Gloria Truscott as she continued her descent and igniting a joyous roar and wild applause from the audience. She wore an ornate robe in the same shade of red as the projected letters. Diagonal white text, "Terra for Terrans!", was emblazoned across each side of the garment in an angry font that looked as though it had been slashed into the robe.

"Terra for Terrans" was also projected in white above the platform. The letters pulsed as the audience shouted the slogan in unison with the pulses.

"I don't understand the slogan," I said. "Don't they mean, 'Terra for humans?' Isn't every citizen of Terra a Terran?"

"Not to those idiots!" May replied.

The broadcast vid feed switched to a closer look at Truscott. Her hands were on her hips, her fingers pointing inward and down, and each fingertip was adorned with a long scarlet nail. Each finger bore hefty jewel-encrusted gold rings. Thick gold chains, ending in massive medallions hung from her wrinkled neck, its loose skin partly folding over the gilded links. From halfway up her neck to just below her hairline, her skin had been lightened to an off-white tone with a layer of thick powder, moist clumps of it gathering in the wrinkles on and below her cheeks. Her eyelids were painted a cyanotic shade of bright blue, and her eyebrows had been covered in black paint, three times wider than an average human's eyebrows and reminiscent of landing gear skid marks on the university's airstrip. Finally, her natural hair was obscured by a massive crimson wig, its twisting fibers reaching high and reminding me of the occasional "dust devil" whirlwinds I had seen across the mineral plain on Kuw'baal.

As the hoverlift completed its descent, I turned to May. "I can't judge these things accurately, so I'm wondering, would you say that Gloria Truscott's appearance is attractive to humans?"

"That depends on whether you think a clown looks attractive or if a nightmare is your idea of a good time!"

"So, why do you suppose she would choose to look like that?"

"I don't have the slightest idea," May replied. "She's the grossest old hag I've ever seen!"

We continued staring with rapt attention as the hoverlift touched down, and the Humanity Party's new leader alighted. Truscott spread her arms wide, the loose sleeves of her robe hanging level with her waist. She looked up above the audience as if basking in their praise as the hoverlift beat a hasty retreat back into the rafters.

Slowly, she lowered her arms and then her head to gaze out at her worshippers. The instant she opened her mouth to speak, the audience silenced itself, as if a switch had been snapped off.

"My fellow humans," she began, omitting any reference to other beings, "why are there aliens here on Terra, living among us? Why would they ever want to be here when their own planets were created to suit their species?"

I had to pause the vid feed and ask May rhetorical questions of my own. "What is she talking about? Why are 'aliens' on Terra? There are thousands of possible reasons! Why wouldn't non-humans be here? What does she mean when she says that planets were *created* for their species? Is she talking about species being adapted to their planets' environment through evolution?"

"She's nuts," was May's astute reply.

I resumed the vid feed. "I'll tell you exactly why they're here! It's about power! They were all sent here by the Planetary Alliance! Why did our wonderful species ever join that corrupt group?"

I paused the feed. "Because humanity has benefited from the Alliance in terms of trade, culture, and education. And what does she mean about the Alliance *sending* non-humans to Terra? They certainly didn't *send* me! I was invited!"

"Don't worry about it, Pa. She's nuts!"

I resumed the vid. "For centuries we've been groveling before the Alliance. All along we've been saying, 'Oh please, great Alliance, forgive us for being humans. Oh, we're not worthy. Oh, please be nice to us.' For what? All we've ever done is give, give, give while they just take from us! They take our resources, they take our technology, they take our culture, and they take our jobs!"

I paused the vid yet again. "What is she talking about? Terra trades its resources for other resources not found here! Almost all new technology on Terra came from other Alliance planets! In what ways has human culture been diminished? Is she going to give an example? And jobs? What about the hundreds of millions of jobs that resulted from Alliance trade and technology? How does this make any sense?"

"It doesn't, Pa. She's nuts!"

The vid continued. "Today is the most important day in the history of humanity! Why? Because today is the beginning of the end of our oppression! Today I am turning the tide! Under *my* leadership, humans shall be victims no more!

"Humans of Terra, I feel your anger, and I know your outrage! We're going to fight back, and we're going to fight hard! With my leadership, we will take back Terra!" she bellowed, raising a skinny, gold-and-jewel-crusted fist into the air as the crowd screamed.

"Take back Terra! Take back Terra!" they cried over and over.

"I am the only human with the guts, the brains, and the will to stand up to the alien tyranny, and I am the only human who will rescue us!" she roared. "Today begins our march toward victory! As your next prime minister, I will save the human species and cleanse this once-beautiful world of the alien filth!"

The audience roared their frenzied approval as she stepped off the stage and waded into the adoring throng.

Utterly stunned, I turned to May. "What did we just witness?"

"A crazy person," May replied, summing up the tableau with an elegant economy of words.

After several seconds of stunned silence, my Infotab alerted me to an incoming call from Jas.

"Hello, Jas."

"Hi, Kelvoo. Um . . . did you see what Simon and I just saw?"

Under normal circumstances, I would have asked Jas for clarification, but not this time. "Yes, Jas. May and I just witnessed the bizarre spectacle."

"Well, I'm really encouraged by what I just saw!" he said. I was shocked by Jas's reaction until he continued. "After *that* performance, I'm convinced the Humanity Party has just destroyed any chance it had to gain any presence in parliament! I think their political ambitions have ended before they could even start! Anyway, I just wanted to know whether you saw it."

I ended the call, then turned May. "Well, Chancellor Linford thinks the Humanity Party doesn't stand a chance now!"

"I think he's wrong," May replied.

"Why is that? You said yourself that Truscott is crazy."

"Pa, there are plenty of crazy people on Terra these days!"

"Are you sure, May? Do *you* know anyone who is crazy?"

"Coach Chang."

"Oh, yes, well that may be. I suppose you also think your sister is crazy."

"She used to be normal, but she's totally mental now," she said despondently.

"You know, May, I don't feel it's appropriate for us to use the term, 'mental.'"

"You're right, Pa. It's rude to mentally ill people if we compare them to the HIM people!"

EIGHTEEN: THE WARNING

The media had a field day with Truscott. Cartoonists created exotic caricatures that exaggerated her already exaggerated appearance. One such illustration showed her long fingernails replaced by knife blades. The upper half of her skull was open but still attached by a hinge with a red tornado emerging from it and a miniature brain bouncing around atop the whirlwind. The artist drew Truscott's blue eye shadow from her cheekbones up to the skull opening, with her painted-on eyebrows surpassing the boundaries of her face, looking like thick black antennae.

Opinion columnists pointed out the absurdities, misinformation, and outright lies in Truscott's speech. The traditional media seemed uncertain of how to handle their news coverage of Truscott or the Humanity Party. They reported the facts of the announcement, but their professional standards prevented the use of subjective terms such as "bizarre" or "lies."

Even the Veritacity Network appeared unsure how to treat Truscott's announcement. They hesitantly called her speech "interesting" and "attention-getting," but as their discussion panels analyzed it, they suggested that Truscott's style must have been part of a deeper, brilliant political strategy that evaded definition. In one of their panel discussions, Kaley Hart remarked, "Well, she certainly raised many of the legitimate concerns of our viewers!"

The morning after the media's analyses, May and I were watching the early coverage when Truscott went on the attack. "Did you see how the media ridiculed me?" Truscott lamented, "How they made vicious jokes about my appearance? I can't help being attractive!" she blustered. "Every decent human knows deep down that the media can't be trusted. Did you see how they all reported the same stories? They're in cahoots, I tell you! They're just a bunch of lapdogs to the Planetary Alliance! We can't show weakness! We have to fight the lying media hard!" Seeming to remember the "friendly" media, she tempered her remarks somewhat. "Of course, I'm not referring to the *honest* media. If you want the truth, you'll find it on networks like Veritacity. They have newscasters and reporters who have the guts to stand up to the alien tyranny and present the *true* facts!"

I switched the vid feed off when the security escort came to pick May up for school. I rode along and then continued to Jas's office for a scheduled meeting.

Jas was in an upbeat mood, "Did you see glorious Gloria in all her glory this morning?" He laughed. "Attacking the media? How stupid is that? Talk about shooting the messenger when they're just reporting the things she said!"

After Jas's laughter died down, he got down to business. "Anyway, Kelvoo, I don't think we need to worry about the Human Independence Movement or its ridiculous political wing any longer."

"Why is that?"

"Are you joshing me, Kelvoo?"

"Jas, have you ever heard of a kloormar 'joshing' anyone?"

"Fair enough, but people would have to be crazy to believe anything Truscott says!"

"Well, May thinks there are a great many crazy people on Terra these days."

"That May is a good kid," Jas remarked.

"And a bit of a social realist," I added, making Jas chuckle.

The Sagacity Club met the following evening, and I was eager to learn the members' opinions. Of course, I could have called or messaged them earlier, but there are differences in how humans present themselves in person, and I usually found it more informative to communicate directly.

I didn't have to suggest the topic of the Humanity Party or its leader. The moment the meeting began, the club members dived into the topic.

"Did you see that . . . that creature from the so-called Humanity Party?" Dr. Sayed asked.

"Who hasn't?" Dr. Schlenk replied. "Her grand entrance, descending from the ceiling, costumed like the unholy offspring of a demon and a clown? Ridiculous!"

"Kelvoo and I have been discussing the subject, and I must conclude that it's the beginning of the end for the Humanity Party," Jas remarked.

"Well, esteemed comrades, let us examine things from the HP's perspective," Dr. Stark said, ever the devil's advocate. "They're attempting to shock humans into taking their concerns seriously, and Gloria Truscott is shocking, to say the least! HIM believes that our fine colleague, Kelvoo, and others of the non-human ilk are a direct threat to all homo sapiens. Now they have our attention and, I daresay, the attention of all humanity. Perhaps, my friends, their next step will be to explain precisely *how* this scheming fiend," he said, motioning toward me, "is going to subvert us. I look forward to their irrefutable evidence!" he added with a wink.

"But it's clear that they're batty, bonkers, and barmy!" Dr. Sayed exclaimed.

"Really, Sayed? I would have said 'daft, deranged, and demented'!" Schlenk replied.

"Unglued, unhinged, and unzipped!" Jas added. The group laughed, with the exception of me, due to physical limitations, as well as Hoffman, who managed only a wan smile.

"What say you, Hoffman?" I asked, partly out of concern that he was being left out. "As our resident psychologist, which scathing adjectives would you use to describe the mental state of the HIM and HP disciples?"

"I'm uncomfortable with all of the adjectives that you lot have been throwing around. Mental health is something that must be taken seriously, and I'm not going to diagnose anyone without working closely with them."

I was concerned that Hoffman was genuinely offended since he dropped the haughty manner of speaking that we typically employed in our meetings.

"Oh, come now Hoffman," Schlenk said, "you know we're all friends here! I'm sure we weren't attempting to impugn your professionalism with our levity."

In an attempt to avoid awkwardness, I turned to Dr. Schlenk. "Well, Dr. Schlenk, I'm relieved that you find the HP and its leader to be ridiculous. Might we conclude that the movement no longer has a viable shot at gaining power?"

"You *might* conclude that if you wish, but I still fear you might be wrong."

"The good lady stretches our credulity!" Jas exclaimed.

"Surely, it is a stretch to surmise that any person of sense would follow the movement now," Sayed added.

"Then I would suggest that my dear colleagues perform some research into authoritarians in our ancient past," Schlenk said, "You will certainly find despots who were charming, attractive, and well-spoken, but you will find just as many who were strange in appearance and demeanor, lacking in knowledge to the point of anti-intellectualism and outright bananas—if you'll excuse my inexpert adjective, Dr. Hoffman!"

Schlenk's ribbing of Hoffman seemed to irritate him. "Look, Schlenk," he began, "I'm just saying that it's not appropriate to—"

We were startled by a bang, followed by rumbling and shaking.

"I say dear, colleagues, whatever was that?" Stark exclaimed, surprising us all by staying in character.

My security escort, who was stationed in the hallway outside, knocked on the door. "Is everything OK in there?" he asked.

I went to the door and opened it. "Yes, my good man, we are all well," I replied, also remaining in character, "but whatever is going on?"

"Not a clue!"

"Then let us investigate!" Jas declared. Our group, led by the guard, hurried out of the room and the building.

When we stepped into the fresh night air, we saw an orange glow illuminating a cloud of dust and smoke and we heard a distant crowd. The source of the glow and the sound was obscured by several buildings. While it might have been faster to find a vehicle and drive to the scene, our curiosity got the better of us, and we made our way on foot as fast as our slowest colleague would allow.

As we approached, we heard an amplified announcement coming from above the humanities hall. As we turned a corner, we saw that a fifty-meter-wide section of the hall had been reduced to a smoking pile of rubble. I could tell that the epicenter of the blast was the location of the lecture hall where my classes were held. Two students were on the grass, dazed and bleeding from lacerations caused by flying debris. Three students were attending to them while a fourth was on a call with emergency services. In the sky above, a loudspeaker drone hovered, and its repeating message started again.

"This is a warning from the Human Preservation Action Front. We will not tolerate Kelvoo's presence in this place of learning. We demand that all courses involving Kelvoo cease immediately. We have destroyed Kelvoo's place of teaching. We could have done so during a lesson, but out of concern for human life, we destroyed the site of Kelvoo's propaganda while the building was empty. Next time no such courtesy will be extended. You have been warned."

"Oh, bloody hell!" Dr. Sayed muttered.

Several students picked up fragments of plasticrete debris and threw them at the drone, which was out of range. Another student ran out of an engineering building carrying a drone with an attached gas cylinder and a long tube. She threw her drone into the air and guided it up to the offensive aircraft. Then she tapped her Infotab. A whooshing, crackling sound emerged from her drone as a ten-meter plume of flame lit up the night sky and engulfed the target. The loudspeaker drone trailed black smoke as it tumbled to the ground. It kept spewing its message until it impacted the rubble below. A loud cheer and hearty applause rose from the gathered students and staff, followed by defiant fists raised into the air.

The engineering student moved close to Jas as she guided her flying flamethrower to land at her feet. "Hope I'm not going to get in trouble for my unauthorized flight," she said.

"On the contrary, I think you've just earned a scholarship!" Jas said. It seemed like he was joking, but his facial expression remained incredulous. "Besides, what unauthorized flight are you talking about? *I* didn't see anything!"

We had to remain at the scene for a considerable time while the injured students were taken for treatment, and the area was secured. Forensic investigators arrived from outside the campus to interview witnesses and gather evidence. Rescue crews followed detector bots into the ruins to search for possible victims. The investigators were especially interested in speaking with me. They initially assumed that I had been on the scene at the time of the explosion and that I had been targeted. After a while my colleagues were allowed to wander off. Jas had called May to advise her that I would be home late. He stayed with me until the investigators finished their interrogation. After that, Jas and I made our way toward his office, this time accompanied by three security escorts.

Jas sat at his desk. "Do you think we should take Dr. Schlenk seriously, or are you still optimistic about the Humanity Party and HIM failing?" I asked.

"Actually, Kelvoo, while I'm shaken to my core about the bombing, I'm more optimistic than ever. What we just saw was an act of desperation. There is no way that HIM and HP are going to avoid being associated with the bombing. They're bound to lose almost all their support now!"

Jas answered a call on his Infotab. His expression became grim and weary. After the call, he turned to me. "Oh my God, Kelvoo. They just found three bodies in the rubble. One was a Sarayan researcher, and the other two were human maintenance workers. Murdering bastards!"

We stood in silence for a minute before moving to the guest suite where Jas switched the entertainment center on and searched for "Interplanetary University Bombing." A torrent of breaking news stories flowed from the networks, including news of the three victims. None of the news commentators or guests had ever heard of the Human Preservation Action Front.

I received a call from May. "Are you OK, Pa?" she asked in a worried tone.

"Yes, May, I'm fine. Why are you still awake?"

"I heard a bang, and I saw smoke through my bedroom window. I looked at the news on my Infotab, and a little while later I saw that there was an explosion. A couple of minutes ago, I saw a vid, and I noticed you in a crowd beside the place where the explosion happened. Are you sure you're OK?"

I assured May again that I was unhurt and would be home later.

The breaking news that Jas and I had been watching was interrupted by more breaking news in the form of a statement from Truscott. She was no longer wearing her red robe, but her exotic hair and makeup was unchanged. "My fellow humans, it is with profound and sincere sadness that I learned of the horrific bomb attack on the Mediterranean campus of the Interplanetary University earlier this evening. On behalf of the Humanity Party, I extend my thoughts and sympathies to the family and friends of the two humans who were killed," she said, ignoring the murdered Sarayan.

"The Humanity Party seeks to achieve its goals through peaceful, law-abiding means. Despite this our enemies, including the major networks, are suggesting our involvement in this heinous crime." In fact, no such suggestions had been made. "We have no knowledge of the Human Preservation Action Front, but we *do* know that a great many people out there rightly feel oppressed and threatened by the growing alien menace. As such, we can expect more violent attacks as people, who are pushed past their breaking point, lash out against the invaders. Nevertheless, we categorically deny any involvement whatsoever in this terrible attack."

"I think she's lying," I said.

"I *know* she's lying," Jas replied.

We took a moment to reflect. "Since the new semester will be starting in three days, what are we going to do about my class?" I inquired. "Will it be moved to a different venue?"

"The board and I discussed the possibility of violence, Kelvoo. I'm sorry, but your in-person classes will be canceled. You can continue your course if you wish but only via remote connectivity. I'm sorry, Kelvoo, but we can't risk further loss of innocent life."

I knew that Jas had no other choice.

"Jas," I began, pausing to let him know that I was about to broach a difficult subject, "perhaps we should consider the option of my departure from Terra."

"What? No!"

"Why not?" I asked. "My presence here has just cost three lives and destroyed part of this campus. As the most infamous 'alien' on Terra— as the 'alien' whose writing brought about the Correction and now the resulting backlash—perhaps it would be safer and easier for me, for the university, and for all of Terra if I remove myself from the situation."

"But, Kelvoo, what about your teaching? What about all your work here educating our students and the public at large and, in the process, demonstrating your value and the value of all non-humans on Terra?"

"I wouldn't have to stop teaching, especially now that that board has decided to cancel my in-person classes. Since all of my classes will be remote, I can just as easily use the quantum entanglement network to teach from Kuw'baal."

"I don't know, Kelvoo," Jas said, looking down and shaking his head. "This is so sudden and unexpected. It just feels wrong. It feels like handing a victory to the Human Independence Movement."

"Well, Jas, given that the board has already acquiesced to the terrorist group's demands by canceling classes, is it that much worse if I just relocate back to my home planet?"

It took Jas a while to respond. He appeared to be distraught, and his expression suggested that he was struggling to find another angle to convince me to remain.

"What about May?" he asked. "You've told me how well she's been doing here. She likes her school, and she has friends here. Kuw'baal is a cloudy place without beaches or oceans or much in the way of facilities for humans. The kloormari are perfectly adapted to Kuw'baal, but, no offense to your home, Kuw'baal is less than ideal for young humans. Don't you want May to breathe the fresh Terran air, to swim in the sea, or to feel the warm rays of Sol on her face?"

"Yes, Jas, of course I do. This whole idea about leaving Terra is something I still have to think through. I hadn't given it any serious thought until the attack and the cancellation of my in-person classes. I would also have to discuss the entire idea and all of its ramifications with May, but here's what I'm wondering. If I decide to return to Kuw'baal, and May wishes to remain here, would you and Simon consider taking her into your care and raising her as if she were your own child?"

I was surprised by my reaction to my own words. My body felt as if it had been hollowed out, almost like I had suggested scooping out my own internal organs. Jas inhaled sharply as his eyes turned red and watery. He moved his mouth a couple of times as if to speak, unable to find the words.

"I . . . I don't know, Kelvoo. If anything were to happen to you, Simon and I would do anything for May, but I can't make you a promise that makes it easier for you to leave." Jas raised his head to look at me. A tear ran down his left cheek. "There's a lot to think about. I need time to process what you're saying. I think you need to talk with May, and both of you need to give the idea some serious thought."

"Thank you, my friend," I said, extending a hand toward Jas.

Jas grasped my hand with both of his. "Thank *you*, Kelvoo."

I stood and walked toward the door. "Kelvoo, wait!" Jas called after me. "Before you go, there is something the board wants me to discuss with you." Jas sounded almost frantic as he continued. "I'm sorry, but when you started talking about leaving Terra, I completely forgot about it. Kelvoo, the board and I talked about another role for you here at the university, if you're interested. As you know, we've been keeping you insulated from the media through your handler, Victoria Janes, and our media relations center. We thought that if the HIM situation got out of hand, there might come a time for you to represent the interests of yourself, your species, and, frankly, this institution.

"You present yourself well, and your logic is flawless. If you're interested, perhaps you might be willing to present your side—*our* side—to the public via media interviews and commentary. Is that something that might interest you?"

"I can't say right now, Jas. I'm honored that the university would make such an offer, but I must speak with May first."

NINETEEN: THE MAY MELTDOWN

When I finally returned to the house, May was asleep. Her bedside light was still on, and her Infotab was lying on top of the sheets. I turned her light off, put her Infotab on her nightstand, then stepped out.

The following day was a non-school and non-work day, so I let May sleep in. She came out of her room at 10:24 the next morning, and we had breakfast together.

May wanted to know about the explosion. I described the scene, the circumstances, and the subsequent investigation. I was concerned about making May anxious, but I recalled her words before we watched our interviews with Liz Underwood: "I'm not a little kid anymore, but I know that I'm going to be a lot more scared if I don't know what's going on." I also wanted May to understand what I was about to say, so I told her that the attack was motivated by opposition to my presence.

"May," I started, "we need to think about the possibility of me leaving Terra."

"But why would we leave, Pa?"

"For safety, May."

"Whose safety?"

"Yours and mine. I'm a main target of the people who hate non-humans, and with you being close by, you could also be hurt."

"Well, what about the safety of all the other non-humans on Terra? You know, the ones who were born here and the ones who don't want to leave?"

"I don't understand."

"Pa, if bad people are threatening you and then you leave, isn't that going to encourage those people to threaten other non-humans? You're the most famous non-human on Terra. If they can make *you* leave, won't they think it'll work on all the others? Won't you be putting all of the other non-humans at risk?"

"I don't know, May. My judgment is clouded by the fact that I care so much about you. I don't know what to do. Even though I've studied human behavior and I'm supposedly an expert, I don't know what the effect would be on the treatment of other non-humans. I suppose I'm thinking that, if I left, it might teach humans a lesson. Remember that I'm very popular with the majority of humans. Would I be fooling

144

myself by thinking that it would teach a lesson if the bad people forced me to go?"

"I don't know, Pa, but what about Brenna? Would you give up on seeing her again?"

"I don't know what we can do for Brenna. She seems to have chosen her path in life."

"Well, Pa," May took my hand and looked at my eye dome, "it sounds like you need to think about it. You're the one they're threatening, so I guess *you* need to decide. If you want to go, we'll have to figure out how I should finish school and where we're going to live on Kuw'baal."

"But May, for humans Kuw'baal is a cloudy, desolate world. You have many friends here, and Terra has the facilities you need to grow and reach your full potential."

May's mouth opened, and her eyes darted back and forth as if trying to figure something out. "What are you saying, Pa?"

"I'm saying that if I leave Terra, it might be best for you to stay here. I've spoken with Chancellor Linford about you living with him and Simon."

May's breathing told me that she was becoming distraught.

"Please understand, May," I added. "I'm not saying that I don't love you. I love you more than anything in the universe! I'm only suggesting that you grow up on Terra because I want what is best for you. Leaving you here would be the hardest thing I've ever done, but it's *because* I love you that I would put my wishes aside and do only what is best for you."

"How could you?" May demanded between sobs. "First, I'm an orphan, then I get put in some crummy foster home, then you come and take care of me, and now you want to put me *back* in a foster home? Don't you love me at all?"

I reached out to comfort May, but she pulled away. "Don't!" she shouted.

Before she could run, I grabbed May in my arms and held her tight. "May, I'm sorry. I'm so, so sorry!" May was shaking, and I could feel her tears on my torso. "I take it all back, May—all of it! I won't go without you, and there's no reason to go right now anyway."

"Pa, don't ever say anything like that again! Don't you know that I love you?"

"I do, May. I really do. You've told me so many times, but I couldn't know how much. Most humans think a kloormar like me looks hideous or scary, so I always thought that a human could never feel the kind of love for me that they might feel for a human. After Brenna got so mad

145

at me for comparing myself to a parent, I put up a wall and decided that I wouldn't let myself think that I meant that much to the two of you."

"I'm nothing like Brenna!" May declared.

May tightened her grip on me, and I wrapped my upper clasper limbs around her in addition to my arms.

"So, what are we going to do, Pa?" May asked after calming down a bit. "If you want to leave, that's fine, but you're taking me with you! If you want to stay and maybe even fight to protect the non-humans, I'm on your side."

"Even if it's dangerous?"

"*Especially* if it's dangerous! Wouldn't that be even more of a reason to stand up and fight?"

I released May and held her at arm's length, so I could look into her eyes. "May," I began, surprising myself at the depth of my emotions and the difficulty forming my words, "I feel so privileged that someone so smart and so brave is such an important part of my life."

When it came to the bond between a normal human adult and their offspring, I felt, at that moment, as though my understanding had deepened.

"So, Pa, what would you like to do?"

"Well, there's a possibility that involves us staying here on Terra. Would you like to go for a walk on the beach while we talk about it?"

May seemed relieved by the prospect of getting out of the house. I contacted the security office on my Infotab to let them know where May and I would be going. I asked them to keep an eye on us but from a distance, so we could talk in private.

May was barefoot and still in her pajamas. She wanted to remain that way, so she could let the small waves wash over her feet to keep her cool in the late-morning sunshine.

"So, May, what would you think if your pa became a news media personality?" I asked as we waded north along the sand.

"In a way, that'd be cool, but can you handle it?"

"Handle what, May? Answering questions and giving my viewpoint?"

"No. Can you handle being hated? Can you handle people telling lies about you or calling you evil or wanting to kill you?"

May had turned fourteen three weeks prior, and I was surprised that someone so young could already be so . . . not exactly cynical but accepting of the harsh realities that had thrust themselves into Terran society.

"What makes you think that would happen?" I asked.

"I *do* go to school with a lot of other students, you know," she replied, "and a lot of them have parents who are in the government or the media or just have strong opinions. Amy's mom is an immigration expert who helps non-humans move to Terra. She doesn't tell Amy anything, but Amy sneaked a peek at her mom's Infotab, and she's seen some of the hateful messages and death threats that her mom gets. Derrick's dad runs a news infosite. It's just about local stuff mostly, but he's also written what he thinks of HIM and he has exactly the same problems. So, it's really scary for them, but they're humans, so it's probably going to be way worse for you!"

"So you don't think I should do it then. Is that right?"

"I didn't say that, Pa. I mean, at least you'd be doing something! I totally get that you want to help make Terra a better place for everyone."

"Please understand, May, there is no guarantee that I'd be able to make any difference at all."

"Pa, the teacher told us something last week. If you're thinking of accomplishing something, but you need to be *sure* you'll succeed, then don't do it. That way you can be *sure* you won't succeed. Or you can try it, and you might have success. Sure, you might fail, but that would have happened anyway if you'd never tried."

While not taking into account the possible repercussions of failure, the simple words that May repeated to me were a source of inspiration. They were also poignant, bringing an old memory of mine to the surface. I recalled my despondency on *Jezebel's Fury* after the baby kloormar I had once carried was murdered in front of me. In that tragic moment, the fight in me was gone, and I was ready to give up on the struggle against our captors. That was when Kroz had said to me, "I know that it all seems hopeless, and I agree that our chances of success are minimal, but the point is that we are *trying*. If we die trying, at least we'll die with some honor."

I thanked May and told her that I'd do my best.

"I'm proud of you, Pa," she said as we turned around and waded back toward home.

TWENTY: MEDIA BLITZ

At our first meeting, Victoria, my media handler, asked me whether I was sure that I wanted to go ahead. She warned me about blowback as my detractors would twist and distort my words at every opportunity. This was followed by our first practice interview session.

Victoria started by asking simple questions, then she would take what I said, distort my intent, and try to corner me into contradicting myself. She was a skilled debater. More sessions ensued over the following days and I learned how to predict manipulation and verbal traps and to word my statements to defuse rhetorical bombshells. I also learned that, in the media business, there was no such thing as a simple "yes or no" question.

I wanted to avoid sounding like a politician who never answered a question directly, but I learned to appreciate how public figures had to take great care when making statements. The exception was Gloria Truscott, who took no care at all with her answers. Her technique was either to respond with an answer that had nothing to do with the topic or to answer directly and sound like an uninformed fool. Somehow her foolish or incomprehensible answers and statements only encouraged her ardent supporters who called her honest, straightforward, and "telling it like it is."

Victoria tested my knowledge on a wide variety of political and cultural topics. She was unable to stump me due to the extensive knowledge locked away in my perfect kloormari memory.

By the end of our eighth session, Victoria said I was as ready as I could be and that I might as well start making media appearances. She showed me a massive list of requests for interviews, dating back to the announcement of my work at the university. The list had grown by leaps and bounds immediately after my one-on-one interview with Liz Underwood when Brenna ran away.

Jas and I had a meeting before I started my new role. He wanted me to know that the university would be charging the networks an "almost ridiculous" amount for access to me. He asked me again whether I would like an increase in my salary to reflect my new responsibilities. I reiterated that I was already being paid more than enough to fund my requirements as well as May's wants and needs.

Victoria booked my first official interview with my favorite journalist, Liz Underwood, to take place in the university's media center studio. Before mentioning the rise of HIM and the current backlash against non-humans, Liz asked me about my life on Kuw'baal before human first contact. She moved on to my initial impression of humans, and then the horror of my abduction and the mistreatment of my kloormari friends and me on *Jezebel's Fury*. She included questions about the birth of our baby, Sam, and Sam's bravery and heroics in assisting us to overcome our captivity.

"Of course," she said with great sensitivity, "Sam never got to see the results of that bravery." She continued to gently pry more information from me about my feelings regarding Sam.

"I see what you're trying to do, Liz," I remarked. "You're trying to make me relatable by eliciting an emotional response from me. I'm sure you're aware that I am physically incapable of crying, but for what it's worth, Sam's death resulted in devastating sadness and anger. Due to the way that kloormari memories are structured, my sadness and anger are as strong today as they ever were, but over the years I've developed coping strategies."

"I think it's crucial for everyone viewing this to understand what you've been through," Liz replied, "and yes, it's important for humans to relate to your experiences and to identify with you as a fellow being."

Our interview continued, covering the rescue from the Brotherhood gangsters, my return to Kuw'baal, the devastating effects of colonization on my homeworld, and the kloormari's attempts to heal over the years that followed.

The second half of the interview dealt with my relocation to Terra, my relationship with Brenna and May, and finally, how the rise of the Human Independence movement affected me and those I cared about. We ended with the current politics of Terra and, thanks to Dr. Schlenk's insights, my dire warning about human history repeating itself.

After the interview, I thought that Liz was either a person who cared a great deal about me and the future of Terra, or she was a brilliant actor. I decided it didn't really matter either way since she had done an outstanding job in helping me to express my perspectives. I just hoped the interview might sway at least a few million humans away from supporting HIM.

My interview with Liz was followed by similar sessions with James Sulawesi from Vega Network and Laurexia Benjerang from Terra Broadcasting.

All three interviews were broadcast as special primetime news presentations on each network. To my pleasant surprise, the interviews had massive audiences. It seemed that there was a great deal of interest from the public to learn my personal viewpoint on the rise of HIM. Now that I was no longer shielded by the university's media center, feedback from the public was shared with me. As with my arrival on Terra, I was once again bombarded with adoration and praise from the general public as well as celebrities and most political leaders.

Of course, my interviews also produced hatred and complaints from followers and leaders of the movement. Gloria Truscott was furious. She lashed out against the major media networks, alleging that they inflated the size of my audience while downplaying hers. She accused them of treating me with "kid gloves" and throwing me nothing but "softball" questions while unfairly picking on her. I couldn't understand her argument. I had answered a great many questions that challenged my views, and I responded honestly. Her problem was that the media's role in society was to report the facts. To Truscott's detriment, the facts simply didn't support her outrageous and blatantly false rantings.

My three interviews garnered the support of a group that had remained conspicuously silent—the extraterrestrial community. Non-humans who had been living and working on Terra, many of them for generations, had kept a low profile. Most had believed that causing a stir would only embolden the bigots. They felt that the best solution was to wait for enough humans to become fed up with the anti-immigration "fad" and for cooler heads to prevail. Most non-humans chose to believe that, given a bit more time, organizations like HIM would become nothing more than a bump on the road to progress and an unpleasant memory. In the meantime, everyday life was becoming harder to bear. Non-humans—especially those who didn't live on university campuses or other insulated environments—were subject to increasing incidents of insults, mockery, and sometimes violent assault. There had even been a few cases of extraterrestrials being found dead under suspicious circumstances.

There was one incident that I found particularly cruel. I saw a vid in which a group of six human teenagers accosted a Mangor and separated her from her personal hover disc. They threw the disk onto the roof of a building. They poked at the Mangor and mocked her while recording her having to use her natural method of movement to slowly crawl along the ground and up the side of the building. They called her a fat slug as she left her natural trail of slime mixed with dirt and dried grass that had stuck to her rippling foot. The vid had been viewed widely because it was seen within another vid of Gloria Truscott watching it. She and her senior staff were pointing and laughing at the vid screen, relishing the apparent hilarity of the persecution of an intelligent, sensitive individual. The backlash was vociferous and intense, but Truscott didn't apologize or make excuses. Instead, she stated that she had nothing to be ashamed of and would do the same thing again.

Extraterrestrials reported incidents of hate, harassment, and violence to law enforcement with mixed results. There were a few documented cases in which human enforcement officers downplayed incidents or refused to take action.

On a personal level, May and I were disappointed that we could no longer travel safely. We had wanted to visit islands in the South Pacific Ocean, but we worried that I would be harassed as soon as I left university property. Additionally, the university's security team wouldn't even consider the notion.

From the time I had brought the Human Independence Movement into the spotlight until my first interviews as a news media personality, about 20 percent of the non-human residents of Terra had packed up and left the planet. Most had been recent arrivals. The inflow of new immigrants had decreased by 98 percent. Many of the non-humans who remained had been born or hatched on Terra and raised on Terra and would likely have had difficulty integrating if they moved to their species' homeworlds. Many were engaged in work that they were passionate about, with accomplishments that distinguished them as individuals. Many also felt that their departure would represent a surrender to evil. They had loved Terra and its multi-species society. The prospect of seeing that society destroyed was unthinkable.

The timing of my interviews coincided with most remaining extraterrestrials, realizing that HIM was not going away any time soon. They started to understand that life was going to become far more hazardous before the movement faded into oblivion. As a result, the media center passed along messages of thanks from countless extraterrestrials. More non-humans than ever started coming forward and speaking with the media, thanking me publicly and stating their solidarity with my views. I quickly came to be seen as the "spokesbeing" for Terra's extraterrestrial residents despite my lack of intent to assume such a role.

After my three interviews, Victoria scheduled various appearances. Sometimes I was a guest on talk shows, and sometimes I was part of an on-air panel analyzing the political situation or the latest outrageous statements by Truscott or her minions. I was invited to appear on hundreds of networks of all sizes, with the exception of Veritacity and similar outlets, whose invitations I would have refused anyway.

As my media presence grew, so did the idea of a one-on-one pre-election debate between Gloria Truscott and me. Although I wasn't interested in giving Truscott yet another platform from which to spew her lies, the university's media center negotiated the conditions for a possible debate. In public, no one was more vocal in their wish for a debate than Truscott. In reality, though, no matter the conditions presented by the university, they were never acceptable to Truscott's team. Of course, she repeatedly raised the issue, claiming that I was too cowardly to do battle with her in public.

There had already been several debates between the party leaders, which May and I watched intently. The debates started with an opening statement by each party leader. Matthew Scott of the ruling Integrity Party would speak of his party's accomplishments over the past decade. He would provide statistics to support his views and would pledge to "stay the course" for future stability. April Sanchez, leader of the Unity Party, offered alternative economic and social policies and admonished the Integrity Party for missing some of its previous targets by 1 or 2 percent. Both party leaders were united in their criticism of Gloria Truscott and the Humanity Party, but they held back from using Truscott's scathing rhetoric and obscenities, wanting to be seen as rising above the vulgarity.

Matthew Scott and April Sanchez praised the advancement and enrichment of humanity through contact with other species and cultures. Both embraced the multi-species world that had been integral to Terran society for centuries and invoked the phrase, "strength through diversity."

Overall, it was hard to distinguish the policies of either established party in any significant way. If the debates had just been between Scott and Sanchez, there would have been a civilized exchange of ideas highlighting areas of agreement and disagreement, using facts and reasoning for the purpose of helping the electorate to make a decision. A great many humans hadn't become involved in politics because they were bored with the entire process.

Of course, the inclusion of Truscott made the debates anything but a civilized exchange of ideas. Her opening statements consisted of her usual diatribes and fabrications. Despite her bizarre clothing, hair, and facial paint, she would insult the physical appearance of her opponents. Regardless of her inability to follow logical thoughts to their conclusion, she accused her opponents of being imbeciles. And despite her delusional perception of reality, she accused Scott and Sanchez of spreading hateful lies.

When opening statements were over, the proceedings would plunge into chaos. As soon as Sanchez or Scott were one sentence into answering a question, she would interrupt, screeching her objections, and drowning out any civilized attempts by anyone else—moderator or opponent—to be heard. She treated time restrictions on answers as though they were just something that applied to other people as she'd continued shrieking until her microphone was cut off. Scott and Sanchez just stood and looked annoyed, not knowing how to react. I guessed they were willing to let the spectacle unfold in the hope that the public would be swayed against Truscott by witnessing her apparent insanity.

As the weeks passed, Truscott's persona became more outrageous and downright cartoonish. In spite of that, her relative popularity remained constant. It was as if a segment of the human population placed the entertainment value of her performances above good government and the norms of a civil society.

As election day neared, Truscott's insincere demands to debate me continued. The interest of the networks also increased with the belief that such an event could draw record viewership. Even Jas started to press me to consider going up against "the dragon."

"Jas, would such a debate benefit the university?" I asked.

"Well, yes. The networks are offering us an astronomical sum for your participation. On the other hand, the Humanity Party keeps putting ridiculous conditions on Gloria's participation. That's why it might be extremely helpful to simply call their bluff. We could get their final offer, agree to their terms, and watch them chicken out in front of all of Terra!"

Only two weeks remained until the election. The networks, the university, and Truscott made offers and counter-offers until a final agreement was hammered out.

Truscott's acceptance statement had all of the grace that Terra had come to expect. "I accept the challenge to debate the hideous alien, Kelvoo. I look forward to wiping the floor with its face!"

I was with Jas when we saw Truscott's response. "What an odd thing to say," I remarked.

"What?" Jas asked. "Do you mean the part about debating the hideous alien?"

"No. I mean the part about wiping the floor. Doesn't she realize I don't have a face?"

TWENTY-ONE: THE GREAT INTERSPECIES DEBACLE

Seven days before the election, I traveled to the agreed-upon neutral location—a broadcast studio in Lagos, on the Atlantic coast of the African continent. Each side could select a co-moderator and invite ten guests. My moderator was Liz Underwood. HP selected Kaley Hart. Although Kaley lacked the experience and professionalism of traditional media journalists, HP's choice was, in my estimation, intended to distract and unnerve me.

I had invited Jas and the four other members of the Sagacity Club. I invited the journalists from Vega Network and Terra Broadcasting who, with Liz, had attended my original announcement on Terra. Last, and certainly not least, I asked May to accompany me. Finally, Jas invited Simon as his personal guest. I asked Jas to select someone for the last remaining seat. Jas told me that whomever he invited, about twenty other people would be annoyed that they weren't chosen. "I might as well have twenty-one people mad at me instead of twenty," he said, so we left the remaining seat vacant.

The Terran debates commission had chartered a semi-orbital to take me and my entourage on the fifty-minute flight to the Lagos spaceport. As our group boarded, I saw that thirty of the seats were filled with security personnel to ensure our safe travel between the university and the debate venue.

When we landed at the Lagos spaceport on Snake Island, we were directed to a line of cars. Our group was split up with no more than two of us plus two or three guards in each vehicle. The remaining guards rode in a small bus at the front of the procession and another bus at the rear. May was my companion in one of the cars.

The convoy proceeded east over inhabited areas, swamps, and waterways toward a building overlooking Tarkwa Bay. As we approached, the need for the security force became obvious. At least a thousand Humanity Party supporters surrounded the building, holding signs and banners, not so much in support of HP but stating their opposition to non-humans, often laced with obscenities. They seemed to know that I was in the approaching convoy as they hurled insults, raised fists, and threw objects toward us.

The entrance to the building's underground parking was blocked by a large number of menacing Truscovites. The cars hovered above the entrance, out of range of projectiles, while the first bus touched down on the building's roof. The first contingent of guards exited the bus and formed a perimeter around the center of the roof. The cars descended rapidly to spots inside the perimeter. The guards in each car jumped out to reinforce the cordon. Each guard deployed an expandable shield, which they used to deflect a few projectiles that had been hurled onto the roof from protestors on the ground.

"I'm not sure it was a good idea for you to come, May," I said while we waited for the go-ahead to leave the car.

"No, Pa, it's good that I'm seeing how angry and ignorant these people are. It makes me more proud of you than ever!"

A guard ran up to each car, hustled the passengers out, and guided us to the top of a stairwell, which we descended to a short hall and then into a production studio. The studio featured a raised, brightly lit stage with a curving apron. A podium was positioned on either side of the moderators' table. The rows of studio audience seats gently sloped down toward the stage. They were arranged in two sections with ten rows of five seats on each side. Only the first two rows of seats would be occupied by the invited guests during the broadcast.

Eight of Truscott's ten guests were seated on the far side of the studio. I didn't recognize any of them. Two empty seats in Truscott's section were in the front row next to the aisle. The backrests bore "Reserved for Special Guest" signs.

A member of the technical crew introduced herself as Rosemary and asked my group to take a seat in our section, where my guests sat in the first two rows. Rosemary told me that I could proceed to the green room, located backstage on our side.

"Thank you Rosemary," I replied, "but I would prefer to wait here with my supporters."

"Um, I guess that's OK," Rosemary replied.

As I chatted with my group, we stole glances at the Truscovites. They were murmuring or whispering to one another. Sometimes they would stare at me and snigger. Jas and I went over my main talking points, which served to fill the time and reduce my nervousness. May and my other guests repeatedly gave me words of encouragement.

As debate time drew closer, hovering cameras moved to their respective positions around the stage while the broadcast technicians and bots performed various tasks.

Rosemary guided me to one of the podiums. Next, she opened the door to Truscott's green room and invited her to the other podium. Truscott's appearance was as outlandish as ever, and she was once again dressed in her signature red robe. As Truscott approached, I extended my hand paddle to her in greeting. She responded by jabbing the open palm of her hand toward my eye and then flicking the back of her hand dismissively. Her guests laughed.

Liz and Kaley emerged from backstage and took their seats behind the moderators' table. Their assistants followed, adjusting their hair and applying finishing touches to their faces.

A technician counted down, "Live in five, four, three, two . . ."

Urgent music played, and the monitors showed a wide shot of the stage while animated letters formed the words, "The Great Interspecies Debate." I thought the title was misleading since only two species were present.

I felt nervous but ready as the music faded and Kaley spoke into the camera. "Welcome to our viewers across Terra and the Planetary Alliance for this special broadcast event, the Great Interspecies Debate! I'm Kaley Hart from the Veritacity Network."

"And I'm Liz Underwood from Atlantic News. Unlike the political debates that we've all been following, tonight we present something different. As we are all well aware, one of the Humanity Party's goals is to remove extraterrestrial species from Terra—"

"All of 'em!" Truscott shouted. Her microphone wasn't active, so to the broadcast viewers, her interruption would have sounded like somebody shouting from offstage.

"As a moderator, I strongly advise our participants to hold their remarks until it's their turn to speak," Liz asserted in a firm, clear voice. "As I was saying, the Humanity Party seeks the removal of non-humans. Since there are no political parties that specifically represent non-human citizens, this special debate has been arranged to present a non-human viewpoint from someone widely considered to be the best-known extraterrestrial on Terra."

Truscott's audience booed and jeered at me, and once again, Liz interjected. "In the interest of providing a fair debate, the audience members will silence themselves!"

"Thank you, Liz," Kaley said, taking her turn. "Before I introduce our participants, I would like to advise the audience that they may applaud after each introduction. Apart from that I remind the audience to remain quiet until the conclusion of this event."

At that point I was pleasantly surprised that Kaley was observing generally accepted debate procedures and conducting herself confidently, though the fact she was reading from a holo-prompter must have been helpful to her. "First, representing the Humanity Party and its extraterrestrial deportation platform," she said, "I am pleased to introduce Gloria Truscott."

Truscott's audience members leaped to their feet, hooting and screaming their support. My group looked at one another tentatively. Jas nodded slightly, and my group applauded politely while remaining seated. The Truscovites kept clapping and shouting while Liz tried to interrupt them. "In the interest of getting this event started, I'm asking the audience to settle down," she said. A moment later, Truscott held a hand up toward her acolytes, and they ceased their din.

"Representing the extraterrestrial beings on Terra, the opposing viewpoint will be presented by Kelvoo," Liz announced, followed by booing and jeering from Truscott's side, which drowned out the applause from my supporters.

Kaley proceeded to outline the rules and the debate process while Truscott and her followers looked bored.

Then Liz took her turn. "Our pre-debate random selection process has indicated that Kelvoo will speak first, meaning that Gloria Truscott will have the final word. Kelvoo, please make your opening statement."

"Thank you, Ms. Underwood. I would also like to thank the debate organizers, Kaley Hart, and my worthy opponent, Gloria Truscott," I said with as much sincerity as I could muster, "for providing me with this forum and this opportunity. I would like to begin with one minor correction. Ms. Underwood, you told our audience that I represent the extraterrestrial beings on Terra. I must respectfully disagree. There are seven non-human species on Terra, and my species is just one of those seven. We extraterrestrials are not a single, monolithic entity. We are a diverse group of individuals, and we vary in our values, hopes, and dreams just like every one of the billions of humans watching us now."

The Truscovites started shifting and looking at one another. Before they could voice their objections to being compared with "aliens," Truscott raised a hand toward them in what I mistakenly thought was a sign of respect for me. I realized I felt quite serene, unlike my initial announcement when I joined the university. I thought I must have been calm due to my confidence that I was representing the righteous side of the argument.

"As I stand before you," I continued, "I represent only myself and my views. I'm doing so in order to let the audience relate to me as an individual, one might even say, as a 'person.'"

The Truscovites grew more restless, but with a motion, their leader managed to keep them under control.

"What some movements, political parties, leaders, and a *minority* of humans fail to recognize is that we are all intelligent, living beings who deserve equal treatment."

Gloria Truscott turned to face the green room on her side of the stage. She gave a slight nod in that direction. A crew member opened the door to the room as I continued speaking.

"Again and again, human history has clearly demonstrated that the subjugation of—" I stopped short as I saw Griffin Taylor exit the green room, followed by none other than Brenna. He was holding her hand and almost pulling her down the five steps from the side of the stage to the audience level. He propelled Brenna toward the two reserved seats on Truscott's side of the room. All of this action was outside the view of the cameras. Now I understood why Truscott had been keeping her audience at bay. She didn't want any distractions from her choreographed effort to distract me.

When Brenna reached the audience level, she and May locked eyes. May was aghast. Brenna reached her hand toward May and opened her mouth as if to speak. Brenna advanced in May's direction, ahead of Griffin. May leaped from her front-row seat and strode toward the exit farthest from Brenna. Jas jumped up and intercepted May just short of the doors. At the same time, Griffin shifted his grip from Brenna's hand to her wrist. He yanked her backward and placed her in her seat. Jas led May to the seats several rows back, and they sat together, away from the rest of the audience.

During the theatrics in the audience, I stood at the podium with my thoughts in complete disarray. I felt as lost as I had at the start of my original announcement at the university, and I suffered the same stress-induced vocal paralysis, darkening of vision, tingling, and quickening of respiration. It felt as if all of Terra was closing in on me.

"Having a little difficulty, *alien*?" Truscott inquired.

"I am warning the audience, here and now, to refrain from actions that may distract our participants, moderators, or crew!" Liz admonished.

My fear transformed to anger, and I decided to deviate from my plan. "It's alright, Liz," I said, doing my best to remain calm. "I was distracted and rattled just now, and I'm sure that the audience watching this broadcast would like to know why."

Truscott furrowed her brow as if she had assumed I wouldn't want to draw attention to her antics.

"As most viewers will be aware," I continued, "a young human, Brenna Murphy, was in my care when I moved to Terra. Back before HIM was well known and before the Humanity Party was formed, someone named Griffin Taylor convinced Brenna that the Human

158

Independence Movement was just and righteous. One evening, Brenna and I had a confrontation, and she ran off to be with the humans who had, in my opinion, poisoned her mind. I was frantic. I didn't know whether she was alive or abducted or dead. I believed that, at the very least, she was being used. Frankly, I still believe that.

"When I lost my train of thought a moment ago, it was because Gloria Truscott brought Griffin Taylor and Brenna Murphy into the studio."

"I did no such thing!" Truscott shouted.

"There are many cameras in this studio," I retorted, "and there will be a vid clip showing my opponent nodding toward the door to the green room that she had just occupied, followed by the emergence of Griffin Taylor and Brenna Murphy. In fact, Griffin practically dragged Brenna into the studio. I haven't seen Brenna in person since she disappeared, and now she is sitting here, right in front of me. Let it be known that Gloria Truscott just *used* a human who is very dear to me to distract and fluster me."

Truscott crossed her arms and glowered at me as I continued. "Tactics such as this are the hallmarks of a cheat and a coward!"

The Truscovites exploded with boos and roars of indignation while the moderators called for order.

"In her past debates, we have all seen how my opponent tries to drown out her opponents by shouting over them," I shouted over the noise. Then I raised my volume another notch. "But what my opponent does not seem to appreciate is that she has but one vocal outlet while I have eight!"

The booing, jeering, shouting, and calls for order didn't stop, so I allowed my anger to transform into fury, and I let loose with all eight of my voices, "I shall be heard!" Every being in the studio, and perhaps anyone else on the same floor of the building, jumped in alarm and covered their ears. The poor sound technician in a booth behind the audience flung his headphones off as if they were causing severe electric shock. The microphone that had been floating in front of me started flashing red and moved away to a safer distance at the far wall behind the audience.

Not letting up, I continued at full volume. "Who else but a coward is so afraid of the facts and the truth that, instead of engaging in an exchange of ideas, she tries to drown out her opponent? Who else but a coward presents misinformation and outright lies as if they were facts, as she has done in every speech and debate in her campaign? Who else but a coward would fear beings like me, beings who have lived in peace and obeyed the laws of this planet for centuries? Who but a coward would be so insecure in her beliefs that she spreads fear to people so

159

gullible and weak-minded that they actually believe her? Who but an utter coward would cheat in a debate by trying to unnerve her opponent through emotional manipulation instead of supporting her arguments through logic and reason?"

When I stopped, the studio was silent. Many eyes were wide, and many mouths hung open with shock. Brenna was an exception. She looked down and blocked her eyes with her hand. As for Truscott, she looked rattled. Her whirlwind of dyed red hair had been knocked askew, its upper level tipped forward like the pointed hat of an elf from old Terran lore.

I took advantage of the silence and stepped toward the stage's apron, squatting in front of Brenna. "Look at me, Brenna," I said as the mic edged back in front of me, and cameras hovered behind me. "Come on, Brenna. You can do it."

Brenna's clothing was impeccable, her hair was neatly styled, and her jewelry was exquisite, but beneath it all, she looked weary. Brenna kept her eyes downcast, not wanting to look at me. Griffin squeezed her upper arm. "Do it!" he commanded between clenched teeth. Struggling to maintain a neutral expression, she finally met my gaze.

"Brenna, are you still in love with this person?" I asked, motioning to Griffin. "If so, can you truly say that he loves you back, or is it possible that you are being manipulated, used, and exploited simply because you were once close to me? I refuse to believe you despise me so much that you would continue to support the Human Independence Movement or that you would choose to follow the hatred being spewed by my opponent.

"Brenna, I was given the opportunity to bring ten guests with me tonight. Instead I brought nine. That means there is an empty seat on my side of the studio. Right now, or at any time during this debate, you have the option to get up and walk over to the other side and step away from the manipulation that you have been subjected to.

"Every day I think about you and all that you must have been through since you left our home. You must be so exhausted by all of the turmoil."

I knew that Brenna's brave façade had started to crack when I saw a tear on one of her lower eyelids. "Brenna, I know that you, like so many humans, think that a kloormar is incapable of feeling love for another being in the same way as a human can. Having never been a human, I have no way of knowing whether or not that is true. Just know that I love you very much, and in spite of her feelings of betrayal, so does your little sister, May. All you need to do is take a few steps to the other side of this studio, and you can be free again."

As I let the silence between us linger. Griffin dug his fingertips deeper under Brenna's bicep.

"I can't," she whispered, a tear rolling down her cheek.

I stood and made my way back to my podium. "I apologize to the organizers of this event, to the moderators, and to the audience for my diversion from the intended format. I have no further statement at this time, and I relinquish any remaining time for my opening statement." I hoped that the impact of my unplanned diversion was far greater than my rehearsed opening statement would have been.

I stood and waited while Truscott made her opening statement. Full of fire and vitriol, her diatribe was little more than a regurgitation of talking points, slogans, and anti-immigrant disinformation from her previous speeches and debates. Only at the end of her statement did she diverge from her prepared material, pointing to my verbal outburst and claiming it demonstrated the anger and violence inherent in all alien species.

The next phase of the debate consisted of the moderators asking us questions. As Truscott's selected moderator, Kaley's questions for me were blatantly biased and sometimes impossible to answer directly. For example: "Kelvoo, when you and your alien co-conspirators grow to outnumber the humans on Terra and dominate the Terran government, what will the role of the humans be in serving their new rulers?"

For each of Kaley's questions, I had to deconstruct the multiple facets of the question, rejecting the premise of each, along with an explanation of my rejection. Then I had to make my counterpoint before my allotted time was up.

I noticed a peculiarity in Kaley's approach not so much in the questions themselves but in her delivery. I had never viewed her as a talented journalist, but her tone during the debate was flatter than normal, as if her enthusiasm or interest was slowly draining away.

There were times early in the debate when Truscott tried to interrupt or shout over me. All I had to do was increase my volume to the point where she would give up, unable to endure another ear-splitting sonic assault. She had no choice but to allow me to continue, which must have been immensely frustrating for her and a great relief for all other beings in the studio.

The questions and answers continued. I will not go into the specifics here since I have no interest in providing a platform for falsehoods and hate. There were, however, two segments of the debate that are worth repeating. They both occurred during an open forum segment of the debate where propositions and rebuttals could be exchanged. The first segment illustrates the degree to which Truscott could lie and the gullibility of her followers.

"Every human knows that Kelvoo's writing, Kelvoo's so-called 'testimonial,' is a pack of lies!"

"Please," I replied, "provide us with a single example of a falsehood in my story."

"Gladly! The entire part about you being abducted for seven years, but it seeming as if only six months had passed. Ha! You were gone for seven years, and you had those seven years to plot and conspire with your alien friends to overthrow Terra!"

"Ms. Truscott, for much of my abduction I was held captive on a vessel that was traveling close to the speed of light. It was the relativistic effect of time dilation that made only six months pass for the occupants during our various voyages."

"Ooh! 'The relativistic effect of time dilation,'" Truscott repeated in a mocking tone. "What a crock! Everyone with a brain knows that there's no such thing as time dilation!"

I stood at my podium in utter shock. "What? What are you talking about? For centuries, every species in the Planetary Alliance has known about time dilation. The concept is taught to every child by their fifth year of education! Time dilation has been confirmed science for centuries. It is measurable, it is observable, and it is established scientific fact!"

"And there you go! Ooh! It's a *scientific* fact! If there's one thing even less trustworthy than the major media," she snarled, looking at Liz, "it's the scientists! Their lies have wormed their way into the schools where those lies are implanted in the brains of our innocent children! The scientists, the intellectuals, and the aliens are all in the same bed together! Aided and abetted by their enablers in the media, looking to poison the minds of children and groom them to spread their lies and hate!"

I had heard Truscott spread misinformation, fallacies, and outright lies before, but I had never seen such a direct attack on the very pillars of knowledge. I hoped her statement would lead to a loss of support for HP, but by that time I had no such expectations.

In the second notable part of the debate, I was putting forward a series of rhetorical questions, aimed at Humanity Party supporters. I asked them to try to think logically about their political affiliation and whether it made any sense. I asked them to think back to the time when they decided that the Human Independence Movement was the path that they wanted to follow, and I wondered aloud how such a hateful movement could have started in the first place.

"You stupid kloormar!" Truscott replied, shaking her head at me. "You don't get it, do you? You don't even realize that the Human Independence Movement was started by *you*!"

"Given that HIM is opposed to my very existence, it is beyond ludicrous to suggest that I had anything to do with HIM's creation," I replied. "On the other hand, making statements that are beyond ludicrous is one of the hallmarks of my opponent's incomprehensible strategy."

"Wow! You still don't get it! Let me spell it out for you. It was *your* Kelvoo's Testimonial pack of lies that led to the so-called Correction when our stupid government decided that we must bow down to the Planetary Alliance and beg forgiveness. If you had never written that garbage, none of this would have happened! Still, I said nothing, and the decent humans of this planet did nothing because we were tolerant and patient and willing to endure the unjust humiliation.

"Don't you understand, you alien freak? *You* opened our eyes, and *you* inspired us to take action when *you* had the audacity to immigrate to the human homeworld and pollute it with your presence! Your relocation to Terra was the final straw! It was the trigger that inspired a few brave humans to say, 'enough!' It was those courageous humans, including the kind and generous Taylor family, that led to the Human Independence Movement, which gave rise to the Humanity Party, which finally resulted in me standing here on this stage, with the most vile, hideous, despicable alien ever to set its stinking foot on this beautiful planet!"

The Truscovites couldn't restrain themselves as they broke into cheers and applause while Liz once again called for order.

Truscott smirked as I delivered my response, which consisted of me explaining that I had come to Terra because I was invited and that my arrival was being used as an excuse for a power grab by a minority of hate-filled humans.

Despite the fact that the personal attack had come from an utterly disreputable source, it still stung me.

Not a moment too soon, the event reached its scheduled conclusion. The moderators looked immensely relieved as Kaley thanked the participants and the organizers.

"That concludes what has surely been one of the liveliest and, quite honestly, strangest debates ever broadcast to such a wide audience," Liz said. She bid the viewers goodbye as theme music started to play, and most of the cameras moved back for a wider shot.

Wishing to demonstrate fairness and graciousness to the viewers, I approached Truscott, but I stopped when she shrank back. "You stay the hell away from me!"

I extended my hand paddle toward her in greeting. In response, she bounded toward me and, with all of her scrawny might, shoved my torso, sending me flailing to the floor.

163

"It tried to attack me!" Truscott screamed, pointing at me. "Did you see that? It tried to attack!"

All of the Truscovites, with the exception of Brenna, leaped to their feet and stormed the stage.

The AI that controlled the camera and audio bots sensed a sensational, newsworthy event in progress and sprang into action. The closing music stopped, and the broadcast continued as the cameras swirled around the room to take in the scene.

Truscott ran into the green room and slammed the door behind her as her supporters clambered onto the stage, followed by my team. Rather than throwing punches, my defenders, including Liz, tried to place themselves between the infuriated Truscovites and me, serving as human shields, but not until several blows struck me.

My main concern was for May. When I got back to my feet, I looked over the crowd and saw that Brenna had intercepted her as she had made her way to the stairs at the side of the stage. I tried to move toward them, but a Truscott supporter who was lying on the stage in the midst of the brawl had a tight grip on one of my ankles. I saw Brenna begging May to leave with her.

"Hell no!" May shouted back. Brenna grabbed May's left wrist and pulled May toward her. May reached her right hand across her body and then backhanded Brenna across the face with a clearly audible slap. Brenna released May and ran off, sobbing, while clutching her stinging cheek.

By that point my security team were pouring into the studio as both podiums were being tossed, along with any loose equipment. Kaley just stood behind the upended moderators' desk with a stunned, wide-eyed look on her face. It was not lost on me that the entire violent, shameful tableau was being broadcast live across Terra and via quantum entanglement relay to worlds across the entire sector of the galaxy.

Within seconds the security team managed to end the havoc by restraining each combatant. I was also restrained, even though I had thrown no punches. As the security contingent was about to march my team and me through the exit doors, Kaley snapped out of her panicked state. "Wait, I'm coming with you!" she shouted. She was at the tail end of my group as we rushed up the stairs to the roof.

Sol was low in the sky and casting an orange glow as we made our way toward the waiting vehicles. The air was alive with the angry shouts of the pro-Truscott mob surrounding the building. They would have been watching the debate on their Infotabs and must have been furious.

We fastened ourselves in the vehicles, though we left the doors to each car open, anxiously waiting for our security escorts to board. May and I sat together and listened as the security guards huddled to discuss the situation.

The security team leader decided it was unsafe to leave at that moment in case the crowd started hurling objects at us. They contacted Lagos law enforcement, but they were already fully occupied combatting the crowd and were unwilling to use lethal force. At the same time, another guard contacted traffic control to obtain override codes for our vehicles. Then the guard moved to each vehicle and entered a code into each control console.

We all took out our Infotabs and watched our situation play out live on the networks. For fifteen minutes we watched the protest crowd, which had grown into the tens of thousands. That's when furious groups of anti-HP protestors started pouring down the main avenues toward our location. Angry scuffles played out on our screens as protestors and counter-protestors clashed.

"Move out!" the security commander barked, taking advantage of the distraction below.

The guards ran to each assigned vehicle. "Hang on!" our driver shouted as our vehicles shot straight up simultaneously. The g-forces pushed us toward the floor as we ascended several hundred meters. Next, we were jolted and then pressed toward the rear as the cars shot toward the spaceport on a trajectory far above and outside the established traffic patterns, thanks to the overrides provided by traffic control. As the inertial forces jostled and jolted us, I hoped that Kroz's work would lead to inertial dampening fields for small vessels sooner rather than later.

We were practically in freefall as the vehicles descended and then we were jolted again as they slowed to a halt just above the spaceport tarmac and right outside the semi-orbital, which was prepped, pre-cleared, and ready to go. We were hustled into the vessel, followed by our security escort, as we saw and heard an angry crowd of Truscovites shouting just outside the spaceport's force-fence.

The moment the hatch closed, and even before the guards were fastened into their seats, the semi-orbital rolled along the runway, then ascended toward the final red remnants of the sunset in the west. The craft banked to the northeast and powered its way out of the atmosphere and toward what we hoped would be the relative safety of the university campus.

TWENTY-TWO: COUNTING DOWN

After escaping the sorry excuse for a debate, relief and fatigue set in during the flight back to the university. The security people sat in silence and, for the most part, so did my supporters, some of them nursing bruises or cuts acquired in the melee.

A group of seats located in the forward section of the semi-orbital's cabin served as the de-facto media section. There were two pairs of seats facing each other across a small, low table. Liz was in a seat beside James Sulawesi from Vega Network, and Laurexia Benjerang of Terra Broadcasting sat across from James. Each journalist alternated between checking their Infotabs and closing their eyes due to fatigue.

May sat in the next row aft of the journalists, and I squatted beside her in a space where the seat had been removed and a supporting frame had been installed.

The moment the craft started coasting above the atmosphere and the graviton field was activated, Kaley walked over and took the empty seat across from Liz.

"What are you doing here?" Liz asked.

"I'd like to talk," Kaley replied.

"No, I mean what the hell are you doing on our vessel?"

"I need to make a statement, and I want all three of you to record it on your Infotabs."

"Why should we?" Laurexia asked. "So you can spread more trash and alarmist lies about the so-called 'alien menace'?"

"Please," Kaley said, looking at the cabin floor, "I have information that will interest you. If you don't like it, you can delete your recordings. I'm asking you this favor as a fellow professional journalist."

The term "professional journalist" made James snicker. Laurexia smirked, and Liz rolled her eyes.

"Fine! Go for it," Liz said as the three of them pointed their devices toward Kaley.

"My name is Kaley Hart, and I'm a former employee of the Veritacity Network."

The word "former" got the group's attention as they moved their Infotabs slightly closer to Kaley.

"When I was at a low point in my career," she continued, "I found a home and family at Veritacity. They took me in, they paid me well, and they gave me a new start. Unfortunately, that family turned out to be highly dysfunctional. For years, I ignored Veritacity's sensationalism and loose relationship with the truth. I rationalized my support of the network with the thought that we were just providing a different perspective, and I chose to believe that the public could gain a balanced viewpoint by watching us along with all of the other sources of news.

"I always had lingering doubts, but who else was going to hire me? My doubts turned to regret when the Human Independence Movement started getting attention, and Veritacity became little more than the movement's propaganda arm.

"The Humanity Party *uses* people. Today, they used Brenna Murphy as a prop to try to unnerve Kelvoo. They also used me. I don't have the experience or, honestly, the skill to host major debates with audiences in the billions, but they chose me in the hope that my presence would distract Kelvoo due to my clandestine interview all those years ago—a professional choice that led to the Correction and a choice I regret to this day.

"In today's so-called debate, I watched Gloria Truscott try to blame Kelvoo for the formation of HIM. Contrary to her claims, Kelvoo's decision to move to Terra did not create the hate and the hunger for power on which the movement is built. I think that Kelvoo is very courageous for remaining on Terra, and I admire Kelvoo's willingness to share knowledge and insight at the university. Gloria Truscott's performance tonight was the tipping point for me, and that is why I am making this statement.

"I condemn the Human Independence Movement and the Humanity Party and the mindless hatred that they embody. I also condemn the Veritacity Network and any similar propagandists for furthering fear and ignorance. Today's event and its violent ending was a sickening travesty. I humbly and sincerely apologize for the part I played in it. That concludes my statement."

James and Laurexia started peppering Kaley with questions, but she responded to each one the same way: "No comment."

Liz took a different approach. She got out of her seat and knelt in the aisle next to me. Pointing her Infotab at me, she asked whether I had heard Kaley's statement and what I thought about it.

"I am grateful for Kaley Hart's statement," I replied. "Assuming it was sincere, I admire her courage. I will require time to digest her statement, and I will discuss it with my colleagues."

Before Liz could try another angle, a chime sounded, and an automated voice commanded us to fasten our restraints in preparation for reentry.

Later that night when we were back at home, May got up to go to her room to sleep. "I'm proud of you, Pa," she said.

"Are you sure about that, May? With the terrible way everything ended, I was concerned that you would be embarrassed by me."

"Oh, it was embarrassing alright," May replied, "but not because of you. I think your arguments were great. All Gloria Truscott did was lie and throw fits! And her supporters were so rude! They made me embarrassed to be the same species as them!"

May fiddled with the sleeve of her pajamas and then looked up. "I'm sorry I belted Brenna. I hope you aren't disappointed in me."

"Well, it looked to me as though she was trying to physically pull you over to the HP group," I replied.

"That's what I thought!"

"Then why don't we just put that down to self-defense?" I asked.

"Thanks, Pa. Love you. Goodnight."

"Love you too, sweetie, and thanks for all your support. Have a good sleep."

I had a surprisingly restful meditation that night despite the absurdity of the events in Lagos. I took comfort in the knowledge that I had made a strong case for the non-human minorities of Terra and that I had taken a stand against ignorance.

The next day I met with my media handler, Victoria. She had watched the debate intently. "I was hoping to analyze the points and counterpoints and come up with a strategy for future appearances," she remarked, "but the whole thing was so surreal that I couldn't concentrate. I ran an AI analysis on the recording, but even the AI was confused!"

"I'm not sure we should be concerned about future appearances," I replied. "I made my points, and I don't think there's anything further to be gained through additional appearances before the election."

Victoria was pleased to hear my opinion. She had come to the same conclusion but was worried about how I would interpret her thoughts.

In the evening, the Sagacity Club gathered. Dr. Stark had invited a special guest, Dr. Peter Probst, a statistician and polling expert. We welcomed him and introduced ourselves with our usual linguistic flourishes.

"How long hast thou 'probst' public opinion?" Dr. Sayed asked, demonstrating great amusement at her own wit.

Dr. Probst opened his mouth to speak, then paused as though trying to find the best wording. "What's wrong with you guys?" he said, shaking his head. He was smiling, so I assumed he wasn't overly perturbed. "Seriously, Dr. Stark has been suggesting that I try to become a member of your group, but first you'd have to drop all the 'pip pip and cheerio' nonsense!"

"I say, dear fellow," Jas exclaimed, "such expressions would be far too cliché for the likes of us! I recall us uttering nary a 'cheerio' nor a single 'pip'! Isn't that so, Dr. Kelvoo?"

"As a kloormar with perfect recall, I declare that I have not heard such words articulated by any member of this club, with the exception of the 'cheerio' and 'pip' just uttered by the good chancellor whilst refuting your claim, my good Dr. Probst!"

"Oh for eff's sake! You blowhards really need to lighten up!" Probst declared with sincere exasperation this time.

"Perhaps this will help," Jas said, handing Probst a snifter and pouring in a splash of brandy. With that, the meeting got underway, consumed by the topic of the travesty we had witnessed the previous day.

Dr. Sayed's view was that my debating points had been solid and convincing. Dr. Schlenk congratulated me on avoiding the temptation to stoop to my opponent's level, though she did enjoy my ability to counter interruptions by putting all of my vocal outlets to use. "My ears are still ringing!" she added.

Dr. Hoffman remarked that he couldn't say that any side won due to the shameful battle that ended the contest. "Let's just say that the Humanity Party could have done a better job of showing some humanity," he remarked.

Jas told me I'd done a superb job, but I had come to expect such support from Jas.

Finally, Dr. Stark said the debate was a solid win for me. "But rather than wagging our chins with opinions and conjecture, why not let our expert weigh in on this fascinating matter? Please, Dr. Probst, enlighten us."

"Um, yeah, sure thing, Lembe," he said, defying our pretentious delivery by using Stark's given name. "Well, my team began tracking public opinion and voting preferences for this election before campaigning even started and before there was a Humanity Party. So, Kelvoo, we took a snapshot of the level of support before your debate, then we performed real-time tracking during the debate, and we took another snapshot this morning.

"Three factors gave a tremendous boost to the Unity and Integrity Party among undecided voters. First was your debate performance. Second was the new low in atrocious behavior by Truscott and her crowd. And finally, there was Kaley Hart's defection, which hit the news early this morning. As a result of these three events, 89.7 percent of *undecided* voters declared they would now vote against HP, 7.2 percent were still undecided, and the remainder said they'd vote HP. That's the *good* news."

"Wonderful!" Jas said.

"Magnificent" Dr. Sayed added.

"Dr. Probst, you concluded your statement with, 'that's the *good* news,'" I said. "I have grown familiar enough with Terran idioms to conclude that there is a strong likelihood of an imminent statement that counters the good news."

"Yup," Dr. Probst replied with his familiar ineloquence. "The problem is that the undecided made up less than two percent of the electorate."

"Are we *really* that polarized?" Dr Sayed asked, "Are we so entrenched that we have all chosen our allegiance and cannot be swayed?"

"Not entirely," Probst replied. "When it comes to choosing between the traditional Unity and Integrity parties, voters can be swayed. Historically, people frequently switch allegiance between the two. Even now the lead between those parties switches back and forth almost daily. On the broader question of voting for one of the traditional parties versus the Humanity Party, however, our statistics indicate that we are as entrenched as you suspect."

"How could it have come to this?" Jas asked.

"Well, Chancellor," Dr. Probst replied, "without asking you for specifics, I assume you've decided whether to vote for one of the traditional parties or to vote for HP."

"Yes."

"So, what are the chances of you switching?"

Jas thought about it and then sighed. "I see your point."

Dr. Hoffman had been swirling a glass of port and seemed to be waiting for a pause in the conversation. Finally, one presented itself, "Enough of this frivolous banter!" he declared. "What are the numbers?"

"I have thousands of numbers, Dr. Hoffman," Probst replied. "Which numbers would you like?"

"Damn it, man! What percent of parliamentary seats do you predict each party will win? Please break these numbers down pre and post-debate."

"Okee-dokie Doc. Sheesh! All you had to do was ask! Pre-debate, Unity was at 32 percent of parliamentary seats, Integrity was 36 percent, and the Humanity Party trailed at 31 percent. As of three o'clock today, we have Unity at 33 percent, Integrity at 35 percent, and Humanity at

31 percent. In other words, the debate appears to have gained Unity 1 percent and cost Integrity 1 percent."

"That's all?" Stark asked.

Probst nodded. "Yes. That's all."

"To think, just a few months ago, the idea of HIM creating a political wing and winning almost a third of the vote would have been inconceivable," Dr. Sayed said. "The idea of a single hateful HPer polluting our government and spouting their hate in the legislature absolutely sickens me!"

"Well, that's democracy for you," Hoffman retorted. "Perhaps you have a better alternative?"

Before Dr. Sayed could answer, Dr. Schlenk jumped in. "Dr. Probst, without wishing to cast aspersions on the expertise of a gentleman such as yourself, how confident are you in your projections?"

"Not very," Probst admitted. "There are still six days to go with greatly intensified campaigning to be expected. The needle could move in either direction. There are also polling factors that could skew in HP's favor."

"Oh dear!" Dr. Schlenk said. "Are you referring perhaps to social desirability bias?"

"Impressive!" Dr. Probst declared in surprise. "Do you have some experience with polling?"

"No, sir, but as a historian, I have undertaken the study of appalling governments elected into office unexpectedly, often due to social desirability bias." Schlenk turned toward the rest of us and explained. "That's the effect of people being reticent to admit their true viewpoint to a pollster lest they be judged as socially unacceptable."

"Precisely, my good woman!" Probst replied, rolling his "r" and surprising us all with his effort to adopt our style of communication.

"Why, Dr. Probst, are you one of us now?" Jas asked with a smile.

"Nope. Just thought I'd try it. It's not for me!"

After some mild laughter, Jas sought to wrap things up. "Well, I suppose that's it. All we can do is wait for six more days. Shall we change the date of our next meeting and gather here a day early to watch the results?"

The regular members nodded and murmured their agreement.

"And what about you, good Dr. Probst?" Jas asked. "Would you be kind enough to join us and provide your enlightening analysis?"

"Sorry, guys. If there's going to be more of the jolly hockey sticks gobbledygook lingo, I'll have to give that a pass!"

"See here good fellow," Jas remarked. "How could we meet in this charming room with all of its refined elegance if not accompanied by refined language?"

"Could we, perhaps, meet at my home?" I ventured. "I'm certain that Miss May would be interested in witnessing the results with me. Also, those of you who wish to could bring a guest. If such an arrangement would suit you, Dr. Probst, then you would be most welcome.

"Hosting such an event would be a good social exercise for me," I added, "since I have never hosted any human visitors other than the Chancellor and Simon, or one or two of May's friends."

"If we meet at your place, could we drop the flowery talk?" Probst asked.

We all agreed, and I looked forward to the experience of hosting a gathering of adults.

As we parted ways for the evening, Dr. Probst waved to us. "Well, pip pip and cheerio then!"

The other humans laughed as he strode away.

TWENTY-THREE: THE VOTE

In the days between the debate and the election, I wasn't the only one lying low and avoiding the media. Gloria Truscott, of all people, did the same thing. Proponents of the Unity and Integrity parties suggested that her performance in the "Great Interspecies Debate" had shown her true nature, and now she was hiding from view, too ashamed to face the public. I thought otherwise, and I suspect that deep down, Truscott's critics did too.

The entire planet was buzzing with tension. Campaigning was in the home stretch with all of the credible polls showing the Humanity Party within striking distance of their opponents. HP's own polls were a different story, projecting that they would win a staggering 80 percent of the parliamentary seats. HP wouldn't release the sources of their data or the methodologies used, but they didn't hesitate to label all of the other polls as fraudulent.

My theory was that Truscott was itching to intensify her behavior and divisive rhetoric in those final days but was keeping a low profile for strategic reasons. I thought she may have been proud of herself and her supporters in the audience for their behavior at the debate. While most humans were revolted by her hatred and outrageous antics, her supporters seemed to gain energy and emotional sustenance from her vulgar behavior, and she may not have wanted to dilute her impact by saying anything more.

It was interesting to hear the change in tone coming from most HP candidates. They started talking about the Terran economy, social issues, and changes to regulations—exactly the same topics that were the bread and butter of the Unity and Integrity platforms. The traditional media continued to bombard the Truscovite politicians with questions about their anti-extraterrestrial stance. Where possible, the HP candidates side-stepped the questions or diverted to different topics.

When cornered, many HP candidates softened their stance with statements such as: "Of course, we're not suggesting immediate mass-deportation. We want to see a more gradual approach" or "I think we should start with a freeze on immigration, study the situation, and make adjustments as we go."

It seemed clear that HP was keeping Truscott out of the spotlight and scrambling to appear more reasonable and mainstream in a last-ditch effort to lure voters.

Jas and Simon were first to arrive at my home on election night. They came early, laden with a selection of beers, wines, spirits, and other assorted beverages. May was also busy preparing snacks, or as she termed them, "nibblies," for our guests. May had put Pollybot to work, ordering snacks, receiving them from the delivery drone, and arranging them in bowls and on platters.

May also decided she would try baking. Our well-equipped kitchen included an oven for those brave enough to attempt the ancient art of cooking. May had ordered a kit with pre-measured ingredients for the creation of food known as "oatmeal cookies." She needed Pollybot's assistance to blend the ingredients, so our servitor affixed a mixer attachment to one of its limbs, and May added the flour to a mixing bowl. As I walked by, I saw the whirling blades of the mixer head. "Watch your fingers, May!" I warned.

"I shall halt the mixing action if any part of a being enters the bowl below the upper rim," Pollybot assured me.

At one point, a large quantity of flour slid from the bag, hit the top of the mixer head, and billowed into the air, applying a white foundation to May's face and a fine layer of dust to the countertop. "This is harder than it looks, Pa!" she exclaimed.

When the mixing was done, Jas, Simon, and I watched the mysterious process with great interest as May took a flat metallic sheet, coated it with a thin layer of organic oil, and dropped dollops of gooey beige matter with flaky bits onto the sheet. May had obviously done her research as she informed us that back in the old days, it would have taken several minutes for the oven to reach the required temperature, and she would have had to place the sheet in the oven using a special protective glove in case of contact with a hot surface. "Good thing these ovens today get instantly hot!" she remarked.

May turned the oven on and asked Pollybot to alert her when twenty minutes had passed. Twelve minutes later, an alarm sounded, and an urgent message appeared on the oven's console and on every Infotab screen in the house: "Excess smoke detected—appliance shutdown and cooling initiated."

The oven took a full ten seconds to cool every hot surface inside it before unlocking. When May opened the oven door, smoke puffed out and rose to the ceiling. Pollybot's emergency override engaged as the servitor entered its ceiling hatch and retrieved a contaminant evacuation conduit. The bot connected one end of the flexible pipe to an extraction vent in the kitchen's exterior wall, then hovered at the ceiling and moved the pipe around to remove all traces of smoke, though a burning smell still lingered.

Frustrated, May looked at the instructions on the kit. "Dammit! Why am I so useless? I didn't notice the temperature setting! I just set it to the maximum!"

"May, you certainly aren't useless," Simon replied. "You just attempted an ancient practice that would take years to master! I'd never be brave enough to try any kind of cooking myself! So what if the oven was a little hot? In the end, they just came out of the oven *earlier*, so they'll probably turn out the same. Let's try one. Maybe they're really good!"

The oatmeal cookies were the same shape as the ones depicted on the kit's packaging, though the coloration was different. May's cookies were black and hard at the edges and on the bottom and semi-liquid in the middle, but if one took the average of the colors across the entire top surface, it would have come reasonably close to the image on the package.

May, Jas, and Simon each picked up a cookie and waved it in the air to cool it. Then Simon held a cookie up to his mouth and urged the others to do the same. "OK, one, two, three!" They each took a large bite. Then all three of them started sputtering. May ran to the sink and started a flow of water. Jas and Simon joined her as they spat the cookie remnants out, wetted their hands, and rubbed the black crumbs off their tongues. I asked them whether I should summon medical assistance, but they assured me that it wouldn't be necessary.

"The heat must have transformed the carbohydrates, leaving carbon behind," Jas surmised.

"I'm really disappointed in myself," May said.

"Well, did you learn anything from the experience?" Simon asked.

"I learned that I should read the instructions—carefully!"

"There you go!" Jas said. "Let's call it an experiment. With any experiment the results might be unexpected and disappointing, but as long as we learned something, it's a success!"

"Thank you, Jas, I mean Chancellor Linford."

"Just call me Jas."

"OK, Chancellor," May replied.

A few minutes later, the other guests started to arrive. Each sniffed the air, noticing the odor of recent combustion. May explained that they were smelling the results of her attempt at baking. That point of conversation allowed May to introduce herself and reduced her concerns about meeting my guests.

With the Sagacity Club meeting outside of its usual space, all pretentious banter was dropped, and we addressed one another by our given names—or in my case, my only name. Dr. Hoffman was Martin, Dr. Schlenk was Rosa, Dr. Stark was Lembe, Dr. Sayed was Mary, and our pollster was Peter.

When the last guest had arrived and was seated, May started toward the kitchen. "I'll get the nibblies, Pa!" she called back over her shoulder.

"Pa?" Rosa inquired.

"That was May's choice," I replied, "It doesn't mean papa or father. It's just short for parent, since I am May's foster parent."

"She seems like a great kid," Lembe remarked.

I was gratified to hear his comment. For some reason it felt good to know that a child in my care met with the approval of outsiders.

Jas took drink orders and then prepared the beverages while May, Simon, and Pollybot placed bowls and platters of snacks in front of the guests. I switched the vid system on. A panel was discussing the latest polls and developments. In a corner of the screen, a countdown clock ticked to indicate thirty minutes until the polls would close.

May had a lot of questions, and I was surprised she hadn't learned the specifics of Terran elections in school. Peter explained the voting system to her, and our historian, Rosa, provided some of the history of voting.

"Long ago, when democracy was young, it could take hours or sometimes even days to get the final results after the close of voting," Rosa said. "People had to cast their votes by marking paper ballots or using machines, often in buildings that they had to visit physically. Then the votes had to be tallied up in centralized locations, sometimes by hand."

"I'm surprised that worked," May replied. "So, nowadays, since a central AI does the count, and people program AIs, how do we know there's no cheating?"

Peter explained that each voter entered a code of their choice when they voted, and they could use that secret code after the election to check whether their vote was recorded correctly. He also pointed out that all of the voting data was made available to hundreds of third-party organizations that could check it independently.

My guests were impressed by May, admiring her thoughtful questions and curiosity, which pleased me.

Even though we were all tense in anticipation of the election results, the mood was upbeat and jovial. The adult humans consumed their nibblies and drinks and laughed at one another's remarks. They even laughed at my attempts, though I felt bad that I couldn't laugh back. Martin wasn't quite as engaged, often leaning close to the vid console to better hear the network commentators above the chatter.

176

At 18:59, the network started playing dramatic music. A countdown timer appeared in the corner of the screen, and a tick sounded as each second passed.

"Less than one minute remaining! If you haven't made up your mind yet, you'd better do so now because you have only forty-eight seconds left! So, if you've left it till the last minute, better get that Infotab out and lock in your vote right now!"

A buzzer sounded, and a new, five-minute timer appeared under the title, "Voting Closed – Electoral AI vote verification in progress." The technical analyst on the network panel explained the procedures that the AI was following before releasing the final results.

"Well, duh!" Peter exclaimed. "Talk about dumbing it down for people!"

As the countdown neared its conclusion, Mary wrung her hands as if feeling her knuckles for the first time. Lembe's feet tapped nervously. Rosa closed her eyes and repeatedly mouthed the words "It's OK. It's going to be fine." Jas held his palms together in an old-style praying position in front of his mouth as he bit his lower lip. Martin continued staring at the screen, perched on the edge of his seat, and Simon clutched an armrest with one hand and bit the side of one of the fingers of his other hand.

May got out of her chair and sat on the floor next to where I was squatting and clutched my upper arm. I don't think I displayed any outward signs of tension, but I perceived the countdown to be taking longer than five minutes.

Finally, a chime sounded. "We have the results of the Terran government election!" the announcer began. "The percent of seats won by each party is . . ." The screen displayed the results as he recited them. "Integrity Party, thirty-five percent." We all exhaled a sigh of relief with the knowledge that Integrity had exactly the figure from Peter's poll six days earlier. Then the next result appeared: "Unity Party, twenty-nine percent."

My mind could hardly process what I was seeing.

No, it can't be. There's been a mistake! That must be the figure for HP!

The third and final line of white text appeared over a wide shot of the studio, like an obscene joke shouted in the middle of a funeral: "Humanity Party: 36%."

Our group remained almost motionless, stunned by what we were seeing. Mary put a hand over her mouth. Lembe's feet were perched on their toes, shaking nervously. Rosa's eyes were wide and staring into the distance. Jas had his head back, his eyes on the ceiling, his mouth open, and his hands clutching the sides of his head. Martin shifted from the edge of his seat and settled back into his chair. Simon was bent forward, his hands cradling his chin and covering his mouth. May looked up at me and shook her head back and forth.

I remained motionless, but my mind was a frenzy of thoughts as I tried to calculate what the future might hold and attempted to keep my imagination at bay, terrified by the scenarios that it might concoct.

Peter the pollster was the first to break the silence. "Son of a bitch!" he said, his voice barely above a whisper. "We tried to factor it in, but that effing social desirability bias sneaked up and bit us!"

"Oh, Kelvoo. I'm so sorry," Mary said, looking devastated.

"Has humanity just lost its mind?" Simon asked. "I would have expected this to happen years ago on an outlier planet, but this is Terra! We're not like that!"

May turned to me. "Are we going to have to leave Terra now?"

Before I could reply, Jas jumped in. "No! Kelvoo, you're not going to do anything of the sort! Just the thought of you handing a victory to that Truscott creature is unthinkable!" Jas paused and took a deep breath. "Let's all just calm down for a moment. No, Simon, we haven't completely lost our minds because a large majority of Terrans voted for a party other than the effing 'Humanity' Party. Let's all just keep in mind that they're going to form a lame-duck government. I think we all know that the other parties are going to block *any* attempts to leave the Planetary Alliance and certainly any suggestion of deportations."

Most of the group nodded in agreement.

"I'm just so sad," Lembe remarked.

Jas stood and started pacing back and forth. "I'm furious and I want to scream! I just don't know what to do now!"

I don't know how or why I came up with the idea, but I stood. "I'd like to take a nice, calm walk to the beach. Who would like to join me?"

Within two seconds, everyone was walking toward the back entrance. "Hang on, I'm going back for my drink," Jas said. Immediately, all of the other human adults spun around and took the glasses or bottles they had left behind.

"Pollybot, follow us. Bring all beverage bottles that I brought here tonight," Jas commanded.

"Permission required from Kelvoo," the servitor replied.

"Permission granted," I said.

We walked into the still night air under a clear sky and thousands of stars. Luna shone brightly behind us, lighting the way. We walked in silence, despondent despite the lovely scene. As we reached the edge of the sand, Pollybot caught up with us, pushing a hovercart laden with clinking bottles. "You didn't have to bring the empties too!" Jas exclaimed.

"Sorry," Pollybot replied. "Exclusion based on emptiness was not specified." Even the servitor seemed depressed. I had to remind myself that a kloormar would not assign emotions to a machine. *I'm becoming far too much like these humans*, I mused.

We walked to a cluster of benches surrounding a fire pit. May wondered whether we could light a campfire. "I might have left some SimLogs in the shed when I moved out of the house," Jas said.

May asked Pollybot to take a look, and the servitor soon returned with a bundle. Pollybot hadn't been programmed to light a fire, so Simon piled the logs in the pit, then asked the bot for a light. Pollybot opened a flap on its side and pulled out an ignitor attachment. Simon held out a small stick and asked the servitor for a flame. When the stick caught fire, he pushed the burning end into the pile of wood.

"Who's ready to do some serious drinking?" Jas asked, draining the last of the wine from his glass and filling it with whiskey.

"Hear, hear!" Lembe replied as each adult human started imbibing anew.

We all stared at the flickering flames. They illuminated us in a soothing orange glow as we chatted about the state of Terra and the human species.

"I'm embarrassed to be human," May said. I had the urge to tell her that she was talking nonsense, but her feelings at that moment were genuine, and I couldn't bring myself to invalidate them.

"I just can't understand it!" Mary exclaimed. "How can a third of Terrans be so ignorant?"

"Our problem is that we live and work here at a university in a lovely little academic bubble," Peter said. "We don't associate with the type of people who would vote to dismantle the multi-species society that we've built."

"Well, at least none of us voted HP, right?" Mary asked. She looked at those of us on her left. The group shook their heads.

"Don't look at us," I said. "May's too young, and I haven't resided on Terra long enough to vote."

Mary turned to her right to look at Hoffman. His eyes were fixed on the fire.

"Martin?" she asked.

"Hmm?"

"Dr. Hoffman, surely you didn't vote for the Humanity Party?"

He didn't respond. He just kept staring at the fire.

"Oh, Martin, no! You couldn't have!"

"I bloody well did!" he barked.

We all sat there, stunned.

"But *why*, Martin?" Jas exclaimed.

"Well *maybe*, Chancellor, I just happen to like what they stand for."

"They stand for my removal," I replied. "Do you think I deserve to be expelled from this planet?"

"No, Kelvoo, I don't," he said, "but it's never going to come to that." Martin resumed his testy tone. "You're all running around clucking and fretting as if the whole world has ended! Get a grip! All this stuff about expelling all the extraterrestrials, it's just political rhetoric, and it's never going to happen. They just want to restrict immigration, which is fine with me!" Martin was slurring his words as his heavy consumption of alcohol was taking effect.

"Why in the world should non-humans be restricted from moving to Terra?" Simon asked. "Do you think humans are superior? Do you think you're better than Kelvoo here?"

"Of course not, you bloody fool! If the non-humans were inferior, I'd have no problem with 'em. The problem is they're *better* than us, especially the kloormari! Kelvoo is superior to all of us! The kloormari are smarter, they have better coordination, they can do multiple things at the same time . . ." Martin trailed off as he lost his train of thought. "Anyway, we can't just let 'em all in, or we'll end up as second-class citizens on our own planet!"

"But, Martin, if you feel that way, why did you come to our meetings?" Rosa asked. "And why did you continue to associate with us if you disagree so strongly?"

"Because the meetings used to be interesting and fun! I used to love coming and yapping about this and that and everything else, right up to the point that this kloormar started showing up, and we all started talking about damned politics! Every week I hoped the topic would change to something we could agree on, but instead I had to listen to all of your sanctimonious do-gooder 'every being is equal' nonsense. Did you ever notice that I wasn't interested? Did you ever ask me whether I felt differently? Of course not! You just assumed I'd be exactly like you because of your condescension to those who might not share your opinion, so I just sat there and kept my mouth shut!

"Just look at the things you people have said this evening," he continued, "Mary just called a third of humans ignorant! So, I'm ignorant, am I? And Mr. Pollster here, just a moment ago he talked about how we 'don't associate with the type of people' who would vote HP. And worst of all is this poor, impressionable child," he said, pointing to May.

"Hey, I'm fourteen!" May interjected.

"Do you remember what this girl said a moment ago?" Martin continued, undeterred. "She said she was *embarrassed* to be human! I couldn't believe it! And none of you said a word to reassure her!"

180

"*You* could have said something," Rosa pointed out.

"Hmph!" Martin replied, waving his hand in dismissal. "Anyway, I'm done with the lot of you!" he exclaimed, grabbing a bottle of beer, then turning and walking away, zig zagging down the beach.

Mary shook her head, "Dr. Martin Hoffman! Who'd have thought it?" she muttered.

A few human students wandered toward us. Two of the females in the group were crying and walking with their arms around each other's shoulders. The group had a sway in their gait, indicating some degree of intoxication.

"Hi," one of them called out to us.

"Want to join us for a while?" Jas asked.

"Thanks," one of the students replied.

As they drew near, one of the students recognized Jas. "Oh, jeez! Sorry, Chancellor Linford. Didn't recognize you in the dark! We'll move along. Sorry to disturb you!"

"No, I invited you, so now you have to come over and sit with us. I insist!"

As the students gathered to sit, some recognized me as well as a professor or two. "Oh my God! Are you Kelvoo?" one asked. I confirmed that I was, to their amazement.

"Oh no! Kelvoo, I'm so sorry! This must be so awful for you!" one of the teary-eyed girls sobbed.

"Not exactly the best day of my life on Terra," I agreed, "but for the moment, here by the beach, with the soothing sound of the waves, and with Luna and the stars above, it's hard to conceive that anything terrible is about to happen."

"That's so bee-oo-tee-ful!" a student slurred.

"It's so weird to think the whole world has changed, starting tonight," another mused while staring into the night sky.

Jas reassured the student that a lame-duck government wouldn't be able to accomplish their more offensive goals.

A short while later, Simon started singing "Building Bridges," and we all joined in. Just as we finished, Martin staggered back toward us. "Building Bridges!" he shouted in a mocking tone. "What a stupid song fer a bunch o' wusses!"

The shocked students stared at the disheveled man, his shoes and pant legs soaked with seawater, wet sand all over the seat of his pants and the back of his blazer.

"Oh, never mind him," Rosa said. "He's a silly old goat!"

Martin turned and walked back toward the house, weaving from side to side.

"Was that Professor Hoffman?" an astonished student asked.

After a while, the conversation died and the group of students wandered back from whence they came.

By that time, Luna had passed over us, and its reflection shimmered on the water. I asked if anyone wanted to go back to the house. No one did. May was getting tired, so she turned to our servitor, which had been dutifully hovering close by. "Please bring me a blanket, Pollybot," she said.

A few minutes later, May curled up beside me under her blanket and fell asleep. One by one our guests fell asleep, or their booze-soaked brains lost consciousness. Emotionally spent, I entered a deep meditative state.

We remained on the beach until the break of dawn the next day.

TWENTY-FOUR: LIFE GOES ON

We woke up covered in dew. My joints ached, my mind was slow, and I realized I was chilled, almost to the point of unconsciousness, which was the standard reaction of kloormari physiology to hypothermia. Though I was in considerable discomfort, I was in remarkably better condition than the adult humans. Peter held his head in his hands. "I think I might have caught a cold last night."

"More like the 'wine flu,'" Rosa said with a groan.

We stumbled back to the house like a procession of injured combatants returning home from a devastating defeat. May and Pollybot were the only members of our party who, apart from being damp and cold, didn't look much the worse for wear. We found Martin, who must have passed out in the back yard right after leaving us. He was on all fours, crawling from beneath the rear deck and then vomiting under a shrub.

I let my guests inside and then called over to Martin, asking him to join us.

"Gonna pass on that," he croaked. "Too embarrassed to face all of you. Going to call for a ride," he added as he pulled out his Infotab.

Once inside, Pollybot prepared coffee, tea, and plain toast for our guests. Most of them were lying on the floor or a sofa or slumped in chairs.

"Well, I suppose Gloria Truscott's feeling smug and happy this morning," Simon remarked.

"Not really," May said.

"Why's that?" he inquired.

"Well, while you lot were still conked out, I watched the news on my Infotab. The Unity and Integrity leaders gave their speeches. I couldn't believe how polite they were even though they lost. Matthew Scott promised that the Integrity Party would help HP take over, and he even offered his congratulations to Truscott. He must have a really strong stomach!

"Anyway, Truscott came on a little later. I thought she was going to thank her supporters or something, but instead she went off on a rant, saying the election was false and full of cheating! I mean, she won, but she wasn't happy at all! She said she should have won a huge majority!

The only promise she made was to investigate the election and bring the cheaters to justice!"

Mary was lying on the floor with a cushion under her neck. "Ohhh! Do we actually have to go to work today?" she moaned.

"Well, I think we'd better put in an appearance," Jas advised. "Maybe tell your classes that you're feeling ill, then give them some sort of assignment while you zone out at your desk. Let's just say that if you're late to class or you're not having your most productive day, I'm not exactly going to report you to the personnel department."

"It probably doesn't matter anyway," Rosa remarked. "HP isn't exactly big on education. We'll probably all be looking for new jobs next week."

***

The following week came and went, as did many weeks and months after that, without the mass deportations we had all been dreading. There was, however, a general worsening in human-extraterrestrial relations. The Humanity Party's wish for Terra's exit from the Planetary Alliance was self-fulfilling. In advance of election day, the Alliance met and decided that, if a member planet's government could be as toxic as HP was, then that planet's membership would be canceled.

Terra's immediate expulsion came despite howls of protest and pleading from the Terran delegation, the Terran opposition parties, and a great many humans across our sector of the galaxy. I had expected Truscott's reaction to be utter delight. Instead, she labeled the Alliance's actions as grossly unfair. "They just left us in the lurch without even giving us the chance to negotiate the terms!" she whined. The Alliance's response was that the Terran government was not in a position to negotiate and that it had nothing to offer, essentially telling the government that it had made its own bed and could now sleep in it.

The Alliance advised non-humans that it could not guarantee their safety on Terra, sparking a mass exodus that drained Terra of many of its best and brightest scientists, medical professionals, technologists, and business leaders. In addition to the extraterrestrials, in under a year, more than five hundred million humans with diverse talents had also emigrated, many settling on the outlier planets of Exile and Perdition, which came to be viewed as frontier worlds where expansion was welcomed and countless opportunities awaited. The media was filled with scenes of tearful goodbyes between family members and lifelong friends.

The Terran economy sank into torpor. Truscott's response was to blame all of Terra's woes on the "aliens" and saying that their revenge-driven plots were behind the economic troubles. There was no shortage of conspiracy theories from the Humanity Party as Truscott vowed that the "alien enemies" must be arrested, prosecuted, and punished as traitors.

The judicial system and the police had managed to purge themselves of radical elements, and they held firm against the government's demands, refusing to detain or try any individual or group without credible evidence. As a result, vigilante groups became increasingly cruel and violent in their attacks against the non-humans who were unable to leave or refused to depart out of principle.

From the first day of parliament after the transfer of power, the Humanity Party put forward one bill after another calling for the expulsion of all remaining non-humans. Each attempt was rebuffed by the coalition of the Unity and Integrity parties, whose representatives began to develop a newfound passion and eloquence that had been lacking in the bygone days of their effective but mundane governance. As legislation was debated, the opposition was scathing in its criticism of HP and its leader, prompting Truscott to call them lying co-conspirators and brand them as enemies of Terra.

Much to the relief of the great majority of students and faculty, the university was relatively unscathed. Apart from the occasional outburst from a dwindling number of HIM and HP supporters, who were duly ignored, the campus persisted as an oasis of calm on a beautiful but troubled planet.

The Sagacity Club continued to meet despite Dr. Hoffman's departure. We did, however, welcome Dr. Probst who thought he should give it a try despite the grandiloquence of our conversations. Although he grew to enjoy the pompous banter, we gradually toned down our bombast. It seemed we had grown emotionally closer to one another, having shared our post-election devastation, followed by our commiseration on the beach beneath the stars and Luna's pale luminescence.

Several months into Truscott's reign, each member of the club received a heartfelt message from Dr. Hoffman. He apologized for his hostility, admitting that recent events had not unfolded as he had hoped. We invited Martin back to the club, but from his lack of a response, we assumed he remained too embarrassed to face us.

With my classes discontinued and my media appearances curtailed, I had more time to spend with May and pursue activities that interested me. This included corresponding with my old friends from the first-contact expedition. They had kept in touch since my reunion with them, but until the election, I'd only had time to reply in a perfunctory manner. Now I was able to take more of an interest in their lives as we shared our thoughts and news regarding the changes transforming Terran society. Some encouraged me to leave Terra before matters became worse while others shared their admiration and encouraged me to remain.

At one point I reached out to Kaley. I felt pity for her. She was reviled by the majority of Terrans for her past allegiance to HP almost as much as she was now hated by the Truscovites for withdrawing her support. Kaley replied that she was moved by my offer of friendship even though she felt that she didn't deserve it. Kaley's career as a broadcast journalist was over, but she was getting by through speaking engagements and by writing articles describing her personal journey.

During those uncertain times, I took pleasure in visiting Kroz more often. I was nervous whenever I exited the university's security perimeter to visit the aviation center, even though it was just a few meters away. Kroz enjoyed showing me *Midge* and updating me with progress reports.

One day, Kroz invited me to watch a test flight. *Midge* rose inside the hangar, and we walked behind the vessel as it exited through the hangar doors and hovered over the landing strip. Technicians carried sensor-encrusted dummies toward *Midge*. Each dummy simulated a different species through variation in its shape and the density of its ballistic gel body. The dummies were secured inside *Midge* and then Kroz and I returned to the building and entered a room with dozens of monitors surrounding us. Kroz explained that *Midge* would transmit telemetry from the dummies' sensors while following a pre-selected flight path. On its return, *Midge* would be opened, and the dummies would be inspected.

We watched a wide-angle view of the landing strip on a monitor. After a countdown, *Midge* shot straight up to an altitude of five hundred meters so fast that it almost seemed to vanish and then reappear high in the air. After hovering for a few seconds, *Midge* moved horizontally to the east, covering two kilometers in a fraction of a second. The g-forces that would have been exerted on a normal vessel and its contents would have been instantly fatal to its occupants. *Midge* continued to slam itself to and fro, side to side, and up and down repeatedly before touching down on the tarmac.

Kroz and I stood outside and watched as the technicians removed the dummies or, more accurately, pieces of the dummies, which had been ripped apart.

"I'm sorry, Kroz," I said. "It appears that *Midge* is not yet working as intended."

"On the contrary, Kelvoo, the test flight has been a remarkable success!" Kroz replied.

Kroz went on to tell me that my reaction would have been different if I had seen the previous test. "The effect on the dummies was so severe that the ballistic gel had liquefied. The liquid coated *Midge's* interior and then congealed. We spent a week peeling the remains of the dummies from every interior surface!"

Kroz was about as thrilled as a kloormar could be, but Kroz cautioned me that it would take more than a year of adjustments to the dampening field before they would expect any dummy to remain "alive" after a test flight and much longer after that before *Midge* could be certified to carry any living being.

Kroz would often visit me at home where we would discuss technical matters well into the evening, something I found fascinating but which May called "sooooo boring"!

About six months into Truscott's reign, I returned to teaching two classes per week in the rebuilt humanities study hall. I had to be accompanied and guarded by a security team, and access to the building was limited to students with passes, who had to be screened for weapons before entry was granted. The government got wind of my return to teaching, and Truscott railed against me "spreading lies and serving as an enemy of the humans," but without support from the other parties, there was nothing she could do about it.

So, life continued on Terra, Truscott continued railing against imaginary enemies, and the opposition kept blocking her most egregious initiatives.

In her speeches, Truscott kept repeating that the "day of reckoning" was coming for the opposition and the aliens. As time passed, even though her warnings became more intense and frequent, they faded into the background noise of Terran life, dismissed by most Terrans as the ravings of a madwoman.

TWENTY-FIVE: BROTHERHOOD

On the morning of the day of reckoning, Kroz was visiting me in my home over breakfast. While Kroz and I each digested a bowlful of algel, May consumed peanut butter on toast.

My Infotab alerted me to an urgent message from Jas that told me to turn on the news immediately.

May leaped toward the entertainment console and selected the Atlantic News Network. The announcer was in the middle of an update regarding "the sudden arrival of dozens or possibly hundreds of large spacecraft in close proximity to Terra."

Vid feed was coming in from satellites, which used their telescopic cameras to view the visitors.

"We have learned that the visitors are jumping to regions of space about half a million kilometers above the North and South Pole," the announcer said.

"They can't do that! That's illegal!" Kroz exclaimed. Kroz was referring to the fact that there were designated jump points in the Sol system, marked on every star chart, pre-surveyed to ensure they were free from particles that could destroy a vessel that materialized there.

We realized that if a vessel was going to risk a jump to Terra's immediate vicinity, it would be safer to materialize above or below Terra's rotational plane. Nonetheless, there were still plenty of objects, debris, or natural matter that could be in a circumpolar orbit or just passing by.

The network showed the cam sat feed of the northern sector where ships had been materializing. We watched as light from the stars started to waver and flicker, resolving into the shape of a spacecraft just before it appeared in a flash of light. The vessel then accelerated away from the area to avoid the vessel behind it.

We were horrified to see a vessel materialize and immediately break apart, sections of its hull spinning outward in an ever-expanding disc of debris that included the bodies of its crew. Subsequent ships started appearing at a new location, farther from Terra.

"What's wrong with these fools?" Kroz asked. "They keep coming! They don't seem to care that they're losing some of their ships!"

"Joining us is Liz Underwood at a hastily announced news briefing from the Ministry of Interstellar Relations," the newscaster announced.

The vid switched to a split screen. One side showed a nervous bureaucrat walking toward a podium, while the other showed more vessels appearing.

May moved from the sofa and sat on the floor next to me. "Pa, I don't like this!" she said. "What's going on?"

"I don't know anything apart from what we're seeing on the screen," I replied. "Stay close to me, and try to keep calm. We don't seem to be in any danger, and there's probably a perfectly good reason for these ships to visit." I'm not sure whether my response reassured May. It didn't do anything to reassure *me*.

As the bureaucrat reached the podium, a gaggle of reporters shouted questions. The official looked at his Infotab screen, then held up a hand. "Just a moment. I'm still receiving updates."

When he looked up, a reporter shouted above the others. "Who are the visitors, and why are they here?"

"We don't know," the official replied.

"Have you tried to communicate with them?" another reporter shouted.

"We've tried, but they haven't responded."

"Do the visitors pose a threat?"

"We have no information that would indicate a threat at this time."

"Where are the visitors from? Has anyone determined the vessels' origin?"

"We have consulted with outside experts, but they can't agree. What's confusing is that the vessels seem to be pieced together from various components. Most of the ships appear to be based on Terran configurations, but they include plenty of Sarayan components along with bits and pieces of Mangorian, Silupan, and Bandorian technology. We also know that much of the technology is old, some of it going back fifty years. There are also vessel configurations or parts that none of the experts can identify."

Liz Underwood took her turn next. "What does the ministry intend to do about it?"

The official inhaled, held his breath for a moment as if to speak, then closed his eyes and shook his head while exhaling. His action seemed to indicate exhaustion or exasperation. "There is nothing we *can* do next. As I'm sure you're aware, since the change in power, our ministry's budget and staffing levels have been slashed by close to ninety percent. In light of the fact that interstellar relations have all but ended, those of us who remain have been working to shut the ministry down and transfer our remaining responsibilities to other ministries.

"We still have spacecraft that we could send to try to make contact with a few of the visitors, but we can't act without a directive from the minister or the prime minister. We have requested permission to launch, but the higher powers have not given us a reply or any indication of what to do next. We are prepared to deploy our minimal resources, but we are holding for authorization."

"If Terra is in danger, how do we defend ourselves?" another journalist asked.

"You're asking the wrong guy," the defeated bureaucrat replied. "You know as well as I do that, as a member of the Planetary Alliance, protection was always provided by the Sarayans. That's why at least one Sarayan warship would be in orbit at any given time, and a patrol vessel was always ready to screen arrivals at each Sol system jump point."

"Have the Sarayans been contacted? Has their assistance been requested?"

"Not by us. We have asked for permission to contact them, but we have had no direction from the political leadership. Now, I'm sure that all kinds of organizations and individuals across Terra have been burning up the quantum entanglement relays, telling the Sarayans about the situation and asking them for all kinds of things. What we need to understand is that, even if the Sarayans were interested in helping, they would never make an illegal jump. With the nearest jump point being thirteen hours from Terra, they couldn't exactly swoop in like an ancient cavalry brigade. Furthermore, we can't assume that the Sarayans would be interested since Terra is no longer in the Alliance. The bottom line, and what we all need to understand is, no more Alliance means no more defense!"

The pack of journalists erupted, shouting all at once.

"Hang on! Hang on!" the bureaucrat said. "Let's not get all panicky yet! As I said before, we haven't received any indication that the visitors are hostile. We all need to calm down and see what happens."

The half of the screen that was showing the cam sat feed was replaced by the newscaster. Audio from the briefing was turned down as the news anchor spoke. "We have been contacted by Amélie Rosenbaum, an AI programmer and member of the Terran Amateur Observer Club. Ms. Rosenbaum, I understand you've been working with other members around Terra to gather more information about the visitors."

A vid feed of Amélie Rosenbaum appeared. "Yes, thank you," she replied. "I have set up an AI program to receive input from our member observers around the globe as well as a number of orbital cam sats. My AI is tracking the path of each visitor ship and looking for any commonalities between the vessels."

"Have you found anything noteworthy?"

"Yes. The vessels are spreading out over Terra's land masses. They are more concentrated over the more populated parts of Terra. We've been capturing 3D images of each vessel and cataloging them. We're posting the images to the club's infosite. The AI has noticed one thing that the smaller vessels have in common."

"What might that be?" the newscaster asked.

"The smaller vessels have large tube-shaped objects attached to their outer hulls. The bigger vessels with large hatches don't have these attachments, but it's possible that these tubes could be stored inside the larger vessels."

"Just a moment," Amélie said, looking to one side. "I've just received a clearer image of one of the small vessels, and I'm seeing what looks like exhaust nozzles at one end of the tubes."

"So, these tubes, are they rockets or, or maybe missiles?" the newscaster asked.

"I don't know, but it looks like they're built to move!"

"Do you have an update on the trajectory of the visitor ships?"

"Hang on. Yep, they're slowing down relative to Terra's surface. I think they're finalizing their positions. For what purpose, I don't know."

"Pa, I'm getting scared," May said in a tremulous voice.

Moments before, Kroz had activated an auxiliary monitor next to the main entertainment panel. Kroz was viewing the infosite for the Terran Amateur Observer Club and was browsing through images of the visiting spacecraft. As Kroz flipped past it, one of the vessels caught my eye.

"Kroz! Would you please go back five images?"

The fuzzy image of a large supply vessel glared back from the screen.

"Kroz," I said, unsure whether I wanted to confirm my suspicion, "please rotate the image forty-seven degrees left and ten degrees down." Kroz did just that. "No!" I exclaimed, my suspicion almost certainly confirmed. "That's the *Bountiful*!"

"The what?" May asked, turning toward me.

I didn't want to answer, but Kroz jumped in. "The *Bountiful* was a supply vessel that rendezvoused with *Jezebel's Fury*. Most of the crew took shore leave there. It's possible that the visitors are from the missing Brotherhood fleet."

May flew into a full-on panic, and I wasn't far behind. "Oh God no!" she exclaimed between shallow breaths. "We gotta get outta here! We gotta hide! We gotta get off this planet!"

"Please calm down, May," I said. "We need to think this through."

"Don't you see, Pa?" May said as she started sobbing. "They've come back for me! They're gonna kill you to get revenge for *Jezebel's*

Fury, and they're gonna take me back and force me to be a gangster! We gotta get outta here now!"

May started running back and forth in such a blind panic that I had to restrain her.

I needed to share what we had learned with all Terrans. As I held May with my clasper limbs, I grabbed my Infotab and used the tendrils on one of my hand paddles to send a message to Liz Underwood:

From Kelvoo. Recognized a visitor vessel. Name: Bountiful. Origin: Criminal outlier organization known as the Brotherhood.

At that moment, the news anchor interrupted Amélie Rosenbaum. "I'm getting word that the rockets or missiles have separated from the visitor ships and are heading toward Terra!"

"Yeah, my AI has noticed that. They're accelerating, and they're following a straight trajectory. The AI estimates they'll hit the surface in just over three minutes!"

May stopped struggling against my grip, transfixed with terror. "We're all gonna die," she muttered.

My mind raced with horror as memories of my captivity by a Brotherhood gang came to the fore. I relived the degradation, abuse, and torture that Kroz and I and our kloormari teammates endured. Once again I saw the crimes that the human gang had committed against their fellow humans and, worst of all, the murder of little Sam, the kloormari baby that I had given birth to during the terrifying ordeal.

"Amélie, can you tell us where they're headed?" the newscaster asked with great urgency.

Amélie turned and commanded the AI. "Display targets of tubular objects on course to impact Terra based on current trajectories." After a moment, she turned back to the camera. "I'm just getting a series of coordinates. Let me ask differently." She turned again to address the AI. "Is there a commonality between the targets? Answer via audio output."

"Affirmative," the AI replied. "Estimated targets are properties known as devotion centers. All devotion centers are owned and operated by an organization known as the Human Independence Movement."

The newscaster opened his mouth, but couldn't produce a word. Likewise, May, Kroz, and I remained silent and motionless.

Kroz asked rhetorical questions, which was unusual for a kloormar. "Why? Why would the Brotherhood return after going missing for so many years? And why are they attacking HIM? What could they possibly have to gain?"

"I don't know, Kroz," I replied, "but I can't imagine the Brotherhood doing anything without immense gain for themselves."

"Maybe they see an opportunity to take over Terra, with such a weak government in place and no support from the Planetary Alliance," Kroz speculated.

"Perhaps the government found them, and they're attacking to keep their existence a secret," I said. "No, that makes no sense," I continued, correcting myself. "If that were the case, they'd be attacking government facilities, not HIM devotion centers."

May looked up at my eye dome. "Maybe they're here to save the non-humans," she said.

"Oh, May!" I replied, heartbroken. "I wish I could believe you, sweetheart."

From that moment until impact we watched with stunned disbelief as the incoming projectiles rained down on the fragile planet we had come to love.

PART 3: COLLAPSE

TWENTY-SIX: DELIVERY

In the final minute before impact, news coverage bounced from one vid feed to another, from a cam sat tracking an incoming missile to a drone's view above a devotion center to crowds gathered in a major city, their eyes fixed on the sky, watching in silent anticipation.

"Look! The missile's going off course!" May shouted as a satellite camera showed a rocket about to penetrate the outer atmosphere.

"You're right, May!" I exclaimed. "Its engine has stopped, and it's turning! Maybe the missiles are failing!"

"Is the Brotherhood just sending the government a warning?" May asked.

"It isn't turning," Kroz said. "It's pivoting around its center of mass."

We stared as the plunging interloper completed its flip. When its exhaust nozzles were pointing at the ground, drogue fins flipped out at the base of its nose faring, and its engine reignited, slowing its descent.

The newscaster was flummoxed. "Standby," he said. "Just a moment. Word is coming in. It appears that the missiles—I mean rockets—it looks like they're going to land!"

"No kidding!" Kroz remarked with uncharacteristic sarcasm.

A satellite camera zoomed to follow the rocket, which intermittently fired its engines to decelerate as it descended through broken cloud. In the breaks between clouds, we saw the outer walls of a HIM devotion center with the rocket heading for flat land in the center of the compound. Before the rocket touched down, clouds drifted over, obscuring our view.

The network switched to vid from a drone hovering over a different devotion center. The vid feed showed a rocket closing in to land. The compound's courtyard was devoid of beings as landing legs deployed from the rocket's lower body. With a final burst of fire and smoke and a spray of dirt blasted from the ground, the vessel touched down, and its engines shut off.

Against the backdrop of the devotion center, the scale of the rocket became obvious. Its body must have been twenty meters in diameter and ten or more stories high. Over a thousand Truscott devotees in red jumpsuits poured out of the devotion center and ran across the courtyard or rode hoverlifts to the vessel as a hatch opened on each side, a third of the way up from the ground.

Hoverlifts stacked high with crates emerged from each hatch and flew toward buildings that surrounded the courtyard. As the hoverlifts left the rocket, other lifts rose to the hatches and hovered beside them while onboard bots helped the Truscovites to unload additional crates. The offloading operation was extremely efficient with one hoverlift after another taking away a new load. The crates were color coded. White crates were taken to one building, blue crates to another, and so on. Black, red, green, and yellow crates followed. We sat in silence for seven minutes, which was all the time required to offload the rocket.

As new developments were announced, we learned that one or more rockets had landed at each devotion center and were being offloaded in the same highly organized manner. Within fifteen minutes of the first rocket landing, all but a handful of the hundreds of devotion centers had completed their offloads.

May, Kroz, and I watched as the news reports became clearer. At one point, Liz Underwood cited a source's suggestion that the visitors could be associated with the long-missing Brotherhood criminal network. Her statement may have indicated that she received my earlier message.

In some of the more populated areas, police and customs agents had stationed themselves outside the walls of devotion centers. While the unauthorized landings and lack of customs clearance constituted regulatory violations, the authorities had no legal right to enter and perform a search without evidence of criminal activity or intent. All they could do was request permission to enter to inspect the newly delivered cargo. They stood outside and waited for responses from each compound's leadership.

The networks started bringing in experts and a few posers, anyone who could come up with a semi-plausible theory about who the visitors were and what they had delivered and anything to quench the public's urgent need to understand what they were seeing. My assertion that the visitors were likely from the Brotherhood had become just another ingredient in a great mélange of hypotheses.

From the moment it became known that the visitors had targeted the devotion centers, the media began requesting information from the leadership of HIM. Fifty minutes after the first landing, the networks interrupted their coverage to announce that the Humanity Party had given ten minutes' notice that Prime Minister Gloria Truscott would be making a statement.

I received a message from Jas asking if he could come over. He arrived two minutes after I replied.

May, Jas, Kroz, and I waited along with the entire planet. Media outlets and private citizens launched drones to provide vid from above the devotion centers. The networks frantically switched between feeds. Each compound was eerily devoid of movement as the devotees had returned into the buildings while the empty rockets stood in menacing silence.

May was terrified, trembling as she clung to my arm.

Drone vid came in from a compound that was surrounded by police and other authorities. We watched as hundreds of Truscovites swarmed the top of the compound walls. They were carrying objects, but the drone was too far away to discern enough detail.

Balls of blue light flew from atop the walls. I don't think Jas understood what he was seeing at first, but the scene was horrifyingly familiar to May, Kroz, and me.

May screamed while Kroz and I hugged our knees to our chests in dread as the orbs of blue plasma ripped through the flesh of the authorities surrounding the compound. A few of the police drew blaster pistols to shoot toward their assailants, but they were cut down by the far more powerful and accurate blaster rifles in the hands of the HIM disciples. The authorities fled, but they didn't get far. The drone descended to survey the scene outside the compound walls, passing over charred, broken bodies, some dismembered or with their entrails splayed out.

One police officer was alive, hunkered down behind a tree in a plasticrete planter. Whenever she tried to look around the side of the planter, plasma shots tore up the ground beside her. A moment later a projectile arched up from the wall and landed a few meters behind the officer. The plasma mortar detonated, flinging her body parts, mingled with pieces of the planter and tree over a wide area.

For centuries before that day of horror, Terra had been free from war and mass murder. The limited number of weapons on Terra had only been accessible to a small number of law enforcement officers.

Having never seen anything like the mayhem unfolding on their screens, the newscasters, journalists, and guests were overwhelmed. Some broke down and cried while others were nearly catatonic. May sat beside me on the floor, and Jas was on the sofa on my other side. Both were weeping.

The networks switched to a broadcast from an auditorium filled with thousands of Truscovites in red jumpsuits, each one with a blaster rifle slung on their back. They stood in a grid pattern, reminiscent of ancient military vids, chatting excitedly with one another. "Attennn-huh!" a disembodied, amplified voice shouted. The Truscovite troops snapped to attention as military music played, and Gloria Truscott stepped onto the stage with her signature red robe and outlandish appearance.

"Today we celebrate a new beginning!" she shrieked, spreading her arms and shouting over the heads of her assembled soldiers. Her voice echoed as she paused for effect between sentences. "Today we take back what belongs to us! Today the universe shall bear witness to our reclamation of humanity! Starting now, we shake off the shackles of our subservience to lesser species! Starting now we shall, on behalf of all *true* humans, purge the contaminants that have plagued us! Starting now the cleansing begins as we wipe clean the alien filth that has stained our wonderful planet! Starting now we throw the windows open as we let in the fresh air of a glorious new era to rid ourselves of the stench of the oppressors and those who have enabled them!"

Jas wiped a tear from his cheek and cast his reddened eyes toward me. "We need to get you off this planet!" he said. "You too," he added, turning to Kroz.

"Well, I'm coming too," May said.

Truscott was far from finished. "While today is the most glorious moment in human history, our struggle is far from over. Our enemies have been conspiring against us. They have been stockpiling weapons of all sorts with the backing of the Planetary Alliance! They have been planning our overthrow for a long time! That's why we had no choice but to arm ourselves and take decisive action!"

"How can she possibly think we're involved in a conspiracy?" Kroz asked.

"She doesn't," Jas replied. "The only thing we need to know about Truscott and her followers is that if they're speaking, they're lying."

"In the interest of protecting our species," Truscott continued, "I am reluctantly implementing the following *temporary* measures. First, I am declaring martial law. All civilians shall obey commands issued by my troops, which you can identify by their distinctive red uniforms. I grant my brave soldiers full discretion to use lethal force as a consequence to those who disobey.

"Second, I declare a curfew from sunset to sunrise. Only my loyal troops are permitted to be outside after curfew. Violators may be detained or executed on sight.

"Third, all spaceports are officially closed. There shall be no off-world arrivals or departures until further notice. This travel ban will be enforced by our wonderful allies who have made their special deliveries to our devotion centers. They have stationed spacecraft and weapons bots in orbit that will immediately destroy any unauthorized craft that exceeds a semi-orbital altitude."

I turned to Jas. "So much for getting us off this planet."

"Fourth," Truscott continued, "during the tribulations ahead of us, humanity will require strong, decisive leadership. Decisions will have to be made instantly without the inherent delays of legislative bodies or committees. Therefore, it is with great reluctance and the utmost humility that I am stepping forward and taking on the monumental burden of serving you as supreme leader of Terra."

Truscott continued her well-prepared rant. She commanded all existing law enforcement officers to abandon or destroy their weapons and uniforms and stay in their homes. She also ordered all members of the political opposition who were not already detained to go to their homes and remain there. She put all media outlets on notice that they had better stop broadcasting their "biased, fraudulent news stories" or face criminal charges, and she declared that the Veritacity Network was the only officially sanctioned, trusted information outlet.

"I have a message for all aliens on Terra," she declared. "It doesn't matter how many generations your ancestors have lived on Terra, what career you have had, the work you have done, or what your social or economic standing might be. If your species is not human, you are an *alien*.

"I hereby command all aliens to remove themselves from public view and self-isolate indoors, where you are to remain until further notice. While humanity's hatred toward you is fully justified, we are not without mercy. As I speak, arrangements are being made for your safe passage back to your homeworlds where you can live with those of your sort in whatever foul, depraved ways you see fit, never to sully us again. You shall standby for further instructions in the coming days."

Truscott surveyed her gathered troops. "Now go forth and reclaim Terra!" she shouted.

The troops remained at attention.

"Well, what are you waiting for?" she demanded, "Dismissed!"

With the signal given, the soldiers roared their support as they turned and ran toward the exits, jamming their way through the doors and out into a deadly, dangerous world.

"Let's get you out of this house!" Jas said, his tears replaced by a steely determination. "The three of you, get your most important belongings, and let's go!"

"I will not be going with you," Kroz said. "I have to return to the aviation center immediately to preserve my work and my research."

"It's not safe!" Jas said.

"We are a long way from any devotion centers," Kroz retorted. "It will take time for Truscovite militants to arrive. I have places I can go that will be as safe as anywhere else, but my work is of the utmost importance."

"More important than your own life?" I asked.

"Yes. More important than any of you realize and far more important than a single kloormar's life!"

With that, Kroz entered the aviation center car outside the house, which made a beeline for the university's landing strip.

I grabbed my algel incubation vat, May threw her toiletries and some clothing into a bag, and we headed out of the house toward Jas's car. We were all in a state that I would describe as a controlled panic.

"What about Pollybot?" May shouted, looking back at the house.

"I'm sure our bot will be safe," I said with as much reassurance as I could muster. "Perhaps we can come back for Pollybot in a while when things are a little more certain."

"Goodbye house," May murmured.

For reasons I can't explain, I quietly echoed May's farewell to our home.

As the car sped across the campus, Truscott's troops were making their way across Terra. Millions of them spewed out of their devotion centers across the planet, fanning out into cities, towns, and villages, and surrounding, entering, and supposedly "securing" spaceports, hospitals, and other vital locations.

The lethal hordes spread like a toxic miasma, moving like mindless masses but also following a carefully choreographed plan.

TWENTY-SEVEN: WAITING TO LEAVE

The car took a circuitous route to the building that housed Jas's office. "OK, the first thing we need to take care of is locator extractions for the two of you. I'm going to need to find someone trustworthy who can get it done," Jas said.

"Could Dr. Charlie Bergen take care of that?" I asked. "You may remember that he came to May's aid when she almost drowned."

Jas called Dr. Bergen. "I have an emergency situation here, Charlie. Could you come over with a kit for minor surgery? We have a couple of lumps for you to remove, if you know what I mean."

Dr. Bergen arrived a few minutes later and was astonished to see May and me again.

"May," he said, "do you remember where on your body your locator was implanted?"

"Here, on my right arm," May replied, pointing to the midpoint on the lateral side of her forearm.

"OK, I'm going to scan to confirm the exact spot and then I'll give you a local anesthetic and make a small incision. We'll get that nasty little thing out of you nice and fast and then I'll rinse the area and join the sides of the incision back together. It'll be sore for a day or two after that, but it shouldn't be a big deal.

"As for you, Kelvoo," he said, turning to me, "I've never had the occasion to perform any medical procedures on a kloormar. Under normal circumstances, I'd refuse to treat you, but in this case I understand the urgency of your situation. As you're probably aware, what makes this tough is no anesthetics are known to work on kloormari physiology. Sure, we could refrigerate you until you're unconscious, but the risks of that are too great for minor procedures. In other words, this is going to hurt." He looked directly at my eye dome. "A lot!"

May and I assured the doctor that he had our consent.

Dr. Bergen removed a disposable towel from his bag and unrolled it onto a table. May rested her arm on the table where the doctor used a handheld scanner to find the locator implant. He used a microspray pen to paint a line for the incision.

"OK, May, I want you to make a fist and then release it over and over again while I spray a local anesthetic and antiseptic on you."

Dr. Bergen used a short medi-wand to apply the solution just below May's elbow. After pumping her fist three more times, May's hand stopped moving. "I can't feel my arm past my elbow," she said.

"That's exactly what we want. Alright, May, you look away while I make the incision."

"I'd rather watch if it's OK with you."

"Why would you want to do that?"

"I want to get used to seeing gross stuff. There's a lot of gross stuff happening on this planet right now. Things are going to get tough, so I'm going to need to get tough too!"

I observed Jas standing behind May. Her words made him scrunch up his face as if he felt despair that a teenage girl was preparing herself for a world that was now embracing the worst of adult human behavior.

Dr. Bergen cleared his throat and swallowed as if he was also suppressing an emotional response. "You must be very proud of her," he said to me.

"No, doctor," I replied, "pride would imply that I am responsible for May's courage. I can assure you that her bravery comes from her experiences and her character. Instead, I would say that I have tremendous admiration for her and I am privileged to know her."

"Can we get this done, please?" May asked.

She watched intently and Jas looked away. The doctor held a device a few centimeters above the incision mark. A dot from a green laser oscillated over the line. Dr. Bergen touched a button with his thumb, and the green light was replaced by an orange beam that appeared in conjunction with a short "snap," followed by a few wisps of smoke. May's skin parted along the three-centimeter incision, revealing tissue to a depth of about five millimeters. He used a small pair of tweezers to remove a silver capsule that was about the size of a grain of rice. Then he irrigated the opening with a purple liquid, pushed the sides of the incision back together, and covered the area with clear, adhesive tape. He pulled out a different handheld device with a roller on the end of it. The device buzzed and vibrated as Dr. Bergen moved the roller down the length of the wound, leaving behind skin that was now fused together, leaving only the faintest hint of a red line under the clear tape.

"OK, I'm going to give you your arm back now," he said as he pressed another button and rolled the device over the surgical site one more time. "Pump your fist for me."

May regained the use of her arm below her elbow. "Do you feel a bit sore where we took out the locator?" Dr. Bergen asked.

"Yeah, but only a little."

"Alright, May," he said, "Do you want me to pull the tape off nice and fast or gently and slowly, or would you just like to wait a few days for it to fall off?"

May's response was to slip a fingernail under the tape to raise a corner. Grabbing it, she jerked the tape and pulled it off, complete with the arm hair that had adhered to it.

Dr. Bergen's eyes opened wide, and his eyebrows rose to his hairline. "Impressive!" He chuckled. Jas and May laughed, and we all felt better for the brief moment of levity.

My surgery came next. "Before we start," Dr. Bergen said, "I once read a research article about pain management in kloormari patients. I recall there was some kind of meditation technique where the kloormar actually embraces the pain, processes it in the four brain centers, and distributes it over a wider area of the body. Does that make any sense?"

"Actually, I think it might," I replied.

As Dr. Bergen scanned the area of my arm that I had indicated, I closed my eyelid and entered a shallow meditative state. I concentrated on visualizing the redistribution of the pain that I was about to feel. I felt him mark the area and heard him pick up the incision device. "OK, just let me know when you're ready," he said.

"Please proceed," I replied.

The snap of the device and the sharp burn of the incision beam were painful. Instead of trying to distract myself, I concentrated on the intensity of the pain and then thought about my other arm, my torso, my clasper limbs, and my legs. To my surprise, the agony from my arm diminished while a dull ache spread across the rest of my body. As unpleasant as the ache was, it was a considerable improvement.

After the extraction, Dr. Bergen tried to seal my wound with tape, but it wouldn't adhere to my skin. I ended my meditation and was pleased to see that my pain continued to be dispersed. I suggested wrapping the tape around my arm several times, which worked well as the tape adhered firmly to itself. I reminded Dr. Bergen that my kloormari physiology had excellent regenerative powers and assured him that no further treatment would be required.

"Take care, my friends," he said on his way out.

"You too, Doctor," I replied. "I have no doubt that your services are about to be required more than ever before."

"I'm afraid so," he said as the door closed behind him.

He had left our locators on the table on top of the disposable towels. May's implant was covered in drying blood, and mine was coated in slimy circulatory fluid. May picked up a small stone carving from the center of the table. "Mind if I take care of these?" she asked, ready to crush the devices under the carving's base.

"No, don't!" Jas exclaimed. "I'm going to take them to your house and ask your servitor to hold onto them. I'm also going to set the bot's security protocols to 'avoid' mode. If anyone is tracking you, they'll think you're at home. If anyone breaks into the house, your bot will flee and, hopefully, they'll be led on a wild goose chase."

Jas looked into May's eyes. "I'm sorry, but I think we're going to have to leave your 'Pollybot' back at the house for a while."

"That's OK," May replied. "At least she'll still be helping us."

Anthropomorphism is the term used to describe the tendency to assign human attributes to non-human lifeforms or inanimate objects. This tendency had puzzled me a great deal. This time, however, May's attachment to our servitor almost made sense. I saw it as an indication of how isolated May must have felt. She had lost her homeworld, her father, her sister, her house on Terra, her possessions, and her friends and teachers at school. Now on top of all that, her new home planet, which had welcomed us so warmly, was crumbling away. A deep sadness gripped me along with a renewed admiration for the courage, patience, and maturity of this remarkable young woman.

***

For the next several days, May and I camped out in the guest room in Jas's office. We spent most of our time watching the entertainment console and flipping between news outlets but avoiding the propaganda networks.

May and I witnessed one horror after another as a constant stream of news vids showed swarms of red-clad hooligans running rampant in once-peaceful communities. Some of the vids had been secretly recorded by courageous citizens, but far more disturbing were the vids taken by the militants themselves, mugging for the camera while performing acts of vandalism, arson, assault, rape, and murder.

These thugs were led by the devotees who had spent months or years being indoctrinated in the HIM devotion centers. Any shred of empathy, decency, or accountability had been trained out of them. As strong as their psychological conditioning was, they and the louts under their command clearly had little training in the use of weapons. The result was clumsiness and stupidity with the troops shooting, tossing grenades, or launching mortars and rockets at random objects and people. They often missed their targets, which sometimes resulted in fires or debris raining down on their own comrades.

While the Truscovite militants were fond of shouting, their words were often hard to discern and were sometimes incomprehensible. In some cases they were clearly intoxicated as they walked with a swaying gait, taking potshots at signs, buildings, vehicles, animals, and any beings who were foolish or unfortunate enough to be close by at that moment.

Jas checked on us frequently. One day he saw May and me watching a litany of images displaying the aftermath of a rampage through a small town. Mutilated bodies were lying among smoldering ruins and maimed citizens were limping, crawling, or lying outside, begging for assistance. Jas took me aside. "I don't think you should be letting May see that kind of stuff!" he admonished.

"Why not?"

"It's probably going to traumatize her."

"Jas, if she isn't already traumatized, there's something wrong with her. You've seen how resilient she is. She needs to see what's happening. So far we've been fortunate that the Truscovites haven't invaded the university, but I have no doubt they'll be here soon. If they find me and I'm lucky, I will be killed right away."

"My God, Kelvoo! If you're lucky?"

"Yes, given that the alternative could be that I'm taken away and I permanently disappear with May having no idea what happened to me. I want May to witness what's happening, so she will do whatever is necessary to stay safe, either with or without me."

"Kelvoo, I don't even want to think about those possibilities."

"Please, Jas, think about them. If I die or if I'm taken away, will you and Simon please watch out for May?"

Jas sighed. "We'll do whatever we can. But you should keep in mind that I'm also unsafe. I'm the head of an organization that promotes the inclusion and education of non-humans. And here I am, harboring a non-human! We need to forget about what might happen and deal with the here and now. Remember, Kelvoo, there is supposed to be an announcement soon with a deportation plan. When that happens, you and May can leave this hellhole of a planet behind and live in safety far, far away."

During those days of uncertainty, the university barely operated. The non-human students and faculty stayed away. The school that May attended had switched to remote learning. Jas arranged for May to be re-registered with her school under a pseudonym in case nefarious agents were trying to find her in order to locate me.

Jas, May, and I often discussed the situation from a philosophical and practical perspective. We wondered how so many humans could have changed their nature so quickly. We wondered how a movement, which seemed so absurd, could resonate with millions of supposedly intelligent people. We surmised that a portion of humans were predisposed to hate others but kept their tendencies suppressed until a certain threshold of societal acceptance unleashed their underlying nature. In the end there was no plausible explanation, just the realization that such uprisings were a recurring theme in human history and usually came as a shock to a majority of the population.

***

One day, Kroz contacted Jas and met him at the entrance to the campus. Kroz provided Jas with a communications device for my use. The device gave me a direct encrypted link to Kroz, so the two of us could communicate without being monitored or tracked. Like me, Kroz's locator implant had been removed. Efforts to preserve the *Midge* project were ongoing, but Kroz couldn't provide me with any of the details. "If you get captured, I don't want you to have the burden of keeping secrets that would be so useful to our enemies," Kroz said. I didn't know why Kroz thought that a small craft g-force buffering field would need to be so secret, but it didn't seem wise to raise questions.

Kroz and I engaged in the not-very-kloormari practice of speculating about what might come next. "I don't know what's going to happen, but it may happen soon," Kroz said, citing the fact that Ms. Taylor had requested the return of the Taylor Group's *Raven* spacecraft, which had been undergoing upgrades at the aviation center. Despite the high cost, she demanded that it be made ready to fly and returned to a Taylor property immediately, regardless of how it looked or what else still needed to be done.

"The likeliest scenarios are either that she and a group of people want to leave Terra immediately or she is protecting a costly asset that is at risk in the aviation center," Kroz said.

As the days passed, the news continued its grim trajectory. Some outlets continued to broadcast the unvarnished facts. They were the first to be shut down. Most of the time their broadcast signals ended abruptly. In a few cases, armed soldiers burst into studios and arrested or assaulted or executed the journalists during their broadcast for the public to see.

The Atlantic News Network dismissed its staff within twenty-four hours of the coup. They continued to broadcast from Terra, placing an "anchor bot" behind a news desk. The bot read the news, accompanied by unedited vid clips, with the content coming from an external location.

May and I were reading one day with the Atlantic News broadcast on a monitor in the background. We heard an on-air commotion and looked up at the screen to see an armed posse of Truscovite soldiers burst into the studio.

One soldier pointed at an empty seat beside the bot, and a young male soldier sat there. He held an Infotab and started reading a statement from it. The bot continued speaking, providing an update on the current situation in Vladivostok. The soldier at the desk pointed a blaster pistol at the anchor bot's head and yelled for it to shut up.

The bot complied. Then the soldier started again, having difficulty reading the statement. "We claim control of Atlantic News on behallf . . . on beh-ha . . ."

"'Behalf,' you moron," the soldier in charge hissed.

"Sorry, on *behalf* of the Human Independence Movement and the Humanity Party. This braw . . . brawdcah . . ."

"Gimme that!" the higher-ranking militant shouted. She grabbed the Infotab from the blithering soldier, motioned him out of the chair, and finished reading. "This broadcaster's operations are temporarily suspended by order of the Ministry of Communication. Broadcasts will resume in the coming days with *truthful* content."

The broadcast continued as the soldier got out of the chair and milled around the studio with five others, unsure what to do next. Behind the desk, vid content from around Terra continued to play.

"Shoot that goddamn monitor!" someone yelled.

"Sorry, what monitor, sir?" the bemused soldier replied.

"The one behind the desk, you meathead!"

"But, sir, there's just a green wall behind the desk!"

Morons! I thought.

While the confused Truscovites wandered about, the anchor bot started talking again, providing an update from Perth.

The Truscovites threw the bot out of its chair, then kicked and beat it with their rifle butts. It took several blows to silence the bot. In a display of the grace and decorum to be expected from Truscovite humans, two of the militants opened the flies on their jumpsuits and urinated on the hapless automaton. It was at that point that May switched the monitor off.

"I don't think you need to be watching that kind of stuff, Pa!" she said.

One by one, the broadcast media outlets went dark, with the exception of Veritacity and the remaining outlets that aped the Truscovite doctrine.

In the hours and days that followed, the major networks came back online. Their content, however, had been replaced by scrolling text with matching audio that praised Truscott, listed beings wanted for questioning, and made all sorts of dictates.

Finally, twelve days after the coup, the extraterrestrial deportations were announced.

TWENTY-EIGHT: PROCESSING

The first non-humans summoned for deportation were those of us who had arrived on Terra in the previous five years. We were given twenty-four hours to make our way to the port where our initial arrival had been recorded.

Jas had arranged for the university's semi-orbital to be pressed into service. Twenty of the university's remaining extraterrestrials in the first batch had arrived via the Central Plains spaceport on the North American continent. Our flight would include two other faculty members, with the remainder being students. Jas insisted on accompanying our group. Jas, May, and the pilot were the only humans who would be aboard.

May packed a few of her possessions in a backpack. Jas gave me a shoulder bag, so I could carry some fridgepack food storage containers with a few days' supply of algel. I also packed the encrypted communication device that Kroz had provided a few days before.

Jas gave May and me a lift to the reception building at the end of the landing strip. I could tell from May's posture that the still morning air was chilly. Sol was poised to rise above the mountains behind us as we paused to look out over the peaceful campus, the beaches, and the Mediterranean Sea beyond.

My memory turned back to the day when we stood in the same spot for the first time, filled with hope and looking forward to new, vibrant lives as we surveyed our future home below us. I recalled how urgently May had wanted to frolic on the beach and how Jas was eager to take us to our house and get us settled in. Most of all, I recalled Brenna's words: "This is the most beautiful place I've ever seen!" Those words of past hopes and inspiration haunted me. As we prepared to leave, my greatest sadness was for Brenna. On one hand, she was living the natural consequences of her choices, but at the same time, her anger over her father's death and her naïveté, which was so easily exploited by other angry people, made me despair for her and for all of humanity.

We entered the reception building and stepped up to the security desk. Cleon O'Toole must have been called in before his usual shift. "Where to this time, Kelvoo?" he asked, as he had done several times before, though now his kind voice was full of sadness.

"I am off to a faraway corner of space on a great new adventure, my friend," I replied.

"Then you must go far and go fast and don't stop until you're a long, long way from this world," he said. "I wish you a long life full of adventure, peace, and contentment," he added with the saddest grin I had ever seen.

Cleon reached over the counter and shook my hand paddle. May stepped up to the counter. When he looked at May's face, Cleon shook his head. "You remind me so much of my granddaughter," he said.

"Thank you, sir," May replied. "How is she doing?"

"To be honest, I don't know. She cut all contact with the family over a year ago," Cleon said, as tears welled on his lower eyelids. "Last we heard, she was trying to 'find herself' in a HIM devotion center."

May walked around behind the counter, then hugged Cleon. "I'm so sorry," she said as they took a moment to comfort one another.

We proceeded out of the building to the end of the landing strip where the semi-orbital was being prepared. We stood in silence as Sol cleared the mountaintops, bathing the scene in a warm orange light. Other deportees were milling about, waiting to board. Jas was taking a moment with each passenger to listen and commiserate. The kloormari students, Klandon and K'deet, were in the group. Early in my tenure at the university, humans had frequently mistaken us for one another.

Just prior to boarding, Kroz emerged from the aviation center and ran toward us. Kroz stopped and handed an object to Jas before approaching me. "Forgive me for not coming to see you sooner," Kroz said, breathing rapidly. "The other staff and I are still rushing to preserve our work."

"Do you have any word on the timing of *your* deportation?" I asked.

"I imagine I'll be called up shortly since I've been on Terra for just a little more than five years."

"In that case, my friend, I shall look forward to seeing you on Kuw'baal in the near future."

"No, Kelvoo, I don't see that happening any time soon. If I manage to protect my work and escape from Terra, I will likely make my way to the outlier worlds. There's an engineering team on Perdition that would very much like to have me, but honestly, Kelvoo, I think it most likely that the end is close for me."

With great sadness, I felt that any resistance to Kroz's statement would only diminish the value of Kroz's sincerity. "In that case, my dear friend," I said, taking Kroz's hand paddles in mine, "thank you for contributing your knowledge and skills for the greater good, and thank you for your friendship."

Kroz knelt to look directly at May, touching her shoulder. "Please, May, don't give up on your species. When I look at you and I think about everything you must have been through, I see courage, intelligence, kindness, and strength. You represent all of the good things that humans have to offer, and I hope you will find happiness and love and that you will be able to share that happiness and love wherever fate takes you."

Kroz stood. "I must return to my duties," Kroz said, heading back toward the aviation center. "Good fortune be with you!" Kroz exclaimed before disappearing into the building.

Kroz's statements and actions were remarkable. The fact that a kloormar could express the concepts of friendship, happiness, love, and good fortune would have been unimaginable in the recent past.

We were hustled on board where I was positioned close to the cockpit. Semi-orbital flights were often automated, but new regulations required a human pilot, who could be "held responsible" for unauthorized transport of aliens. I heard the pilot repeatedly hailing transport control to request clearance for the trip. The replies ranged from incoherent to downright rude.

"Transport Control, this is vessel *Latakia* filing a semi-orbital trip declaration."

"Um, Latka. State your destination."

"Central Plains Spaceport."

"Yeah, OK Latka. Go ahead."

"What do you mean, go ahead? Are you telling me to lift off? Wouldn't it be normal practice to request my departure point, so you can plot a flight path for me?"

"Oh, yeah, yeah. What's your departure point?"

"The aviation center at Interplanetary University, Mediterranean Campus."

"Um, OK."

"OK, now you're supposed to request confirmation of my transponder ID."

"Yeah, hang on. I'm going to get my supervisor," the "controller" said before closing the com link.

The pilot tried again and again, with a typical response being, "Yeah, we're kinda busy here. Try again another time."

It was clear that the Truscovite coup had thrown Terran infrastructure and processes into utter disarray. We waited for almost two hours as our pilot became increasingly infuriated with each attempt. Her frustration was reflected in the fear and confusion of everyone on board. Finally, she lost her self-control:

"Transport Control, this is vessel *Latakia* filing a semi-orbital trip declaration."

"We're busy right now. Can you try ag—"

"What is your name and rank?" our pilot demanded, loud enough for every passenger to hear.

"Whoa! I'm not telling you that! You trying to get me in trouble?"

"Listen up, Transport Control. I'm recording this message. Am I trying to get you in trouble? That's up to you! I've been sitting here for over two hours with a shuttle full of aliens that I'm supposed to transport for immediate deportation. You *idiots* are stopping that from happening! If I don't get *immediate* clearance, I will provide a copy of this communication to your superiors, and I will ensure that you are held personally responsible for the delay. So, if you don't want to be held personally accountable for interfering with Gloria Truscott's deportation order, then I strongly suggest that you give me effing clearance now, you effing imbecile!"

"Geez, lady," the flustered Truscovite peon replied, "you don't have to get your panties in a bunch! Here's my supervisor."

Two minutes later, clearance was granted, and the flight path was set. Before lift-off, the pilot stood in the cockpit doorway to address us. She took a deep breath, closed her eyes, then exhaled slowly. "I'm sorry about that," she said, "and I'm also sorry about what's happening to all of you. We all just need to do whatever we can to survive."

The pilot took her seat. Moments later the shuttle roared along the landing strip, streaked out over the sea, and bulleted up on our semi-orbital trajectory.

When we were about midway over the Atlantic, Jas stood to address the passengers. "I am so sorry that your time as well as your work or studies on Terra have been cut short. I stand before you, ashamed to call myself human. It is the sad legacy of my people that we fail to learn what history teaches us. Since time immemorial, the planet below us has been wracked with violence, greed, the lust for power, and the urge to hate. Time after time we erupt into senseless orgies of self-inflicted suffering.

"Eventually, we grow weary of the turmoil, the oppression, and the senseless death. When we reach that point, we solemnly vow 'never again.' We hold the responsible parties accountable, we reform our systems, and we erect monuments and hold events to remind us of the terrible cost of evil when it is allowed to fester, grow, and infect us.

"So, time goes on, and we remember. But we also become complacent. Under the banner of freedom and openness, we allow false and hateful statements, dismissing them as the rantings of a few lunatics as we say, 'It won't go anywhere. It's different this time.'

"Then we experience disruption. It may be an economic downturn. It may be a political incident that erodes trust in our leadership. It may be a societal change that was long overdue. Those who don't understand what's happening start looking for causes and placing blame. They invent enemies, taking their own worst attributes and assigning them to their imagined foes. They conjure up conspiracy theories so bizarre that any human with a brain should dismiss them out of hand. Nonetheless, these theories are taken for truth by a subset of humans who enjoy the emotional appeal of such ideas, and who want to feel they have a role at the forefront of something bigger than themselves. Still, we, the majority of humans, say 'It won't go anywhere. It's different this time.'

"In one way, it *was* different this time. Until the coup, we enjoyed centuries of peace, learning, and growth. We reached across the stars, and the stars reached back to us. We believed we had turned a corner and were destined for greatness while we brushed aside our own failings and frailties.

"As you return to your homeworlds or as you resettle on any of the open, welcoming worlds of the Planetary Alliance, please share your knowledge for the betterment of those worlds and their species. Take your experiences at this moment in time on this broken planet, and share our cautionary tale far and wide. At the same time, take the knowledge that most human beings are kind, creative, and caring. Going forward, please treat my species with love and with caution in equal measure. May peace be with you."

Every deportee applauded Jas's statement. His kind words moved me and made our imminent parting all the more poignant.

Our flight had won the race against Sol's rise from the east as we landed smoothly with only a faint red glow on the morning horizon.

We touched down on a vast paved surface at a sub-terminal several kilometers from the main spaceport. Lighting towers had been erected, illuminating the entire area and reminding me of the lights that had been left behind on Kuw'baal as a gift from the human first-contact expedition. A large temporary building stood a few hundred meters away, and I saw cordons of non-humans being led from newly landed craft into the building, which bore the sign "Deportee Reception."

As we disembarked, Jas shook the hand, or grasped the equivalent appendage, of each deportee. Since May and I were among the first to leave the semi-orbital, we milled around, waiting for a chance to say a special goodbye to our great friend. We never got the chance. Reception staff in civilian clothing arrived and herded us toward the building. As Jas shook the hand of the last deportee to leave the vessel, all I could do was shout to him. "Thank you, Jas. We love you!" Jas could only wave, as I noticed the wetness of his cheeks reflecting the harsh tower lights.

The "reception" staff were unlike anything I had anticipated. They were friendly. A member of our group was an aging Sarayan who was struggling to keep up on the walk to the building. A staffer came out on a hoverlift and gave the Sarayan a ride. As we entered the building, an elderly human gentleman looked at May. She was holding my hand, so we wouldn't be separated. The old man looked at me, then back at May. "What are you doing with . . . I mean, do you know this kloormar?" he asked May.

"This is my pa." May said.

"I am this human's legal guardian," I explained.

"Oh, I see," the man said. "Er, well I guess we'll let them sort it out at the main terminal."

A woman wearing a badge that indicated her name was Margaret approached me bearing a folded piece of fluffy fabric. "I know that, as a kloormar, you can't tell when it's cold, so I want you to know that it's pretty chilly this morning. Here's a blanket for you. You should wrap yourself up, so you don't lose too much heat."

I thanked her. When I unfolded the blanket I saw that it was emblazoned with the logo of a Terran disaster relief charity. I realized the humans in the reception building were there voluntarily, trying to make the best of a tragic situation that they deeply regretted.

A male human approached wearing a badge that said his name was Jake. He seemed slightly older than May. He handed a wrapped sandwich and a bottle of water to her. "I'll be back in just a sec," he said to me, returning moments later with a fridgepack of fresh algel.

"Thank you so much, Jake," I said. I hadn't consumed any of the algel in my shoulder bag, so I stowed the new pack in the bag, removed an existing container from the bottom of the bag, and placed its contents into my feeding pouch.

May and I were loaded onto a hover platform along with a few others from our group and many more deportees whom we had never seen before. "Goodbye and Godspeed," a volunteer called to us as the platform started its journey. We traveled several kilometers to the main terminal, where we were thrust into a scene of immense chaos.

A sea of displaced beings, hundreds of thousands strong, were standing around, gradually feeding into the immense terminal. Small groups were huddled at the periphery of the amoeba-like throng, looking as though they were too tired or too despondent to join the horde. Truscovite troops were making the rounds of these groups, screaming at them to move and striking those who weren't fast enough, using batons and electric whips.

Occasional shouts, screams, and wails punctuated the din as May and I were swallowed up in the legions of herded beings.

Overhead, I witnessed a steady stream of departing orbital and interstellar vessels. I thought it was curious that I also saw local or semi-orbital craft, and I wondered why the spaceport's main area wasn't being used strictly for deportation, given the importance of the deportations to the Truscott regime.

Hours later, the cold was replaced by baking heat under Sol's noonday rays. With no room in my bag or May's backpack, I had to discard my blanket, which was promptly trampled under the feet of the refugees behind us.

As we entered the terminal, May and I made our way into one of many corridors that were laid out in a spoke-and-wheel configuration. The spokes converged at a security checkpoint. We were pressed and jostled and swept along among the throng of fearful refugees. On the way we passed intersecting corridors, and I saw that the other spokes were just as packed. When we were within two hundred meters of the checkpoint, I heard the keening wail of a Sarayan in distress along with the panicked screams of a human toddler, shouting, "Mama! Mama!"

Minutes later, one of my fellow kloormari from the university, K'deet, somehow made headway back from the checkpoint against the surging crowd, finding May and me just as we approached the last intersection before the final stretch to the checkpoint.

K'deet practically shoved us into the relative spaciousness of the intersecting corridor. "We have to get you out of here!" K'deet exclaimed. "They're looking for you! They're looking for anyone who played a role opposing them. They asked me where I arrived from. When I told them, they thought I was you! They cut a piece off me," K'deet said, holding up a hand paddle and showing me the site of a missing tendril. "They held me down while they put it in a tissue identification unit. When it didn't match your profile, they pushed me to one side and told me to wait.

"I heard them talking. They have a list of wanted extraterrestrials. They're pulling them aside, so they can be shipped away for interrogation and imprisonment. They were laughing about all the terrible things that were going to happen in the interrogation centers before the prisoners were executed.

"While I was waiting, a female Sarayan came to the checkpoint holding a tiny human. They asked the Sarayan what she was doing with a human child. The Sarayan explained that her family had adopted the boy and were his legal guardians. The boy's biological grandparents were waiting for them on Saraya, so they could see their grandchild. The soldiers accused the Sarayan of lying and trying to kidnap the boy. They said, 'We know all about the things you types like to do to little children, you filthy pervert alien!' The next thing I knew, they snatched the child

216

away. It was horrible, Kelvoo! The Sarayan's screams were so awful and the little boy was calling, 'Mama!' when they took him away.

"Kelvoo, we've got to find a way out of here! They're going to identify you, and when they do, you'll disappear!" K'deet motioned toward May. "They're going to separate you from this human!"

K'deet's report was too much for May. She stood, frozen with dread.

I recalled what I knew of the spaceport, replaying my memories from the moment we had arrived on Terra. "Follow me!" I exclaimed.

I wasn't sure where I was heading, but I had a hunch. We charged through the corridor to the next spoke. I picked May up and held her tight in my claspers as we pushed through the crowd, crossing diagonally to the next connecting corridor. We repeated the process twice more until we came upon a large arrivals area with a huge glass wall. On the other side of the wall, I saw the customs inspection room with the large metal wall sculpture where I had panicked and made a spectacle of myself upon my arrival. On the opposite side of the arrivals lounge, I saw the set of doors that Sheila Yang, the spaceport administrator, had ushered me through so that Brenna, May, Jas, and I could calm down before we boarded the semi-orbital to the university.

I led the way to the doors and covered the control panel with a hand paddle. As my tendrils tapped out the ten-character security code that I had seen the spaceport administrator enter years before, I hoped beyond hope that the spaceport's security hadn't been overhauled.

Relief flooded me as the door opened inward. K'deet and May rushed in. As I closed the door behind me, I heard someone shout at us.

"Where do you think you're going, kloomer scum?" As the three of us fled down the narrow corridor, I heard footsteps rushing toward the other side of the door. I didn't know whether those soldiers had the security code or were able to override it, but if they did, they would be no more than a few seconds behind us.

"Alpha three, code white," one of the soldiers shouted into a com device. "Two kloomers have taken a human girl! Heading to landing pad three in sector sigma!"

We emerged onto the landing pad in bright daylight. To the left a line of shackled extraterrestrials were being led at blaster point into a semi-orbital. On our right was a metal grid fence, separating the landing pad from a grassy area. The fence was topped with razor wire in loops about sixty centimeters across. Shouting Truscovite troops emerged from the building via a different exit and were searching for us.

I noticed a cargo container adjacent to the fence. "This way!" I said. I lifted May onto the container and then climbed onto it, followed by K'deet. "I'm going over," I said to K'deet. "Throw May over to me when I'm on the other side!"

I had been worried that May would object to the three-meter drop, but she didn't say a word. I grasped the top of the fence just below the razor wire, then swung my legs over. Extending my upper limbs to their full length, I reached around the razor wire, grasping the other side of the fence as I released my other arm, arching it over the menacing blades. When my feet touched the ground and I reached up, K'deet threw May over to me. She looked terrified but kept silent.

"There's one of 'em!" a soldier shouted just as K'deet was clearing the top of the fence. A shot rang out, and K'deet slumped. K'deet's foot was tangled in the razor wire, causing K'deet to hang upside down on my side of the fence as smoke rose from a charred wound on K'deet's shoulder.

I ran back, intending to pull K'deet free. "What are we going to do?" May asked in a panic.

K'deet's eye dome turned toward us. "Run!" K'deet replied. An instant later, a ball of plasma tore through K'deet's torso, spraying us with blue bodily fluid.

TWENTY-NINE: RUN TO THE LOST CITY

May and I ran as we never had before. Though the grass was up to May's knees, I was surprised by how quickly she could move. After fifty meters, the ground dipped into a slight gully with a dry streambed at the bottom. The gully wound to our left as the land sloped down from the plateau on which the spaceport was built.

Three soldiers were screaming at us to stop. A moment later, they opened fire through the fence as we jumped into the shallow gully. Balls of plasma shredded the air just above our heads, charring the far bank of the streambed and setting the grass alight. Through the trailing edge of my eye dome, I noticed more soldiers arriving, one carrying a ladder and setting it up so they could cross over the fence. We had no choice but to keep running down the hill. In some spots the gully was deep, and we couldn't be seen, but our heads were visible in the shallower sections where additional volleys were shot at us. I'm sure the shots were aimed at me, but far too many came perilously close to May.

Several soldiers crossed to our side of the fence and raced along the bottom of the gully or the top of the bank. May's frantic running was fueled by adrenaline. Between breaths, she grunted and whimpered in fear. My running was fueled by terror and self-preservation, but most of all, the need to protect my young human companion.

To our right was a section of dense forest, its edge parallel to the streambed but separated by thirty meters of open grassland. If we crossed the open space, our pursuers would have a clear shot at us, but they were gaining ground fast, and we couldn't maintain our pace much longer.

The Truscovite soldiers shouted at me.

"Give it up, kloomer scum!"

"We're gaining on you!"

"Just let us kill you, kloomer. You don't want to know what we're gonna do if we take you alive!"

A volley of five plasma balls tore into the ground ahead in a line extending between the right bank and the forest. The grass and some low brush caught fire, and smoke billowed up, presenting us with the one and only chance we would have for escape.

When we were adjacent to the conflagration, I grabbed May's hand and pulled her up the right bank as a plasma ball hit the ground and threw dirt up close to our feet. We stayed close to the flames, and I maintained a low crouch while we sprinted uphill toward the forest, using the flames and smoke to obscure us.

As we were about to enter the forest, one of the soldiers moved past the fire line. His shot hit a tree just in front of it, shattering the trunk and showering us with hot splinters of wood and bark. Above, a huge branch broke free and came crashing down just behind us, its leaves and twigs scraping my shoulders.

We ran headlong into the forest, dodging tree trunks and tripping over the underbrush, hearing our pursuers' shouts as the occasional plasma ball ripped into the forest ahead or close behind us.

At one point as we ran, a thorny bush caught on May's top, tearing it open at her midriff and leaving a vicious welt with bleeding scratches. She fell to the ground and put her hands out to break her fall, a rough rock scraping skin off one her wrists.

May stayed on the ground, sobbing between heaving breaths. "I can't do it, Pa. I'm sorry, but I can't run anymore! You need to leave me here. I'm a human, so they won't kill me. You have to save yourself, Pa! Please! I can't live if you die!"

I held May close to me. "Listen!" I whispered. "I don't hear the soldiers. I think we've lost them!"

In fact, we hadn't just lost the soldiers, we were also lost. There were no trails in sight. I used my Infotab navigation software and found that we could reach the edge of the forest if we made our way northwest for several kilometers. We started picking our way through the underbrush until we came across a narrow trail running in the direction we were heading.

We paused by a pond to rest. We were glad we hadn't thought of ditching May's backpack or my shoulder bag. May retrieved the sandwich that Jake had given her back at the deportee reception facility. She tore the wrapper off and bit into the soft bread, closing her eyes to savor the nourishment. I opened one of my fridgepacks and poured the cool algel into my feeding pouch.

May's torment was far from over as a swarm of black flies and mosquitoes descended on us. May blew a fly off the last piece of her sandwich before stuffing it into her mouth and slapping insects from sections of her exposed skin. The tiny, savage creatures had no interest in biting me, but a few landed on my eye dome, sticking to its moist surface until I blinked them away.

We got up and pressed on along the trail. The shadows lengthened, and the forest floor darkened as afternoon turned into evening. We didn't talk much. As the temperature dropped, I worried about losing consciousness during the night, leaving May frightened and alone in the dark woods.

As we approached another dry streambed, a voice rang out from behind a thicket. "Halt! Identify yourselves and the business you have at this checkpoint!"

May leaped with surprise, but the voice was reassuring to me, its pitch and accent indicating that the speaker was Bandorian.

"I am a simple kloormar, my Bandorian friend. I'm the legal guardian for this young human. We escaped from grave danger during the deportation process at the Central Plains Spaceport. We became lost in these woods while fleeing Truscovite militants."

A short Bandorian emerged from behind the thicket. "Truscovite militants?" he said. "I've never heard them called that before!"

"What do you call them?" I asked.

"Effing bastards most of the time!" he replied without hesitation. "We have a few more choice terms, but I wouldn't want to use further foul language in front of your young human."

May opened her mouth to object, but I interrupted her. "As you must be aware, I am concerned about losing consciousness as the cold of night settles in. Might you be able to direct us to shelter?"

"Yes. Make your way through that culvert," he said, pointing to a drainage pipe to our right. It was no more than thirty centimeters in diameter.

"I would thank you, my friend," I said, "but I'm afraid that we're too large to fit."

"No, not *that* culvert," he said, "*this* culvert!"

The Bandorian clicked a button on his bracelet. The pipe and surrounding ground was clearly a holographic projection as it wavered and disappeared, revealing a culvert just over a meter in diameter.

We thanked the Bandorian as May led the way into the dark pipe, using the light on her Infotab to see where we were going. May had to bend at the waist to fit through. I found it easiest to go "centipede style," lying down and using all twelve of my limbs to scuttle through. May said my smaller clasper limbs sounded "creepy" as they tapped on the culvert's metal walls. The odors in the tunnel were revolting, especially when May waded through pools of stagnant water and my prone torso skimmed floating patches of slime.

The culvert ended at a grate. Judging by the corrosion on the metal, I estimated it had been fabricated centuries earlier. A deafening screech came from the rusty grate as a Bandorian swung it open for us. This Bandorian was female and much larger than the one at the checkpoint.

May and I took a moment to stretch our limbs after the cramped confines of the pipe. "Follow me," the Bandorian said. "Bruno will see you."

We emerged from a narrow alley between two ancient steel-and-glass buildings and onto a dark street littered with refuse and groups of beings who were carrying bedding or small fabric shelters. They appeared to be looking for places on the sidewalk or in doorways to spend the night. Old-style street lights stood on poles but were not functioning. The only light came from dimly lit spaces on the ground floor of each building. Cables snaked from a small portable fusion reactor and along the sidewalks to each space. Beings worked in some of the spaces using noisy machinery. Other spaces were ad-hoc trading centers where shambling individuals appeared to be bringing items in and leaving with other goods.

"Come on, keep up!" the Bandorian said as May's head swiveled to take in one scene after another. "It's getting dark, so you'd better stay close!"

A scruffy human was sitting on the sidewalk looking unwell, his back resting against a wall. "You look like my little girl!" he shouted at May in a loud, gravelly voice. "Will you be my little girl? How much for the little girl, Mr. Kloormar?"

May was wild-eyed with fright.

"Aw c'mon honey, get back here!" the wretched human demanded as we picked up the pace. "I'll take real good care of you! You'll see!"

"Who was that man?" I asked.

"Who knows?" the Bandorian replied. "Just another human who's been pushed over the edge and lost his mind."

We entered a building through a narrow doorway where the Bandorian led us up a narrow, dark flight of wooden stairs that squeaked with each step. *Wooden stairs!* I thought. *Just how old is this sad, neglected place?*

The Bandorian opened a door and led us into a musty second-story room that looked out over the street below through the few windows that were not boarded up. "Bruno, two new arrivals from checkpoint seventeen!" the Bandorian called out.

Bruno entered the room. He was an unassuming human with short, well-groomed white hair. He was dressed in business attire. He motioned us to a desk where May took a chair, and I knelt. Bruno sat behind the desk. "What have we here?" he asked. "A kloormar and a human girl." He paused and leaned closer to May. "A human girl who looks so familiar! Let me think . . . what would you look like if you weren't so disheveled and banged up?" he asked, looking at May's injured wrist, torn clothing, and scratched midriff. He closed his eyes

222

and tilted his head up slightly, something I'd seen humans do while trying to access a memory.

Then Bruno's eyes snapped open, and he startled us by slapping the desktop. "I know who you are!" he said. "You're May, and your sister is Brenda!"

"Brenna," May corrected.

"Yes! That newscaster, Liz Underhill, interviewed you when your sister ran off to HIM!"

"Liz *Underwood*," I said, also correcting him.

Bruno snapped his head toward me and inhaled through his gaping mouth, "Jesus! Are you Kelvoo?"

"I'm not sure whom you are addressing as Jesus, but yes, I am, in fact, Kelvoo," I replied.

It occurred to me that it might not have been wise to reveal our identities right away, but we were on the run and lost in the dark, menacing ruins of a city. If we couldn't trust Bruno, or whatever his name really was, we were as good as doomed anyway.

"Please enlighten us, Mr. Bruno." I said. "Who are you, and what is this place?"

"I am a friend, and this place is a dump!" he replied. "Tell me a story, Kelvoo. Tell me exactly how the two of you ended up here. If I like your story, I might be a bit more forthcoming with mine."

I told Bruno about our departure from the university, our experience with the volunteers after we landed, the chaos at the spaceport, K'deet's warning as we neared the security checkpoint, and K'deet's horrifying death. I continued with our frantic run down the gully, our escape into the forest, and our good fortune to stumble upon a Bandorian at a "checkpoint."

Bruno listened with rapt attention. "May," he said with a grin, "tell me about the spaceport."

"I don't understand," she replied.

"Describe it to me. Tell me what the exterior looked like, tell me about the areas inside the building, describe the colors of the walls or the patterns on the floor or the signs you saw—anything that convinces me you were really there."

With the trauma she had endured hours before, May had a difficult time. She struggled and was frustrated, but she managed to relate information that was, for the most part, factual. I was annoyed that Bruno was grilling May, and I resented his distrust and his demands for May to focus through her fresh, painful memories.

When the inquisition was over, Bruno thanked us. "I could see that my questions were difficult for you, May. I'm sorry, but I think you understand my need for caution.

"We are in a centuries-old section of a city that was once vibrant and thriving. The old ground-based highways and surrounding rural areas are now covered by the forest where you were wandering. These old streets and buildings aren't exactly a secret—you can find them on most maps—but they've been forgotten by most people. The residents here have taken to calling this place the Lost City.

"This neglected neck of the woods would probably have been redeveloped sooner or later, but the Lost City has never been completely abandoned. Before the coup, the beings who lived here were from the margins of Terran society. Artists, free-thinkers, ne'er-do-wells, and anyone that didn't quite fit and didn't want to fit—all of them found a home here, and all worked together to keep most of the buildings standing and, depending on your living standards, habitable.

"When the Humanity Party took control, some of its victims found their way here. Those who were familiar with ancient Terran history were inspired to start an underground resistance. The long-term residents resisted the influx of beings who were ready to fight back, but they weren't inclined to turn them over to the authorities either. Now that those residents have seen the atrocities on their Infotabs and heard distant blaster fire and explosions, their resistance to us has faded, and *our* resistance movement is strengthening every day."

Bruno went on to tell us that his real name was not Bruno and that it was also not our concern. He was once a high-ranking bureaucrat in the Ministry of Laws and Enforcement, with personal experience as a police officer. He and most of the staff had been purged from the ministry and replaced with virulent HP loyalists. Bruno offered his leadership and experience to the underground resistance, which had cells across Terra.

He also explained that the Lost City had become a weapons acquisition and manufacturing hub. Rather than surrendering or turning over their arms, thousands of law enforcement officers had made their way to the Lost City and other "safe zones" with their weapons. The machinery that we saw in the old street-level storefronts was scavenged or smuggled into the city and was producing blasters and churning out bombs using old-style chemical explosives. Raiding parties were routinely sent out, looking for militants who were out alone or in groups of two or three. The raiders would lie in wait, assassinate the soldiers, and run back to the Lost City with their weapons. It saddened me to know that young humans were dying as a result of being gullible enough to follow a violent, hateful movement, and my mind turned to Brenna as I wondered again where she was and what would become of her.

Everyone in the Lost City was ready to flee at a moment's notice, with the knowledge that the entire operation could be discovered and raided without warning.

"Bruno, given how outnumbered the resistance is, why do you and the other members of the underground take such dire risks?" I asked.

"I think you, of all beings, should understand that!"

"I believe I do, but I'm curious to hear the reasons in your own words."

"Alright, Kelvoo. There are many reasons, but what if I told you that *you* have personally provided us with reasons for resistance along with motivation and inspiration?"

"I would wonder how you could possibly think that!"

"Everyone in the resistance has read your story or is familiar with your fight for survival against overwhelming odds. We are all fully aware of the sacrifices you made. Terra has been at peace for generations, so yours was the most widely known heroic tale from recent times. Your story presents the idea that righteousness can defeat evil, and in these times of great evil, your story serves as a rallying point."

"Bruno, it could just as easily be argued that my story was a rallying point for the forces of evil," I argued. "The Human Independence Movement was created to protest the hardships imposed on Terra by the Correction, and my testimonial was a major cause of the Correction."

"The majority of humans don't see it that way, Kelvoo. Your work was not an inspiration for evil. It was an *excuse*. If your story had never been written, some other excuse would have come along. Some humans are intellectually lazy and are more concerned with the notion of individual freedom to do whatever they want regardless of whoever else gets hurt. Acknowledging their shortcomings, improving themselves, or sacrificing for the greater good are *alien* concepts to them, so to speak. It was that minority of humans who brought the Humanity Party to power, and look at what it's got them: living in a world consumed by violence and ruled by a crazed dictator, living in economic ruin with the best and brightest having fled, and bringing isolation and shame to the human species."

He paused and took a breath. "So, what are we going to do with you?"

"I want to join you and fight for you!" May announced.

"You must be what, fourteen years old?" Bruno asked.

"I'll be fifteen in three weeks!" May retorted.

"Sorry, May, but we fight in compliance with Planetary Alliance regulations. In military conflict, the minimum age for human combatants is nineteen."

"Is there some non-violent way in which we could contribute?" I asked.

225

"There is, Kelvoo. The best thing you can do is to get off this planet safely and pick your story up where you left off. Share what you've experienced since you came to Terra. It's what you're good at. To me it's your purpose in the universe."

"I don't believe in preordained purposes."

"You're right, Kelvoo. Our purpose is whatever we choose it to be. I'm just hoping that you'll *choose* to continue to tell your story."

"Well, since that will only be possible with my safe departure from Terra, do you have any ideas how May and I might make our way to an interstellar jump point?"

As Bruno shook his head and shrugged, it occurred to me that I could use my secure com device to contact Kroz. I explained the device to Bruno. When I retrieved it from my shoulder bag, its screen indicated that a message was waiting for me. I switched to external speaker and then tapped the screen, so we could all hear it.

"Hi Kelvoo, it's Jas here on Kroz's communicator. Hopefully, you haven't received this message and never will because you're beyond Terran orbit and en route to a safe planet. Kroz turned the device over to me just before we boarded the shuttle from the university.

"I got word that the Central Plains Spaceport was in disarray, and I heard stories about all kinds of terrible things happening there. That's why I'm calling. I just want to be sure that you're on your way. I'll take it as a good sign that you didn't answer this call."

The display showed the time of the message, which coincided with the time that May and I had spent transiting the culvert. The reverberating sounds of May's footsteps and my claspers clattering along the walls of the pipe must have drowned out any audible alerts.

I tapped the screen to reply to the message via audio calling. After a few seconds, I heard Jas's voice. "Hello?"

"Jas, it's me."

"Oh no!" he exclaimed. "Kelvoo, you aren't still on Terra, are you? Is May OK? Is she with you?"

"We have both been through some terrifying experiences," I replied, "but yes, we're alive. Where are you? Did you return to the university safely?"

"No. We couldn't get clearance to fly back to the university. We were directed to a small airstrip about a hundred kilometers south of the spaceport. Transport control is in such disarray, we *still* haven't received clearance. Where are you, Kelvoo? If you can send your coordinates, I'll borrow, rent, buy, or even steal a car, and I'll come get the two of you."

"Hell no!" Bruno barked. "Jas, or whoever the hell you are, can you hear me?"

226

"Yes, who the hell are *you*?" Jas replied.

I explained to Jas that Bruno was an ally. I also told Jas that I hadn't looked at our coordinates myself, and giving them away or repeating our ally's name could put him and our "friends" in a bad situation.

"Kelvoo, you're aware that we're speaking on secure devices aren't you?" Jas asked.

"Of course, Jas, but you'd have knowledge that could be of great value to the Truscovites. If you get captured and they decide to interrogate—"

"OK, OK, got it!" Jas said. "We need to get you back to the university. Things are still peaceful there. When Kroz handed the com device to me, we talked about evacuating others from Terra, including me. Kroz is working on a way to do that! So, how can we get you out of there?"

"How about if you give us *your* coordinates?" Bruno asked. "I'll make arrangements to get Kelvoo and May to you pronto."

"What do you think, Kelvoo, can we trust him?" Jas asked.

"In my estimation, yes. Besides, we don't exactly have an abundance of options."

Jas provided his coordinates.

Bruno led us down the stairs, through a dim, narrow hall, and down more flights to an underground space where a car was parked. The vehicle looked well used and worse for wear. When we entered, we saw that the dashboard shell and a center console hatch were missing. Bruno explained that a few modifications had been made or, more to the point, several capabilities had been removed. We would be able to see our destination on the nav map, but all of the driving would be manual, and there would be no broadcast of our origin, destination, or route data.

We drove up a ramp to street level, then out over the edge of the city and the forest that May and I had traversed. We took a circuitous route, ending up traveling south of Jas's coordinates before approaching from the southeast to conceal our origin from any observers. We were fortunate to travel without incident, especially so late after curfew. It was interesting to see an individual driving a car without any automation.

I communicated with Jas as we approached. The pilot had moved the semi-orbital to a pad in a remote corner of the airstrip facility to reduce the risk of me being spotted. Jas remained in the vessel as Bruno landed beside the craft, allowing May and me to board immediately. Jas invited Bruno aboard, and we all discussed recent events and the underground resistance. During our conversation, the pilot was in the cockpit, trying to reach transport control for clearance to return home, and being frustrated at every turn.

"I can't thank you enough for taking care of Kelvoo and May," Jas said to Bruno. "I wish there was some way I could repay you for that."

"Well, chancellor," Bruno replied, "those are some pretty slick com devices! When we send a team out on a mission, we can't use our Infotabs without the risk of eavesdropping or location tracing, so we either have to send teams out incommunicado and hope they return or communicate in code and set up elaborate relay systems. Even having a single pair of secure com devices could save a lot of lives."

"Well, I suppose we *could* part with them," Jas said, "since you've so kindly returned May and Kelvoo."

Jas handed the devices over to Bruno. He also promised to ask "the inventor" about acquiring more devices for the resistance, and Bruno provided instructions on how to contact his people on the sly.

When Bruno left, the three of us moved toward the cockpit. "Ready for plan B?" Jas asked the pilot.

"I'm good and ready!" she replied. "How about our passengers?" she asked, turning to May and me.

Jas explained that plan B was to take off without clearance and get home as quickly as possible, letting the shuttle's nav system avoid other traffic.

"Won't that get us in trouble?" I asked. "Or possibly shot down, given the current state of the planet?"

"Well, it's certainly something I'd never have considered in my wildest nightmares," the pilot replied. "On the other hand, transport control is totally broken right now! There are emergencies around the globe requiring immediate transport. It's become so bad that craft everywhere have given up getting clearance and just flying anyway. I suggest we join them and be just another of the tens of thousands of unauthorized semi-orbital flights in progress right now. Transport control and the Truscovite command aren't exactly able to deal with that many violations at the same time."

"It's up to you two," Jas said to May and me. "Kelvoo, as a kloormar, I know you're naturally risk averse. My question for the two of you is, what's riskier, sitting here and hoping the militants don't come looking for you, or getting the hell out of here?"

"I'm for getting the hell out of here!" May said.

"I'm with her!" I added.

Moments later, we were airborne on a semi-orbital trajectory at full throttle.

"Whoo-hoo!" the pilot cried in what I interpreted as an expression of relief.

When we reached the apex of our sub-orbital glide, I peered through the windows in the ceiling at the Milky Way above. Out over the mid-

Atlantic, Sol would be rising soon, and its angle allowed its light to reflect off the occasional vessel in orbit over us at much higher altitudes and speeds.

"I had expected to see more vessels," I remarked to Jas.

"Most of them have bugged out and jumped away," he explained. "The ones that remain are small armed mercenary vessels, ready to blow away anyone who enters orbit unless they're on a flight that's cleared for deportation. If we increased our altitude by another fifty kilometers or so, we'd be toast! By the way, you were right about the fleet being from the Brotherhood. Truscott has personally acknowledged and thanked the Brotherhood and 'our outlier friends' for their support. A response came from the outlier planets condemning the Brotherhood and the crimes of the Truscott regime. They demanded a full, unequivocal retraction and apology from the Terran government."

"Was an apology forthcoming?" I inquired.

"What do you think?" Jas replied, highlighting the absurdity of my question.

Sol was high in a cloudless sky when we touched down at the university's landing strip. As we disembarked, I saw a flurry of activity at the aviation center. Vehicles were parked part of the way up the steep, rocky hill behind the building. Individuals were using hoverlifts to remove items from the building and transfer them to the vehicles. As we entered the reception building, I saw Kroz scrambling down the hill toward the aviation center. There was no time to greet Kroz, and I had no doubt that Kroz had far more urgent matters to deal with.

"Let's get you back to my office, and we'll figure out what to do next," Jas said as we hurried into a university car.

I asked why Simon hadn't met us. "He's staying with his sister in Tripoli," Jas explained. "He was worried about her, and I insisted that he spend time with her while I attempt to get you off this planet."

All three of us were exhausted, and I was looking forward to a deep, restorative meditation. May wanted a relaxing bath, and Jas needed a shower after being cooped up in the semi-orbital for the last two days.

The university was almost deserted. The campus provided an oasis of calm and tranquility in contrast to our recent experiences and the descent into hell across most of Terra. Instead of driving beneath the administration building, Jas pulled into an outdoor parking area close to a side entrance. We stepped from the car and took a moment to stretch our sore bodies and breathe the fresh air. I closed my eye dome and breathed deeply as I listened to the waves breaking along the beach just a short walk away. I released my pent-up tension, almost to the point of lapsing into a meditative state.

My auditory senses picked up a growl that sounded like distant thunder. The sound took my mind back to a time on Kuw'baal when I was meditating by the algel falls outside my village. The rumbling had turned out to be coming from the rockets on a probe, sent by a human expedition and ushering in the new era of contact between the kloormari and the rest of the universe.

I returned my mind to the present and opened my eye dome to see smoke rising from the landing strip up the hill. A few seconds later, I saw flaming debris shooting out from a central point, followed by a column of flame and smoke that rose and spread outward in a shape resembling a kloormar's eye stalk and dome. That was followed by a shock wave that rent the air and shook the ground as it passed above and below us.

We stood in stunned silence as the aviation center was reduced to rubble.

THIRTY: TAKEN

Jas, May, and I took shelter in the main administration building, not knowing whether the destruction of the aviation center was an isolated attack or the start of something bigger.

"Let's get you into safer quarters," Jas suggested. "There's an unused space on the ground floor at the opposite end of the building. It was used for storage, but I had it cleared out a few days ago, just in case. I don't want anyone else to help us because the fewer people who know your location, the better."

We went to the loading area and took a hoverlift to Jas's office. The three of us loaded furnishings and supplies from the office and then descended to the lowest floor at the north end of the building. Our new space was a single, windowless room. The walls were reinforced plasticrete, and the door had thick metal plates attached to it.

As far as we could tell, we were the building's only occupants, so we were confident that our new location was known only to the three of us.

"This is for as short a time as possible," Jas promised. He called campus security, which had only six remaining staff. "I'm going up to the aviation center, or at least what's left of it," Jas said after his call. "I want to find out whether Kroz is OK and if there's still a plan to get you two off planet."

"Unfortunately, Jas, both prospects seem to be unlikely," I said.

From the time of the explosion until May and I were settled into our new quarters, we had been too busy to contemplate our situation. When Jas left, we fell into deep states of stress and sadness. We attempted to reassure each other, but there wasn't much to say. An hour later, exhaustion got the better of us. May entered a deep sleep, and I had a fitful meditation session.

Three hours later, Jas returned, looking utterly shattered. He sat on the corner of May's bed and put his head in his hands. "It was so terrible! So terrible!" he said. "The whole reception building is broken glass. Cleon was bleeding badly and had to be taken away to the medical center. The aviation center was much worse. There was nothing left! Just dust and rubble and," he inhaled sharply, "and burned body parts all over the place."

"Was Kroz there?" May asked, fraught with worry about the answer.

"They found part of a kloormar's hand paddle halfway up the hill," Jas replied. "It was badly burned. Security had a tissue identification unit. Oh God! I'm sorry," he said, sobbing. "It was Kroz. Kroz is gone."

May also started weeping. She sat beside Jas and hugged him.

That night, May and I rested intermittently. We talked in the intervals when we were both awake. May talked about dying.

If I had been a human parent, I might have advised May not to think such thoughts, or I might have reassured her and told her to hold on to hope regardless of my own mental state. I was not a human parent, however, so I didn't dismiss May's concerns. Doing so would have felt disingenuous. Death seemed like a better option than many of the alternatives percolating through my imagination.

"Well, May," I said, "if we die, we should take comfort now in knowing that we stood by our principles, and if our lives end soon, we will have no regrets about the things we've done."

"Yeah," she said, "I've been thinking about what an amazing experience my life has been. Before we met I was just an illiterate outlier kid on a dirty spaceship. If my dad and I survived, and if you'd never written your story, nothing would have changed on the outlier worlds, and I'd probably be married off in a couple of years, doing housework and having babies."

I noticed that May had left Brenna out of her musings, but I wasn't about to interrupt her heartfelt train of thought.

"Instead," May continued, "I learned how to read, I got to live and go to school on your planet, and then I got to live on the human homeworld! When we came to Terra, I loved having a life that was close to what a 'normal' human would experience. I also loved traveling with you and seeing so many amazing parts of Terra. Thank you, Pa. Thank you for the adventure."

Once again, May's courage and maturity was deeply moving.

"Thank *you,* May, for always being there for me," I replied. "I hope we'll leave a positive impact—perhaps not for Terra but for the Alliance and other species as well."

As I listened to my own words, I paused. Was I giving up? Back on *Jezebel's Fury,* I had given up hope, and it was Kroz who made me realize we needed to fight back against our captors so that, even if we didn't survive, our efforts would have meant something. On further reflection, I realized we were not giving up at all, and if there was any opportunity to escape, we would take it. At that moment, all we were doing was making peace with the reality of our situation.

The next morning, May was rummaging through a pile of clothes that she had brought from the guest suite in Jas's office. She was determined to wear her green jacket. "I remember I left it in the office. It's in the closet along with my other pairs of shoes."

I wanted to call Jas, but I didn't dare use my Infotab in case of eavesdropping or location tracking, so May and I left the room to check whether Jas was in his office. We peered around each corner as we made our way to the opposite end of the building. We saw no one else along the way. We tried to open the double doors to the office, but they were locked, so we knocked. A moment later, Jas opened the door. "What the hell are you two doing here?" he asked, his eyes wide with alarm.

We explained that May had left some personal items behind. "Well, you'd better grab them and go," Jas said. "I have to deal with some extremely urgent stuff right now, including how to hide you better."

It turned out that May had several items in Jas's closet. We didn't have a hoverlift or cart with us, and there was too much for the two of us to handle. May and I each grabbed a pile. "We'll be back for another load," I said.

"No!" Jas declared. "The last thing we need is for you to be roaming the halls again. Look, Kelvoo, why don't you take some of May's stuff and go back right now? If May can wait, I'll help her carry the rest of her belongings in a moment. We'll be just a couple of minutes behind you."

I made my way back to my new quarters and put the pile of clothes on May's bed, with her green jacket on top.

After a minute went by, I felt uneasy and began to worry. I dismissed my concerns, thinking I was being irrational as a symptom of spending too much time with humans and becoming more like them.

Suddenly, my body was picked up and slammed into a wall. For a moment, I wondered why. I heard a bang and a rumble and I saw a flash, followed by bright daylight. Through a cloud of dust and smoke, I saw debris where the rear wall of my quarters had been. Flames roared through the room, consuming May's bed and her belongings. A wall of fire raged in front of the door, preventing me from reaching it.

As smoke filled the room, horror filled my mind. I crouched in a corner where a diminishing pocket of breathable air remained, but the ceiling of black smoke descended lower and the flames started spreading. Given no other choice, I scuttled on my twelve limbs, climbing over the rubble toward the hole in the side of the building, all the while agonizing over May and Jas.

Did the whole building collapse? Is the entire structure on fire? Is Terra coming to an end? Is May aware of what's happening here? Stay away, May! Stay away! It's too dangerous here! What if I die now? Who will take care of May? Will May feel guilty for not being here with me? No! No! No! I thought as I fought against crumbling plasticrete debris.

When I reached the top of the rubble heap under what remained of the external wall above me, I stood up and picked my way down the rubble outside the building. A loud "crack" issued from the wall above. Additional debris rained down as more chunks broke away from the building's exterior, knocking me over. A section of wall fell outward and pinned my leg to the pile of debris. In the distance, I saw explosions, fire, and smoke coming from various buildings. I was pulling my leg from the rubble when I heard a voice.

"Hey, look what I found! It's a goddamn kloomer!"

A Truscovite militant in a red jumpsuit scrambled up to me, pointing a blaster rifle at my torso. Another militant, perhaps fifty meters away, was running toward me.

"What should I do with it?" the Truscovite beside me shouted.

"Kill it, obviously! Cut its bloody head off!" his comrade yelled.

I heard the sound of a blaster rifle switching to "slice" mode.

While under extreme stress, even a kloormari mind is liable to think strange thoughts. In that moment, with my death a certainty, I could only think to shout one thing: "But I don't have a hea—"

Pain. Utter, unbearable pain ripped through my entire being. Pulsing back and forth, the agony echoed and built upon itself. The pain became visible as intense white. The whiteness of the pain was all I could see as it enveloped me and blocked my other senses. My mind scrambled into random, incoherent thoughts as I lost consciousness.

Moments later my ability to taste, smell, and hear returned, but my vision was gone. I remained immersed in indescribable pain and whiteness.

I extended my arms and felt my surroundings, letting the tendrils on my hand paddles explore the area around me. As I pulled my leg out from beneath the fallen section of wall, I reached down the rubble pile and felt a rubbery object. It was hemispherical and had a partial covering that slid over a smooth surface. The covering moved, extending itself over the dome and returning to its previous position. It started to twitch violently. Horror engulfed me as I realized I was feeling my severed eye dome, its eyelid still moving autonomously. I curled into a ball and pulled my detached eye toward me, hugging it as if it could somehow make me whole again.

I reached up to my shoulders and felt the flaccid, withered remains of my eyestalk. Most of the stump was charred and cauterized from the heat of the blaster beam, but I felt a narrow stream of slippery circulatory fluid spurting from it. My mind shut down again as it retreated back into the whiteness.

Then I came to a full realization of where I was and what had happened. I was alone, probably left for dead. Then I heard two voices shouting.

"Pa!"

"Kelvoo!"

May and Jas! They were outside the building, looking for me!

"May! May!" I cried.

Then I heard a new voice. "That's her! That's the kid the kloomer stole! And that's the chancellor!" The voice belonged to Coach Luna Chang. "What are you waiting for?" she bellowed. "Grab them!"

"Run, May! Run!" I screamed through all of my vocal outlets.

"Get 'em!" a voice shouted.

I flailed helplessly as I heard a dozen feet stampeding toward the location of May's and Jas's voices. May's screams filled my mind. "Pa! Pa!" she shouted with wrenching desperation.

"Kelvoo!" Jas screamed.

"Get 'em in a car and outta here!" someone commanded. I heard May and Jas's screams and shouts getting fainter as they were apprehended and taken away.

"Now, the two of you, go get the kloomer!" the commander yelled.

Two humans approached me. "Oh, gross!" one of them said as he came upon me, thrashing all of my limbs except the one holding my severed eye.

"May! May!" I screamed.

"How can that *thing* still be alive?" the other human said.

"Should I put it out of its misery?"

"Are you kidding? That guy was calling it Kelvoo. Think about it. We can be the ones who captured Kelvoo! If that doesn't earn us a promotion, nothing will! Hell, they'll probably give us medals and our own command! Let's take it back to base."

"I don't want to touch it! It's disgusting!"

"Suit yourself. I'm happy to take the credit."

I felt myself being lifted and slung over the shoulder of one of the humans. "OK, hang on," the more squeamish human exclaimed. They put me down and then one of the soldiers picked me up under my arms and the other held onto my legs to take me away.

"You won't need this, you freak!" one of the militants said, wrenching my eye dome from my grip. He must have tossed it as I heard it squelch when it hit the ground some distance away.

I wanted to struggle and break free, but I could only flail weakly or shake with agony as I was carried off. In that instant, everything was taken from me: my freedom, my sight, my sanity, and my friend, Jas.

My foster daughter, Brenna, had fled from me. And finally, May—who mattered far more to me than my own life—was gone.

THIRTY-ONE: RECUPERATION

A gentle human voice was the first thing I remember after I was blinded and taken away.

"Can you hear me?"

I was weak and in agony. Given the effort required to speak, I tried to respond by nodding my eye dome before realizing it was gone. I took a deep breath. "Yes."

"You've been through a lot, my friend," the voice said. "Now that I know you're responsive, there is no need for you to speak. Just listen while I explain where you are and what's happening.

"My name is William Castillo. Most of the time, I'm called Dr. Bill. I'm a physician who is trained to provide basic care to all sentient species on Terra, though I must confess that you are my first actual kloormari patient. I am told that you are Kelvoo. If that's correct, please lift one of your hands—just a little bit is fine."

For a moment I wondered whether I should respond or try to mislead the doctor, but I didn't have the mental acuity or energy to do so. *At this point, what does it matter anyway?* I thought as I bent my wrist to lift a hand paddle.

"That's excellent, Kelvoo. You are in an infirmary where it's my job to take care of you and ensure your recovery. You're in a private room with around-the-clock monitoring. If you need anything, just call out. There are sensors attached to various parts of your body, and some are wired directly to diagnostic equipment. Please keep still, so the devices can function properly.

"What I'm going to do first is to try giving you a little algel. Our staff managed to locate an incubation vat. It's in the room, growing a nice batch of food for you."

I heard Dr. Bill move a couple of steps toward my feet. "I'm going to scoop up a little bit on a spoon and place it in your feeding pouch."

The doctor returned, pulled my pouch open, and placed the nourishment inside.

"I'm going to leave you for a while, so you can get some rest," he continued. "Before I go, I have a question for you, though you don't have to respond. I just want to ask, is there anything I can do to help you right now?"

I took a deep, painful breath. "Dr. Bill, do you care about me?"

"I care about you very much, Kelvoo," he replied.

"In that case, doctor, I declare that I am of sound mind, and I request that you terminate my life," I said.

"I respect your wishes, Kelvoo, but I can't do that right now. We can talk about your options after we have dealt with your pain and evaluated your mental state. I'll be back to check on you later. In the meantime, please rest." He held my hand paddle for a moment. "It's going to be OK, Kelvoo. I promise."

I heard Dr. Bill's receding footsteps and the whispered hiss of a door closing. Then I retreated into the white world of my blindness and lost consciousness again.

Several hours later, I returned to a semi-lucid condition. I realized I was lying on a padded platform—a bed of sorts—which had no center section, allowing space for my downward-facing respiration inlet and vocal outlets. I didn't want any of the staff to know I was conscious, so I moved one of my hands very slowly to check for my Infotab. I discovered that my belt, which contained my Infotab and identification, had been removed. Never before had I felt more alone and exposed.

My thoughts turned to May and Jas. I tried to suppress my imagination to avoid thinking of the terrible things that could be happening to them, if they were still alive. I thought about summoning Dr. Bill or anyone else who might have news about May or Jas. More than that, I wanted May and Jas to know I had survived and was clinging to life. In the interest of their safety, I resisted the notion of mentioning May or Jas to anyone. The greatest threat to their well-being was their relationship with me. If I drew attention to that connection, I could endanger the two beings who meant so much to me. I suppressed my thoughts of them to the best of my ability, even though doing so tore me up inside.

I heard the door to my room open and footsteps approaching. "Good afternoon, Kelvoo," Dr. Bill said. "How are you feeling?"

"Not well."

"Your vital signs seem to be much better, not that I know much about interpreting kloormari vital signs. In which ways are you feeling unwell?"

"I am emotionally unwell, Dr. Bill. As you may be aware, I was almost killed when an explosion hit the building I was in, I was nearly burned to death or overwhelmed by smoke, I was injured by falling debris, and then I was blinded in a soldier's failed attempt to murder me. I wonder whether you might feel unwell if you had experienced something like that."

"Forgive me, Kelvoo. I wasn't informed about the specific cause of your injuries, and I didn't mean to downplay the effects of such a terrifying experience."

"I'm surprised, Dr. Bill, that you wouldn't have been briefed when I arrived."

"When you were brought here, all they told me was your name," he said. "My assignment is simply to aid in your recovery."

"And then what happens?"

"What do you mean?"

"What happens when I'm deemed to have recovered? I assume I'm being treated in a government facility. What is the Terran government's plan for me? Do you think they're just going to let me walk out of here?"

"Listen, Kelvoo," Dr. Bill said in a hushed voice. "We're all just doing what we need to do to survive. There's a vast chain of command above me. They're not inclined to share their plans, and I don't ask them any questions. Things don't go well for people who ask questions. All I know of any plan is that I'm supposed to heal you, then they'll ask you a few questions, and then you'll be deported to your home planet.

"You may not believe me, Kelvoo, but I'm on your side. I truly am. I'm familiar with your story and your background. There's a lot of ignorance about non-humans. A good example is the fool who tried to kill you. He must have thought he was decapitating you. He was too uninformed to know that you have four brains, and they're all located in your torso. Your best hope is to lie low and let me do what I can to keep you comfortable."

Dr. Bill switched to his normal manner of speech. "Now, let's try a normal feeding, shall we?"

He went to the algel vat and removed a full serving of algel. He handed me the scoop he had used and let me deposit the algel into my feeding pouch. Then he left, promising to return as soon as possible.

Weeks passed. Three or four times a day, Dr. Bill visited me. He knew that, as a kloormar, I required an ongoing stream of new knowledge to prevent a further decline in my mental health, so he would sit with me and let me ask questions. In almost every case, he used his Infotab to look up the information and provide it to me via audio output.

"Perhaps you could provide me with an Infotab," I suggested.

"I'm sure that would be frowned upon," he replied.

I was greatly restricted in the topics that I could inquire about. When I asked questions that were related in any way to current events or even history, Dr. Bill refused, often admonishing me to stick to approved topics and then whispering that I shouldn't be trying to get both of us in trouble. I knew better than to try to find out about May and Jas. On some level I just didn't want to know what terrible things had happened to them.

Over the course of my treatment, Dr. Bill seemed to enjoy talking about his family. He was one of two adult males in his relationship contract, and they were partnered with two adult females. Between them, they had three children: Mary, Jack, and Belinda. He referred to Jack as the smart one, Mary as the sweet one, and Belinda as the spunky, rebellious child. He talked of their vacations to see some of Terra's natural wonders as well as special off-world trips to Saraya and Mang. "Of course, all those trips were before the coup," he whispered.

Each day he visited with news of his family, such as the reopening of the children's schools or the charity work that one of his wives was doing or news from his other wife's workplace. I learned that the other adult male was having a dispute with his parents over politics. While I found Dr. Bill's stories mundane, I was sure to be polite by thanking him for sharing such "interesting" parts of his life. As time went by, he would whisper stories of his dismay at the state of the world. During the family trip to Saraya, his daughter, Mary, had fallen in love with the planet and been accepted to study at one of their interplanetary universities, but the election and Terra's expulsion from the Planetary Alliance had put an end to that dream.

"You know, Kelvoo," Dr. Bill said one day, "for days now, I've been spouting off about the people in my life and completely ignoring you. Please tell me about the beings that were close to you. They must have felt lucky to be with you. I'd love to learn more about them. Who knows? Maybe you'll see them again one day."

My defenses went up. "Actually, Dr. Bill, I haven't been especially close to anyone since my arrival on Terra. I have immersed myself in my work without much time for anything else."

"Look, Kelvoo," he whispered, "I know you had a human girl, May, in your care. I also know that you came to Terra at the urging of Chancellor Jasmit Linford. You spent considerable time with him on Kuw'baal before leaving your homeworld. I know this because, like most intelligent humans, I followed the news about you. I read your testimonial, and I saw your interview when your other foster child, Brenna, ran off. I'm a huge admirer of yours. I'm not a psychologist, Kelvoo, but it may help you to heal if you talk about your emotional pain. I've come to realize that you are a very private being, but I'm one of the good guys, and I hope you will eventually realize that you can trust me."

"Bill," I said, dropping his professional designation, "I know you're good, and I trust you implicitly. I'm just not ready to talk about it."

That ended the conversation.

For most of my time in the infirmary, I was alone. The room must have been soundproofed since the only sounds were from inside the room itself: The faint humming of equipment, the passage of fluid through tubes, the flow of air from the ventilation system, or the occasional spray of water into the algel incubator.

In those extended times of solitude, my mind replayed many scenes from my past, and my thoughts turned to the remarkable beings I had known. One of those beings was the esteemed kloormari elder, Kwazka. Kwazka had died five years after my rescue from *Jezebel's Fury*.

Several years before that, an automated probe landed near my village, ushering in my species' first contact with humans. When my fellow villagers and I gathered around the probe, I saw Kwazka using a rare and special ability. The probe had a defense mechanism that administered an electric shock to any being that approached too closely, but Kwazka was able to determine some of its physical characteristics by emitting pure tones at various frequencies and analyzing the sounds that reflected back from the probe.

After the first two weeks of my recovery, I was disconnected from the large pieces of medical equipment and I was able to move around the room. With my complete blindness, I had to go slowly and feel my surroundings. I felt the walls and the floor, the bed and the equipment, the algel vat, and the locked door.

Once I knew the relative location of each major object, I tried to develop my own echolocation skills. I started by using high frequencies beyond the range of human hearing. By the end of the first day, I could sense the walls and the largest objects but only a crude approximation of distance and size. I began to experiment with lower frequencies. When I started, Dr. Bill burst into the room asking me whether I was alright. I told him that my vocal outlets hadn't been the same since I suffered my injuries, and I was producing tones to exercise my voice. To my relief, he believed me.

In the following weeks, I trained my mind to analyze the complex echoes that bounced off objects, and I was able to visualize basic shapes as well as the distance of objects. I also learned to hone my skills using only ultrasonic frequencies.

In terms of my physical recovery, every day Dr. Bill would soak my eyestalk stump with warm water and a sponge. Next, he would debride the wound site, removing dead tissue and scabs. Sometimes the detritus would stick to new living tissue and would have to be torn away, which caused considerable pain. Fortunately, the pain was short-lived and greatly diminished whenever the procedure ended, and Dr. Bill massaged a soothing gel into my stump.

One day a tiny dot interrupted the total white of my blindness. It lasted for a fraction of a second, but it led me to feel my stump. An excess of skin had built up around its severed end. It felt like a donut that was swollen to the point that the hole was closed over. I stuck one of the small claspers on my hand paddle into the hole. Then I opened my pincers to widen the hole. As I pulled the skin back, I saw the tiny black dot in the center of my field of vision. As I widened the hole or let it shrink back, the dot enlarged or shrank. I was overwhelmed with relief that my eye was starting to regenerate, and my sight would return. However, I decided to keep that information to myself.

During a deep meditation one night, my mind was cross-referencing my experiences involving fear, reaching back to the days of first contact. Humans might use the term "nightmare" to describe such memories. Nonetheless, my recollections resulted in a personal epiphany.

It dawned on me that I was no longer afraid, at least not to the point of being incapacitated. During my abduction by the outlier gang on *Jezebel's Fury*, my fellow kloormari and I had been paralyzed with terror and revulsion when we watched a crew member called Brawn undergoing extreme corporal punishment. The same emotional trauma happened when the outlier crew was sentenced to death by the Sarayans and executed in front of us. I also meditated about my panic attack when I first arrived on Terra, and I saw the customs officer's blaster pistol.

Next, my thoughts turned to more recent horrors. On newscasts I had seen terrible atrocities being committed when Gloria Truscott's armies were set loose on society. As we fled from the Central Plains Spaceport, May and I were sprayed with poor K'deet's bodily fluids when K'deet was killed. That was followed by running for our lives while being shot at. We were back on the university campus when I saw the aviation center destroyed, just before being blinded and captured while May and Jas were screaming and being taken away to what was, in all likelihood, a terrible fate.

During the most recent incidents and in the aftermath, I had felt as fearful as ever, but somehow I had remained in control of my own mind and body. I can't explain the change in my psyche. Perhaps I had built up a tolerance for extreme stress through repeated exposure. It could be that having a house, a job, and a young dependent to take care of had shifted the focus of my subconscious. It might even be that I had learned to cope and be brave by witnessing May's courage and determination.

The day came when I was to be discharged from the infirmary. Dr. Bill entered the room to deliver the "good news." I told him that it wouldn't be easy for me to let myself out into the world due to my blindness. He told me not to worry. "You will be well taken care of,

Kelvoo," he assured me. "Some people just want to ask you a few questions and then you'll be returned to your home planet."

Dr. Bill also told me how much he would miss me. He said he respected my courage and expressed regret over the terrible things that had happened to me. After he bid me goodbye and the door closed behind him, I reflected on the weeks that had passed since my capture, and I took inventory of what I had learned during my recuperation.

I had come a long way since I had asked Dr. Bill to terminate my life. I had learned to use echolocation, I had improved my pain-management abilities, and unknown to anyone else, my sight was slowly returning. Most important of all, I realized I had developed the mental toughness and determination to cope with whatever was about to be inflicted upon me.

THIRTY-TWO: MARCUS AND BILLY

I was standing in the room to stretch my limbs when the door hissed open. I heard three sets of footsteps, and I caught an unpleasant whiff of stale human sweat.

"Hands behind your back, feet together, and keep your voice holes shut!" a human female barked.

My wrists were bound, and my feet were hobbled. "Guess we won't need the bag this time," a male remarked. I assumed they would have put a bag over my eye dome to blindfold me. I was grabbed by the middle segment of each arm and frog-marched from the room onto a hoverlift.

"Given my blindness, are the restraints really necessary?" I inquired.

"I already told you to shut your voice holes!" the female said as she struck one of my shoulders with an unknown object.

"Clearance requested for incoming kloomer," a male voice said.

"Granted," someone replied over the communications unit.

I had expected to be loaded onto a semi-orbital or a small craft to be transferred to some other location on Terra, but I was surprised to be moved to a nearby building. Along the way I smelled hot, humid air, and I felt Sol's rays on my skin. I also heard birds calling, mixed with at least a hundred human feet marching in unison and commands being shouted in the distance.

Using my echolocation skills, I determined that we were crossing a courtyard, surrounded by buildings of various shapes. Beyond the buildings were high walls that surrounded everything else. The muffled echoes from beyond the wall suggested tall vegetation. Based on all of the inputs, I deduced we were inside the compound of a Human Independence Movement devotion center, likely located in a remote, tropical forest. I also sensed we were approaching a low building with thick hard walls. The building jutted out from the base of the wall that surrounded the compound.

The hoverlift entered the building. Two humans propelled me from the lift and down a corridor into a room. They removed my restraints, threw me to the floor, and closed a door behind me with a reverberating slam. My echolocation indicated that the cell was approximately 1.1 meters wide, 1.9 meters long, and 1.4 meters high, requiring me to stoop when standing. There was no source of algel, no equipment, and no

244

furniture. The floor sloped toward a small drain hole in the middle of the cell.

The walls, floor, and ceiling sounded and felt like cold stone, as if they may have been formed from the old building material, concrete. The door was made from thick metal. Unlike my room in the infirmary, the cell was not soundproof. I could hear the muffled sounds of human footsteps, shouting, and distant screams of terror or agony, but those external sounds were soon drowned out.

A few minutes after my incarceration commenced, I was startled by an almost deafening din. Loud human music started playing in my cell with lyrics that were screamed rather than sung. The "songs" seemed to address the subjects of rage, violence, and death, but the words were hard to distinguish. I surmised that I was being subjected to some form of psychological abuse. After several minutes, the noise stopped for a few seconds, then burst forth again. The treatment continued, with the noise randomly starting and stopping.

I soon learned to cope with the abuse by focusing on the noise and analyzing its component tones, instruments, and voices. This activity kept my mind nimble. Soon, I realized the torture playlist consisted of the same twenty songs, repeated in random order. Due to my polyphonic speech capabilities, I was able to vocally reproduce each song, including all of the instruments. As each song played, I "sang along" at a higher volume than the actual playback. Then I portioned off a section of my mind to act autonomously, and I sang each song as a background activity. This freed the rest of my mind for meditation and rest.

Overall, the noise torture was only a minor inconvenience. The isolation took a greater toll, as did my hunger. Once each day, the music would stop, and I would hear a metal-on-metal screech as a slot in the door slid open. A blob of algel on top of a plastic slab would be pushed through the slot. Sometimes it would land on the floor with the slab under it, but most of the time it would land upside down with the algel picking up some of the filth from the floor. The quantity of algel was insufficient to provide long-term sustenance, making me physically weaker as the days passed.

After seven days, two guards entered the cell. They shackled me and led me along a corridor. My echolocation and my overall hearing told me that I was walking past cells on either side of the hall, with bars instead of front walls. I heard beings moving around in the cells, sometimes speaking to one another in quiet tones. I heard whispers and murmurs in Terran, Sarayan, Bandorian, and Silupan. I heard my name spoken as I passed some of the cells.

I was led to a room at the end of the corridor where my wrist and ankle restraints were tied to a metal ring in the floor. The chain that attached the restraints to the floor was about a meter long, allowing me to shift position but preventing me from standing.

Once again I used echolocation to determine that the space was long and narrow, and I was positioned in the center of the room. The place was sparsely furnished, with a desk and a chair on top of a rectangle of soft material, likely a rug. A four-legged stool was located closer to me. A set of shelves was positioned along one of the longer walls to one side of me, containing objects that I couldn't clearly discern using soundwaves. Light fixtures were positioned on the ceiling in a row running the length of the room. An especially large fixture hung from a cord directly above me.

I was left alone and shackled for over two hours. I wasn't using echolocation, and I didn't hear a door open or approaching footsteps when I heard a man's voice within a few centimeters of my auditory receptors say, "Good morning, Kelvoo." I was startled, and my body jerked in response.

"Allow me to introduce myself," the man said. "I'm Marcus, and I'm looking forward to working with you."

"Do you know why you're here?" he asked.

"I've been told that I'll be asked a few questions and then returned to my home planet."

"Well, Kelvoo, you have the first part correct. The second part will depend upon the answers to my questions. I know you're highly intelligent, so I'm sure your answers will be more than adequate for us to send you on your way.

"I would like to start by telling you how much I admire you and what an honor it is to have the opportunity to work with you. I'm sure that I'll be learning a great deal from you. That privilege is not lost on me.

"Our meeting today is just a 'get to know you' kind of thing. I'm going to explain my purpose and what you can expect from our work together. I'm a gatherer of information who will seek your knowledge. Since you'll be leaving us, I want to learn as much as I can from you while we still have an opportunity to exchange ideas and information. As a renowned teacher, would you agree that the exchange of information is beneficial to all beings?"

"Yes," I replied.

"Excellent! I don't know much about kloormari emotions or responses, but I must say that you *seem* to be quite calm. For some reason many of the beings I have worked with are terrified when they meet me. I hope that isn't the case with you. After all, things will work far better for both of us if we are calm, open, and truthful at all times. Tell me, Kelvoo, are you feeling at all uncomfortable?"

At that point I was feeling helpless, frightened, and most of all, angry. I felt what I think humans would call hatred toward my questioner. I wasn't about to give him any satisfaction.

"Yes, Marcus, I'm feeling uncomfortable. Perhaps if you could unshackle me for a few moments I will be able to stretch my limbs and feel some relief."

"Ah, Kelvoo, I would have no qualms about doing so. Unfortunately, I am required to follow certain procedures. When I asked whether you were feeling uncomfortable, I was referring to your mental state. Do you fear me, Kelvoo?"

"I have no reason to fear you, Marcus," I lied. "You have been perfectly affable. You have kindly introduced yourself, you have explained who you are and what you want, and I will be pleased to share whatever information I have with you. You have even expressed concern for my comfort and emotional state. For these reasons I am not afraid."

"I am so happy to hear that," Marcus said in a tone that I interpreted as utterly deceitful. He stepped away from me. I used echolocation to sense Marcus walking to the shelves and picking up a cylindrical object. I heard a click and then a soft hum coming from the object.

"So, Kelvoo, a moment ago I was explaining that there are procedures that I am required to follow."

In a flash, Marcus touched my shoulder with the end of the cylinder. A shock raced through my body, and a few seconds later, sharp, agonizing pain surged through me. My limbs jerked uncontrollably. When the initial pain passed, a deep ache remained in my shoulder.

"The sensations you just experienced came from a device called a motivation rod," Marcus said.

I heard the rod hum with a different tone. Marcus touched one of my feet with it. My leg felt as if it was being incinerated. I was convinced I was on fire. To the extent that the restraints allowed, I slapped my leg to extinguish the flames. The scalding agony passed suddenly, but my leg was in pain from the areas that I had struck.

"I should have mentioned, Kelvoo, that the motivation rod has three modes. The first is called 'pain,' which is not very imaginative if you ask me. The second mode is 'incinerate.' Much better. It produces the *feeling* of being on fire without actually consuming the flesh. What do you suppose the third mode is called?"

My physical and emotional agony made me want to scream with rage. I wanted to break the restraints, grab the rod, and kill Marcus as painfully as possible. It took every fiber of my being to control myself.

"Chill," I replied, my voice calm.

"Excellent guess, Kelvoo! It's actually called 'ice.'"

The rod's hum changed to a higher pitch, and Marcus pressed it to my hip. Mercifully, I felt nothing except the pressure of the tip. Perhaps Marcus didn't know that a kloormar can't sense cold. It was clear that the device was intended to simulate the *feeling* of cold without actually lowering the victim's temperature. Doing so would have rendered me unconscious.

I thought it would be best to feign extreme suffering. I knew that the initial human response to hypothermia was to curl up and shiver uncontrollably, so I made myself shake violently. I laid down and pulled my limbs in close, tightening them as if they were cramping. I formed a tight ball around the restraining ring in the floor and continued to shake spasmodically. Wanting to perform realistically, I continued to tremble for a time after the rod was withdrawn.

"So, Kelvoo, which mode was your favorite?" Marcus asked.

I responded with meaningless slurring sounds, hoping I was simulating the aftereffects of hypothermia.

"OK, Kelvoo, I'm going to step out and give you a few moments to compose yourself," Marcus said. "Be right back!" he added in a sing-song voice.

When Marcus returned, I detected him taking a seat on the nearby stool.

"Kelvoo, allow me to apologize for our unpleasant introduction. I need you to understand that procedures require me to begin by demonstrating the consequences of non-compliance. What can I say, my friend? We can't escape bureaucracy!

"The good news is that I'm sure there won't be any need to put you through such discomfort again. In our remaining sessions, I will ask a few questions, and I'm sure that you will provide satisfactory answers.

"Our time is up for today, but I look forward to our next meeting. In the meantime, is there anything you'd like to say?"

"Yes, Marcus," I replied, "I have a question. Do you enjoy your work?"

"Oh, Kelvoo! Certainly not!" he said with mock indignation. "I gain no enjoyment from interrogating alien species or their human collaborators. It is not pleasure that drives me to perform my important work. My motivation comes more from a sense of duty. You and I are more similar than you may think, Kelvoo. As a member of the intelligentsia, you are motivated to find the facts and learn the truth. My goals are the same, my friend. Only my methods are not as . . . conventional. Until next time!" Marcus said cheerfully as he left the room, and two guards entered.

The guards disconnected my shackles from the floor and pulled me to my feet. I was surprised by how weak my legs were as they collapsed under me. The guards had a grip on my upper arms, and my feet dragged behind me. They took me to a hoverlift, transported me back across the quad, and placed me in the infirmary.

My physical and emotional exhaustion forced me into a non-responsive state. I was not unconscious since I was still aware of sounds and the feeling of the padded platform on which I was lying. I would characterize my condition as an involuntary meditative state.

I was returned to alertness when a human hand jostled me.

"Are you alright, Kelvoo?"

I recognized Dr. Bill's voice, but I did not reply.

"I really didn't expect to see you again," he continued. "You have some external injuries on your shoulder, and I've been asked to take a look. What happened, Kelvoo?"

"I was subjected to severe pain by one of your torturers. Surely you've seen this before, Doctor."

"Oh, Kelvoo, I'm so sorry. That's terrible!"

Dr. Bill poked at the injury site on my shoulder and then applied a numbing agent. After that he proceeded with a full physical examination.

"Oh, you poor thing!" he said. "You don't deserve to be treated like that."

His words of concern put me over the edge, and I was having none of it.

"No, Dr. Bill or William Castillo or whatever your real name is, you're not sorry at all!"

"What do you mean, Kelvoo? How could you think that?" he replied as if hurt.

"Well, 'Billy,' do you really think I couldn't tell you were a fraud from the moment we met?" I asked as calmly as possible. First, you pretended to sympathize with my situation, and you promised me that everything was going to be alright. I may be blind, but it didn't take me long to figure out that we were inside a Human Independence Movement compound. It is rather unlikely that they would let you work on the inside if you hadn't proven your loyalty over and over again. That was clue number one."

"Kelvoo, I must advise you to watch your tone and show a little more respect."

My anger increased, but at the same time, I felt a new sense of satisfaction. "Once you thought I was convinced by your phony friendship, you attempted to get me to open up about the beings who are close to me. No doubt your masters ordered you to obtain a list, so those beings could be used as leverage against me. How disappointed you must have been when you learned there is no one special in my life. That was clue number two."

"That's enough, Kelvoo," Billy replied, his tone sharp.

I increased the volume of my rant in step with my rising fury. "In your pathetic attempt to relate to me, you manufactured a story about members of your family. That was the most ham-handed part of your pathetic ploy. You told me you had a son named Jack—that's Jack with a 'J,' as in 'Jasmit.' Then you claimed you had a daughter called Mary— 'M' as in 'May.' Finally, Belinda—your equivalent of 'Brenna.' 'Jack's the *smart* one,' you said, 'Mary's *sweet*, and Belinda's the *rebellious* one.' I figured out exactly where you were going after you brought up Jack and Mary."

I could hear Billy's respiration rate increase. "I'm warning you, Kelvoo, you need to shut up now!" he said, on the verge of shouting.

"You were actually stupid enough, *Billy*, to think that *I* was stupid enough to fall for such a transparently obvious lie! Oh, and while we're on the topic, all of your fake stories about your family were *boring*, Billy—unimaginative, mundane, insipid, colorless, and utterly tedious! *You* faked your family, and *I* faked interest! Do you really think I could care about one of your wives' charity work or the other's workplace gossip? Why would I give a damn about your co-husband's differences with his parents? Oh, and your sob story about poor little Mary being denied entry to a university on Saraya? Do you remember what you said? Let me replay it for you."

I changed my voice to mimic Billy's previous statement: "'When the Planetary Alliance expelled Terra, they put an end to Mary's dreams.' You really slipped up there *Billy*! You spoke as if your fake daughter's problems were the fault of the Alliance. You are so disconnected from reality; you couldn't even connect the dots to grasp the fact that the Human Independence Movement, the Humanity Party, and the obscenity named Gloria Truscott are the reasons for your misery!

"Human Independence Movement indeed!" I shouted. "Independence from what? A thriving economy? Interplanetary travel and opportunity? Having the respect and admiration of other planets and civilizations? Those things are all gone now, Billy! All because of a self-centered, power-grabbing dictator, her minions, and tiny-minded, toadying, bootlicking, fawning, flunkies like you, Billy!"

"Shut up! Shut up, you effing kloomer!" Billy hissed, indicating that he was speaking with his jaw clenched.

I had crossed a point in my rage where I was taking pleasure in Billy's emotional distress. "How utterly worthless your life must have been for you to be doing a job like this! You're not here to relieve suffering or cure ailments. You're only here to prepare beings to be tortured! You're only examining me now so you can tell your buddy, Marcus, that I'm ready for another round!"

"You're goddam right I am, you kloomer scum!" Dr. Bill screamed. "You're gonna die here, you know! I hope it happens slowly and painfully! You deserve it! All you alien scum deserve it!"

I took on a slower but firmer tone because I wanted every single word to stab its way into his memory. "Speaking of Marcus, he may be a violent sociopath, but you know what, Billy? I hold him in far higher esteem than you! Marcus may use a smarmy, casual manner when he interrogates his victims, and he may even enjoy torturing them, but at least he's honest and upfront about who and what he is. But you, you're just a two-faced double-dealing fraud and failure! You're even a failure as a fraud! You're not even fit to do Marcus's job. What would you do? Tell fake stories about your phony family to bore your victims into submission?"

"You want to die? You want me to kill you right here and now, you piece of garbage?" Billy roared.

"I'll bet you don't even have a family, Billy! I'll bet you're too pitifully deplorable to attract a partner, and you're just a lonely, bitter loser! That's it, isn't it, Billy? You do this job because it makes you feel clever, trying to outsmart beings who you know are smarter, kinder, and more capable than you and the rest of the vile, worthless, pitiful Truscovite scum whom you associate with."

Billy roared. He didn't form any discernible words; he just roared. I heard him leap to a spot just past the foot of the bed. Using echolocation, I sensed him opening a drawer in a mobile cabinet. Above his continued roar, I heard the clank of metal on metal, indicating that he had probably removed a tray full of instruments. I detected that he was holding a long, thin object in one hand. He used his other hand to sweep the tray off the top of the cabinet, causing a din as the instruments bounced off walls and clattered or shattered on the floor.

"Die, you effing bastard!" he shrieked as he lunged toward me with the object in his raised fist.

My echolocation tracked Billy's head. I extended my arm to its full length, placing it diagonally across my body. Before Billy was close enough to strike me, I swept my arm toward his head, connecting the back of my hand paddle across Billy's cheek with a satisfying wallop that sent him sprawling across the floor.

Billy must have been stunned as it took a second or two for him to leap back up to his feet. At the same time, I heard the door open behind him. "Stop! Stop it right now!" someone shouted. I detected two people grabbing Billy from behind.

251

Two more humans entered, grabbed me, and led me out of the room as Billy continued shouting. His voice broke, indicating emotional distress. "You think I enjoyed pretending to like you?" he bellowed. "You think I liked pretending to respect you and care about you? It made me sick, you disgusting kloomer!"

The door to the room started closing behind me. "Shut up and settle down, you idiot!" one of the humans said. "Marcus still needs that thing alive!"

I was placed onto a hoverlift and taken back toward the torture prison. Along the way I had a moment to think about what had just transpired.

There was a time not long before my capture when I couldn't have conceived of saying things to beings just to hurt them. Much more than that, I never would have believed I could feel enjoyment from causing emotional distress. In the time leading up to my capture, if I had ever hurt someone, or worse, enjoyed hurting someone, I would have been deeply concerned about my mental well-being, and I would have felt the kloormari equivalent of guilt.

As the hoverlift floated over the quad, however, the joy of revenge filled my mind and washed over my entire being. I had beaten one adversary, and I was ready to take on another. Since I believed I would be dead soon, my long-term mental health was irrelevant. I took comfort knowing I would die defiant and unbroken.

From the time of my first contact with humanity, my life had been a journey of new experiences, new feelings, and new emotions that would never have entered the day-to-day life of any pre-contact kloormar. My experiences with Dr. Bill and Marcus had taken me past a new milestone in my emotional development.

I had crossed the Rubicon and experienced the lust for vengeance and the intoxicating joy of exacting it, and I had no qualms about it whatsoever!

THIRTY-THREE: QUESTIONS

I was thrown into one of the cells lining the hallway that led to the interrogation room.

"Welcome, Kelvoo," a Sarayan voice said. "We've been expecting you."

"Yeah, welcome to hell," a human voice added.

I had six cellmates in all. Four of them were human. Donna was fifty-two years old, Pete was forty-two, Dave was thirty-one, and Stan was twenty-two. My other cellmates were two Sarayan males, Vertuma and Preeta. Sarayans don't keep track of their ages, but Vertuma calculated that he was about twenty-seven Terran years old, and Preeta guessed he was between forty-five and fifty.

My companions treated me with excessive reverence as though I was some kind of legendary figure. They wanted to know how I was captured and everything that had happened to me since then. I told my story, but I only mentioned Jas, Brenna, and May in passing as if they were characters who were only tangential to my life. I didn't know whether any of my cellmates were government agents, so I didn't reveal how deeply I missed the humans in my life and how worried I was about them. The last thing I wanted was for Marcus to use threats against my loved ones to "motivate" me. I found it easier to cope if I assumed that Jas and May were dead, and Brenna was living in luxury, insulated from the barbarity of the world.

My new friends guided me around the cell, so I could feel the three solid walls and the bars as well as the toilet and water faucet. I used echolocation to create a mental map of the cell, but I didn't want anyone to know about my "special power" in case they let the information slip out.

I had many questions for my fellow inmates. I wanted to learn everything I could about the prison, the routine, the guards, and especially Marcus. My cellmates were willing to tell me everything they knew.

Twice in my first day among the inmates, prisoners were removed from cells and taken to the interrogation room.

"There goes Tom," Pete observed. Moments later, I heard muffled screams from behind the door at the end of the hall. Then Tom was dragged back out and returned to his cell.

"Poor bastard," Stan remarked.

Later that day, a Bandorian was taken from a cell at the opposite end of the hall, dragged past my cell, and taken to the interrogation room. In less than a minute, I heard a blaster shot, followed by the sound of a corpse being dragged past us. "If there's one good thing about being blind," Preeta said, "it's that you didn't have to see that."

"What's even worse," Stan added, "is that sooner or later, you get used to it."

I used the mention of my blindness to ask my new friends a favor. "As you probably know, a Kloormar can regrow severed body parts. I recently noticed a small part of my vision returning. If there are no guards watching, could you please gently draw back the skin covering the end of my eye stalk and let me know what you see?"

I demonstrated by grasping my stalk and sliding the loose skin part of the way back.

"Oh hell no!" Pete exclaimed. "It looks just like a dick!"

Fortunately, my Sarayan cellmates had no such qualms. Vertuma started peeling the tube of skin back, but it offered some resistance toward the end, and he was concerned that it might be painful if he continued.

"Go ahead," I said. "It may hurt a bit, but the skin needs to become accustomed to stretching as my eye dome grows back and enlarges. You might even split some of the skin, but it will heal in a looser configuration."

As the skin was pulled back, it stretched and it split in two places, but the pain was relatively mild.

"Interesting," Vertuma observed. "When I look into the end, I can see a bluish-white disk with three yellow triangular segments."

"Yes," I replied, "I could see your face. It wasn't in sharp focus, and I was seeing triple, but as my eye dome grows, the images will combine into a single, detailed image."

When Vertuma released his grip, the skin closed back over my eye bud, and I returned to my world of white. I was relieved that I was regaining my sight, but I asked my cellmates to keep my progress to themselves.

On my third day in the crowded cell, I was hauled out for interrogation. Marcus was waiting for me. He asked the guards to use a longer cable to fasten me to the floor. "No sense you being more uncomfortable than necessary," he said.

My anger and fear returned along with my determination.

"So, Kelvoo, tell me something new and interesting," Marcus said.

"What sort of things would you find interesting?"

"Anything, Kelvoo, anything at all. You don't know the routine yet, but I like to start each meeting with that question. It's amazing how well it can set the tone for the rest of the session. In this case perhaps you'd like to tell me how you're settling in and how you're getting along with the others."

"I'm getting along fine, Marcus."

"Do they have interesting things to say?"

"Sometimes."

"Like what?"

"Stan's favorite color is blue. Vertuma has been to the same beach on Saraya that I once visited, and Pete has a brother who was killed by HIM soldiers. I haven't learned any facts from my three other cellmates."

Marcus must have realized his line of questioning was going nowhere, so he changed the subject.

"So, Kelvoo," he said, "when did you first learn of the AHA?"

"I am not familiar with that acronym."

"Sorry about that. I'm talking about the Alien-Human Alliance. You know, the underground group that has been advocating for aliens to recruit humans to their side to help overthrow the duly elected Terran government. There is no doubt in my mind that you could tell me all sorts of interesting things about the AHA."

Marcus took a few paces toward the shelves. I sensed him picking up the motivation rod. "This sound should be familiar to you," he said. Marcus switched the rod on, so I could hear it humming. "I'll tell you what, Kelvoo, I'm going to give you some time to search your memory. Perhaps after a few days, it will all come flooding back, and you'll have lots of interesting things to tell me about the AHA. I think we've done rather well today. That will be all, my friend."

I didn't feel any relief when Marcus left and I was taken back to my cell. I was certain that a great deal of pain was in store for me.

I wondered whether Marcus was so ignorant that he wasn't aware that a kloormar has perfect recall, and I wouldn't have needed any amount of time to search my memory. I suspected he was trying to "mess with me," and I was ready to return the favor.

Every day of my captivity, new prisoners arrived, and others left. Some were carried away as corpses. Others were taken away and not seen again. My cellmate, Dave, was taken and didn't return.

"What do you suppose happened to him?" I asked my friends.

"Well, they want us to believe that some prisoners are set free in exchange for their cooperation," Donna replied. "They want to motivate us to tell them whatever they want to hear."

"What do you think the chances are that Dave was freed?" I asked.

"Zero," Donna said. "Absolutely zero."

Dave was replaced by a human newcomer, Sue. When we introduced ourselves to her, she was incredulous. "You're Kelvoo? But you're supposed to be dead!"

"How so?" I asked

"Your death was announced on the broadcasts! The government issued an official statement. It said you were killed while you led a gang of murderers in a raid on a primary school!"

The news further cemented my suspicion that I was marked for death in the near future.

According to Stan, prisons like ours weren't supposed to exist. "Everyone here is officially listed as dead or missing," he said. Truscott would look pretty stupid if we all turned out to be alive. Sue agreed. She brought us up to date with the latest news from the outside.

The Terran economy was in ruins. Food production was crippled due to a dire lack of equipment and transportation. In the worst affected regions, people were hungry and increasingly desperate. Riots were erupting, and society was breaking down. Pockets of armed resistance were emerging, conducting raids and sabotaging military equipment, institutions, infrastructure, and anything else that aided the government.

At the same time, the government was announcing "spiritual reforms" by reintroducing their own form of religion, with Gloria Truscott declared to be the "God-appointed adjudicator of the faith."

"They're trying to revive superstition?" I asked. "To what possible end?"

"It's pretty obvious to me," Stan replied. "Once you can convince some people that magical beings are calling the shots, you can convince them of anything!"

Sue reported that one of the first religious proclamations was the condemnation of homosexuality.

"That makes no sense!" I exclaimed. "There must be countless non-heterosexual humans who support the government, including millions of high-ranking officials!"

"There are!" Sue replied. "Well, there *were*," she added. "There are purges going on as we speak."

"But, Sue, why would they attack so many of their own people?"

"With things going badly, I bet they're looking for scapegoats," Donna said. "They've always blamed extraterrestrials. Now they're looking for anyone else who's different in some way."

My thoughts turned to Jas, though he was likely dead. I also thought about Simon, and I became greatly concerned for his well-being.

As for government officials who weren't being purged, Sue said they were busy enriching themselves and their cronies, lavishing themselves with looted luxury items. At the same time, the officials realized their lifestyle was unsustainable over the long term, so they started reaching out to the Planetary Alliance for aid.

The Alliance nominated the Sarayans as spokesbeings and the Sarayans had been pleased to oblige. They offered Terra emergency aid in exchange for the immediate resignation of the Terran government, the disbanding of all armed forces, the surrender of all weapons to the Planetary Alliance, and the restoration of individual rights. Planetary Alliance officials would form an interim government on Terra and oversee a transition to an elected government that met the standards of the Alliance. To put it mildly, the Truscovites found the offer to be lacking.

When I was taken for my third session with Marcus, he began with the usual demand. "Tell me something interesting." I decided to cut to the chase.

"I assume, Marcus, that you want to know about the Alien-Human Alliance, especially now that I have had time to rest and search my kloormari memory."

"You know, Kelvoo, I admire your practicality and straight-shooter approach to things. Like you, I'd rather get this session over with quickly and painlessly. So, tell me what you know about the AHA."

"Thank you, Marcus. With me being perhaps the highest profile non-human on Terra, I can see why you would turn to me for information about a topic that certainly would have come to my attention. Fortunately for both of us, an organization called the Alien-Human Alliance never came to my attention until you told me about them. I have analyzed the possibilities. The most likely conclusion is that we do not have to worry about the AHA since it doesn't exist."

"Oh, well you see, Kelvoo, my superiors aren't going to be very happy about that," Marcus said as he fetched the motivation rod from the shelves. "The problem is that I'm going to have to tell them *something*. So, help me out here, Kelvoo. Tell me something—anything—about the AHA."

Marcus switched the rod on. I could tell from the tone of the hum that he had selected pain mode. I prepared myself accordingly.

"Alright, Marcus, why don't I tell you how the AHA was conceived? The organization's name is a dead giveaway! You see, we non-humans consider the word 'alien' to be a derogatory slur. The word is often used to describe something that doesn't belong—something strange and unwelcome or offensive or damaging. That's why beings like me tend to use terms such as 'extraterrestrial' or 'non-human' instead. The possibility of extraterrestrials associating with an organization with 'alien' in its name is virtually non-existent.

257

"So, here's what you can tell your masters. Tell them that the AHA was invented to distract and to divert attention from the ignorant, despicable actions of the Truscovite government. Tell your masters that the whole thing was made up by one of their talentless, sadistic, sociopathic pawns who only knows how to inflict pain and not how to do anything noble or productive!"

The jolt of agony from the motivation rod tore into my side, making my body and limbs convulse, but I was prepared. I dissipated the pain by distributing it throughout my body. The pain was still intense but not unbearable. I made my limbs spasm, and I was sure to keep shaking as if I was being tormented with intolerable agony.

Marcus continued to administer the pain for at least half a minute. "I suggest you apologize, Kelvoo," he said.

"Alright, Marcus. Sorry," I gasped.

"You know, Kelvoo, you could have chosen to answer me differently. You might have simply said, 'I don't know,' but instead you chose to be rude and belligerent. Frankly, I would have thought that you'd be more interested in returning to your homeworld. Don't you miss your freedom? Don't you miss living with others of your kind?"

"Yes, Marcus. Unfortunately, the prospect of being returned to Kuw'baal is not something you can use to motivate me. You see, I am utterly convinced that I will be killed as soon as you determine I am no longer of any use to you."

"And why would you suppose that?"

"Because of my past experience. When my fellow kloormari and I were abducted by an outlier gang, the gangsters promised to return us at the end of the voyage. We learned they were actually planning to kill us, so we couldn't report their crimes and movements. Likewise, your overlords aren't going to give me an opportunity to describe the barbarity of this place and those who work here."

"You are wrong, Kelvoo, but let's suppose, for the sake of argument, that you really are doomed to die here. Let's also suppose that you have a choice: You could die in excruciating agony, or you could be put out of your misery quickly and painlessly. Your cooperation would ensure the latter. Wouldn't that be preferable?"

"Of course it would, Marcus. I would be pleased to cooperate because I am secure in the knowledge that I hold no information that would compromise the safety of others. So, if you ask me questions that I am capable of answering, I will answer truthfully. Unfortunately, you aren't after the truth, are you, Marcus? I suspect that you are seeking information that reinforces the dogma of your superiors."

Marcus seemed to ponder my words for a moment. "You may find this hard to believe, but I like you, Kelvoo, or at least I enjoy our banter.

You know, most interrogators would see you as a mere alien who is beneath contempt, but you are quite fortunate to have someone as kind and open-minded as me."

"I'm glad to hear that, Marcus, though I think that our definitions of 'fortunate' and 'kind' may differ."

***

My sessions with Marcus started happening on a daily basis. He continued his ruse of being interested in me, and his questioning was more along the lines of having me recount the events in my life since my arrival on Terra. Each day he would repeat many of the same questions, phrasing them differently, and each day I would repeat the same answer, worded differently but with the same facts, down to the finest detail. This seemed to confirm my assumption that Marcus didn't know about kloormari memory. When Marcus questioned other species, he may have heard variations in stories due to defective memories and an inability of those beings to keep their stories straight. No doubt, Marcus would have dealt with such inconsistencies with the utmost cruelty.

I withheld some information from Marcus. For instance, I downplayed my friendship with Jas, and I didn't mention my involvement with the Sagacity Club. When Marcus asked about my relationship with Brenna and May, I treated it as though I was simply their legal guardian with certain responsibilities, with little or no feelings toward them. I doubted that Marcus was aware of my interview with Liz Underwood shortly after Brenna's disappearance. Perhaps he had only seen news from Veritacity and other "approved" sources. If he had seen the interview, he would have known about my deep attachment to the girls.

Between the daily interrogations, the interactions with my cellmates, the dragging of other prisoners to the interrogation room, the arrival of new prisoners, and the disappearance or brutal executions of others, there were moments of relative silence and solitude, especially when my cellmates were sleeping. In those intervals, when I was free from distractions, I would think about Brenna and May, deeply saddened that I would never see them again.

THIRTY-FOUR: THE FALL OF THE WALL

As the days passed, my eye grew larger, and my vision improved. When my cellmates assured me that no guards were close by, I moved to the cell's rear wall and pulled back the excess skin on my eyestalk. It felt good to stretch the skin, and it provided an opportunity to look around.

Each day one or two new segments would appear on the dome. The muscles between my shoulders and the stalk started to heal, and before long I could tighten the muscles to withdraw the stalk skin and pop my eye out of its sheath. When I relaxed the muscles, my eye would withdraw again. An eyelid had also formed, but at that stage it was a thin band of skin that could wipe over my eye dome but couldn't be extended to cover it entirely. As the dome grew in size, the skin at the top of the stalk started bulging, but Marcus hadn't noticed.

I knew it wouldn't be long until my eye dome grew so large it could no longer be hidden inside the stalk. One day it would pop out and be impossible to withdraw. I wanted to keep my healing secret for a variety of reasons, including fear that my captors would blind me again. I also wanted to provide as little information as possible since even the smallest snippet of data might be used against me or to advance Truscovite goals.

One day, Donna remarked that my eye dome was about the diameter of a plum. When I asked her to clarify the species of plum and level of ripeness, she shook her head. "Jeez, why do you have to be so literal? About five centimeters, OK?"

My vision had resolved enough that I could blend the image from each segment into a single, unified image, but I still felt impaired by my field of view. Instead of having 360 degrees of horizontal vision, I was limited to an effective range of about 120 degrees. With my stalk in its natural position, I was looking at the ceiling. By bending and swiveling my eyestalk, I could look around. At that stage even though I could see my surroundings, I felt frustrated by my reduced field of view, and I was anxious for my full sight to return. That's when it occurred to me that I was seeing about as well as any human could. I marveled at how humans were able to function with such limited vision.

As I looked around, Sue watched me intently. After the morning meal, she took me aside. "What's the smallest thing you can see?" she asked.

"Well, although my field of view is reduced, the resolution of what I can see is back to its original state. As long as I'm looking directly at something, I can perceive its fine details."

Sue shook her head. "I have no idea what that means."

"I can see things that are slightly smaller than a human can discern."

"Good," she said.

Sue excused herself to use the toilet. As always, my cellmates turned away from Sue, and I retracted my eye to provide her with a degree of privacy.

When she was finished, Sue took me aside, telling the others she had to speak with me alone. "Kelvoo, I have something for you," she whispered. I pushed my eye back out of its stalk as Sue passed me a silvery metal capsule. "Read it!" she said.

I saw tiny letters engraved into the capsule's surface. I whispered the words to Sue as I read them. "Keep this hidden in your body. May it bring you good fortune."

"What is this?" I inquired.

"No idea," she said.

"Where did you get it?"

"We have a friend on the inside. I got it a few days ago, and I was told to give it to you when your sight returned."

"Where have you been keeping it?"

"You really don't want to know!" she replied.

I didn't completely trust Sue. She was the most recent addition to our group, and she claimed not to know what she had given me. The capsule could have been a transmitter to track me in the event that I escaped. Perhaps it was designed to poison me.

"I'm not interested," I said.

"Why not?"

"Because when you arrived you appeared to be surprised to see me alive. Isn't it rather convenient that you just happened to be placed in the same cell as me, and now you've suddenly got a connection to an insider? It doesn't add up."

"Yes, Kelvoo," she replied with exasperation, "I knew damned well that you were alive before I came here and our insider placed me in your cell. I had to act surprised, so I wouldn't blow my cover! There's more text on the capsule, so why don't you read it before you accuse me of being a Truscovite? I don't have a clue what it means, but maybe it'll make sense to you!"

I rolled the capsule to find an additional inscription on the other side: "Ke soo ko manago dimay."

I was jolted. Excitement and terror, hope and regret, and joy and sadness coursed through every fiber of my mind and body.

I stuffed the capsule deep into my reproductive pouch. Then I grabbed Sue's hands in my hand paddles. She recoiled at my touch, but I continued undeterred, pointing my partially formed eye dome close to her face. "Thank you," I whispered.

As I was taken to the interrogation room early the next morning, I had a sense that change was imminent, and something big was about to happen. I'm unable to explain the basis for my confidence. I just seemed to be using another acquired human trait—a gut feeling.

When I was shackled, Marcus entered. "So, Kelvoo, tell me something new and interesting," he began, as usual.

"May I *show* you something new and interesting instead?" I asked.

My echolocation told me that Marcus was walking around me, looking me up and down with suspicion. "Sure, Kelvoo, why not?" he replied with mock cheerfulness.

I tightened my shoulder and eyestalk muscles, and my eye dome popped out with a "plop."

"My, my, Kelvoo! You *are* full of surprises!" Marcus exclaimed.

During my blindness, my echolocation was good enough to know that Marcus had a close-to-average body size and shape for a human male. I had used my imagination to try to picture Marcus's face. I had pictured a scarred, grizzled visage with beady eyes and misshapen or missing teeth. Instead, I was struck by how unremarkable Marcus looked.

"So, Kelvoo, why did you choose to reveal your hideous eyeball now?" he asked.

"First of all, it formed overnight," I lied, "so this is the first time I would have been able to show it to you. Second, I wanted to see whether your face was as unappealing as I thought it would be. It most certainly is!"

I swiveled my eye dome to watch Marcus walk to the shelves and return with the motivation rod. For the first time, I saw that it was bright red and adorned with images of skulls, knives, demons, and monsters. I assumed the images were supposed to intimidate Marcus's victims.

Marcus activated the rod and held it with the business end close to my new eye. "You know, Kelvoo, I wasn't insincere when I told you that I like you, and I enjoy our conversations. If we had just met, I would be going to town on you right now, and then I'd lop off that stupid kloomer eye, so you could start growing a new one all over again!

"The fact is, you're only alive right now because I like you. After our fifth meeting, I realized I wasn't going to get anything useful out of you. I've only been keeping you around because you're amusing. Well, for an *alien* anyway.

"So, Kelvoo, would you like to rephrase what you said about my face?"

"Yes, Marcus. Thank you for the opportunity. I was not being honest when I said that your face was unappealing. What I meant to say was that your visage is the most vile, grotesque, grisly, beastly, deformed, foul, loathsome, repellent, repugnant, hideous sight that this eye, or the one before it, has ever beheld!"

Marcus had burst out laughing before I was halfway through my list of adjectives. When I finished, he struggled to get his words out between spasms of laughter. "You know what I hate the most about this job, Kelvoo? The begging and pleading. I have no patience or respect for whimpering fools. But you, Kelvoo! You're something else! Before you started growing your new eye, I'll bet you were growing a big pair of balls!"

"If I were human," I replied, "I'm sure that I would perceive your remark to be exceedingly funny."

Marcus seemed to find my logical deadpan kloormar persona charming, perhaps because it fit with his preconceived notions.

Marcus settled his laughter as he returned the rod to its place on the shelves. Then he sat on the stool and told me to relax. He said he wasn't going to subject me to further pain. I didn't know whether he was referring to our current session or future encounters.

Marcus started speaking in a tone that was markedly different than I was used to. He talked about his life before the coup, and he asked me about my life before first contact. "Better times for both of us, eh?" he said.

"Certainly better than this moment," I replied.

As Marcus opened up to me, my hate and revulsion toward him did not diminish, but for a moment it was tempered by pity. Clearly, Marcus was uncommonly cruel and sadistic, but those tendencies had probably been dormant before the rise of the Human Independence Movement. I wondered whether HIM had awakened the malevolence in Marcus and given him a perfect excuse to express his repressed urges. I also wondered what would happen to Marcus if he ever faced justice, and I thought that, on some level, Marcus was being exploited and was, in his own pathetic way, another victim of HIM.

"So, Kelvoo," Marcus said, "I can't keep up the pretense of interrogating you much longer, and I'm convinced you have nothing to tell me that would interest my superiors. What the hell am I going to do with you?"

I was planning to tell Marcus that he should switch allegiances and find a way to set me and all of the prisoners free. As I was about to speak, however, we were distracted by a low rumbling that seemed to come from the other side of the room's outer wall.

One second later, a large section of the wall fell away. There was no bang or roar, just the sound of plasticrete chunks falling and piling on top of one another or rolling downhill.

Marcus was stunned, as was I. Marcus didn't cry out or make a sound when an armed man entered through the hole in the wall, aimed a weapon at him, and blasted away half of his face and head. I watched, dumbfounded, as Marcus's body slumped to the floor. For some reason I recalled something I once heard Bertie Kolesnikov say in a moment of astonishment during the first-contact mission: "Well, butter my butt and call me a biscuit!"

In that instant, my Marcus problem was solved, but a new and immediate set of hazards lay ahead.

Twenty-four armed, masked humans and three Sarayans poured into the room and crouched beside the door that led into the hallway. One of the raiders knelt beside me. He put a finger to the part of the mask covering his mouth to indicate that I should remain silent. Using a plasma slicer, he cut through my shackles in less than three seconds. Then he pulled me to the exterior wall and had me squat next to the new gaping exit. He waited with me while the others poured through the door into the cellblock.

I heard two initial shots from plasma rifles. *That would be for the two guards who are usually roaming the corridor*, I thought. I heard shouting and screams that would have come from the main staff area off the hallway. Those sounds were silenced with blaster fire as the raiders moved through the prison with unrelenting efficiency.

I can't describe what I felt in those moments. I didn't know the identity of the raiders or what their allegiances were. I wanted to feel joy and intense relief, but I was also deeply fearful. If a rescue attempt was underway, I feared the consequences if it failed. I was terrified that my fellow inmates could be hurt or killed.

After a few moments of silence, I heard someone yell, "Secure!" More voices sounded from different parts of the prison as additional raiders repeated, "Secure!"

"Who *are* you?" I asked the raider who was waiting with me.

"Your salvation," he said. "I'm going to guide you through this, so stay close to me."

In the hallway, plasma slicers made short work of the bars on each cell, and I heard them clang to the floor. I heard two more rumbling sounds at about the midpoint and far end of the hallway. Three of the raiders led a group of inmates into the room, followed by three more to guard the rear. That was when a piercing alarm sounded throughout the building.

It was clear that the mission had been meticulously planned, but with the alarm wailing, events took an urgent turn as the first trio of raiders exited through the hole. "This way!" one of them shouted. "Just run, and don't look back! Get down into the forest, and wait by the river."

"Let's go," my guide said.

We burst out of the hole and over a pile of rubble. I felt a joyous rush of freedom, tinged with intense fear.

The ground fell away into a steep, grassy slope that plunged into a deep ravine. The edge of a dense tropical forest started half way down the hill.

Before my capture, the command to not look back would have been impossible to obey, but now with just a partial eye, I could only look in one general direction. I did, however, briefly swivel my eye to the side, spotting two additional holes in the compound's outer wall, with inmates and raiders dashing out of them.

My coordination was impaired by my tunnel vision and the brilliant daylight, combined with the fact that I hadn't run in the previous weeks, yet there I was, charging headlong down the side of a ravine. I stumbled and fell twice, rolling along the ground. As we ran, the grass became longer and was punctuated by scrubby vegetation, slowing my progress. That's when a ball of plasma ripped overhead, striking one of the fleeing inmates who had overtaken me. I slowed to assist him, then realized there was nothing I could do when I saw that the plasma had torn through his back and exploded out of his chest.

"Keep running!" my guide screamed, grabbing me by the shoulders and shoving me ahead.

Without warning, a barrage of plasma fire erupted from multiple positions ahead of us, just inside the forest. I stopped short. "It's a trap!" I shouted.

"They're ours!" my guide bellowed, shoving me forward again. The moment we entered the woods, he grabbed my upper arm. "Get down here."

We crouched behind the trunk of a huge mahogany tree, and I peered around the side to look up the slope. I saw the dead inmate and at least two other bodies. The last of the group was barreling down toward us as more Truscovites moved into position along the top of the compound wall above the holes that we had used to escape.

265

As the final surviving raiders and escapees reached the forest, Truscovite reinforcements took up positions at the top of the hill, unleashing a barrage of plasma fire and mortars that shook the trees and sent branches crashing down. This was answered by three missiles from the raiders' side, which impacted the wall above the three holes. The wall collapsed, sending screaming soldiers plummeting to their deaths and crushing many of the soldiers at the top of the hill. The collapse also had the unfortunate effect of sending chunks of the wall sliding, rolling, and bouncing down the slope toward us.

My guide and I made ourselves as small as possible as we cowered behind the tree trunk and watched plasticrete boulders smashing through the forest. One of the boulders struck a Sarayan raider, sending her bloody corpse flying past us.

When the last of the detritus had settled, a raider stood up. "To the river, now!"

We resumed our run, heading through the forest with the defending raiders laying down covering fire as more Truscovites moved in to replace their fallen comrades. The jungle floor was dark enough that there was little ground vegetation in our way, so we leaped with giant strides, dodging tree trunks as we descended. A small, muddy river came into view at the bottom of the ravine, winding along the valley floor. Freight pods lined the riverbank where human coordinators waited. As each escapee arrived, a coordinator asked their name and then directed them to a specific pod. My guide took me directly to my assigned pod.

"OK, Kelvoo, climb in!" he said.

My pod was a box about 2.5 meters long and less than a meter in width and height. A streamlined nose cone was attached to the leading edge. Since I arrived on Terra, I had seen tens of thousands of freight pods zipping overhead, delivering cargo to every corner of the planet, but it hadn't occurred to me that they could be used to transport living beings.

I stepped into my assigned pod through a hatch on its top surface. I held the sides of the opening as I slid my legs down and forward. I was relieved that a slightly raised, cushioned platform was attached to the floor with a center strip removed for my comfort.

When I was fully reclined, my guide looked at me through the hatch, then pulled his mask down. "Take care of yourself, and tell everyone your story." I recognized his face immediately, although he looked like much more of an adult than when we had last met. His voice was deeper, and he spoke with confidence. He was the son of Sam Buchanan and Lynda Paige.

"Kelvoo!" I exclaimed.

Kelvoo Buchanan-Paige gave me a thumbs-up and a smile that was tinged with sadness as he slammed the hatch shut.

The pod hummed to life, then rose and hovered for a moment. I had never seen the inside of a freight pod, but this one had been customized for the delivery of living beings. Two vid screens were located on the ceiling, just aft of the hatch. One displayed the view from a forward external camera, and the other showed the ground below the pod along with the rear view in a split-screen format. The walls were lined with numbered storage compartments, starting at a point that was level with my eye dome and extending forward to just past my upper elbows.

The pod started moving forward above the center of the river. "Welcome, Kelvoo," an automated voice said. "I am here to assist you. If there is anything I can do to aid in your comfort, please state your requirements.

"You have been issued a secure communication device with a belt and holster, located in compartment S-1. For your security, the device can only *receive* communications. It will be used to provide you with instructions when the time comes for your extraction. Please take it with you at the end of this trip.

"Compartments P-2 and P-3 are refrigerated and hold containers of algel. Please start consuming the algel now, and ensure you are fully fed before the end of this trip. It is important that you are alert and well rested when you arrive. Is there anything I can do for you now?"

"Yes, please tell me who arranged for me and others to escape today."

"I am sorry, Kelvoo, but that information has been withheld from my database to prevent its discovery. I can inform you that your escape was organized by beings who share your values and goals."

"What is our destination?"

"I am prevented from revealing a precise location, but I can tell you that our destination is a clandestine encampment in a relatively safe location."

"What is the purpose of the encampment?"

"To process political refugees for extraction from Terra."

"What is the expected duration of the trip?"

"Our estimated time of arrival is five hours and forty-two minutes from now."

I opened compartment P-2 and removed a chilled container of algel. I had entered the pod with my feeding pouch facing down and my reproductive pouch up. I had to struggle a bit, but I managed to flip, so I could pour the algel into my pouch without any of it spilling and going to waste. Unlike humans, I don't have a sense of taste, but the algel was fresh and energizing, and it made me realize how poor the prison algel had been.

"I watched the monitors as the pod followed the river. Shortly after we departed, the water started flowing faster with many sections of rapids. The tree canopy hung over us along much of the river, giving the appearance of flying through a tunnel. Suddenly, the view ahead was clear. I watched the downward-facing vid feed to see the river drop over a spectacular waterfall. The pod veered to the left, skimming over the forest canopy as it followed the contours of the land, down to plains and fields dotted with towns and villages. Later, I saw vehicles moving below and humans walking. The scene looked like a normal day on Terra before the violent upheavals began. Only the occasional ruin or column of smoke belied the apparent calm.

For the first time that day, I had an opportunity to ponder. I thought about how I was feeling, and I wondered why I wasn't full of intense joy and relief. The entire rescue had been so fast that I hadn't had time to process it emotionally. The experience had been so surreal that I even doubted my senses. My intense stress, combined with the lack of regular, undisturbed meditation over the preceding weeks had likely impaired my ability to sort out my feelings.

I reached deep inside my reproductive pouch until I located the capsule that Sue had given me. I turned it over to read the inscription once more: "Ke soo ko manago dimay." Seeing those words again invoked a blissful sense of freedom and, for the first time since my capture, hope. I didn't feel relief because I didn't know what challenges might be ahead of me. I didn't know whether the capsule might still be needed, so I put it back inside me for safekeeping.

My joy was tempered with intense worry about the humans whom I loved so much. When I told Dr. Bill and Marcus that I had no special attachment to May, Brenna, or Jas, I had, on some level, convinced myself that my concerns had diminished. But I was lying to myself. I struggled to suppress my imagination but found it pointless as I thought about the terrible fates that could have damaged or destroyed each of them. I wished there was some way I could channel the universe to bestow good luck upon them, and I came to understand why prayer and the belief in benevolent supernatural forces might appeal to some beings.

I thought about my human namesake. Kelvoo Buchanan-Paige would have been barely older than May—younger than the minimum age for combatants. I wondered how he could have become an armed rebel, and I thought about his lost youth and the sacrifices he was making.

The journey afforded me the opportunity to examine my behavior during captivity. When I spoke to Dr. Bill with the intention of causing him emotional pain and when I diminished my attachment to May, Brenna, and Jas, I did it with the belief that I would soon be dead and would never have to reconcile my actions. Now that I had a sliver of hope, I realized I had let the human traits of vengeance and deception drag me down toward the values embodied by my captors. I wondered whether my choices would have been different if I had known that survival was possible.

Soon enough my exhaustion got the better of me, and I realized the time was not right for in-depth self-reflection. I closed my eye to the extent that my partly regrown eyelid would allow, relaxed my body, cleared the tumult from my mind, and drifted into the soft respite of a deep and healing meditation. As I entered my altered mental state, I was soothed by the sound of rushing air and the movement of the freight pod as it whisked me toward the next phase of my adventure.

THIRTY-FIVE: LYSERA AND TONE

The voice of the AI in the freight pod woke me up. In my meditation, I heard my name being spoken over and over, each repetition louder than the last.

"Kelvoo! Wake up!" the AI said, louder than before, finally snapping me out of my reverie. "Pardon the intrusion, Kelvoo, but we will arrive at our destination in approximately seven minutes. I suggest you consume more algel." I did as the AI instructed.

The display panels showed that we were once again flying over forest, but the trees were not as tall, and a lighter type of vegetation filled the gaps between them. Flatter terrain was interrupted by mountains with nearly vertical sides, thrusting their way through the canopy. Sol was low in the sky, casting a warm orange glow over the peaks. I didn't know which direction the pod had been heading, so I couldn't tell whether Sol was rising on a new day or setting on an old one. The scene reminded me of the landscapes that May and I had enjoyed around the headwaters of the Yangtze River, and I was filled with a sense of wonder and what humans might call nostalgia.

The pod entered a narrow gap between two spires of rock, then turned a corner to enter a tunnel that wouldn't have been visible from farther away. The tunnel was straight, but it angled downward into a mountain peak. When it emerged, I realized the pod had entered a valley running between the peak behind me and a far higher mountain up ahead. The valley was covered by the forest canopy, obscuring any view from above.

The pod floated along a well-defined path and into a circular clearing. A mixture of anxiety and relief took hold as the pod settled onto a patch of crushed gravel. The forward camera caught a glimpse of two humans as they approached from each side. The hatch opened, and I inhaled the cool, clean, fresh air.

"Greetings, Kelvoo. Welcome to Sanctuary," a female human said, offering me a broad, friendly smile. I sat up and thanked her. Then I reached over to the storage compartment and pulled out the belt with the communication device in its holster and fastened it around my waist.

The human male grinned and offered his hand. Each human grasped one of my hands and used their other hand to support me at my lower elbows as I slid my stiff, sore legs out of the pod and stepped onto the ground. My greeters wore flowing white robes and seemed to be the very picture of serenity. Their calm, peaceful demeanor had a similar effect on my state of mind.

As I turned my eye to take in my surroundings, I noticed two kloormari behind the male human at the edge of the clearing. They stepped forward and greeted me warmly in my native language, which gave me immense comfort.

The human female introduced herself. "In this place I call myself Lysera."

"Does that name have a special significance?" I asked.

"No, it just sounds peaceful to me and has a vibe that fits with this place. Besides, who uses their real name in these times?"

The male told me his name was Tony, but in our location, he was just Tone.

One of the kloormari was Krootoo, and the other one was K'lalo.

"You referred to this place as a sanctuary. Is that its name or its function?" I asked.

"It is both," Tone replied.

"Please, tell me more." I said.

"Let us *show* you," Lysera replied.

As we ambled along a path, the trees gave way to a forest of bamboo, at least ten meters tall. It was morning, as indicated by the brightening sky and glistening droplets of dew on the leaves. Swallows swooped overhead, and unseen birds filled the air with a chorus of chirps, tweets, and calls.

We entered another patch of forest that led to a rock face. Carved into the rock was a terraced structure, three stories high with glass walls facing outward and trees and vegetation planted on top of each terrace. A waterfall cascaded from the top of the rock face and then flowed along the top terrace, falling onto the second and then the lowest terrace before it flowed into a pond at ground level and continued as a crystal-clear stream.

When our group entered the building's ground level, I saw multiple beings of five species—six if I included myself and the two other kloormari. Some beings were standing, and others were sitting on chairs or cushions. Tables lined the far wall. A kitchen was located at one end of the wall, and breakfast items were laid out on the tables. My olfactory receptors came alive with the smells of the food being prepared for the various species. Some of the beings were standing along the table, helping themselves to breakfast, while others were consuming their meals. An algel vat and dispenser were placed at the end of the table.

As soon as we entered the building and the occupants noticed me, they broke into applause. The Sarayans dipped their heads toward me in their traditional show of respect. The Bandorians extended their hands with their palms turned up, and the Mangors landed their hover discs on the floor before joining the applause of the humans and the Silupas. Many of the beings welcomed me by name.

I felt overwhelmed with the love and acceptance of my fellow beings. I also felt embarrassed. My captors and the rulers of Terra had blinded me, separated me from my loved ones, imprisoned me, tortured me, and treated me as a lesser life form. Although I had known they were wrong, and I had resisted at every turn, their treatment still had an effect on my feeling of self-worth. To be welcomed by so many to a place of such tranquil beauty humbled me and filled me with joy.

Lysera touched my shoulder and asked me to walk with her. She explained many things as she showed me around the building and the grounds, including the places where Sanctuary's food was grown.

"Let me start by telling you a bit about this place," Lysera began. "Sanctuary is a way station for beings who need to leave this planet. Tone and I built this place almost ten years ago. We both came from prosperous families. We spent our younger years managing and building our wealth. We never had to work hard or struggle to get by, and we certainly didn't realize just how privileged we were.

"When we were in our forties, we found ourselves bored with living to acquire money and goods, so we started traveling—not to the usual luxury resorts or on interstellar cruises but to places that were off the so-called beaten track. We had some great adventures in all corners of the Alliance planets, and we became thrill seekers of a sort. One day on a trip to Bandor, we met a traveler who was about to take a trip to Perdition as part of an unsanctioned humanitarian aid group. The idea of visiting an outlier planet with its primitive culture was terrifying, but we were also excited to experience a 'forbidden' world.

"Our trip was eye opening to say the least. It was unbelievable to see how women were treated as property and often abused. The corruption on Perdition was endemic, and it led to a few families enjoying wealth that was comparable to Tone's and mine, but the overwhelming majority struggled to survive. We saw the devastating effects of the ancient practice of religious worship. The powerful used it to take advantage of the poor's gullibility with the promise of a blissful afterlife in exchange for the hardship that was all part of their god's divine plan. Of course, Kelvoo, this was before your story became known across the Alliance and before the resulting reforms swept across Perdition and Exile.

"Despite the hardships on Perdition, the people there welcomed us with open arms and shared whatever food or comfort they could. They were so grateful to us and genuinely interested in getting to know us and hearing our stories.

"Our mission was to deliver and set up a portable fusion power source for a small village, but first we had to assemble a building to house it. Tone and I had never worked so hard in our lives. No builder bots were available to the villagers, so we had to create the whole structure by hand, with only one hoverlift to haul material. Tone and I unloaded supplies, helped set the foundation, and assisted when the wall panels were raised. I can't say we were much help since we weren't used to physical labor, so we made up for it with a generous financial contribution to the aid organization.

"We returned to Terra as changed humans. We had made new friends on Perdition, and we learned of other wealthy benefactors. We banded together with them to use our resources to alleviate poverty and injustice. We had always moved in the same circles as other wealthy families and organizations, but we saw that most of them were focused only on acquiring power. Oh sure, they backed charitable causes, but only the ones that would benefit them somehow. Their social and political views were all about consolidating their positions, even at the expense of others. They looked down at us and, frankly, we weren't exactly thrilled to be associated with them. In the end we split into two groups and avoided one another.

"Tone and I could see how society was starting to fracture. We heard the rumblings of discontent, with non-human Terrans labeled as the cause. That's when we decided to build Sanctuary here on this property, which has been in my family for three generations. We would invite our friends to visit and discuss the state of the world and the causes that we wanted to support. Before anyone visited, we had them agree to keep the location a secret, so we could have a peaceful place if the situation deteriorated in the outside world.

"Despite thinking that we were prepared, we were shocked when the Human Independence Movement was formed and started gaining widespread support. It didn't surprise us that the Taylor family was their main backer. The Taylors were the most ruthless and callous of all the powerful families."

"Do you have any news regarding the Taylors?" I asked.

"Oh Kelvoo!" she said. "I know how worried you must be with your foster daughter in their presence, but I have heard nothing about her. All I know is that the income and power the Taylors had before the coup pales in comparison to their present wealth and influence. They funded HIM more than anyone else, and now they're reaping the benefits of Truscott's corruption to an astronomical degree."

Lysera's insight was an epiphany to me. "Is that what it all comes down to?" I asked. "Is it actually about the 'alien menace' and threats to human civilization, or is it just about the accumulation of wealth and power?"

"Now *that* is the question that everyone should be asking!" Lysera said as she touched my arm.

I pondered Lysera's words and then apologized for interrupting her. She continued her story about the founding of Sanctuary.

"When the Humanity Party was elected," she said, "Sanctuary became a crucial meeting place for our closest allies. That's when we built the hidden tunnel through the mountain, so visitors could come and go without revealing our location.

"When the coup happened, some of our friends were able to get up here. Some remain, helping us run the place. Others were forced to pledge loyalty to the HP and Gloria Truscott. Many said what they had to, but they are working with us in secret. Those who refused to bend the knee have disappeared.

"As a well-connected group, we were able to establish contact with beings who were ready and able to organize and lead resistance groups. One of those courageous leaders told us of your escape from the Great Plains Spaceport. I believe he was calling himself 'Bruno' when he met you. You and Chancellor Linford provided him with secure communication devices that were of immense help to the resistance, especially since Bruno's team was able to reverse-engineer the devices and start producing them in quantity.

"Many of our friends joined the fight, and many have died or gone missing. Some of our friends were pacifists like Tone and me. We wanted to help the cause using peaceful means. For us it was only natural to let the resistance use Sanctuary to evacuate refugees, both extraterrestrials and the humans who supported them. That's why you're here with us, Kelvoo."

"Lysera, I am deeply honored that you and Tone and your friends would put yourselves at such risk to help others," I said.

"No, Kelvoo, *we* are honored to host *you*. The impact of our work pales in comparison to the good that you have done and have yet to do."

I didn't know what Lysera was referring to when she referenced the good that I had yet to do, but my emotions were starting to build, and I didn't know what to say.

"How long have the refugees been here?" I asked.

"Most of our guests stay for a few weeks or a few months. Some of them never want to leave, but sooner or later they must, for their own safety. Getting safe passage off this planet isn't easy, with the Brotherhood patrols ready to blast unauthorized vessels out of existence. The only methods are to pay exorbitant bribes or to make a run for it in an exceptionally fast vessel. For you, Kelvoo, there's no bribe that Tone and I could afford that would outweigh the bounty on your head—um, I mean, on *you*. Your evacuation requires an exceptional vessel."

"That's alright, Lysera. This is a beautiful place for me to heal. I could stay here for months or years or as long as it takes. I will be pleased to assist in the wonderful work that you are doing."

"Kelvoo, I think you underestimate your importance. If our plan works out, you'll be leaving us later this week. Since your destination will be Kuw'baal, Krootoo and K'lalo will be accompanying you."

"No!" I exclaimed. "I can't possibly leave before other beings who have been waiting so long! It wouldn't be fair to them!"

"On the contrary, Kelvoo, your story needs to be told and it must be told by *you*. Millions of beings have lost their lives to Truscott's thugs, and millions more are languishing or being tortured in prison. Most beings in the Alliance want their governments to launch rescue missions, but none of the Alliance governments want to be the first to act. Since Terra was expelled from the Planetary Alliance after the election, the Alliance governments want to claim they have no jurisdiction here. Your story could help sway the Alliance and save untold millions of lives!"

"That may be," I replied, "but I would think that many of your guests have endured even more abuse than I have. Can't they be evacuated to tell *their* stories?"

"Yes, Kelvoo, they can, and many of the beings we rescued *have* told their stories. Those individuals have garnered great sympathy from the general population on their worlds and across the Alliance, but it hasn't been enough. Again, Kelvoo, you underestimate yourself. Your original story—your 'testimonial,' as it was called, was a *pivotal* element in the reforms on the outlier planets, in the Correction on Terra, and in the general outlook of the Planetary Alliance.

"The difference with your story is that it will come from *you*. You may not like it, Kelvoo, but you are viewed as a legendary, heroic figure across the Alliance. When you were captured, your legend only grew. If you survive to tell your story, I have little doubt that the Planetary Alliance will be pressured to act immediately"

"It's not right!" I replied. "The entire idea of me being a hero is absurd! The whole 'hero' label has been thrust upon me! I have resisted that title from the beginning! I haven't earned it, and I don't deserve it!"

Lysera grasped my hand paddle and looked at me intently. "Kelvoo, you may not like being seen as a hero, and it isn't for me to say whether you are heroic or not. Personally, I see every resistance fighter and every refugee in this place as heroic. Nonetheless, you are in a unique position to have an impact that could result in every refugee being safely evacuated in a short amount of time."

"And if I fail?"

"Then at least we will all know that we tried."

"I don't know," I said. "It doesn't feel right to jump the queue ahead of the others."

"Kelvoo, I challenge you to talk to every refugee here and find a single one who doesn't want you to escape this broken planet as soon as possible. You'll find that every one of them would be overjoyed to delay their departure and give up their place for you."

Once again I was honored and humbled but also ashamed to be so loved and admired. I had no further argument that I could make, so I relented and accepted the privilege that was so generously handed to me.

Lysera and I walked back to the ground level of the main building. Tone came to greet us. "Kelvoo, come quickly," he said. "There's someone who would like a quick word with you before she leaves."

We walked into the main hall. "Sue!" I exclaimed when I saw my former cellmate.

She rushed over and held my hand paddles. "I just wanted to wish you luck, Kelvoo. I'm about to head back to my unit for my next mission."

"What about our cellmates?" I asked. "Are they all OK?"

"All except Donna, I'm afraid," Sue said, her smile dimming. "They cut her down just as she reached the edge of the forest."

"That's so tragic!" I said. "I wish I'd had the chance to say goodbye to her and all the others. Where did everyone else end up?"

"Well, most of them came from the resistance, so they're back in the fight alongside their comrades. The rest of them are at different way stations while they wait to get the hell off this planet!"

"What about the capsule you gave me? Did you find out what it is?"

"It's a simple locator beacon with an encrypted signal. If you still have it, don't worry; it's been deactivated remotely. Its location was being monitored from a resistance camp down by the river. They knew the layout of the prison, so they knew when you were in the interrogation room. That's when they planned to strike."

"OK, but why *me*? Why wait until *I* was being interrogated? Why not anyone else?"

"You don't get it, do you, you big lug?" Sue asked as her smile returned. "The resistance unit didn't just wake up one morning and say, 'We should do a prison break today!' They don't have the resources to break into a devotion center compound and bust everyone out! They did it for *you*, Kelvoo! That's how important you are! They decided that, while they were rescuing you, they might as well free as many prisoners as possible. It would provide cover for your escape, and it would be a nice bonus to reclaim more fighters. The unit knew there would be losses, but your escape was worth the cost."

Sue's statement left me, once again, feeling guilty and embarrassed. I decided not to burden her or bring her down by arguing, so I just thanked her again and wished her the best for a happy, safe, and successful life. It felt good to have the opportunity to say a proper goodbye to Sue.

I spent the next five days in the healing presence of Lysera, Tone, the many volunteers who ran Sanctuary, and my fellow refugees. We shared stories, and we listened—really listened—to one another.

Many of the volunteers and refugees took advantage of the beautiful surroundings to learn how to meditate—not in the kloormari sense of the word but as a technique that clears the mind and provides a sense of peace, balance, and emotional health. Lysera and Tone had practiced meditation for several years and were pleased to lead sessions on Sanctuary's beautiful grounds.

I took advantage of my time at Sanctuary to meditate in my own kloormari way. Sometimes K'lalo and Krootoo would join me, and other times I would find a quiet place under the forest canopy or in the bamboo. My meditations were deep, restful, and wonderfully restorative. I thought about many things and I processed my feelings about being treated as a hero and my shame at so many lives being risked when others tried to save me.

By the time I left Sanctuary, I had come to realize that other beings, especially humans, *needed* heroes. In their quest to better themselves and in their struggles to overcome evil, heroes gave them something to aspire to. Heroes were an embodiment of courage, integrity, and justice. I came to the pivotal decision that, whether or not I deserved to be a hero, I was not going to deny others the opportunity to be inspired by my efforts. I resolved to do whatever I could to live up to the impossible standards that would be expected of me.

***

At mid-morning on my sixth day at Sanctuary, my communication device alerted me and displayed a message. "Kelvoo, K'lalo, and Krootoo are to proceed to the bottom of the Heavenly Path for extraction details. Time is short. Proceed immediately."

I hurried to the bottom of a steep trail at the signpost that read "Heavenly Path." I had explored many paths at Sanctuary, but not that one. Tone was waiting by the sign, and I saw K'lalo and Krootoo arriving just ahead of me.

"Do we have to leave right now?" I asked Tone. "I just want a moment to say a proper goodbye to Lysera and all my new friends."

"Sorry, Kelvoo," he replied. "The extraction vessel is on its way, and it will take you about twenty minutes to reach the boarding location. There isn't even time for *me* to say a proper goodbye to all of you.

"You must hurry. This path ends at the top of a precipice. That is where the vessel will meet you. The location is exposed, but there's a bamboo thicket where you must take cover to avoid detection from overhead observation. The extraction vessel can't remain there for long and will not wait for you. Go now, my friends! Hurry! May good luck and good fortune be with you always!"

K'lalo, Krootoo, and I hurried up the path. The mountainside was steep, and the path included many switchbacks and stepping stones over rushing streams. On the final sections, we glimpsed the view between trees where we saw other steep mountain peaks.

We reached our destination in just under fifteen minutes. I was awestruck by the view from the precipice. Below us the world was covered in puffy white clouds, like an ocean of seafoam, frozen in time. Sol's rays dazzled my partial eye as the light bounced off the clouds and up into a sky of the deepest blue. The cloudscape was broken by steep mountain peaks like the one we were standing on, their black rock faces and deep green vegetation piercing the soft fluff around them. I stood, taking in the scene before me, drinking in the beauty that still remained on Terra.

"Shouldn't you join us here in the bamboo?" K'lalo asked. Snapping out of my trance, I concealed myself with my kloormari companions.

As the three us stood just inside the thicket, we allowed ourselves to extend our eye domes out of the vegetation to watch for the extraction vessel. With my tunnel vision, I had to keep swiveling my eye to scan the horizon while my companions could remain still and take in the entire spectacle. Twice we saw vessels crossing the sky far overhead, but we could tell that they were destined for other places.

"I see something." Krootoo reported.

"Where?" I asked.

"At the top of the cloud layer, twenty-one degrees left of the nearest peak ahead of us."

With great excitement, I concentrated on the location. It took a moment, but I saw what appeared to be a tiny piece of cloud separating from the main formation and then rising, a tiny white dot against the pale blue of the sky at the horizon. With almost inconceivable speed, the dot sped toward us and arrived in a fraction of a second.

Even Krootoo and K'lalo were dumbstruck as the brilliant white object came to a sudden stop at the top of the cliff.

There it was, hovering and shimmering before us in the full light of day: an honest-to-goodness flying saucer!

THIRTY-SIX: LIKE A BAT OUT OF HELL

A hatch opened from the saucer's lower section, and a ramp extended, almost touching the top of the cliff.

"Please board carefully," a female voice said.

"*Midge!*" I exclaimed.

"Greetings, Kelvoo, and greetings to Krootoo and K'lalo as well," *Midge's* AI voice replied.

I motioned for my kloormari companions to board first. I was shaking with anticipation and excitement as I strode up the ramp, wondering whether the experimental vessel had been saved or reconstructed and how *Midge's* AI had been preserved. My excitement was tinged with sadness, as I missed my friend, Kroz.

As my kloormari companions entered, *Midge* told them to select support frames and secure themselves. As I entered I saw something even more astonishing than my initial sighting of *Midge*.

"Kroz!" I blurted in amazement before thinking that I must have been letting my hope override my logic. "Forgive me," I said. "You resemble a kloormar who was very dear to me and was killed tragically."

"What would make you believe that I am deceased?" the kloormar replied.

"Kroz! Oh, Kroz!" I shouted. "But you died! They found your body at the aviation center!"

"No, my old friend. They likely found a charred body part or two," Kroz said, showing me an arm that was partly regrown from the lower elbow down. "I don't have to remind you that the kloormari species has the ability to regenerate missing parts," Kroz added, motioning toward my partial eye dome.

"I was evacuating equipment from the aviation center," Kroz explained, "and I was most of the way up the hill on a hoverlift when the explosion hit, sending me flying and severing my lower arm and two of my auditory cones. I managed to make my way to a vehicle and leave."

Kroz turned to a human who was seated slightly farther along the console. "Any interlopers?" Kroz asked.

"Nothing on sensor scans yet, commander," the human replied.

"Very good," Kroz said. "Now, Kelvoo, we must get underway momentarily, so we'll have to catch up later. In the meantime, please take your place in the support frame next to me."

I squatted inside the metal frame. Safety restraints extended from the frame and wrapped around my waist, upper legs, and ankles in preparation for the trip.

From the moment I boarded *Midge*, I kept my partial eye dome fixed on Kroz, fearing I was in the midst of a wonderful delusion that would vanish if I looked away. As I stared, I saw Kroz's human crewmate as well as Krootoo and K'lalo in their support frames. Beyond them I saw a figure in a chair, covered by a blanket.

"Before we go, Kroz, I have to ask whether you have any news about May or Brenna. I have come to terms with the possibility that May has lost her life, but if you know anything at all, please tell me now. I know it sounds strange coming from a kloormar, but I loved those girls more than I can possibly express."

"There certainly is news, Kelvoo," Kroz began. I steadied myself to absorb whatever Kroz was about to say. "But there is someone more qualified to deliver such news."

Kroz leaned forward as if to see something hidden behind me. That's when I heard a voice breaking with tears of joy.

"Don't I even get a 'hello'?"

I snapped my eyestalk around to see May's grinning, tear-drenched face!

"May! Oh my dear, dear May!" I exclaimed.

May unfastened her safety restraints and threw herself toward me, landing in my lap. She clung to me, resting her head on one of my shoulders. I extended my eyestalk and partial eye dome, wrapping it over May's head as I used the tendrils on my hand to stroke her hair. I rocked back and forth as we took comfort in our reunion. May's tears soaked my shoulder and flowed down my upper arm.

I was so overcome that I had no idea what to say. All I could do was whisper her name over and over again.

Kroz leaned toward the human crew member. "Status?" Kroz asked.

"Still no bogeys, Commander," he replied.

"Kelvoo, May, I'm sorry to interrupt this important moment," Kroz said, "but you must take your places now. We have got to get underway immediately!"

"We separated ourselves. As May stood and turned to return to her seat, I grasped one of her hands. "May, I have to know—what happened to Brenna? Have you heard anything?"

"Why don't you ask—"

May was interrupted by Kroz's crew member. "Two bogeys closing fast from sectors 19-272 and 17-233. Twenty seconds until we're in their sensor range!"

May leaped back into her chair as its restraints fastened around her.

"*Midge*: single hyper-jump into cloud cover!" Kroz commanded. "Select location to avoid incoming vessel vectors!"

"Hang on, Pa. You're not gonna like—"

Once again, May was cut off as our bodies were wrenched to one side and then snapped back into an upright position. The terrifying experience lasted for less than two seconds. I was shaken, but not nearly as much as my fellow kloormari passengers who were making rasping sounds of primal fear.

"Kroz," I gasped, "I thought *Midge* was equipped with an inertial dampening system!"

"Oh, she is," Kroz retorted. "We flew 50.7 kilometers in just over a second. If not for the dampening field, we would be in a liquid form, dripping down the wall. As I told you back on Kuw'baal, *Midge* is a work in progress, and that hasn't changed!"

"My apologies for any discomfort that you may have experienced," *Midge* said in its calm AI voice.

"Alright," Kroz announced after the threat had passed, "we're going to ascend vertically. To avoid injury, bend at your waist, and grasp your ankles. Humans, if you have difficulty breathing, push off the floor to give your diaphragm more space."

"Are you launching fast to avoid detection by the Brotherhood vessels in orbit?" I asked.

"No, Kelvoo," Kroz replied. "They *will* detect us, and you can expect that we will be pursued! Remember, large vessels can accelerate just as fast as *Midge*, and the size of their dampening fields lets them do so in comfort. Our only advantage is maneuverability. We are going to zig and zag and rise and dip and do whatever we can to avoid their weapons."

"Isn't that risky?" I asked.

"Extremely! But so is staying on Terra," Kroz replied. "What's your preference?"

In addition to my personal risk on Terra, I thought about May and my kloormari companions. "Let's fly like a bat out of hell!" I exclaimed.

Midge began a countdown to the high-velocity launch. "Three . . . Two . . . One . . ."

I felt as if I was being crushed, and my partial eye dome was threatening to burst. I tried to close my eyelid, but it hadn't grown enough to completely cover my eye, so I braced my eye dome between my upper knees.

Much of the light in the vessel came from display panels showing the scene outside. I couldn't look up at the panels during acceleration, but the light they cast changed from the blue of the sky to bright orange as *Midge* burned through the atmosphere, fading to black as we entered space. The entire transition took no more than two seconds.

After ten seconds, acceleration slowed enough to allow the crew to move their limbs and for all aboard to maintain or regain consciousness.

"Two vessels on intercept course," Kroz's crew member announced. "Thirty-one seconds to weapons range!"

"Initiate jump field generation!" Kroz ordered.

"How long until we're at an official Terran jump point?" I asked.

"Are you trying to make a joke, like a human would?" Kroz replied.

"No."

"The requirement to jump *from* a designated point is a rule in Planetary Alliance sectors. Since Terra is no longer in the Alliance, the rule doesn't apply. Also, Brotherhood ships are stationed at the jump points, so they'd just be waiting for us. We do, however, have to jump *to* a surveyed point to avoid materializing in a dust cloud or debris field. So, we're not exactly playing by the usual rules, but let's just say the Alliance has granted a special dispensation for refugee evacuations."

"Fifteen seconds to weapons range," the crew member announced.

"Why can't we jump now?" I asked.

"Because we're too close to Terra. The jump field is initiated but won't stabilize until we're in space that's absent of all micro particles in the field radius. We need to be about half a million kilometers perpendicular to the Terran ecliptic plane."

"Ten seconds!" the crew member shouted.

"*Midge*: Initiate enemy avoidance maneuvering!" Kroz commanded. "OK, listen," Kroz continued. "*Midge* can avoid plasma fire without a problem, but directed energy beams travel at light speed. She can see the direction that these weapons are pointing, and they emit a glow just before firing. That's when *Midge* is going to start veering in random directions. Prepare to be flung around like a leaf in a hurricane!"

The moment Kroz had issued the warning, we were all wrenched in what felt like a downward direction and then whipped to the starboard side. On the monitors I saw the linear distortion of a directed energy beam that had passed close by. Less than two seconds later, the next evasive maneuver flung us again. As the process continued, my muscles grew sore from resisting the jarring movement, and my internal organs were in pain.

"How much longer?" Krootoo gasped.

"Just under 350,000 kilometers to go!" the crew member shouted. "Problem is, we're not traveling in a straight line with all this evasive action!"

"Have they caught up to us yet?" Kroz asked.

"Almost, commander. They're on either side of us and closing in!

"*Midge*: utilize predictive model, Kroz-22," Kroz commanded.

Looking at the display panels, I saw both Brotherhood ships, and I was concerned to see that *Midge* was positioning us directly between the enemy vessels. My concern turned to terror as I saw the barrel of a directed energy weapon pointing at us and starting to glow. The instant the tip became white hot, our bodies were flung forward as *Midge* reversed direction for half a second.

I looked up at the forward display panel and beheld a sight that was tragic and beautiful. An energy beam had passed from the enemy vessel that had been above us and on the port side, through the spot that *Midge* had just left, and straight into the midsection of the other Brotherhood ship. Atmosphere was venting into space as a bright ice mist, accompanied by debris of all sizes. The ship was pitching on its horizontal axis while it rolled and died.

"OK, just one last jolt!" Kroz exclaimed, taking control of *Midge* and blasting us along a straight trajectory toward clear space, fleeing the vicinity of Terra like my proverbial bat fleeing hell.

"Estimated arrival in clear space in one minute and fifty-three seconds," the crew member reported.

It took about twenty seconds for the inertial dampening field to stabilize, returning us to a feeling of normality.

"Alright, we'll be ready to jump in about a minute and a half," Kroz said. "But before we do, there are a few things you should know. Kelvoo, do you recall what it was like to jump when we were aboard the *Pacifica Spirit* and when we were on *Jezebel's Fury*?"

"You know I do! As a kloormar you are fully aware of my perfect memory."

"Yes, of course, Kelvoo. My question is rhetorical, for the benefit of our other passengers. So, Kelvoo, without getting into great detail, how would you compare the two experiences?"

"I would call a jump on the *Pacifica* disconcerting at first but quite interesting. On the other hand, a jump on *Jezebel's Fury* was pure terror!"

"Well," Kroz said, "as I mentioned before, *Midge* is a work in progress. We were able to remove *Midge* from the aviation center and hide her in a cave that we had secretly excavated in the mountains. We were in the process of ferrying equipment to our clandestine facilities when the missile struck. That was when five of my co-workers were killed, and I lost my lower arm.

"We were able to continue working on *Midge*, and we got her dampening field refined to its current level, but we didn't have the resources for anything but the crudest jump technology. This means our jump will feel the same as it did on *Jezebel's Fury*."

"What will the experience be like?" K'lalo asked, sounding nervous.

"It is best described as an 'out of body' experience," I replied. "Do your best to stay calm, and take comfort in the knowledge that the jump is our portal to freedom."

"Clear space arrival estimate: forty-five seconds," the crew member reported.

"Kroz, can we unfasten ourselves now?" May asked.

"Yes," Kroz replied. "In fact, I recommend that all of you prepare for the jump by making yourselves as comfortable as possible."

May left her chair, and I removed myself from the metal frame. We crouched on the deck and clung to one another. "I'm not afraid of the jump, Pa," she said. "I did it many times before on *Jezebel*, but I was only four years old. I'm scared of remembering all the things that happened back then."

"Me too, sweetheart. Me too," I replied, not because I could have forgotten my past experiences on *Jezebel's Fury* but because I was afraid of how I would react if the jump brought my past trauma to the surface.

I swiveled my eye to see Kroz and the crew member monitoring their consoles. K'lalo had taken up a squatting position against the central pillar, and Krootoo was lying on one side, curled into a ball. I became curious about the being seated on the opposite side of the cabin, still fastened in place and still huddled under a blanket.

Kroz started the jump countdown. "Jump in five, four, three . . ." May and I tightened our grip on one another. "Two, one, jump!"

All sounds were sucked from the cabin and then *Midge* and May and my own body vanished. There is no way to describe the utter loneliness of a jump from a vessel that is not equipped with jump mitigation technology. As the seconds passed, not only was I without May or any other beings, I was bereft of my own body. I couldn't move or breathe, but since I didn't have a body, there was no need. I simply existed as the essence of my consciousness.

Surprisingly, since my damaged eye didn't exist in the hyperspatial dimensions, I could see everything around me. Terra was a small sphere, half of it in light and half in the dark. With the bright white Antarctic continent facing me, Terra took on a slight resemblance to the white cloud-shrouded planet of my origin. Luna hung against the starry backdrop, barely more than a dot.

As I had anticipated, the physical, auditory, and visual aspects of the jump brought my experiences from *Jezebel's Fury* to the forefront. Although the memories were vivid and visceral, they no longer frightened me. After all that I had seen and experienced recently, my memories had become integrated into my being. My memories were just another part of me, and my experiences were just milestones on the journey that had led me to become the individual that I was.

I let my memories wash over me as I marveled at the raw universe that was wrapped around me.

I'm unsure how much time passed. Sometimes I recall it taking seconds and sometimes minutes, but at some point the second phase of the jump took hold. Terra and Luna vanished, and Sol became a rapidly receding dot as the surrounding stars were transformed into streaks of light. I would describe the sound that enveloped me as a cosmic "whoosh." My essence was carried across vast expanses of space until, in an instant, the universe and my "presence" came to an immediate halt in front of a vast wall hanging in space.

The wall ranged from black to dark green, and it bristled with weapons and technology. I never would have anticipated feeling such relief to be in the looming presence of a gargantuan Sarayan warship. An instant later, *Midge's* hull and interior formed around me, and then I was my physical self again, crouched on the cabin floor in a flying saucer, clutching May, and overcome with relief and joy.

My kloormari companions were respiring rapidly, but their breathing was starting to slow as their soft sounds of fear diminished. The figure on the other side of the cabin was still under a blanket but was slumped over more than before and was whimpering.

May's breathing was deep and rapid. I was concerned by the degree to which the jump might have traumatized her. Slowly, May released her grip on me. As she looked up, I saw her wonderful smile. "That was amazing!" she said, laughing.

"Welcome to the Kuw'baal jump point," Kroz announced, explaining that the Sarayan warship was stationed there to defend against enemy vessels. Additional warships were positioned at other jump points and in orbit around Kuw'baal.

"We're being hailed by the *Montiba*," Kroz's crew member announced.

"Responding and switching to speaker," Kroz replied.

"Vessel with disc configuration at jump point Kuw'baal-3: this is Sarayan warship *Montiba*. Your configuration matches vessel *Midge*. Request you send confirmation code or indicate otherwise."

"Confirmation sent," Kroz replied.

"Kroz! Great to see you again!" the voice from the *Montiba* said. "We have to know, were you able to extract the target?"

"Affirmative. Target extraction successful. Four additional refugees are also aboard."

"That's wonderful news!" the Sarayan crew member exclaimed. We also heard excited Sarayan chatter in the background.

"Requesting clearance to land in the vicinity of Newton," Kroz said.

"Kroz, take *Midge* to Newton Plain. Landing pad Newton-Alpha will be cleared for your arrival. Proceed at standard cruise speed, and take approach vector two seventy-seven by forty-eight."

Midge started moving. I watched a display panel as the *Montiba's* hull slid by. As we cleared the ship and the space behind it was revealed, I saw the most beautiful orb of pure white. *Midge* began a leisurely cruise toward my original home.

"May," I said, "what's the first thing you'd like to do when we land?"

"Get on my knees and kiss the ground!" she replied.

"For some reason that sounds appealing," I remarked.

"No, that's not enough!" she added. "When we land I'm going to roll around in the dirt and cover myself in Kuw'baal!"

"Now you're talking!" I said, surprised that I might have said something humorous.

May and I talked for a while. We spoke of the things we appreciated about Kuw'baal and the ways in which we would enjoy our newfound freedom. Best of all, May was smiling throughout.

"May, I'm sorry you got cut off earlier," I said after a brief lull in our conversation. "What happened to Brenna? Have you heard anything about her?"

May's expression took a serious turn. She stood and reached out a hand. When I grasped it, she led me to the far side of the cabin.

"What I was going to say earlier, Pa, is, why don't you ask her yourself?"

With that, May reached over and tore the blanket off the huddled figure.

"Brenna! Oh, Brenna!" I exclaimed, thunderstruck.

Brenna was curled up with her head down and her long, dark hair hanging between her knees. She was dressed in nightclothes and clutching the sides of her head.

I knelt down to see Brenna's face, but her chin was tucked against her chest, and her forearms blocked the view from the sides.

"Brenna," I said, "are you alright?"

I reached out to touch Brenna's shoulder, but she flinched and twisted away from me. I looked up at May. "What happened to her?"

May was looking down at Brenna with a degree of contempt. "She's a total mess, Pa, and she deserves every bit of it!"

I didn't know what to do. "Well, we're almost home," I said. "Once we're there perhaps we'll have an opportunity to help Brenna."

I turned back to Brenna. "Brenna, I know a lot of bad things have happened, and I have no idea what you've been through. I just want you to know that I'm here for you. You might not want to hear this, but I love you, Brenna."

Brenna responded to my reassurance by gripping her head tighter and rocking.

"We're going to give you some space now," I said as May and I retreated to take up positions beside Kroz. Then we watched as Kuw'baal grew to fill *Midge's* entire forward view.

Kroz took us straight down and then slowed *Midge*. Kroz switched to a sloping trajectory that lined up with the approach instructions. As we reached the top of the cloud layer, Kroz made a slight adjustment so that we were skimming the cloud tops and passing through the occasional vertical column of cloud.

"This reminds me of our first flight on the *Pacifica Spirit*," Kroz remarked. "We were all so terrified that the sky was solid, and we were going to collide with a cloud and plummet to our deaths!"

Even though Kroz was recounting a moment of terror, my recollection of those early days of discovery brought me great comfort.

"Alright, let's go home!" Kroz added.

A moment later, we were engulfed in Kuw'baal's cloud layers, which were several kilometers thick. Within a few minutes, we broke through the clouds as my wonderful home revealed itself. The first terrain to appear was the geological wonder of Sam's Lake and the valley surrounding it. May and I watched with joyous fascination, knowing that the mineral plain was about to come into view with the kloormari village to our left and the town of Newton on the right.

When the scene revealed itself, it was truly beautiful, but it had changed. I saw lines across the plain, indicating that channels had been dug, and I saw small shelters all over the plain and throughout the hills behind my village and Newton. Small spacecraft and surface vehicles were taking off, landing, hovering, or moving to and fro. I asked Kroz to explain.

"You must understand, Kelvoo, Kuw'baal has been undergoing a great transformation recently."

"The last time that happened, things didn't go well for our species," I replied with great concern.

"It is different this time," Kroz assured me. "This time our species is in control. We are, as the humans like to say, 'calling the shots.'"

"You need to understand that, as one of the less populated inhabitable planets, Kuw'baal has become a major transit hub for Terran refugees. Hundreds of millions of displaced souls have passed through. Some have even decided to settle here. Our planet and our species have provided the means to save untold millions of beings. Our species and our world is truly loved and appreciated beyond measure!"

Kroz's words filled me with a deep pleasure that has remained with me ever since.

Midge banked to her port side and approached the landing pad. Beings of many species lined the sides of the pad, and thousands more were assembled on the plain around the pad and along the village hillside, overlooking the pad. We hovered, then descended to the pad.

"Kroz, why have those beings gathered?" I asked. "What are they doing here?"

Kroz seemed perplexed by my questions.

"Witnessing the incredible return of their hero, of course!"

PART 4: RECONNECTING

THIRTY-SEVEN: A WONDERFUL AND WEIRD RETURN

The ramp folded out from *Midge's* lower section and extended down to the landing pad's surface. May and I stood ready to disembark, as did Krootoo and K'lalo.

"Kelvoo will exit first," Kroz announced. "The rest of you will remain on board until Kelvoo has been formally greeted on the landing pad."

"That hardly seems fair," I replied. "I'm sure that every refugee has an equal desire to enjoy the safety of Kuw'baal."

"I do not doubt the veracity of that statement, Kelvoo. I'm just conveying my instructions from the welcoming committee."

I asked May what she thought and whether she and Brenna should accompany me since we were, after all, a family. "Um, I really don't think Brenna's ready for that kind of attention," May pointed out.

"Arrangements have been made for Brenna," Kroz interjected. "A mental health counselor will come aboard, and Brenna will be taken to a nearby clinic for evaluation. After you have been greeted outside, you and May will also go to the clinic for a debriefing and to give you some privacy and time to adjust."

A light, warm breeze wafted up the ramp as the feeling and the smell of the humid air filled me with a renewed appreciation for my home. I could also hear the sound of thousands of beings eagerly waiting to see me. That motivated me to get the spectacle over with.

"If you would like to join me, May, please follow me down the ramp," I said. "I would be grateful for your support."

"For sure! Thanks, Pa!" May replied.

As I made my way down the ramp, the throng applauded, waved, and roared with excitement. The humans clapped and cheered, the Sarayans dipped their heads toward me, the Bandorians extended their upturned hands, and the Mangors, Silupas and xiltors simply clapped. I was surprised to see my fellow kloormari bowing their eyestalks slightly in what must have been a recently acquired mannerism.

I paused at the bottom of the ramp, and May waited a short way up. Cameras were hovering over me, above the crowd, and over the general area. I had mixed feelings. On the one hand, it was fascinating to be part of such a significant historic event. On the other hand, being the subject of such an event was disconcerting.

I waved at the crowd, and the intensity of their cheers and applause grew. I was delighted to see old friends and acquaintances lining the railing around the landing pad. A podium had been set up on a platform at the spot where the path to the village began. My old friend, K'tatmal, was waiting beside the podium.

I took two steps away from the bottom of the ramp and extended my hand paddle toward May. When she stepped onto the landing pad and took hold of my hand, the cheers subsided, and I saw individuals looking at one another and murmuring. It must have seemed strange to see a kloormar exhibiting a human sign of affection toward a human being. I chose to hold May's hand because I wanted to signal that my experiences had changed me, and I might not fit the image that the crowd had built up. I also wanted to make a symbolic gesture to show that heroes come in all shapes and sizes, and, if I was a hero, I certainly wasn't the only one.

May and I walked toward the podium, and K'tatmal motioned us onto the platform. K'tatmal stepped up to the podium and spoke into a hovering microphone to address me along with the crowd.

"To all gathered beings," K'tatmal began, "and to all beings watching via vid broadcast, it is my profound honor to have been chosen to say, 'Welcome home, Kelvoo!'"

The crowd roared its approval, and K'tatmal had to wait for the commotion to subside before turning toward me and continuing. "Kelvoo, as a kloormar, I know there is a four-letter word that will make you uncomfortable. Nevertheless, you will hear that word frequently directed toward you. That word is 'hero.'"

K'tatmal turned back to the crowd. "Whether or not you see Kelvoo as a hero will depend on the traditions and values of your species, along with your individual viewpoint. We kloormari have never understood the concept of heroism, but we have learned that many cultures embrace it because it sets examples that others can strive for. Heroes demonstrate courage. Heroes have the courage to stand up to tyranny. Heroes have the bravery to state the truth despite the consequences. And heroes are willing to make sacrifices for the betterment of others.

"Kelvoo, you were just over one year old when I crawled from my host's reproductive pouch, so I have known you my entire life. I'm not going to call you a hero, but with my own eye, I have witnessed your courage in the face of tyranny. I have also seen you speak and write the truth of our species, and I know just a few of the terrible sacrifices that you have made on behalf of *all* species in your fight for justice.

"Finally, old friend, I must assume that you are exhausted and in need of meditation, healing, and a nice big bolus of fresh, homegrown algel! As such, I will not subject you to further talk except to say once again, welcome home!"

The horde of well-wishers stood and cheered again as K'tatmal stepped away from the podium.

"I assume you are weary," K'tatmal said, pulling me close, so I could hear, "but if you want to say a few words, you have an opportunity to do so now."

I was surprised to find that I was eager to make a statement, so I sprang to the podium. The crowd's cheering reached a fever pitch, and I had to wait for the roar to settle before I could address them. As I waited, I recalled how nervous I had been when I spoke to the large crowd that had welcomed me to the university. This time I had an important message that I was eager to deliver. *I'm such a different being now!* I thought. *Where did this self-confidence come from?*

"Thank you," I began. "Thank you for taking time out of your busy lives to greet me so warmly. K'tatmal was correct with regard to how I, as a kloormar, would feel about being labeled a hero. I have come to accept that this is the lens through which many of you wish to view me, so I will not offend you by rejecting your perspective.

"Think of me as a hero if you wish, but please do not think of me as *the* hero. The hatred and violence consuming Terra, has produced millions of victims, but it has also produced *millions* of heroes. I would like nothing more than to list the heroes who risked everything to liberate me, so that I could stand before you at this historic moment. Sadly, I can't acknowledge these wonderful beings. I can't put them at risk by telling you their names or their locations or anything about them. That is because, while I stand here enjoying my freedom and soaking up your praise, millions of unsung heroes remain on Terra fighting the oppressors every single day despite the extreme danger to their lives and well-being.

"There is, for example, one very brave, brilliant kloormar who was instrumental in building this incredible vessel," I said, motioning toward *Midge*. "That kloormar and a courageous human crew member rescued me from Terra, along with two other kloormari and two humans. Those humans are dearer to me than I could describe in any language. My rescuers fly this amazing vessel on mission after mission to rescue *true* heroes. With each mission, their lives are in great peril, but still they fly time after time after time. That, my friends, is *real* heroism."

The crowd applauded politely.

"I can also tell you about a human who is my personal hero. She was born into a life without status or privilege, but her tenacity, her character, and her bravery have inspired me. During my capture and imprisonment on Terra, I thought about her all the time, and when I felt weak and helpless and ready to give up, I drew strength from my memories of her.

"I met this human when she was four years old. I was one of several kloormari assigned to teach her and her sister to read. Through a series of tragic circumstances, which many of you will be familiar with, these young humans came to be in my care. Initially, my hero learned from me, but as I have watched her grow into the brilliant young woman that she is now, I have learned so much more from her.

"Over time my human friend came to think of me—a kloormar—as her parent. That's when she started referring to me as her 'pa.' That was a far greater honor than any sort of formal recognition I could possibly receive. You can call me courageous if you wish, but if you wonder where that courage comes from, look no further than my human hero, May Murphy."

I extended my arm toward May and invited her to step forward. She did so, smiling and waving at the cheering crowd. Then May hugged my arm while I concluded my speech.

"In closing, I would like to take this opportunity to address the Planetary Alliance and the delegations from each member world. I know you are under pressure to compel the Terran government to release its prisoners and to allow the safe evacuation of its opponents. I also know that you can provide the necessary incentives and potential consequences to make that happen. At the same time, I understand that none of your worlds want to take the lead on this initiative because to do so will put you at risk. But ask yourselves, what is the nature of that risk? The answer is 'political.' So, you debate, you delegate, and you delay to defer the *political* risks of taking action. Meanwhile, millions of heroes on Terra are taking the *ultimate* risk and thousands every day are paying the *ultimate* price to uphold the very principles on which the Planetary Alliance was founded. I pledge to you that I will not rest until every being that wishes to escape Terra is given the means and the opportunity to do so. Thank you all so much!"

As the Terran expression goes, "the crowd went wild!"

K'tatmal ushered May and me from the landing pad. We made our way along the elevated walkway over the mineral plain and adjoining stream to the path that led up the hill and into my home village. A black vehicle hovered beside the path, partway up the hill. A large crowd of well-wishers formed around May and me as we stepped from the raised walkway onto the path, where we stopped.

"This way to the car," a man said, encouraging us forward.

"There's just one thing I have to do first," I said.

I released May's hand and made my way down the embankment to the stream, beside the pilings that supported the walkway. May followed me partway down while the crowd looked confused and a bit concerned. At the stream's edge, I used both of my hand paddles to scoop up a mound of cold, fresh algel. Then I stuffed as much of it as I could into my feeding pouch. I felt wonderful as I closed my pouch, the excess algel spilling out and dripping down my legs. May chuckled.

The human who had directed us to the car came partway down the embankment and offered his hand to assist me up the loose gravel along the bank. I took his hand and thanked him. When we were back at the foot of the path, May stopped short.

"There's one thing *I* have to do first," she said.

With that, May got down on her knees, just off the path. She bowed her head and kissed the ground. When she raised her head, her lips and cheeks were covered in reddish dust. Then May rolled back and forth in the dust before returning to a kneeling position and rubbing dirt over her arms and body.

The beings around us looked perplexed and unsure of what to do. I paid them no heed as I joined May, dropping to my knees, scooping up dirt, and covering my arms and my sides. My hand paddles and lower limbs were still wet with stream water and algel, so I was smearing myself with a mixture of mud and dust. I threw dust over May, and she responded in kind as the witnesses to the spectacle became increasingly concerned.

At one point, some of the dust thrown by May entered one of my vocal outlets, causing the kloormari equivalent of a cough as the dust burst forth from my outlet, forming a cloud between us. May erupted in squeals of laughter. Despite the fact that I was incapable of laughing, I decided to join May by simulating the sound. I knew I didn't get it quite right. If anything, I must have sounded maniacal. As a result, May's laughter became even more intense and uncontrollable.

Our human guide bent over to talk to us discreetly. "OK, you two," he said, "let's get you into the car and take you where we can get you some help."

We climbed into the passenger compartment.

May turned to me, smiling. "They must think we're crazy!"

"I don't think so," I replied.

"No?"

"No, I'd say they must think we're *cuckoo*!"

"Loony!" May said.

"Barmy!" I countered as we took turns coming up with synonyms.

"Unhinged!"

"Unglued!"

297

"Kloofed!"
"Delirious!"
"Deranged!"
"Demented!"
"Daft!"
We continued trading adjectives all the way to the clinic.

THIRTY-EIGHT: BRENNA'S SAD STORY

I recognized the location of the clinic. A small medical facility once stood there. That facility was where my fellow kloormari and I had been taken years before after our rescue from *Jezebel's Fury*. Now an entire multi-species hospital had been constructed around the original building. The sprawling hospital had been expanded by joining temporary buildings together, further evidence of a planet that was struggling to cope with the sudden influx of millions of temporary visitors and immigrants.

We drove past a wing of the hospital marked by a sign that read, "Mental Wellness Center." A lineup of beings stretched from the main entrance. Most were human, but every Alliance species was represented. Some had vacant looks, some were shaking or exhibiting tics, and a few were talking or shouting to no one in particular.

The car rose and then landed on the hospital roof next to an access door. May and I got out and were escorted down a set of stairs. A staff member led us into a room with a wall of windows looking out over the lower part of the village, the landing pad, the mineral plain, and the town of Newton in the hills beyond.

"Please make yourselves comfortable," the staffer said. "Somebody will be with you as soon as possible."

May and I gravitated to the wall of windows, where we stood and watched the hustle and bustle of what was once a calm, and some might say, boring landscape. The plain, which used to be a stark white expanse of crystalized minerals, was nearly covered with portable shelters. The smallest structures would accommodate one individual, and the larger ones could have housed families of up to ten beings. The plain was crisscrossed with drainage ditches. In the past the afternoon rains would temporarily flood the plain, so the ditches served to make the area habitable, if only temporarily.

The plain wasn't the only area being used; it was just the most striking since it had once been an almost vacant expanse. The distant hills were dotted with shelters for as far as we could see.

Transport vessels were constantly coming and going, carrying shelters or aid for the refugees. The air was thick with passenger vessels; many seemed to be on a trajectory to or from the spaceport, twenty-six kilometers upstream from the village. A majority of the vessels and equipment appeared to be Sarayan, but there was also plenty of human and other technology. Most of the vessels and larger equipment bore symbols of Planetary Alliance relief agencies. The scope of the relief efforts amazed us. As we watched, *Midge* departed from the landing pad, and a bus touched down in its place.

"Out of all your friends, I think I like Kroz best," May remarked as we watched *Midge* disappear behind a building on her way toward the spaceport.

"How did Kroz rescue you?" I asked, "and, for that matter, how did Kroz rescue Brenna?"

May proceeded to describe her situation after she was taken by the Truscovite troops. She had been separated from Jas and hadn't seen him or received any news about him since then.

May had been taken to a processing center and crammed into an overcrowded cell. A few hours later, she was transported and dumped outside a small house somewhere in the European Alps. Brenna had run from the house toward May. Her arms were outstretched, and she was smiling with joy at being reunited with her little sister. In return, May greeted her with a right hook to the chin, knocking Brenna flat on her back. May had jumped on top of Brenna and landed a couple of additional blows.

"I'm outta here!" she said, then walked away.

Brenna followed May as she walked along a mountain path away from the house. Brenna was crying and pleading with May, explaining that she had been rejected by the Taylor family and had been exiled to the mountain house. She told May that she still had a few well-connected friends who had been keeping a lookout in case May was captured, so they could "pull some strings." Thanks to those friends, May had been delivered to her. Brenna also told May that she hated the Taylors, and she had been used by them to stir up hatred against non-humans. Above all, she expressed her regret at the way she had treated me, and she swore to May that she would do anything and everything possible to make things right.

May didn't believe a word that Brenna was saying, including Brenna's assertion that they would be stopped and forced to turn back to the house if they walked much farther. Minutes later, a perimeter guard bot sped over and hovered in front of them, ordering them to return to the house. When May shot an obscene gesture toward the bot, it responded with a ball of plasma that blasted a hole in the ground just in front of them. With Sol starting to set and the thin mountain air getting cold, May had no choice but to storm back toward Brenna's house, with Brenna struggling to keep up.

Exhausted, cold, and hungry, May devoured a warm supper at Brenna's home. She didn't want to hear any more from Brenna, but she had little choice as Brenna regaled her with a tale of woe. Brenna told May about the pressure that the Taylors had subjected her to. Griffin had constantly belittled her and mocked her humble background. If she complained, he pointed out all the things his family had bought her and the luxurious life she was living, telling her she should be "damned grateful."

The lowest point for Brenna came after the debate between Gloria Truscott and me. As the debate began, Griffin pulled Brenna into the studio and made her sit in the front row. Truscott's team had envisioned that seeing Brenna would fluster me and throw me off balance. When I called out their tactics and stepped to the front of the stage to talk directly to Brenna, and Brenna broke down with emotion, I ruined their plans and negated the impact of Brenna's presence.

After the debate, when Brenna and Griffin returned to the Taylor estate, Griffin verbally accosted Brenna and slapped her. The family didn't know what to do with her, so they exiled her to one of their properties in the mountains where she had limited contact with the outside world.

When Brenna finished telling May her story, May had reacted not with sympathy but with anger.

"Well, boo-hoo!" May replied. "You were taken in by a bunch of rich people who bought you nice stuff! Then they were mean and took advantage of you! Then you got moved to this place in the mountains! Oh, how sad!

"Do you want to know what *is* sad, Brenna?" May shouted. "First off, I have a sister who's so ungrateful to Kelvoo—the being who loved us and took care of us—that she took off out of the blue to hang out with the people who would do anything to hurt anyone who isn't like them, but you already know that! What you don't know is Kelvoo and I tried to leave when it was Kelvoo's turn for deportation. We were herded like cattle through the spaceport. We found out that they were looking to capture Kelvoo, so we made a run for it with a kloormar called K'deet. K'deet was shot, and K'deet's guts were splattered all over us! Can you even imagine what that was like?

"Then we ran from a bunch of soldiers who were shooting at us. They didn't want to capture us; they wanted to kill us, and they almost succeeded! They chased us into a forest, where we got lost. We were saved by a bunch of rebels who are risking their lives and dying to fight back against the killers that you thought were so wonderful.

"Chancellor Linford took us back to the university where we had to hide and wait for your murdering friends to attack. We were just sitting

301

there, waiting to die. Do you remember our friend Kroz from the aviation center? Or have you forgotten every decent being you ever met? Well, the aviation center got blown up by your friends! The searchers only found pieces of Kroz! What the hell did Kroz ever do to deserve that? Huh?

"Quit looking away Brenna! Look at me! Have some guts for once in your miserable life because I'm not even at the 'best' part yet!

"Kelvoo and I were moving to the basement of the administration building to hide out. Those bastards bombed the building while Kelvoo was down there alone. Somehow Kelvoo managed to get outside. That's when they found Kelvoo. Want to know what they did to Kelvoo? Huh? Those bastards cut Kelvoo's eye off! When we got there, Kelvoo's 'blood' was squirting out of the eyestalk, but Kelvoo wasn't dead yet! Kelvoo was screaming for me to run! That's when more of your scumbag friends grabbed the chancellor and me.

"Want to know the last thing I saw when they carried me away? Kelvoo's body, twitching and shaking, holding on tight to Kelvoo's own eye! You know what I hope, Brenna? I hope Kelvoo died, and the chancellor was executed, because if they weren't, they're probably being tortured right now!

"How's that for a sad story, Brenna? Is *that* sad enough for you, or are you just going to keep on saying 'Oh, boo-hoo, poor me'?

"Want to know who I blame for this, Brenna? You! I blame you! It's *your* fault! I hate you, and I think you're a disgusting, self-centered brat!"

As May recounted her outburst, she became increasingly upset. By the end her hands were clenched into fists, she was shaking, and she was on the verge of shouting.

"You must have been so angry," I observed, "and I can see that you're still very upset."

"No kidding!" May replied.

"So, do you really think that Brenna's to blame for all the things we experienced?"

"No, Pa, but I wanted to hurt her for being so stupid, and I guess I succeeded."

May and I were still looking out through the clinic windows, waiting for a counselor to show up. I thought it might be useful for May to speak her peace in the presence of a mental health professional.

"What was Brenna's reaction?" I asked.

"She ran to the kitchen and grabbed a knife and pointed it toward herself. The kitchen servitor bot set off an alarm and kept repeating, 'Danger! Stop your action!' I walked in and said, 'Don't you dare, you coward! Killing yourself is cheating! If you have a shred of decency and

302

you actually feel bad about what you've done, you're going to live! I want you to live every single day, full of regret at how you treated the people who loved you and took care of you. I want you to live, so you can feel shame and maybe even face justice someday!' Brenna dropped the knife and curled up in the corner and cried and cried."

"So, is that when Brenna shut down? Is that when she became the way she is now?"

"No, not quite. She could still talk and kind of respond, but she got worse when Kroz showed up."

"Do you mean when Kroz showed up in *Midge* and rescued you?"

"No, we saw Kroz well before that! The morning after my first night in the mountain house, I was walking outside, trying to figure out how to get past the perimeter bots and run away. That's when a freight pod dropped straight down out of the sky. It landed in the meadow right in front of me, and Kroz climbed out!"

"You must have been so relieved that Kroz was alive."

"For sure, but Kroz looked kind of gross with the missing lower arm. It hadn't started healing yet, so the stump had a bunch of loose, dangling bits on the end. I asked Kroz how it had been possible to find me and get past the guards. 'It all comes down to who you know,' Kroz said. 'Knowing a bit about technology also helps.' I figured that Kroz wanted to protect me by keeping the details secret.

"Kroz told me to stay put. Kroz was working on a plan for your escape, but it would take a few weeks or months, so I needed to stay in the house. When you were freed, the plan was for Kroz to come back for Brenna and me. I told Kroz that Brenna should be left behind because she was a dirty traitor.

"We talked for a little while about Brenna, and I told Kroz how she was feeling guilty and stupid now that she had been betrayed. We talked about humans and how so many of them used to be kind and smart but had been swept up in the Human Independence Movement and lost their minds. Kroz couldn't understand it but said that humans seem to have a deep fear of change, and immigrants were part of that change. Kroz said that HIM seemed to make sense to people who wanted to be part of something big, especially humans who held a grudge against extraterrestrials. The part about holding a grudge made sense, with Brenna blaming you for our dad dying. Kroz said that if I wanted to be with you on Kuw'baal, then Brenna had to come along too.

"I wasn't about to forgive Brenna, but I decided to ease up on her. She and her HIM friends wanted to blame extraterrestrials for all of their problems, so I figured that if I blamed her for all of our problems, I wouldn't be much better than the HIM people."

"So, the next time Kroz came to you, was it for the rescue?" I asked.

"No. Kroz came to the house and visited Brenna and me. Seeing Kroz upset her, especially when she saw Kroz's partly regrown arm. Kroz told us about a plan to get a locator beacon capsule to you. The resistance had an insider in the devotion center, but Kroz was worried that you wouldn't go along with the plan because you might think it was a trap. Kroz said you trusted me more than anyone, so Kroz asked me to come up with a message that you would recognize but no one else would know the meaning.

"Since my Infotab had been confiscated when I was taken, I had been using Brenna's. I remembered that she had been working on a 'simplified kloormari' language that humans would be able to speak. I transferred a copy of the documents to Kroz's device and we came up with 'Ke soo ko manago dimay,' which Kroz was going to engrave on the capsule."

"I will meet you again. From May," I said, repeating the words in Terran. "I'm glad you didn't write 'from Brenna' because then I would have suspected a trap!"

"That's what we figured, so we put my name on it," May replied. "Kroz gave us a new secure communication device, like the ones we gave to Bruno's rebels. Kroz said that if everything went according to plan, I'd get a message on the device in a few days. When that happened, we needed to be ready to go."

"You must have been excited to know I was alive and that we might see each other again."

"Yeah, Pa, I was glad you were alive, but I was also scared of what you might be going through. You haven't told me anything about that yet, and I'm not sure I want to know."

"How did Brenna react to the plan?"

"She was terrified. She kept saying, 'I can't face Kelvoo! Not after what I did! I can't do it!' As each day went by, she became more scared. She wanted to be alone, and she hardly spoke, except to say 'Go without me. Leave me here.' I was worried she'd run away and hide when Kroz got there. I used the com device to let Kroz know what was happening. We agreed that I wouldn't tell Brenna when Kroz was coming, so we would both be there to convince her to leave with us.

"I got the message from Kroz just twenty minutes ahead of time. It was 04:15, so Brenna was asleep. *Midge* landed quietly in front of the house. I let Kroz in, and we burst into Brenna's room. She flipped out, screaming that we couldn't take her. She clung onto the top blanket, so we pulled her out of bed, blanket and all. She struggled and fought, but somehow we managed to haul her up the ramp into *Midge*, just as the crew member shouted that vessels were approaching. We got out of there just in time!"

"That's an incredible story, May," I said. "You never fail to amaze me!"

At that moment the door to the room hissed open. A harried-looking counselor entered. Behind her, a hover chair carrying Brenna was pushed into the room by a member of the clinic staff. May and I turned to see the counselor standing there, gawking at us. We were still covered in mud and dust from our earlier antics, with much of the dirt having dried and dropped in piles on the clinic floor. When May saw the counselor's startled look, she burst out laughing. I can only imagine what the counselor must have made of the bizarre tableau.

THIRTY-NINE: MOVE IN, CATCH UP, AND BREAK THROUGH

Our first family counseling session was not especially noteworthy. Brenna remained non-responsive while May and I answered questions and shared parts of our stories. When May spoke, she was far more measured and matter-of-fact than when she had been speaking with me. She and I were subjected to a variety of psychological evaluations.

At the end of the session, a course of treatments was offered. Weekly sessions were scheduled for me, and daily sessions were set up for May to deal with her "anger issues." Brenna was evaluated as "non compos mentis." As her former guardian, I agreed that she would remain as an in-patient until she could function without risk to herself or others. As Brenna's only blood relation, May was legally required to agree, which she did without hesitation.

The clinic sent a message to the kloormari elder, Kahini. I knew Kahini from my days in the village before human first contact. Kahini walked with us to a house that the village had provided. Our new home turned out to be the same dwelling where we had lived prior to leaving for Terra. When we arrived, a kloormar was moving out while an aid organization was moving an algel vat in for me, along with a few human furnishings for May and perhaps Brenna in the future. The dwelling was also being stocked with donated food and clothing for humans, and Kahini handed a new Infotab to May.

I objected to the arrangement, and May agreed with me. "No, Kahini!" I said, "We can't displace the current occupant, especially when so many refugees are living in temporary shelters!"

"The clinic said it would be best for you and the young humans to recover in familiar surroundings," Kahini replied.

I was about to object to all of the special treatment we were receiving when the former resident approached. "Kelvoo, please honor me by letting me turn this dwelling over to you. I insist!"

"But where will you go?" I asked.

"K'riti will be staying with me in my home," Kahini said. "Besides, if you were to be placed in an emergency shelter, there would be an outcry about how the courageous hero of Kuw'baal was being treated so terribly." May and I were too exhausted to argue, so we capitulated and moved back into our former home.

The sky outside was darkening, and the village lights came on. Still covered in dust but too weary to bathe or change clothes, May laid down on top of her new bedsheets.

Before she fell asleep, May glanced over at me. "Pa, when you made your speech, you called me a hero. Why did you say that? What did I ever do that would make me a hero?"

I took her hands in my hand paddles. "May, you have been loyal to those who love you, you have been true to your principles, and you have shown kindness toward others."

"Is that all it takes to be a hero?" May asked.

"Yes, May. That's all it takes."

With that I went downstairs and squatted in front of the main windows, overlooking the village and the plain. I closed my eye and descended into a deeply restful meditative state.

I remained at rest through the night, the following day, and the subsequent night. Three times I was aware that May had woken up, used the washroom, and taken some food and drink, but she went back to bed each time.

In my meditation I processed and cataloged information from the last several days. I analyzed my options for fulfilling my promise to pressure the Planetary Alliance to evacuate innocent victims from Terra. It turned out I had already succeeded.

When I finally emerged from meditation, I saw that the window coverings had been drawn shut. May was devouring breakfast. She bounded toward me with a smile and handed me a bowl of algel. May sat beside me and showed me news clips that she had saved to her Infotab. My speech at the landing pad had been broadcast across all of the Alliance worlds. More importantly, my pleas to the Alliance for the Terran evacuation was heeded to such a degree that the Alliance delegations were practically tripping over one another to be the first to act or the one to commit the most resources.

A few days before, I would have bristled at being labeled a hero, but the news made me appreciate the incredible influence and power that I wielded now. I decided I would remain humble, but I would use my influence for the betterment of all beings, especially those who were marginalized or oppressed.

After I had seen enough of the news coverage, May suggested that I look outside. I peered through a gap in the window coverings and was amazed to see a cordon of security surrounding the house, keeping a horde of media and well-wishers at a respectful distance.

"Should we let them know we're alright?" May asked.

I opened the window coverings, and May and I waved at the crowd. It took a moment for them to notice us and for word to spread farther back in the group, but soon they erupted in cheers and waved back. We would step outside and say hello at some point, but not until we had spent a few hours of quality time together.

***

Over the subsequent months, planets kept turning, events continued to unfold, and my life and the lives of those I loved went on.

The day after my return to freedom, the Planetary Alliance contacted the Terran government, advising them that an evacuation fleet was on its way. The response was belligerent until a fleet of Sarayan warships jumped to Terra, causing the Brotherhood vessels to flee "like rats from a sinking planet," to use a phrase May had coined. Gloria Truscott remained defiant. She told the Alliance to do something to themselves that would be physically impossible for all but two member species. Her attitude changed when the warships entered a low Terran orbit, making them clearly visible from the ground, even in broad daylight. Truscott then claimed to welcome the evacuation since it would cleanse Terra of the alien filth and the human "species traitors" who supported them.

The evacuation took several months and involved every Alliance world. Vessels and volunteers from the human outlier planets also joined the fleet. The Truscovites attempted to hide prisoners whom they considered to be "high value" or those with grievous injuries from torture, but the evacuation force thwarted these attempts with their superior surveillance technologies. Information was also forthcoming from regretful Truscovites who saw the wreckage of their once beautiful world and were more than willing to switch sides in exchange for their own evacuation.

Hundreds of millions of humans in the resistance refused the offer to leave Terra, preferring to risk their lives and well-being to fight tyranny and restore peace to a world that was integral to their identity. They said that leaving Terra would be like losing a limb. Given that humans have only four limbs and are incapable of regenerating lost body parts, I found the statement especially powerful.

Millions of extraterrestrials had been born and raised on Terra and wanted to stay behind and fight, but the humans in the resistance encouraged them to leave since they wouldn't be able to blend in with the general population and would be killed on sight by Truscovites. In the end, almost all extraterrestrials felt they had no choice but to leave Terra. Their only comfort was a promise that they would be welcomed back someday when peace was restored.

When the evacuation was fully underway, the impact on the Alliance worlds was massive. Each planet grappled with the logistics of relocating, housing, and feeding refugees who had left behind their possessions, friends, and livelihoods.

At the peak of the evacuation, five million refugees were transiting through Kuw'baal each day. Every capable kloormar joined with aid providers, volunteering or otherwise contributing to the relief efforts. May and I assisted with food distribution and setting up shelters, but we were limited since our celebrity status required the constant presence of our security contingent. A management team had been assigned to us, so every aspect of our lives outside the house was carefully choreographed. While the situation was annoying, we realized we had duties far greater than our personal wishes, and we never lost sight of how fortunate we were compared to the evacuees.

An infobase was set up for missing Terrans. May and I used it to look up beings whom we had met on Terra. For the ones we couldn't find, we posted their names and whatever we knew about them. I learned that many of my human friends and colleagues had been able to find their way off Terra. Most of the university faculty had left after the university was effectively shut down but before the mass deportations of extraterrestrials. Most of my first-contact friends had relocated to Perdition, Exile, or Saraya or were serving on interstellar Alliance vessels. My fellow Sagacity Club members had left Terra, with the exception of Martin Hoffman.

Dr. Hoffman was one of many listed as "location unknown," which didn't necessarily mean he had disappeared. For their safety, members of the resistance were shown as "location unknown." For example, while Lynda Paige was living on Saraya, her son—my namesake—Kelvoo Buchanan-Paige, was still on Terra, fighting the Truscovites.

Lysera, Tone, and the beings who lived and worked at Sanctuary were shown with "location unknown" until the end of the evacuation, when I was relieved to see that they had relocated to Exile.

Sadly, the database also revealed many tragedies. Several refugees had updated the status of Chancellor Jasmit Linford. After his capture, and during my imprisonment and torture, a sham trial was staged. As an educator, Jas was found guilty of corrupting the minds of human students. As a human who tried to save my life, he was also convicted of harboring enemies of Terra. This intelligent, compassionate man and leader was executed immediately. It was difficult for me to break the news to May. Both of us were devastated.

A few days later, an update to the database revealed that Jas's intimate partner, Simon, had been arrested shortly after Jas's execution. Under the new religious doctrine, Simon was tried and found guilty of homosexuality and conspiracy to pervert society. He was executed in public as a warning to others. *Surely, madness has overrun Terra*, I thought as I pondered the pointless tragedy of it all.

The news of Simon's death was more devastating to May than I would have anticipated.

"Do you remember when I burned the cookies on election night?" she asked.

"Of course I do."

"Simon reassured me and then he tried to eat a cookie along with the chancellor and me before we all started choking and spitting them out. Then by the fire later, he's the one who started us singing 'Building Bridges.' He was such a nice person. What kind of humans would want to hurt him?"

I had no reply for May.

May's routine included visiting the clinic every morning. I had weekly sessions, and Brenna remained in the facility for the first ninety-two days.

My sessions were mostly geared toward updating my counselor about how May was doing and providing information about events that added or relieved stress for May and me.

May's sessions were aimed at resolving her anger toward Brenna and other humans who had fallen under the spell of the Human Independence Movement. May's counselor informed May about Brenna's deep-seated resentment over the death of their father and how that resentment attracted her to HIM's simplistic black-and-white dogma.

After eight weeks, Brenna was brought into May's sessions. Initially, Brenna was unable to contribute much, but with the counselors' guidance, the sessions allowed May to speak her peace to Brenna while the counselors guided May on how to explore and channel her own anger in a more positive way.

The counselors suggested that May's anger had sprung from Brenna's disregard for May's wish to "protect" me from my naïveté and the humans who might seek to exploit it.

Brenna's treatment started with medication along with brain scans and neural stimulation. She started speaking again, first with the counselors and then with May, but only about the most benign subjects. Over time, Brenna could talk about past events on Terra or stressful subjects with May as long as a counselor was present. After three months, Brenna reluctantly accepted the counselor's recommendation to spend the occasional day and night at home with May and me. Brenna couldn't bring herself to talk to me or even to look at me, but she would talk with May in whispered conversation.

One day I received a message from my first-contact friend, Bertha Kolesnikov. Bertie had joined a relief effort on Kuw'baal, serving as a cook at a refugee feeding station. She had a two-day break and wanted to visit me. My security team was reluctant, but I insisted that every arrangement must be made to accommodate Bertie in my home.

Bertie arrived on a morning when Brenna had just stayed overnight. That afternoon, Brenna was scheduled to return to the clinic for a few days, so Bertie had a brief opportunity to interact with Brenna. I was apprehensive due to Bertie's penchant for direct, unconstrained honesty, but I was curious to know whether she and Brenna would connect and what form their conversation might take.

"Kelvoo!" Bertie shouted as she stepped through our door. She wrapped her muscular arms around me and pulled me in tight, unperturbed that she was blocking my upper vocal outlets and throwing me off balance. May walked up to Bertie and was startled when Bertie grabbed her into a bear hug, followed by a sloppy kiss to the cheek. Brenna didn't move from her seat and was looking down at the floor.

"Hiya, Brenna!" Bertie said. "Little bit shy, are ya? That's OK, hon."

I invited Bertie to sit on the sofa. "Sure, I'll sit next to this lovely lady," she said, plunking herself down next to Brenna. "C'mon over here, sweetie, an' sit next to me," she said to May while patting the cushion next to her.

With the girls on either side of her, Bertie asked me how things were going. I didn't want to upset Brenna by recalling anything before our return to Kuw'baal, so I provided an upbeat assessment of our lives. Then Bertie changed the subject.

"One thing I wanna do is to get to know the two of you better," she said while patting Brenna and May's knees. "After all, I only metcha fer a minute or two at Kelvoo's welcome party back at the university. Hey, do you remember me teachin' Kelvoo how to dance?"

"I'm still trying to forget that!" May exclaimed as Bertie stood and started bouncing around, twirling her arms and extending her head back and forth. May burst out laughing and then I noticed something I hadn't seen for years. A hint of a smile crossed Brenna's face. I never would have thought that I could feel such relief or so much hope from a brief facial expression.

With the ice broken, Bertie sat back down and turned to Brenna. "So, hon, how've you been?"

Brenna shrugged.

"Look," Bertie continued, "I know things have been rough for ya, but it looks like you've got people who care about you and love you a whole lot. I just wanna know how yer life's goin'."

"Umm," Brenna said, glancing toward me with a strange expression.

"Isn't there something you should be doin'?" Bertie asked, turning to me.

"No, Bertie, not that I'm aware. I—" I stopped short, realizing what Bertie meant. "Oh, yes, Bertie! I need to go into the kitchen and read my Infotab for a while!"

I went into the kitchen, pulled out my Infotab, and squatted by the counter. I could still see Bertie and the girls, and I could hear them speaking. I thought it was important for me to be aware of anything Brenna said, but I hoped the semblance of privacy would help her to open up.

"So where were we, hon?" Bertie asked. "Oh yeah, how's life?"

"It's too good for me, Bertie. I don't deserve it," Brenna said in a near monotone.

"You don't deserve to have a good life?" Bertie asked.

"I don't deserve to live at all!"

"Aw geez, hon. I hope you haven't thought about hurtin' yerself!"

May shot a look at Bertie that I interpreted as, "Please don't go there!" I was also alarmed that Bertie might be planting thoughts of suicide into Brenna's fragile mind.

"Yeah, I've thought about it a lot," Brenna replied without emotion, filling me and May with dread.

"Well," Bertie replied, "I've known people who've chosen that route. Sammy Buchanan was a wonderful man and one of my best friends. He was also Kelvoo's best friend. Sam didn't think he deserved to live, so he offed himself. Do you think that made things better for anyone, or did it just create a whole lot more pain and sufferin' for everyone who'd ever loved him?"

Brenna didn't reply, but I could tell she was weighing Bertie's words.

"Brenna told the counselors she should turn herself in and be punished," May interjected, "but they keep telling her that she hasn't committed any crimes."

"Look," Bertie said to Brenna, "I followed the broadcasts, so I know a bit about what happened with ya. You were in a bad place. Then along comes a guy! The guy acts real nice, he treats you special, an' he's a slick talker. He gets you to do stuff you'd never think of doin' and then he takes off an' leaves ya hangin'!" Bertie chuckled. "Hon, if that's a crime, I'd be servin' about twenty life sentences right now!"

Once again, I saw Brenna's beautiful smile.

"So, you really think you should be punished?" Bertie asked.

Brenna's smile twisted, and her eyes closed tight, squeezing out tears that ran down her cheeks. "Yeah," she said between sobs.

Bertie reached over and hugged Brenna in a comforting, motherly way that I will never be capable of. As Bertie rocked Brenna, Brenna's tears soaked into Bertie's blouse.

"If you were gonna be punished, who would that help?" Bertie asked.

"It would help me," Brenna said, "because I deserve to pay for what I did, and it would help other people because it would show that justice works."

"OK, so let's say you should pay for your mistakes," Bertie replied, causing May to lean over and shake her head with concern.

"It's OK, sweetie," Bertie said to May. "I'm just sayin' it for the sake of argument. So, Brenna, let's say you should pay. There are two ways you can do that. You can do something to hurt yourself, or you can do something to help others. So, if you're convinced that you need to *atone*—I think that's the right word, then why don't you make that your goal? Why don't you think about what you can give to others, to make up for your one little mistake that any of us could've made?"

Brenna clung to Bertie, crying unabashedly in a catharsis that was both painful and joyful to witness.

May also started crying. She put an arm around her sister as Bertie held both girls. "I'm sorry I was mean to you," May said to Brenna, sobbing.

When the time came for Brenna to return to the clinic for a few days, she thanked Bertie. Bertie transferred her contact information to Brenna's Infotab and told her that she could call "Auntie Bertie" any time. I walked with Brenna back to the clinic and had my first actual conversation with her since she left our home at the university. We didn't talk about her feelings or any "difficult" subjects; we just made small talk, and it felt wonderful.

The next morning, I received a call from one of Brenna's counselors. "I'm happy to report that we might have a small breakthrough," the counselor said. "Brenna has been talking about atonement for what she thinks are her wrongdoings. We have been assuring her that she has done nothing wrong, but we think it might be good for her healing if we helped her channel her wish to atone into contributing to society."

I told the counselor that the idea sounded wonderful. I added that I was so impressed with their insight and strategy, knowing full well that the breakthrough was Bertie's doing.

The following morning it was time for Bertie to leave.

"Bertie, you have got to be one of the wisest humans I have ever met!" I said.

"Aw, shucks," Bertie exclaimed, "better not say that too much, or it'll go to my head!"

"Have you ever considered becoming a counselor?"

"Naw. If I did, they'd be outta business lickety split!"

"How so?"

"Thirty minutes with me, an' the patient would be cured! If I trained other counselors, and they listened to me, they'd run outta patients in no time!"

While I still didn't understand humor, I knew that Bertie was joking. Her crusty, no-nonsense persona and direct approach was a protective shell that housed a wise mind and a tender heart. We said our goodbyes and promised to keep in touch. As Bertie ambled away, I added her to my internal list of humans whom I loved deeply.

FORTY: A PROPER GOODBYE

By the time we reached the one-year mark after our return home, the situation had eased into a "new normal." Schools had reopened, and May was completing her basic education through a Terran language program. Brenna had also settled into a new normal to the point where we could have interesting, enjoyable conversations. She had become a far calmer person who no longer took offense as her default reaction. We had both learned how to define and exert our personal boundaries, and I learned how to back off when Brenna signaled that I should change the subject.

Brenna wasn't interested in continuing her education and earning a degree. She found employment with a multi-species institution that was establishing a new justice system that was compatible with all of the species that now inhabited Kuw'baal. As one of the directors of the institution, K'tatmal enjoyed any opportunities to work with Brenna.

Brenna made it clear that she intended to leave Kuw'baal to take on humanitarian work as the atonement aspect of her healing. Until then, Brenna's work allowed her to live in her own home over in Newton, and her time at the clinic was reduced to one session per week. Independent living was another building block in Brenna's recovery. From our home, May and I could see Brenna's house in the distance.

Brenna had her own home because refugees were no longer transiting through Kuw'baal, leaving many semi-permanent structures uninhabited. The Planetary Alliance had done a remarkable job removing old shelters and refuse from Kuw'baal and restoring the natural environment. On the mineral plain, the temporary drainage ditches had been filled in, and once again the bright white vacant plain reflected the diffuse daylight. As before, the afternoon rains would flood the plain. May and I enjoyed wading in the shallow, salty floodwaters after a downpour. We both found great peace and contentment standing ankle deep in the water as the shallow lake sank into the crystalline ground, and wisps of vapor rose up to the clouds above.

I was able to resume my teaching career by continuing my previous course, "Human Nature – An Outsider's Perspective," albeit with material updated to reflect my experiences and the tragic demise of Terran society. I limited my engagement to two classes per week, working from my home and interacting with students remotely via the quantum entanglement network. I worked with all manner of educational institutions across the Alliance. I contributed my course materials and recorded sessions at no charge in the interest of providing education and perspective to displaced beings who were struggling to make new lives for themselves. I did ask my students and their families to donate whatever amount they considered fair but only if they had the means to do so. The revenue was enough for me to purchase the necessities for May as well as a few comforts, including a vehicle.

May and I used the car to explore the area around the village or farther afield, including other villages and burgeoning immigrant settlements. Sometimes we would visit the park at Sam's Lake and admire the natural beauty. We visited Brenna once in a while, and sometimes May would use the vehicle so it could drive her to school on windy, dusty days or whenever a heavy rain pelted down at an unusual time. She also took the car when she visited Brenna without me. May liked visiting Brenna for gab fest bonding sessions. May had suggested to Brenna that she could call me "Pa" if she wanted to. Brenna replied that it was nice that May and I were close, but she wasn't comfortable calling me anything other than Kelvoo.

Three months after Brenna moved into her new home, she sent a message asking to meet May and me at our house. When she arrived, Brenna let both of us know that she had come to a decision about how to atone for her mistakes.

"I'll be leaving in four weeks," she said. "I've accepted a volunteer position on Exile. Things are still chaotic there, so I'll be staying in a relief camp where I won't be able to communicate with you."

"So, you're going to help settle refugees on Exile?" May asked.

"No. I'm going to help people who were already living on Exile, older people and mostly women."

"Why would *they* need your help?" May inquired.

"Because they're just like you and I were, May. They can't read. They're living in one of the communities that used to treat girls and women as property. You were very young then, but you probably remember that the only expectations for our future were housework and having babies.

"When I made my selfish choice to run away on Terra, I was used and rejected by evil people. I thought my life was so awful, and I felt so sorry for myself. When I learned what *you* went through, it put my problems into perspective. And when I learned what happened to *you*, Kelvoo," she said, turning to me, "I realized how much worse things *really* could have been for me.

"May and I were so fortunate that you and the other kloormari taught us how to read on *Jezebel's Fury*. Sure, we might have ended up getting some schooling after the Terran Correction, and May was young enough that she might have learned, but I would have been starting much later, and I doubt my life would have amounted to much. That's why I've decided to volunteer to teach basic literacy skills to adults. I'm able to do this because of you and your friends, Kelvoo. I'm going to do this as a tribute to you and to try to repay the universe for bringing you into my life. I just want to show some appreciation for everything that you've done for May and me."

Brenna's statement stirred profound emotions in me.

"Brenna," I replied, "there are no words in any language that can describe how touched I am. The choice you have made is truly beautiful. By passing along the gift of literacy to strangers, you will honor me far more profoundly than you can ever know."

Brenna came up to me and hugged my upper arm. I nestled Brenna's head under my eye dome as May wrapped her arms around her sister.

As we basked in the glow of our loving family, I cast my mind back to the time when Brenna and May were passengers on *Jezebel's Fury*, brought along by their father, Murph, after the death of his wife and the girls' mother, Sally.

When my abducted kloormari teammates and I were asked to teach the girls how to read, we agreed in order to please the crew in the hope of receiving better treatment during our captivity. Our decision was not based on kindness or affection toward those small, motherless, illiterate urchins. At that time we were not even fully familiar with such concepts.

As I reminisced about teaching Brenna and May, I realized how one small act can stay with an individual for the rest of their life and then expand beyond that life to bring knowledge, comfort, and success to the lives of so many others. This realization filled me with joy.

***

The day before she left us, Brenna packed her belongings, moved out of her home, and spent the night in the house with May and me. Brenna and May talked long into the night while I entered my meditative state and focused on my memories of Brenna. I contemplated the inner pain that she must have been dealing with when she ran away, and I thought about how she had come back to us and started healing, transforming into the stronger, selfless, beautiful person to whom I was about to bid farewell.

Early the next morning, the air was still, and the village was silent, with the kloormari residents still in their full meditative states. A small hoverlift waited outside my door as Brenna, May, and I stepped out into the fresh morning air and placed Brenna's bags onto the lift. We watched while the lift floated away toward the landing pad. Then we followed the path down the hill, the only sound being the crunching and scraping of our feet on the grit and gravel.

"Are you sure you won't be able to keep in touch with us?" May asked, breaking the silence. "We're going to miss you so much!"

"Like I said, May," Brenna replied, "where I'm heading, I don't think I'll be able to connect to a quantum network, but even if I could, I need to spend time focusing on my personal journey. I need to separate from my past for some time, so I can understand myself better. I also need to make up for my mistakes without support from anyone else. I know that probably doesn't make sense to you, and I can't explain it, but it's just what I need to do for a while."

"For a while?" May asked, brightening. "So you think you will contact us someday?"

"Count on it," Brenna replied.

"When you're ready, do you think I could come visit you? I mean, Kuw'baal is OK, but I'm going to get sick of the cloudy weather every single day. I'd love to come soak up some daylight with you."

"I'd love that!" Brenna declared.

When we reached the end of the path, the spaceport shuttle was already on the pad. Baggage was piled up, and an attendant was loading it into the shuttle's cargo bay. We were a few minutes early, so May and Brenna had time to hug each other. I stepped back a few paces to give them some privacy while the sisters said their tearful farewells.

When they separated, Brenna held her hand out toward me. "Walk with me to the shuttle?" she asked.

I looked over to May, who nodded, indicating I should have a moment with Brenna. She waited while Brenna and I took the walkway over the stream.

When we reached the pad, the baggage had been loaded into the shuttle, and the other passengers had boarded. The attendant stood to one side of the shuttle door, leaving it open for Brenna. As we stood by the railing at the edge of the pad, Brenna held my hand paddles and looked at me with her wet, reddened eyes. "I am so, so sorry for everything I've put you through. I hope you can forgive me."

"My dear, dear Brenna," I replied, "there's nothing to forgive."

"Promise me that you and May will take care of each other."

"We will always be there for each other, and we will always be here for you, whenever you need us."

Brenna hugged my arm and nestled her head against my shoulder. Then she stepped back with a sad smile and walked up the three steps into the hovering shuttle. Once inside the shuttle door, she turned back toward me with fresh tears rolling down her cheeks.

As the steps retracted and just before the door closed, Brenna had four final words for me. She spoke them with a strong, yet quavering voice. No words have ever been as beautiful or as devastating to me.

"I love you, Pa."

Did you enjoy this book?

I can't begin to tell you how valuable a positive online review or social media post is to an independently published book like Kelvoo's Terra. Good reviews and positive mentions are the fuel required to compete with millions of other titles – especially when those titles are produced by massive publishing houses with huge marketing budgets and distribution networks.

If you leave a review or make a post, please let me know where to find it and I promise to read it. Your feedback helps me to understand my readers and to improve as a writer for any future books that I may write and you may enjoy.

By aiding in my future success, your reviews or posts will help to enable me to continue my writing and create more books.

You can visit my website and find my social media links at:

www.kelvoo.com.

THANK YOU so much,

-- *Phil Bailey*

Made in the USA
Las Vegas, NV
26 May 2024